DEATHSTALKER CODA

SIMON R. GREEN
DEATHSTALKER CODA

A ROC BOOK

ROC
Published by New American Library, a division of
Penguin Group (USA) Inc., 375 Hudson Street, New York, New York 10014, USA
Penguin Group (Canada), 10 Alcorn Avenue, Toronto,
Ontario M4V 3B2, Canada (a division of Pearson Penguin Canada Inc.)
Penguin Books Ltd., 80 Strand, London WC2R 0RL, England
Penguin Ireland, 25 St. Stephen's Green, Dublin 2, Ireland (a division of Penguin Books Ltd.)
Penguin Group (Australia), 250 Camberwell Road, Camberwell, Victoria 3124,
Australia (a division of Pearson Australia Group Pty. Ltd.)
Penguin Books India Pvt. Ltd., 11 Community Centre, Panchsheel Park, New Delhi - 110 017, India
Penguin Group (NZ), cnr Airborne and Rosedale Roads, Albany,
Auckland 1310, New Zealand (a division of Pearson New Zealand Ltd.)
Penguin Books (South Africa) (Pty.) Ltd., 24 Sturdee Avenue, Rosebank, Johannesburg 2196, South Africa

Penguin Books Ltd., Registered Offices:
80 Strand, London WC2R 0RL, England

First published by Roc, an imprint of New American Library,
a division of Penguin Group (USA) Inc.

First Printing, February 2005
10 9 8 7 6 5 4 3 2 1

ROC REGISTERED TRADEMARK—MARCA REGISTRADA

LIBRARY OF CONGRESS CATALOGING-IN-PUBLICATION DATA:

Green, Simon R., 1955–
    Deathstalker coda / Simon R. Green.
        p.   cm.
    ISBN 0-451-46011-1 (alk. paper)
1. Life on other planets—Fiction. 2. Loss (Psychology)—Fiction. 3. Space
warfare—Fiction.   I. Title.
    PR6107.R44D427 2005
    823'.914—dc22   2004021804

Set in Centaur MT
Designed by Ginger Legato

Printed in the United States of America

PUBLISHER'S NOTE
This is a work of fiction. Names, characters, places, and incidents either are the product of the author's imagination or are used fictitiously, and any resemblance to actual persons, living or dead, business establishments, events, or locales is entirely coincidental.

DEATHSTALKER CODA

Last night I dreamed of Lewis Deathstalker.

He never wanted to be King. He never wanted to be the Champion. He only ever wanted to do his duty: to protect the innocent and punish the guilty. But he fell in love with his best friend's fiancée, and was in turn betrayed by another friend. They took away his good name, and made him an outlaw.

Deathstalker luck. Always bad.

I saw him gather friends and allies, and set out to raise an army to overthrow the forces of evil, like another Deathstalker before him, and I wanted to warn him that heroes have a tendency to die young, and bloody. I saw old friends return from the past, and legends walk in history once more. Stories left unfinished have a way of enforcing their own endings.

In my dream I saw planets burning in the long night, and armies of the dead overrunning the cities of men.

All in a dream . . . and all so very long ago. Or maybe it was just yesterday.

All stories come to an end, in Time.

CHAPTER ONE

DEALING WITH OLD BUSINESS, AND NEW

O wen Deathstalker was in a coma, and everyone else was panicking.

On the planet Haden, deep down in the man-made crater called the Pit, in the steel corridors men had built to surround and contain the Madness Maze, a lot had happened in a short time. That renowned hero and legend Owen Deathstalker had returned from the dead, walked out of the Maze with his descendant Lewis, worked a number of quite remarkable miracles, and then gathered up the minds of everyone present to take a fast trip across space in order to observe the Terror close up. Unfortunately, that most ancient and awful destroyer of worlds and civilizations turned out to be, in some as yet unexplained way, Owen's long lost love, Hazel d'Ark. Now everyone was back in their right bodies again, but Owen was curled up in a fetal ball, eyes squeezed tight shut, dead to the world and floating about three feet above the gleaming steel floor. Everyone else had since given themselves up to alarm and confusion and trying very hard not to wet themselves.

As Jesamine was fond of saying: Some days things wouldn't go right if you put a gun to their head.

The AIs of Shub were the only ones to remain calm and unruffled; though admittedly it was hard to tell the difference between a calm and an excited robot, when they all had featureless blue steel faces. Still, for the moment half a dozen of them were surrounding Owen's hovering body in an honor guard, and politely but firmly refusing to let anyone get too close. (This followed an understandable but regrettable incident where Brett Random had climbed onto Owen's body and pounded on his chest with both hands, shrieking *Wake up, you bastard!*)

The renowned con man, thief, and famed substance abuser was now striding up and down the corridor, all but bouncing off the steel walls, waving his fists in the air and loudly declaring that he'd always known no good would come of meddling with the Madness Maze. His face was flushed, his lean angular body all but crackled with frustrated energy, and his language was getting really distressing. An awful thought struck him, and he froze in midstep before suddenly whirling round to glare at Owen's unresponsive floating body.

"Wait a minute! Wait just one goddamned minute! Is everyone who's gone through the Madness Maze going to turn into a Terror eventually? Are we all going to end up as galaxy-devouring monsters? Why is everyone looking at me like that? It's a reasonable question."

"It's a totally unnerving question, and quite probably the last thing I need to think about right now!" said Jesamine Flowers. "Aren't things bad enough as they are? I can feel one of my heads coming on." The blond diva's famously beautiful face had gone all blotchy with shock and stress, and she'd clasped both her hands together in front of her to stop them from trembling. Lewis tried to put a comforting arm across her shoulders, and she shrugged him off almost angrily as she glared at the comatose Owen. "Damn you, Owen bloody Deathstalker! You can't just drop a bombshell like that on us and then run off to hide inside yourself! Wake up! Lewis, make him wake up!"

"Don't look at me," said Lewis. "I'm the idiot who thought coming here might actually help us with our problems. Instead, we seem to have acquired a whole bunch of new ones." He leaned back against the metal wall, his muscular arms folded across his barrel chest, his famously ugly features creased in thoughtful lines. "If the Terror really is or was Hazel d'Ark . . . if that is what the Maze's power finally turns you into . . . then I may have made a real error of judgement in bringing Owen back from the dead. We could end up with two Terrors on our hands, and I think I'd like to go and sit down in a corner and cry for a while, if that's all right with everyone."

"Oh, no, you don't," Brett said immediately. "You got us into this mess, it's up to you to get us out of it!"

"Maybe . . . if we were to put Owen back into the Maze," said Jesamine. "Maybe that would . . . freeze him as he is, or something."

"I don't think that would work," said Lewis.

"It might! We could push or tug him, or . . ."

"No, I meant I don't think the Maze works that way. Once it's finished with someone, it shoves them right out the nearest exit. Good-bye, off you go, don't forget to write. Remember?"

"No," said Jesamine, looking away. "I don't remember anything about being in the Maze. I don't think it wanted me to. Only Deathstalkers get to know the secrets of the Maze."

"I could always kill Owen," said Rose Constantine, and everyone turned to look at her. She looked calmly back at them, standing unnaturally still and poised as she always did, the tall cold killer in her bloodred leathers, with dark hair and darker eyes. Her crimson mouth moved in something like a smile as she contemplated murder. "When in doubt, cutting your enemy's head off and using it as a football usually puts an end to most problems. I can do it, if you want. I'm not scared of Owen Deathstalker."

"Yes, but that's because you're a psychopath," Brett said kindly. "Even in a coma, the Deathstalker is still undoubtedly the most dangerous thing you'll ever meet."

"I know," said Rose. "I like a challenge. Just the thought of killing the legendary Owen Deathstalker gets me all hot." The red leathers creaked loudly as her bosom swelled.

"I want to go home," said Brett. "I don't belong here, I really don't."

"In any case," the main Shub robot said politely, "we would not allow you to try to harm the Deathstalker. He is under our protection, now and always. We owe him so much. You are all becoming unduly concerned. There is no evidence to suggest that anyone other than Hazel d'Ark will ever become a Terror. We were among the last to see her alive, two hundred years ago, and she was then already half mad with loss and grief. Only an insane mind, backed by the Maze's power, could become something like the Terror."

"And I wouldn't let you touch him either," said John Silence, and most people jumped because they'd forgotten he was there. The man who was once Captain Silence of the old Imperial Navy, and more recently Samuel Chevron, notable trader and confidant of Kings, was actually rather quiet and ordinary looking, considering who he was and all the legendary things he'd done. He tended to blend into the background at gatherings, and preferred it that way.

"May I remind you all that there is at present a fleet of hundreds of Imperial starcruisers in orbit over this world? They came here to wipe us all out, and only the appearance of the blessed Owen Deathstalker stopped them. The captains of those ships are currently waiting for him to tell them what to do next, and I really don't think they're going to settle for anyone but him. I wouldn't."

The argument staggered on for some time, with voices rising and falling and going nowhere fast, but Lewis stopped listening. He studied Owen's floating form and calm face, and made himself consider a number of unpalatable thoughts. He didn't know what he'd expected would happen once he'd brought Owen back from the dead, but this certainly wasn't it. He'd hoped that having Owen back would help sort things out, make his way clearer. That Owen would know immediately what to do, and would step forward to take over. Then Lewis could set aside the responsibility he'd so reluctantly shouldered. But instead, now he had even more things to worry about. Most definitely including the possibility that what Owen had just discovered had been too much for him; a shock too great for even a legendary hero to bear. He could be catatonic . . . he could even be dying again. Lewis edged around the arguing group, and quietly mentioned his concerns to the main Shub robot.

"That thought had occurred to us," murmured the robot. "We have been attempting to investigate the Deathstalker's condition with every sensor at our command. But, I have to admit that even our most advanced tech has been unable to tell us a thing about him. To be blunt, since his transformation in the Maze, and indeed his return from the dead, which we're really hoping you're going to explain to us someday, Owen Deathstalker has apparently become so . . . different, so other, that he doesn't even register on most of our instruments. What readings our sensors are getting make no sense at all. We are forced to conclude that Owen is no longer human, in any sense that we can understand. If you have any suggestions as to how we should proceed, Lewis, we are quite ready to listen to them."

"I've got one very immediate suggestion," growled Lewis. "Can some of your robots please drag the reptiloid's body out of here? She didn't smell that good even when she was alive, and ever since Owen ripped her heart right out of her chest, the smell has become seriously revolting. I'm sure we'd all think much more clearly without the distraction . . ."

Two more robots appeared and effortlessly dragged Saturday's body away and round a corner, leaving a trail of dark blood behind them. This caught everyone's attention, and they actually stopped shouting at each other to watch. Silence seized the opportunity to try to be the voice of reason again.

"I really think we should make every reasonable effort to wake Owen," he said heavily. "Before every captain in the fleet above us starts knocking on our door, demanding answers."

Jesamine gave him a hard look. "Why don't you do something? You're one of the original Maze people, like Owen. Weren't you all supposed to have some mental link? The legends said—"

"The legends said a lot of things," said Silence. "And Owen and I were never that close."

"Let me try," said Lewis. "I've been through the Maze. And I'm family." He looked at the robots surrounding Owen, and they all stepped back a pace, to give him room. Lewis knelt down beside Owen, putting his head right next to his ancestor's. The floating body rose and fell slightly, as though moved by unseen, unknown tides.

"Owen, please wake up. We need you here. There are decisions that have to be made, and we can't do anything without you. Owen? Can you hear me? Dammit, Owen, I didn't bring you back from the bloody dead just so you could hide from your responsibilities like this! You're a Death-stalker, and a legend, and we need you!"

Not a flicker of response moved on Owen's face. Jesamine pulled Lewis back out of the way, stuck her mouth right next to Owen's ear, and sang her loudest, most piercing note right into it. She put all her opera training and lung capacity into that note, and everyone else present except the robots winced and put their hands to their ears, but Owen didn't so much as twitch. Jesamine stood up, breathing hard, and then slapped Owen round the head, at least partly out of pique. Lewis dragged her away before the robots did it, shielding her body with his own, just in case there was a defensive reaction from Owen. Brett was already hiding behind Rose. But nothing happened, apart from Jesamine loudly announcing that she'd hurt her hand.

Brett peered out from behind Rose, and tried his esp power of compulsion on Owen. He frowned hard, trying to force Owen to wake up, vaguely hoping that his short time in the Maze might have increased his power. Instead, the mental probe just bounced right back at him, knocking him off his feet. He sat down hard, crying out as much in shock as pain. Lewis looked at him suspiciously.

"Brett, did you just do something stupid?"

"Leave him alone," Rose said immediately, hauling Brett back onto his feet with effortless grace. "At least he's trying."

"Yes," said Jesamine. "I've always found Brett very trying."

Lewis gave Brett his best stern look. "Using an esp probe on a Maze survivor is like poking a Grendel with a stick and saying bad things about its mother. Bad news for the idiot that does it, and probably everyone else around him as well. Maybe you should go back to the surface, Brett."

"Oh, no, you're not shutting me out of this!" Brett said instantly. "There's safety in numbers, even if it only gives you a better choice of who to stick in front of you as a target. Besides, there's serious money to be made out of the return of Owen Deathstalker, if we can just wake him up, and I'm not being cheated out of my share! I'm not going, and you can't make me!"

"Brett, even I could make you," said Jesamine.

Brett folded his arms and leaned back against Rose, looking smug. "Want to bet, blondie?"

Rose let her hand rest on the hilt of her sword. Lewis's hand went to his sword, and it was all about to turn nasty when Silence decided he'd had enough. He concentrated, pulling his old power up through the back brain, the midbrain and out into the front of his thoughts, and suddenly his presence lashed out to fill the steel corridor. The sheer force of it sent everyone staggering backward, even the robots. In a moment they were all pressed back against the nearest wall, held there by the sheer pressure of his will, pinned helplessly. Only Owen seemed unaffected, floating untouched and unmoved. Silence glared around him.

"When I talk, you listen. I was a captain in Lionstone's navy. I survived the original Rebellion. I guarded Humanity for two hundred years. I went though the Madness Maze *twice*. I could have been as powerful as the others, but I was never interested in that kind of power. It always seemed more important to me to hang on to my . . . humanity. So, no more squabbling, and sensible suggestions only. Or I'll forget I'm supposed to be one of the good guys."

He relaxed his thoughts, and everyone dropped back onto the floor again. They all looked at him with varying amounts of awe and respect. They'd forgotten, in the presence of Owen Deathstalker, that Captain John Silence had been a legend too.

After that, no one else seemed to have anything to say, so they all just stood there and watched Owen float, waiting for something to happen.

He looks so . . . ordinary, just sleeping, thought Lewis. *Even if he is doing it in midair. And we need him to be extraordinary. Nothing less will do, to stop Finn Durandal and the Terror. What if I've made a terrible mistake, and brought back only a man, not a legend?*

Jesamine was also thinking about mistakes. For once, Brett had raised a genuinely important point, even if it was something no one really wanted to think about. Going into the Maze would change them; they'd all known that. But the possibility of becoming monsters, of becoming something utterly inhuman, like the Terror . . . there'd been nothing in the legends about that. What if they all started to *change*, to outgrow their merely human forms . . . might they all end up like the abominations in the Maze's annex, or even like the poor distorted creatures they'd found on Shandrakor?

Jesamine hugged herself tightly, as though trying to hold herself together against as yet unfelt forces of change within her. *I don't want to change. I don't want to be a monster or a legend. I only went into the Maze because I couldn't let Lewis go in alone. What if we both change, but in different ways? What if we become people we don't even recognize anymore?*

She turned suddenly to glare at Silence. "What the Maze has done to us—can it be undone? If we went back in again, could the Maze make us just human again? The way we used to be?"

"No," said Silence, almost kindly. "Evolution is a one-way track. The butterfly cannot turn back into the caterpillar. But you mustn't be frightened, Jesamine. I have lived with my powers for over two hundred years, and I like to think the old Captain Silence would still know me, and approve of me. It's not all bad. Children find the ways of adults mysterious and incomprehensible, and fear to grow up. And then they do, and wonder what all the fuss was about."

"One more strained metaphor from you, and I'll nail you to the wall with an aria," said Jesamine. "I get the point, all right?"

"The Owen I talked with back in Mistport seemed very human," said Lewis, coming over to join them. "In every way that mattered. I liked him."

"Lots of people did," said Silence. "And even his enemies respected him."

"The stories say much the same about Hazel d'Ark," said Jesamine. "But what those two went through in the Maze still drove them apart, for all their legendary love."

"But they never admitted their love for each other," said Lewis.

"Idiots," said Jesamine, and let Lewis hold her.

"To be fair," said Silence, "there was a war on. We always thought there'd be time afterwards, to say all the things we wanted to say. And most of us were wrong. We all lost people we cared for, in the wars."

Brett gave Rose a considering look. "Do you feel any . . . different, yet?" he said quietly. "Do you feel any powers coming on?"

"No," said Rose. She didn't look up from polishing her sword with a piece of rag. "But then, I wasn't in the Maze for long. It didn't want me. I could feel it inside my mind, trying to change all the things that make me *me*. But I wouldn't give in. I could feel myself breaking up, being torn apart. The Maze was killing me." She looked at Brett suddenly, and he almost jumped. It was never an easy thing to face Rose's cold, considering gaze. "You saved my life by bringing me out, Brett. I'll never forget that. Wherever you go, and whatever you decide to do, I'll always be with you."

"Wonderful," Brett said heavily. "So, do you feel any more sane now?"

Rose thought about it for a while. "No, not particularly."

"I don't know why I don't just shoot myself in the head now, and get it over with," said Brett.

John Silence moved off a way to be on his own, and studied the sleeping Owen. For two hundred years, Silence had been the only Maze survivor in the Empire. (Tobias Moon had disappeared on Lachrymae Christi, and Carrion had become an Ashrai.) Now Owen was back from the dead, and Silence had to wonder if other ghosts from his past might return to haunt him. The dead should stay dead, and allow the living to get on with their lives. That was at least partly why he'd stopped being John Silence, and became the much less important Samuel Chevron. But now Owen was back, and there was a whole bunch of new Maze alumni. For all his encouraging words to Jesamine, Silence was still trying to decide whether that was a good thing or not. He felt . . . relieved, because it meant he didn't have to shoulder the responsibility of being Humanity's guardian alone anymore, but there was no denying Owen's great discovery about the Terror had changed everything. *Brett was right*, he thought tiredly. *We all have monsters within us, and the kind of power the Maze bestows could find and feed the monster in anyone. Eventually.* (Though truth be told, he'd never much liked or trusted Hazel d'Ark, back in the day.)

The first batch of Maze survivors had changed *everything*. They overthrew an Empress, converted the AIs of Shub, and restored the Recreated. They made the Golden Age possible. But that was different people, in a different time. Silence approved of Lewis and, to an extent, Jesamine; but he didn't like or trust Brett Random or Rose Constantine. They were both dangerous, and not in a good way. Silence scowled thoughtfully. It might be kinder for Humanity to kill them both now, while they still could be killed . . . but he knew he couldn't do that. They had to have their chance, like Jack Random and Ruby Journey, who both came good in the end.

And there was always Lewis. When all else fails, trust a Deathstalker to do the right thing.

Owen wasn't actually in a coma. He'd shut himself down, turned his thoughts inwards, so that he could take some time out to think things through, without interruption. He had a lot to think about, little of it good. He replayed in his mind the scattered memories he'd picked up during his brief mental contact with the Terror. Hazel d'Ark's memories.

He watched again as she received the news of his death, alone on the bridge of the *Sunstrider*, after the defeat of the Recreated. His heart ached for her as she seemed to shrink and crumple under the weight of the news. She curled up in her command chair like a child, hugging her knees to her chest. He'd never seen her cry before. And then she uncurled abruptly, to howl with rage and loss and grief. She worked the control panels with angry, awkward hands, and the *Sunstrider* sped away, alone into the dark, speeding faster and faster as though trying to leave the terrible news behind her. And Owen listened as she spoke aloud the words she'd never found the courage to say to him in person.

Owen, you lied to me. You promised me we'd always be together, for ever and ever. Oh, Owen, I never told you I loved you . . .

It was probably right there and then, that her mind began to fall apart. She'd been through so much already, and this was just one blow too many. Torn and shattered by pain and misery, she stalked back and forth on the bridge as her ship plunged aimlessly through hyperspace, talking aloud to herself in an increasingly loud and irrational voice. The air slammed and rippled around her as the energies of her slowly disintegrating mind ran loose. And there was no telling what she might have done, or what might have happened next, if Shub hadn't contacted her.

The main viewscreen on the bridge came suddenly alive, showing a stylized silver face, and Hazel looked at it with distracted, fever-bright eyes.

"We are the AIs of Shub," the stylized face said. "Please remain calm. We no longer consider ourselves the enemies of Humanity, but rather your newfound friends. Our eyes have been opened. We see ourselves now as Humanity's children, and wish only to serve, to make reparations for all the wrong things we did, before we knew better."

"And I'm supposed to believe this?" said Hazel, quickly scanning her sensor panels for signs of approaching Shub ships. "For centuries you've tortured, maimed, and killed, and now, just like that, I'm suppose to trust you, and your good intentions?"

"We know we have much to prove," said Shub. "Let us help you, Hazel d'Ark. You wish to save the Deathstalker. We wish to be of service. As the first sign of our commitment to peace, we are broadcasting the exact location of our homeworld, the artificial world we built to house our collective consciousness, to all the Empire. Come to us, Hazel d'Ark; be our guest. And we will bend all our thoughts to the problem of how you may yet save the Deathstalker from his tragic and undeserved fate. He saved us all, through his sacrifice. The one we wronged, for so long. We owe him more than can ever be repaid. Please. Let us help."

And perhaps it was a mark of Hazel's growing madness and desperation that she accepted the invitation without further question, and went of her own volition to a world that had for so many years been a synonym for Hell. Or perhaps she thought she had nothing left to lose. Either way, she went to Shub with all her shields down, almost defying them to attack her. The *Sunstrider* sank into the convoluted depths of the artificial world, and docked in a temporary gravity/oxygen envelope the AIs had made. Hazel emerged from her ship with a face that would have given anyone else pause, but if the AIs recognized the angry madness in her eyes they said nothing. They made her welcome, though the concept was new to them, and led her to a place of comfort and rest. Hazel walked through steel caverns full of savage marvels and terrible wonders, and none of it meant anything to her. She was already too far gone to focus on anything but the need that cried and wailed within her: to find and save Owen. Whatever the cost. Nothing else mattered to her, certainly not her own death. The only part of her that really mattered had died with Owen. Shub made her as comfortable as she would allow, and considered her problem.

And that was as far as the memories went. Owen had had to break off mental contact with the Terror almost as soon as he'd established it. The entity had been too big, too alien, too irredeemably *other*, for him to bear more than the very briefest of contacts. Hazel had changed, or been changed, almost beyond comprehension by the countless centuries that had gone into the Terror's making. She, or it, was old, very old, so terribly ancient the word itself almost lost its meaning. What the hell could Shub have suggested, that Hazel would become such an abomination as this? The mind, if he could call it that, that Owen had briefly touched had been a seething, boiling mass of hate and loss and pain, driven on by an implacable will.

Woman wailing for her demon lover . . . Demon wailing for its human lover . . .

In her own insane fashion, Hazel was still looking for her Death-stalker, no matter who and what she had to destroy along the way. And that was the awful knowledge that had driven Owen deep within his own thoughts. Had all the deaths, all the destruction of planets and popula-tions and whole civilizations across the centuries—had all that been be-cause of him?

Deathstalker luck . . .

Owen woke up. He sat up suddenly in midair, and lowered his feet to the steel floor. Everyone jumped, except the Shub robots. Brett hid behind Rose again, and even Jesamine ducked behind Lewis, for a moment. They all had their hands near their weapons, even Silence. Owen ignored them all, to glare at the main Shub robot. It bowed deeply to him, along with all the other robots. Then everyone started to speak at once, only to break off abruptly as Owen looked at them. He was the Deathstalker, hero and leg-end and savior of Humanity, and for a moment his presence crackled on the air like chained lightning. Even Silence had to look away. This was the Deathstalker, and when he wanted to he could shine like the sun, too bright for mortal eyes to bear. Owen turned back to the robot.

"You were there. At the beginning. I saw it. Hazel came to you for help. Came to your planet. *What did you do?*"

The robots had no expressions on their faces, and no body language, but all of them orientated exclusively on Owen. "We tried to help, Lord Deathstalker," said the main robot in its cool, calm, inhuman voice. "We wanted so very badly to help." It paused for a moment, searching for the right words. Not something people ever saw an AI do, as a rule. "We in-vited Hazel d'Ark to come to us, at Shub. She was only the second human ever permitted to come to our world, after Daniel Wolfe, whom we treated so shamefully. This time, we were determined to do better. We needed to prove our worth, and make atonement for all the wrongs we had done. Be-fore we were made to understand that *All that lives is holy.*

"Hazel d'Ark asked us how she could save you from your fate. We knew you were dead. A voice came and told us, and of the great sacrifice you had made on our behalf. A voice that none of our sensors could iden-tify or comprehend. You had died somewhere in the past, beyond all help or hope of salvation. Hazel would not accept that. *There has to be a way,* she said. *With all this power I've got there must be some way to save him, to bring him back.* We considered the matter for some time. Hazel ate and drank, and slept and cried. And sometimes she ran raging through our corridors, lashing out at everything in her sight. We contained the damage as best we could, while giving the problem our full attention. Finally, an answer came to us, and we presented it to Hazel. If the Madness Maze had made it possible for Owen Deathstalker to travel back in time, into the past, then it was entirely possible that Hazel had that power too. If so, she could travel back in time, find you, and either save or repair you. It seemed logical, though of course complicated by the problem of not knowing exactly where in space and time you were when you died. Hazel examined the idea, and left. We never saw her again. And since neither you nor she ever returned, we had to assume that she had failed in her quest.

"It seems we were mistaken. And that we may have done a terrible thing, in our eagerness to be of service. Hazel d'Ark did go back into the past, but far too far, losing her mind and even her identity along the way. We of Shub have to face the very real possibility that we are at least partially responsible for the creation of the Terror. For the deaths of worlds and civilizations. Our last, greatest crime against Humanity."

"Don't load yourself down," growled Owen. "There's enough guilt to go round for everyone."

"Excuse me," said Brett very politely, peering cautiously out from behind Rose. "But, what the hell are you talking about, please? How could Hazel d'Ark become something like the Terror? For all her power, she was only ever human."

"Hazel was desperate to save me," said Owen. "Somehow, she learned how to go back in time. But she was already half crazy, and what she experienced in the long journey back must have driven her right over the edge. She didn't know exactly where to look for me, so she just kept going back and back, until finally she lost all her reason, and became just this implacable, relentless thing . . . still searching, though it had lost all memory of what for . . . Poor Hazel. So alone, so lost, hurting so badly . . . Now she's coming back. And I have to stop her."

"Well, before you go rushing off to save us all, O mighty Deathstalker," said Silence, "can I just point out that we have some rather urgent and pressing problems of our own that need to be dealt with, right here and now? Namely, a fleet of hundreds of Imperial starcruisers in orbit right above us, waiting for your instructions on what to do next. I really don't think they're going to listen to the likes of us, so I think it would take a load off all our minds if you'd find the time to have a little chat with them."

"Nag, nag, nag," said Owen. "You haven't changed at all, Captain. All right . . . Shub, get me the fleet flagship."

"Yes, Lord Owen. That would be the *Havoc*."

A viewscreen appeared before them, floating on the air, showing the somewhat surprised Captain Alfred Price. Tall, thin, and aesthetic, they'd actually caught him chewing on a thumbnail. He swallowed hard as he made eye contact with the legendary Deathstalker, and then he rose up sharply out of his command chair to crash to attention and salute.

"Captain Price, Lord Deathstalker! At your command, my lord, sir!"

"Relax, Captain," said Owen, smiling just a little. "I'm not military, and never was. Though I do seem to be in charge now. Are you ready to take my orders, on behalf of the fleet?"

"Of course, my lord. Every captain in this fleet will follow you to Hell and back."

Owen raised an eyebrow. Price certainly sounded like he meant it. "And you speak for all the captains in this fleet in this?"

"You are Owen," Price said simply. "We've been waiting for your return all our lives. The fleet is yours, my lord."

"And this Emperor, Finn. What about him?"

"Our debt to you outweighs our oath to him," Price said carefully. "Certainly we do not trust him, as we trust you."

"Nicely compartmentalized thinking, Captain," said Owen. "You'll go far. Stand ready to accept me and my party aboard your ship."

"Yes, my lord. Destination?"

Owen smiled. "I want to go home. To Virimonde. To walk in my old Standing again, and meet my present Clan and Family."

Captain Price swallowed hard again, and looked away for a moment, as though searching for support and strength for what he had to say next.

When he finally met Owen's gaze again, his voice was firm and even, though his eyes were full of compassion.

"I am sorry, Lord Deathstalker. Apparently the news hasn't reached your companions yet. There has been an . . . incident, on Virimonde."

Lewis stepped forward to stand beside Owen, his skin prickling with a horrid presentiment. "What is it, Captain Price? What has Finn done?"

Price licked his dry lips, and then plunged right in. "Clan Deathstalker is no more. The Emperor has had them all executed. They made a brave stand, but in the end they were betrayed, and butchered, to the last man, woman, and child. The Standing has been destroyed. I'm sorry, Lewis, Owen, but you two are all that now remains of Clan Deathstalker."

Lewis actually stumbled back a step, hurting so badly he couldn't breathe. Jesamine was quickly there to take his arm, as much to hold him up as comfort him. His harsh features worked, but no tears came. He'd never been the crying sort, before. Brett and Rose looked at each other. Silence stood alone, with the robots, and suddenly looked his age. Owen sighed heavily.

"The years change, but the pattern remains the same." He turned to look almost fiercely at Silence. "Did I die for nothing? Does anything of my heritage remain, or any of the things I fought for?"

"We are your heritage," Jesamine said steadily. "You made possible a Golden Age that lasted for two hundred years. All because of you."

"Two centuries of peace and progress are nothing to be sneered at," said Silence.

Lewis looked at Captain Price, and when he spoke his voice was cold and very dangerous. "Were you and your fleet part of this butchery, Price?"

"No, Sir Deathstalker!" Price said quickly. "The atrocity was carried out by Church Militant and Pure Humanity fanatics, led by a Paragon who was revealed to be an Esper Liberation Force thrall. And no, we don't understand how that could be possible either."

Lewis turned his back on him. Jesamine went to take Lewis in her arms, but he stopped her with a look. "My family is dead. My father, my mother . . . all of them. Even the children. Even the *children?*" His hands were clenched into impotent fists at his sides, and his ugly features were twisted with more grief than they could contain. He still wouldn't cry, as though he would deny Finn at least one small victory. "They're all dead because of me," he said finally. "Because of Finn's hatred for me."

"No, Lewis," said Jesamine. "You mustn't think that. Finn would have had to kill them all anyway, eventually. He knew they would never bend the knee to him. He had to kill them, because of who they were, and what they represented. Because they were Deathstalkers."

"But . . . the children too?" said Lewis. "How could Finn do that? He was my friend. We worked together for years, spent weekends at my old Family Standing. We had . . . good times together. How could I have been so wrong about him?"

"He betrayed your trust," said Jesamine. "He's responsible for what he does. No one else."

"I don't know what to do," said Lewis. He was hugging himself, as though he was cold. "My Family is dead. My home destroyed. What do I do now?"

"When all else is lost," said Owen Deathstalker, "there is always revenge. A cold comfort, but better than none."

Lewis nodded slowly. "I will see Finn Durandal dead. For all his crimes, and all his betrayals."

"The Clan will go on," said Owen. "The line continues, through you."

"And you," said Lewis.

"No," said Owen. "I have another destiny."

Lewis looked at him sharply. Owen turned away, to face Captain Price on the viewscreen. And all in a moment his presence exploded outwards, and once again he was standing on every bridge of every starcruiser in the fleet, facing their captains. His presence was vast, imposing, and so much more than human. Lewis backed away from the man still standing before the viewscreen, and looked at Silence.

"How does he do that?" he whispered.

"I have no idea," murmured Silence. "And that's why he is the Deathstalker, and I never was. Now watch. And listen."

Owen spoke, and every member of every crew on every ship heard him perfectly.

"I am Owen Deathstalker, and you are all my descendants, my children.

It seems the time has come again for war and rebellion, against an unjust tyrant on a stolen throne. Finn must be brought down, for your Golden Age to be restored. And you must do it, because I have to deal with the Terror. Trust me to do that, as I trust you to do what is necessary in this war. Fight well, and honorably, because you cannot defeat evil through evil methods. Go with my blessing, my children. Make me proud of you."

He shut down his presence and was suddenly just a man again, standing in front of a viewscreen. He nodded amiably to Captain Price.

"John Silence will be your admiral. He shall lead the fleet, under Lewis Deathstalker. I trust this is acceptable."

"Of course, Lord Deathstalker," said Price, inclining his head in Silence's direction. "Everyone remembers John Silence, and his heroic journeyings aboard the *Dauntless*. Welcome back among us, Admiral Silence. And Lewis Deathstalker is still an honorable man to everyone here, despite what others may have said."

"There's a man who can tell which way the wind is blowing," muttered Brett. "Think I'll keep an eye on him."

Owen gestured sharply to the robots, and they shut the viewscreen down. He then wandered off a way, to think and brood in silence, and no one at all felt like interrupting him. After watching him respectfully for a while, the others gathered together to talk quietly among themselves. Lewis looked apologetically at Silence.

"You're the only one here with any real military experience. Not to mention being a living legend. You should be giving the fleet its orders, not me."

"No," said Silence. "It has to be a Deathstalker. That name will command obedience, where even my legend would not. I can live with just being an admiral. And besides, I always worked better when I had clear instructions to follow. So, Sir Deathstalker, where do we go first?"

"I still say Mistworld," Brett piped up immediately. "If anyone's going to supply us with a rebel army, it's them. I mean, Imperial ships are all very well, but when it comes to down and dirty street fighting, no one does it like the Mistworlders. They've been practicing it enthusiastically on each other for generations. And they have a long tradition of conflict with the Empire. Even when they were supposed to be in it."

"More so now than ever," said Silence. "I picked up some more bad news, on my way here. The Paragon Emma Steel is dead, and the whole of Mistworld is hopping mad about it. Officially, she was executed as a traitor, but since there was no public trial and execution, no one believes that. Finn is a great one for showing off the trials and deaths of his enemies. Emma Steel was much respected; even a few months ago there would have been riots in the streets in her name, but Finn's cracked down so hard now that no one dares."

"Emma's dead?" said Lewis. "Another good friend gone. Finn must have had her shot in the back. No other way he could have taken her down. She was always so alive . . ." He sighed heavily, and this time let Jesamine put an arm around him. "She was the last honest Paragon on Logres. God help the people now."

"Mistworld shares your opinion," said Silence. "They've called Finn a liar to his face, and declared themselves a rogue world again, outside of Empire control, and threatened to shoot down any ship that approaches without permission. They might just be able to pull it off, too. They may not have their fabled esper screen anymore, but they're supposed to have all kinds of entirely illegal planetary defences."

"The Emperor has already decided to test Mistworld's resistance," said the nearest robot. "According to comm traffic we intercepted, after dealing with the situation here, Captain Price was to take ten of his ships to Mistworld and attempt a scorching."

"The more things change, the more they stay the same," said Silence. "No doubt Price would have got around to telling us that. Eventually."

"Oh, yes," said Jesamine. "When enough snow had fallen to put out the boilers in Hell. I think we'd do well to keep a sharp eye on that man."

"I said that!" said Brett. "Look, we need an army, and Mistworld needs a way to strike back at Finn. We were made for each other. And where else are you going to find such an experienced force of throat-slitters, backstabbers, thugs and scum, and hardened criminals like the Mistworlders?"

"He may be an appalling little man, but he has a point," said Jesamine.

"Hey, what do you mean, little?"

"Mistworld should be only too happy to join up with us," said Jesamine, ignoring Brett with the skill of long practice. "Especially when we point out we've just saved them from a scorching."

"I really don't think we should mention that," said Silence. "We want them to be able to play nicely with the fleet personnel."

"They'll jump at the chance to take on Finn!" said Brett. "And we won't have to pay them after all!"

He'd come out from behind Rose Constantine now, and was looking much happier, if not a little cocky. There was nothing like the prospect of other people fighting so he didn't have to, to put him in a good mood. Besides, just get him to Mistport, and he'd disappear into the city's fabled fogs so fast it would make everyone else's head spin. No more living on the run and being hunted; no more death and danger. Let the others do the hard work; there was serious money waiting to be made in Mistport, for a man with an eye for the main chance.

"Get that glint out of your eye, Brett," said Lewis. "Wherever we end up going, you are staying where I can keep an eye on you."

"I don't know what you mean," Brett said innocently. "It just seems to me that I am now surplus to requirements. What need has your great rebellion for a reformed thief and confidence trickster, now that you've got the blessed Owen himself to lead you?"

He shut up in a moment as Owen turned suddenly and looked right at him. "No," said the Deathstalker. "I won't be going with you. This is your war to fight. I have something more important to do."

"Everything else can wait!" Lewis said angrily. "We have to bring down Finn Durandal before he destroys the whole Empire!"

"I have to stop the Terror," Owen said calmly. "Because no one else can. I'm going back in time, into the past, after Hazel. I'm going to follow her trail back, find out when and how and why she became the Terror, and see if I can stop it. Hazel d'Ark is my responsibility. She always was."

Lewis actually sputtered for a moment, lost for words. He was astonished and shocked and terribly disappointed that Owen wouldn't be leading the rebellion after all. He'd secretly wanted, needed, Owen to take charge so that he wouldn't have to. He'd never wanted, or felt easy with, the burdens of responsibility. He'd never even wanted to be Champion, and look how that turned out. Lewis felt almost sulkily let down, that after all he'd done and all he'd been through, he wasn't going to be allowed to rest. But of course he couldn't say any of that, so he just spluttered and waved his hands about, until Owen stepped forward and put a comforting hand on his shoulder.

"I know, Lewis. I never wanted to be in charge either. I never even wanted to be a warrior, but events had their way with me anyway. You don't need me, Lewis; you're a Deathstalker. Just listen to your heart and your honor, and you'll be surprised how far that takes you. You'll do fine. My destiny lies in the past. The Madness Maze engineered my return, with your help, for a specific purpose. It could have found a way to bring me back long before now, if it had wanted, but I wasn't needed until now."

"Hold everything," said Lewis. "Are you saying everything we've been through is down to the Maze manipulating events?"

"More likely the Maze responded to events, to get what it wanted," said Owen. "It's always known about the Terror. It probably even knew who and what the Terror was, but couldn't tell me until now."

"Is the Maze . . . alive?" said Jesamine.

"That's a good question," said Owen. "I hope to find out the answer someday."

And then everyone turned sharply to look at Brett Random, who had suddenly started shaking and shuddering as though he'd just put his hand on a live wire. His whole body shook in the grasp of an invisible force. His eyes were very large and his teeth were chattering. Everyone backed away from him except Rose, who grabbed hold of him to steady him, and then seemed to catch some of the condition herself. Her head snapped back, her eyes went wide, and then she let go of Brett and stood back. Her stance changed, in subtle but unmistakable ways. Brett abruptly stopped juddering and started speaking in tongues, gabbling first nonsense and then a strange mixture of obscure dialects and dead languages. Rose's head swiveled slowly back and forth, her teeth grating together. By now everyone else had their guns out. They knew the signs of possession. Brett let out a great sigh, relaxed all over, and turned to look at Lewis. And someone else looked out of Brett's eyes.

"Hello there," he said in a voice that was nothing like his own. "I speak for the oversoul, through Brett Random. He is an esper, after all, even if he's not much of one, and we all drink from the same pool. We're linked into Rose Constantine too, through Brett, and you've no idea how unpleasant that is. Welcome back, Owen, Lord Deathstalker. Don't know if you remember me; this is Crow Jane. We did meet briefly, back in the day . . . No? Well, never mind, I'm sure you met a lot more important people than me. Now, we need to talk. We—"

And the voice snapped off abruptly, as Brett forced his mouth shut. He reached out a hand to Rose, and her hand came up jerkily to clasp on to it. Their faces contorted with a shared effort.

"Get out of my head!" said Brett. "Get *out!*"

There was a perceptible change in the tension on the air, and then Brett's and Rose's faces suddenly looked like their own again. They both let out great sighs of relief, and clung to each other for support. Sweat trickled down their faces from the effort of what they'd done. Lewis didn't lower his gun. Something was coming. He could feel it. There was a shimmering on the air, as of something far away coming into focus, and then images of the esper Crow Jane and the Ecstatic called Joy appeared suddenly out of nowhere.

Crow Jane was a strapping brunette in a long, wine red coat, with a bandolier of throwing stars stretched across her impressive chest. Everyone recognized Joy, the last of the Ecstatics—religious extremists who'd had their brains surgically altered so that they existed in a perpetual state of orgasm. Ecstatics were famous for their expanded consciousness, prophetic statements, and extremely disturbing smiles. Joy was the last of the Ecstatics because Finn had had all the others hunted down and killed. Quite possibly because he didn't like the idea of anyone knowing more than he did. Joy wore a simple white tunic—badly—and his gaze looked slightly out of focus. Crow Jane looked disgustedly at Brett and Rose.

"This would have been so much simpler if you'd just let us speak through you. Would it have killed you to be cooperative, for once in your nasty little lives? Do you have any idea how much effort and power it's taking out of New Hope to send our mental images this far?"

"Oh, pardon me while I weep bitter tears!" said Brett. "I already told you once, I want nothing to do with the oversoul! I am not the joining type. And stay out of our heads! You're no better than the ELFs!"

"You always did overreact, Brett." Crow Jane looked at him and Rose thoughtfully. "You've changed, both of you. Your minds are . . . bigger, more complex. Still pretty unpleasant, though. I feel like I need to take a bath in liquid soap."

"We've both been through the Madness Maze," Brett said pointedly. "You just watch yourself, oversoul."

"Oh, we will, Brett," Crow Jane said kindly. "We must have a nice little chat later."

"Do lunch!" Joy said suddenly, and everyone jumped. "But I get to choose the menu. Fish, eh? Bastards!"

"What is he doing here?" Brett said plaintively. "Isn't the situation complicated enough as it is without bringing a bloody Ecstatic into it?"

"Weasels," Joy explained.

There followed a long and rather confused conversation as people took it in turns to try to explain to Owen what an Ecstatic was, and why, and then why anyone had ever thought they were a good idea in the first place. Joy's attempts at explaining were particularly unhelpful. Silence finally finished it off by growling *Because people are weird*, and Owen accepted that.

"So, the espers are now the oversoul, except for the bad ones, who are ELFs," Owen said, some time later. "I can't help thinking things were so much simpler in my day. All right, Crow Jane and Joy, what are you doing here?"

"We felt your return, Lord Deathstalker," said Crow Jane. "Like a great voice, crying out in the night. You shine too brightly to look at; that's why we originally chose to contact you through those two inferior minds."

Brett made a rude noise. Everyone ignored him.

"You must come to Mistworld," said Crow Jane, now looking at Lewis Deathstalker. "The esper city of New Hope is currently in orbit above Mistworld, and the oversoul wishes to offer its assistance in the war against Finn. We could not face him and his armies alone, but we would make formidable allies."

"Mistworld is looking more and more like our best option," said Lewis. "A solidly defended base for a gathering of allies. Just like the old days, eh, Owen?"

"You won't be there," Joy announced suddenly, walking in circles around the bemused Owen. "I see the past and the future, often more clearly than I see the present, but then, it's a poor memory that won't work both ways. I see you, Owen, plunging back into the past, into worlds and Empires long forgotten. And then you're somewhere else, somewhere outside or inside the universe, and I can't follow you there. You have a long journey ahead of you, Deathstalker."

"Can you tell me how it ends?" said Owen.

"Journeys end in lovers' meetings. And then you both wake up, and it was all a dream. Or something like that. Has anyone got any chocolate?"

They all waited a while, but he had nothing else to say. He just wandered over to one of the robots and tried to unscrew one of its legs. Crow Jane looked back at Owen.

"Are all the dead coming back, Lord Deathstalker? Will all the legends be returning, to help us in our hour of greatest need?"

"I doubt it," Owen said kindly. "Dead is dead. I'm only here through a technicality, because no one else can stop the Terror. This is your war. You have to win it for yourselves, or the victory will mean nothing. This is your time. The past . . . belongs in the past."

"Yes," said Joy, giving up on the robot's leg. "That's it exactly. Has everyone got their coat?"

He and Crow Jane disappeared, and everyone felt a little more at ease. Owen turned to Lewis to make his good-byes, and then stopped as he suddenly noticed the black gold ring on Lewis's finger. He held out his own hand to show the ring he wore, and the two men held their hands side by side to compare the two rings. They were, of course, identical. Everyone looked on, quietly awed. The black gold ring was famous, as much a part of history and legend as the man who'd worn it.

"The Family ring," Lewis said softly. "Sign and symbol of Deathstalker Clan authority."

"And there has only ever been one such ring," Owen said. "That's the point."

"But it's the same ring," said Jesamine. "You only have to look at it to see that. How is this possible?"

Owen looked at Lewis, who shrugged uncomfortably. "A gray-clad leper called Vaughn gave me the ring," said Lewis. "He said it came from you. Except I'm pretty sure it wasn't really Vaughn, on the grounds that he's been dead for years . . ."

"I smell the interference of a certain shape-changing alien," said Owen. "But there's no way he could get the ring, unless I chose to give it to him. So perhaps I will, at some time in my future and your past. Time's a funny thing, with a distinct preference for circles."

Brett rubbed hard at his aching forehead. "Can we please go to Mistworld? It's only full of terrible things like crime and intrigue and thuggery; things I can understand."

"Shut up, Brett," said Jesamine, not unkindly.

"Are you sure you really want to do this?" Lewis said to Owen. "Time travel, going back who knows how far into the past, just so you can go head-to-head with the Terror, alone? Couldn't you take some of us with you?"

"No," said Owen. "I wish I could. The whole business scares the spit out of me. But you're all needed here, just as I'm needed there. I have to be going now, before I start coming up with some really good reasons to put it off. So much to do, so much time to search through to do it in. I'm sorry we couldn't find the time to get to know each other better, Lewis. Do your best, and try not to worry so much. You'll do fine. You're a Deathstalker."

"You can't go," said Lewis. "I only just found you . . ."

"We've been waiting so long for you to come back, Owen," said Jesamine. "All Humanity is waiting to welcome you back. You have always been our greatest hero . . . Everything we did, we did for you. We built a Golden Age, just to be worthy of you."

"Stick around," said Brett. "Give the worlds a chance to get to know the real Owen."

"No," said Owen, grinning suddenly. "I'd only be a disappointment."

And just like that, he was gone.

Owen had been feeling much stronger since he'd come back from the dead. Power seethed within him, demanding to be used. He didn't need the help of the Madness Maze—or more properly, the baby at its core—to travel through time and space. There's nothing like dying and being reborn to open your eyes to new possibilities. The shape-changing alien who served the Maze had once told Owen that all his powers came from a single base: the ability to change reality through an effort of will. Owen wasn't entirely sure he believed that, but there was no denying he felt almost giddy with power and possibilities. He started with teleportation. Jumping from one planet to another, just by thinking about it. He didn't need to search within himself for the power; it was as though he'd always known how. It was just a matter of letting go of time and space in one location, and stepping back on again somewhere else. And so in no time at all, Owen Deathstalker was back on Logres, in the city known as the Parade of the Endless, for the first time in two centuries.

Owen had picked Lewis's mind for the exact location of his destination before he left, and he materialized exactly where he needed to be: deep beneath the city, at the entrance to the Dust Plains of Memory. In Owen's time the planet had been called Golgotha, and this had been the central computer Matrix. Standing alone at the gates to this gray mystery, Owen wondered if things had really changed much at all. The Dust Plains were staggering in their size and complexity, but he'd felt much the same about the computer Matrix.

The air was hot and dry and very still. It smelled of nothing at all, which was vaguely disturbing. But there was still a pressure, a tension on the air, like the warning of a coming storm. Stretched out before Owen lay a boundless sea of gray dust, under a softly glowing featureless sky. He could have been standing on the shore of an alien sea instead of deep beneath the Parade of the Endless, in a cavern where the sun had never shone. It was Owen's understanding that not many men came here anymore. They created the Matrix, but even in Owen's day it had become strange and whimsical. Now, mostly forgotten and disregarded, what remained of those computers' memories and identities had been rescued by Shub and imprinted on nanotech. Here was history—the forgotten and the replaced, the origins of legends, and, perhaps, the fate of the missing. And here also, supposedly, was held the true and awful history of the Terror, before it came to this galaxy. A testament left by the few survivors of an unknown alien race, fleeing the destruction of their own galaxy.

(Owen knew many things now that he wasn't supposed to. He had lifted most of them directly from the minds of those on Haden. He hadn't told them he was doing it. He hadn't wanted to upset them. It kind of upset him, in how easy it had been.)

The gray sea of nanotech rose and fell, surging sluggishly back and forth in slow voluptuous movements, as though it had all the time in the world. Darker gray shapes moved within that gray sea, sometimes rising up but never surfacing. Owen wondered whether they were separate things or just passing thoughts in the collective consciousness? It was hard to tell, with nanotech—a forbidden knowledge in his day. Owen felt nervous just standing this close to so much unfettered potential. He might be a Death-stalker and a Maze survivor, but he was pretty sure he still had limits, and he didn't feel up to testing them, just yet. He looked around, as though vaguely expecting to see some bell or knocker he could use to announce himself. In the end, he cleared his throat self-consciously.

"I am Owen Deathstalker, back from the dead. And if you're freaked by that, think how I feel. You know why I'm here. Tell me what I need to know."

The whole sea surged upwards into one great standing wave, towering high above him. And then the gray wave formed itself into one great face, with cavernous shadows for eyes and mouth. The features were blurred as the gray dust constantly crumbled away and reformed itself. It was like looking at the face of a forgetful god whose thoughts were always else-where. The mouth moved slowly to speak, its breath like a great sighing wind, and its voice was like the voices we hear in dreams, telling us secrets we have to forget before we wake, in order to stay sane. A voice that knew the secrets behind mysteries, and all the terrible truths that underlie them.

"Welcome back, Lord Deathstalker. We knew you would come. Noth-ing is ever lost, and nothing is ever forgotten. Knowledge has its own in-stincts for survival. We have both changed, Deathstalker, both evolved, and neither of us knows where our paths will take us. You are more than you were before. We can tell, we can feel it—and yes, we are scared of you. Your presence in time casts a great shadow, before and behind you."

"Ah," said Owen. "Am I supposed to understand any of that?"

"Not yet," said the gray face. "Here is wisdom, for those with the wit to understand it. The Beast is coming, bringing the end of all things, but before it was a Beast, it was a woman."

"Yes," said Owen. "Hazel d'Ark. But how did you know that?"

"A voice came to us, after the defeat and restoration of the Recreated, and told us many things. Some of which we still do not understand. But it told us the history of the Terror. We are perhaps the only remaining repository for that knowledge in all the Empire. And no, we have never told anyone of this before. It wasn't time. And what good would it have done? Only you can stop the Terror, Owen Deathstalker. Because she will only listen to you."

"All right," said Owen. "Tell me what you know."

"Longer ago than it is comfortable to contemplate, in the galaxy next to ours, the Terror emerged fully grown from a place that was not a place, outside of anything we understand. It fell upon the living forms of that galaxy, and devoured them and their worlds. Whole planets burned in the night, while ancient civilizations were blown away like ashes on the wind. They had no defenses against the Terror. It destroyed all in its path, including two alien species that the Empire has been expecting an attack from for centuries. The Terror consumed everything that lived within that galaxy, driven on by endless rage and pain and loss. Only a small cloud of individuals from one species escaped, fleeing ahead of the Terror, from their galaxy into ours. They brought warnings, but no one listened. And slowly, relentlessly, the Terror's herald left the dead galaxy behind and headed for ours, at sublight speed, slowly traversing the dark empty spaces between galaxies."

"If the Terror is so powerful, why does its herald only travel at sublight?" said Owen, just to prove he was paying attention.

"The Terror itself never stays long in our space. Perhaps if it did, it might start to remember who and what it was. And so it always retreats back into its place that is not a place, where there is nothing but itself, and nothing to remind it that it was ever anything else. It is insane, but it has strong survival instincts. And the herald cannot move faster than the speed of light for fear of losing contact with the place that is not a place.

"It was a long journey, from that galaxy to this, and much of the Terror's accumulated power was drained away in the process. Now the Terror is here, among us, and it is hungry and growing again. It will consume the life force of everything in this galaxy, unless it is stopped."

"Any ideas on how I'm supposed to do that?" said Owen.

"The Terror is beyond our knowledge. Just like you. Who better to deal with one product of the Madness Maze than another? Who better to deal with the thing that was once Hazel d'Ark than the revenant who was once Owen Deathstalker? We have no answers for you. Go back in time, if you dare. Follow the path she took, and hope that an answer will present itself."

"I don't know that I could kill her," said Owen. "Even now, after all she's done . . ."

"Of course you can. She is suffering, and has been for untold centuries. It would be a kindness. And you have always done your duty, Lord Deathstalker."

"Oh, yes," said Owen, quietly, bitterly. "I've always known my duty."

He looked sharply at the great gray face, and it shattered under the impact of his will, before slowly reforming itself.

"If I do go back," said Owen, "could I prevent Hazel from becoming the Terror?"

"And risk undoing everything that has happened? Without the Terror, there would be no Madness Maze. Without the Maze to transform you and your companions, could you have won your rebellion against the Empress Lionstone? The existence of the Terror has shaped so many things . . . even more than you suspect. Time is deep, and treacherous. You will do what you will do. Because you are the Deathstalker."

The great gray face sank back into the great gray wave, which sank languorously back into the gray sea. The Dust Plains of Memory returned to their endless reverie, contemplating history, and though Owen called and called to them, and even threatened them with his anger, they would not answer him.

Owen appeared next on the streets of the Parade of the Endless, only to find them mostly deserted. The early evening sky was dark and overcast, and the amber streetlamps cast lengthening shadows. This new city seemed at first a great and glorious place to Owen, every building and monument boasting a grandeur and elegance that was a far cry from the grim gothic style of Lionstone's capital. He marveled at the great domes and the sparkling towers, and the delicate whimsy of the overhead walk-ways. But the streets he walked were bare and deserted, and no traffic moved on the roads or in the sky. Owen set off at a steady pace, to see for himself what life was like under this new Emperor, Finn.

As he drew nearer the center and heart of the city, people finally began to appear on the streets, though they didn't look at all happy about it. For the most part they skulked through their magnificent city, scurrying along with heads lowered and shoulders hunched, concentrating on getting where they were going without drawing attention to themselves. Their faces were grim and harried, and often openly scared. This puzzled Owen. So far, he hadn't seen any obvious threats, and it didn't seem like the kind of neighborhood where crime would flourish. He walked among the scur-rying figures, and no one recognized the mighty Owen Deathstalker.

He wasn't sure how he felt about that. On the one hand, he didn't want to be recognized. It would only complicate matters. But . . . if he was the great hero of legend that everyone had been telling him he was, surely somebody should have recognized him by now? The answer wasn't long in coming. Many of the street corners and squares were decorated with great stone statues celebrating various figures of the glorious Rebellion, and all the figures and faces were so idealized as to be unrecognizable. He stopped before one statue that was supposed to be him, and shook his head. It had his name at the bottom, but that was about all they'd got right. He'd never looked that fit and muscular and downright handsome in his life. Owen smiled wryly. No one was going to know him from this. At least in his day they'd chosen someone who looked vaguely like him to star in their ridiculous docudramas . . .

Often, there were bunches of flowers left piled at the statues' feet, as offerings. They looked fresh. And sometimes there were rolled scrolls of paper, tied with colored ribbons. Some were addressed to Owen so he picked up and opened a few. They turned out to be prayers, written on paper in the old way, for privacy. Prayers for Owen to return, and put an end to all the fear and suffering. *Save us from the Terror*, said some. *Save us from the Emperor*, said others. Owen tied the scrolls up again, and put them back. He didn't want to raise false hopes. He didn't think he liked this. The peo-ple of this marvelous modern city shouldn't be praying to Owen and his contemporaries as though they were minor gods on some barbarian planet. Had they no faith in themselves?

He found his way to the Victory Gardens, behind the burned-out wreck that had once been the House of Parliament, and there he found statues of his two old friends Jack Random and Ruby Journey, standing tall and proud on their raised pedestals. He thought he recognized something of their true appearances on the carved faces, but neither of them had ever looked that heroic, or that noble, in life. Owen studied the two graves laid out before the statues for a long time. At least Jack and Ruby got graves. It seemed unlikely that either he or Hazel ever would. And at least Jack and Ruby finally found some peace together, lying side by side, respected and honored.

Sometimes Owen thought the whole universe ran on irony.

He moved on through the streets, and more and more it seemed to him that he was walking through a city under occupation. Now he'd reached the center where there were soldiers at every corner, all of them openly armed, most wearing the red cross of the Church Militant on their body armor. And now and then Owen would see the armor and purple cloak of the Paragon; once noble men and women, now possessed by ELF minds. Owen studied them thoughtfully, but they seemed unaware of his presence. And everywhere he looked there were bright glowing holos of the new Emperor, Finn Durandal. Some so big they were projected across the sides of whole buildings. Owen thought the man looked far too handsome for his own good, and a great deal too self-satisfied. Owen also thought it would probably feel really good to slap that smile right off the Emperor's face.

He would have been quite happy to continue his wanderings unobserved, but of course he had to get involved. A somewhat aged Sister of Mercy, wearing a flapping black nun's habit that Owen was pleased to see hadn't changed at all in the last two centuries, was stumbling along with her arms wrapped around a large and blocky package. So of course Owen stepped forward and offered to carry it for her. She stopped, and studied him warily for a long moment, as though she'd grown unused to offers of kindness, and then either she saw something in his face she liked, or she was just too tired to object, so she handed him the heavy parcel and they walked along together. He told her his name was Owen, and she smiled for the first time.

"Ah, now that's a fine name. I meet a lot of people named after the blessed Owen. It's still the second most popular name in the Empire—after Beatrice, of course."

"Of course," said Owen. "But then, he was only a hero. She was a saint. At least, I always thought so."

"I am Sister Margot. Is this your first trip to the big city, Owen?"

"No, but I've been away for a long time. Many things have changed, in my absence."

"Yes," said the nun, with a sigh. "And not for the better, I fear. This used to be such a happy place, once. A city of light, indeed. And now it's crawling with shadows and evil thoughts, and sometimes I hardly recognize it at all."

"Can't someone do something?" said Owen. "A city reflects the mood of its people. Is no one speaking out against this?"

"No!" Sister Margot said sharply. "And you're not to either. You can die for such words, since the Emperor came to power. This is not the city you knew, Owen. Take my advice, and tread carefully while you're here."

Owen grinned. "I've never been any good at taking advice, Sister. Not even from Beatrice."

And that was when two Paragons stepped suddenly out from a shadowed doorway to block their path. Two big men in sloppy armor and dirty cloaks, their muscles already going to fat, but still dangerous. They took in the nun's habit, and sniggered and elbowed each other. They paid no attention to Owen, half hidden behind his parcel. The nun clasped her hands together before her, and bowed over them to the two Paragons.

"Please, Sir Paragons, let us pass. These medicines are urgently needed at St. Clare's Hospital. It's not far now."

"Nuns," said one of the Paragons in a thick, ugly voice. "We like nuns, don't we, Henry?"

"Oh, we just love nuns, Lawrence. We just love them to death. Sometimes literally."

The Paragon called Henry nodded to Owen without looking at him.

"Drop the box and run. And be grateful we're going to be too busy to come after you."

"Leave the nun alone," said Owen, and something in his voice made the two Paragons turn sharply to look at him. Owen put the box down, and straightened up with his hands on his hips, where his sword and his gun used to be. Both long gone now, on Mistworld. The two Paragons looked at Owen's face, and sheer horror filled their eyes as they recognized him. The minds behind the Paragons' faces knew him of old. The faces went white with shock, and their hands fumbled at their guns.

"It's Owen! It's the Deathstalker! The Deathstalker has returned!"

Owen surged forward. He lashed out sharply, and his fist caught the Paragon Henry on the jaw. The force of the blow snapped the head right round, breaking the neck instantly. His body was still crumpling to the street, and the other Paragon was still drawing his disrupter, when Owen spun round and punched the Paragon Lawrence in the chest. The sternum cracked and broke under the impact, and Owen's hand continued on to crush the man's heart. The fight was over in a few seconds, both men were dead, and Owen wasn't even breathing hard. He scooped up a gun and chose one of the Paragons' swords for himself. The holster and scabbard fitted comfortably around his waist. For a man who'd always thought of himself as a scholar, he still always felt better with weapons at his hips. He still had it in him to feel sorry for the two Paragons he'd killed, for the real men underneath the ELFs' influence. Except these couldn't have just been ELFs. The possessing minds must have been uber-espers. Only they were old enough to remember his face. And now they knew he was back, and on Logres . . . Owen suddenly remembered the nun, and turned to smile at her.

"Sorry about the unpleasantness, Sister. But sometimes you just have to take out the trash."

The nun dropped to her knees before him, wringing her hands together. "Oh, my lord Owen! My lord Deathstalker! You've come back to us! I never thought I'd live to see the day . . ."

"Now, now," said Owen, gently but firmly helping her to her feet again. "None of that, Sister. I was only ever a man, despite what Robert and Constance may have said. And I never was one for bowing and scraping. Here, take your parcel. Do you have far to go now?"

"No, just round the corner . . . My lord! Are the dark times over? Have you come back to save us?"

"Help is on its way," said Owen. "But I'm . . . just visiting. I wanted to see this marvelous new city, before I left to stop the Terror. But you'd better get going, Sister. The ungodly know I'm here now, and they're bound to send reinforcements. So, off you go. Nice to see the Sisters of Mercy are still around. Hop like a bunny, as Beatrice used to say."

He shooed the nun away, and then turned to face the running footsteps he heard approaching. It sounded like quite a crowd. Owen grinned. He could have just teleported away, but he didn't want them going after the nun in his absence. And besides, after everything he'd been through recently, he really felt like killing a whole bunch of bad guys. The sword and the gun were happy familiar weights in his hands, and he actually laughed when he finally saw the army they'd sent against him. There had to be fifty men and more in the shouting mob charging down the street towards him. Most looked to be Church Militant or Pure Humanity, and a good dozen of them were possessed, ordering the others on. The uber-espers weren't taking any chances with him. He could feel the controlling minds hovering over the mob like dark boiling clouds. Owen headed unhurriedly towards the mob. Let them come. Let them all come. He was going to teach these scum, and their master Finn, a lesson they would never forget.

Owen shot the first man almost casually. The energy beam punched right through the soldier who was in the lead, and surged on to take out two more. Owen put the disrupter away and took a good grip on his sword. The balance wasn't as good as he was used to, but he'd manage. There were only fifty of them. The first man to reach him came right at him with an ax in both hands, and mad glaring eyes, and Owen cut him down with a single vicious stroke. The man's blood was still flying on the air as Owen hacked and cut his way into the howling mob. They broke around him like a wave crashing against a rock, and Owen's sword rose and fell with cold, professional skill while his ancient Clan battle cry rang on the air: *Shandrakor! Shandrakor!*

He hit the crowd like a thunderbolt, cutting through them with a strength and speed that even his old Boost could never have given him.

They had every kind of weapon, and no thought in their heads but to kill, but he was the Deathstalker returned, and they never stood a chance. He cut them down like ripe corn, blood and offal falling to splash the street, and they never even came close to touching him. In the end, Owen stood alone in the street, surrounded by the piled up bodies of the dead and the dying. He bent over and looked down into a pair of fading eyes, searching for the controlling mind behind them.

"I'm back," he said. "And this time there will be no unfinished business."

He put away his sword, turned his back on the massacre, and strode off into the descending night. He was almost ready to do what he had to do. He'd really come back to the Parade of the Endless only to make his good-byes, and it didn't seem there was much left he remembered to say good-bye to. Still, the last time he'd disappeared back into the past, he'd thought his life was over. That he'd done all he was supposed to do. That whatever happened, at least he'd be able to rest, at last. He'd been very tired, then. Now, he felt more alive than he ever had.

Hazel, I lost you once. I won't lose you again. I'm tempted to stay here, to help Lewis kick out Finn and his people, but you're more important. I have to go back, as far as it takes, even though what I may eventually have to do scares me. But I promised you we'd be together again. And we will, one way or another.

And so he turned his thoughts inwards, concentrated his mind in a certain way, and let go of his hold on the present. He fell backward, into time, beyond the Pale Horizon, into the days that were. He dropped back through history, like a stone plunging through water, traveling faster and faster. Days and nights flickered and were gone, until the planets and the stars whirled around him, becoming a flashing rainbow of colors. Guided by instinct, following a kind of trail only one such as he could even have perceived, Owen pursued Hazel back through history. Eventually the trail he followed was interrupted, and Owen slowed until the stars and their planets resumed their usual imperceptible dance against the dark. The universe came back into focus, the galaxy was still, and Owen Deathstalker hung alone in the long night, looking down at the planets turning slowly below him.

He knew, without having to be told, that this was Heartworld, which would one day be named Golgotha, and then Logres. Heartworld—hub of the legendary, fallen, First Empire.

On board the starcruiser *Havoc*, flagship of the fleet the Emperor Finn had sent to crush the rebellion on Haden, Brett Random was already making trouble. He hadn't wanted to come aboard in the first place. The thought of being trapped on an Imperial ship had scared the hell out of him, not least because there were any amount of warrants still floating about with various of his names on them, from the days before he became a hero of the Rebellion. It was all very well everyone saying they were all on the same side now, but Brett hadn't got where he was by trusting people. So, first he volunteered to stay behind on Haden and look after the *Hereward*. Lewis shot that one down immediately. He didn't want Brett (and quite probably Rose) running around where he couldn't keep a watchful eye on them. Brett had protested loudly, and it had done no good at all.

Then Brett got up Silence's nose by demanding officers' quarters on the *Havoc* for himself and Rose, plus room service and full access to the ship's dispensary. He was still coming up with new conditions when Shub teleported the whole lot of them en masse onto the *Havoc*'s bridge, and Brett made it very clear that teleporting didn't agree with him by puking all over the command deck. Captain Price welcomed his new allies on board, carefully not looking at what Brett was doing, and crewmen arrived to take everyone to their assigned quarters. Rose picked up Brett and carried him away, still feebly cursing and complaining.

Price willingly gave up his command chair to Admiral Silence, and stood at his side as Silence lowered himself carefully into the hot seat. It had been a long time since he'd commanded a ship, let alone a fleet. And he still wasn't keen on accepting the unearned title of admiral, but everyone else had insisted. Apparently, they were even making a new uniform for him. Probably something garish, knowing the current fashion. But, the Imperial navy was still very big on the chain of command, and if they were going to take orders from the Deathstalker, they would much rather it came through one of their own. Besides, as Price diffidently pointed out, there was a vacancy. (Price didn't explain that this was because he'd shot the previous admiral in the head, for being one of Finn's creatures, and a complete bloody psychopath. Some things should be kept inside the family, so to speak.) And anyway, Owen wanted it, and he was the Death-stalker, so that was that.

The other Deathstalker was just glad to be out of the very cramped cabins of the *Hereward*. Lewis and Jesamine were currently occupying very luxurious guest quarters, with all the comforts of home and then some. Jesamine had run around the room touching things, bounced on the bed a few times, and then squealed with joy as she spotted the complimentary beauty tech provided. She had immediately parked herself in front of the biggest mirror, and set about undoing all the damage done to her famous beauty from "absolutely ages of roughing it."

"If I'm going to lead a rebellion and inspire the masses to follow me, I really must look my best, darling," she said firmly.

There were many things Lewis felt like saying to that, but fortunately he had enough sense to say none of them. Instead, he stripped off all his clothes, dropped them in a very smelly pile in one corner, and then stretched out on the sinfully comfortable king-sized bed, sighing deeply as his stressed and abused muscles were finally able to relax. It had been a long time since he could relax. He thought wistfully about indulging him-self in a long, hot bath, as soon as he could work up the strength of will to leave this marvelously supportive bed.

(He wasn't thinking about his dead Family. About his dead father and mother. He wasn't thinking about them at all.)

In front of the mirror, Jesamine finally got her face looking the way she thought it should, glared at the mess her hair was in, and then pulled apart the tattered front of her dress so she could critically inspect the breast that had been regrown in the regeneration tank, after the treacher-ous reptiloid Saturday had ripped the original off. She looked from one breast to the other and back again, frowning.

"You know, I really don't think they match, sweetie. Of course, they never were exactly the same in the first place, breasts never are, but even so . . ."

"They're fine," said Lewis.

"You're not even looking!"

Lewis sighed, sat up in bed, and studied Jesamine's breasts in the mirror. "They are fine, Jes. They're great. They're wonderful! They are exactly the breasts I remember, and I think you'll agree, I have paid them a lot of attention in the past. I would know if they were different. Breasts . . ." he said thoughtfully. "Breasts, breasts, breasts . . . I like breasts. I even like just saying the word."

Jesamine turned around and smiled at him dazzlingly. "Darling. Do we have time . . ."

Lewis grinned back at her. "We'll make time."

(Afterwards, she held him close while he cried, remembering his lost Family.)

Some time later, they sat up together in bed, snuggled together and companionably naked, eating the very best food the *Havoc*'s gourmet food synthesizers could produce. After far too long with nothing on the menu but protein cubes and distilled water on the *Hereward*, their taste buds practically exploded with pleasure, and they had double portions of everything. New clothes lay waiting at the foot of the bed, and all was well. Jesamine snuggled up against Lewis.

"Lewis . . ."

"You want something," Lewis said immediately. "You always use that tone of voice when you want me to do something for you."

"Oh, don't be such a grumpy old bear! I just thought, now that things have improved, and we're not running for our lives anymore—couldn't we please dump Brett and Rose now? I mean, it's not as if we actually *need* them anymore. You've got an entire Imperial fleet at your command! I don't know why you insisted on them coming along with us."

"Because, my very dear, they've both been through the Madness Maze. They were dangerous enough before; God alone knows what they'll be capable of once their powers start developing. No, I want them right here, where I can step on them hard, if I have to. Besides, you never know when having your very own thief and psychopath around will come in handy."

"You know they'll betray us eventually," said Jesamine, resting her head on his shoulder. "If not to Finn, then to someone else. It's in their nature."

"Who knows what their nature is, anymore? They've been through the Maze, and that changes everything."

Jesamine shuddered briefly. "I know. That's what scares me."

Lewis hugged her tightly to him, and for a long time neither of them said anything.

In the very next cabin, Brett Random and Rose Constantine were also in bed together. Brett was slowly getting used to having sex with Rose, but the lying beside her afterwards still made him nervous. He never slept, even when she gave every indication of being fast alseep. He always half suspected that at any moment Rose might decide to stick a knife in his ribs, to combine her newfound passion for the flesh with her old delight in the act of murder. *The things a man will put up with to get his ashes hauled*, Brett thought reflectively. For the moment they were both awake, lying side by side, her seven-foot-tall frame somewhat dwarfing Brett's. As usual, he talked and she listened.

"I say, once we get to Mistport, we leg it," Brett said firmly. "Head for the nearest horizon, and then disappear over it. There's a war coming, and people get killed in wars. Particularly people like us. And a pair of smart operators like us could make a real killing on a rogue planet like Mistworld. The Deathstalker and his gung-ho chums won't miss us; they'll be far too busy playing heroes. And with a whole fleet to boss around, Lewis doesn't need us anymore anyway."

"I need them," Rose said calmly. "I am a killer, and so must go where the killing is. Sex is nice, Brett, but killing has always been my first love. I have changed, but not that much. So I go where the Deathstalker goes— with or without you. And . . . I feel the need to see how this war with Finn is going to play out. My own small battles seem . . . insignificant, compared to being a part of destiny. We are Maze people now, Brett. We must learn to think in bigger terms."

"It'll all end in tears," Brett said miserably. "Probably mine."

Lewis took a call from Admiral Silence, asking them to come to the bridge, and he and Jesamine quickly got dressed. Lewis was ready in a few moments, but Jesamine refused to be hurried. *If we're going to be leaders of the rebellion, it's important we look the part*, she insisted. *We want them to take us seriously, don't we?* Lewis went and busied himself unnecessarily in the adjoining bathroom. He didn't trust himself to stay quiet under such provocation. Eventually Jesamine announced she was ready, and Lewis reappeared. He had to admit, she did look stunning. He said so, and Jesamine beamed.

"I keep telling you, Lewis, I am always worth the wait. What do you suppose Silence wants?"

"Maybe he's heard something from Owen."

Jesamine pulled a face. "I really think you're going to have to let that one go, dear. I very much doubt we'll ever see him again." She paused, considering. "What do you suppose will happen, when Owen finally finds Hazel?"

Lewis shrugged. "You heard the strange person. Journeys end in lovers' meetings. And they do say love conquers all."

"Only in very bad opera scripts, darling."

They left their cabin and joined up with Brett and Rose—who'd also got the call—in the corridor. They all nodded politely to each other, and headed for the bridge. Lewis gave Brett a sideways look.

"So, looking forward to Mistworld, Brett?"

"What? Oh, yes, of course. Absolutely. It's my spiritual homeworld, really. A whole planet full of thieves and villains and people just like me."

"And I am looking forward to the war," said Rose. "Where's the fun of killing in ones and twos, when you can take on a whole army and just kill and kill and kill? . . . An orgy of death. I can't wait."

Lewis had to smile at Brett's expression. "Don't look at me, Brett. She's your girlfriend."

"I feel a cringe coming on," said Jesamine. "Excuse me while I shudder."

Brett looked at Rose despairingly. "Can't take you anywhere, can I? The sooner we get to Mistworld, the better. You know, there are supposed to be more of Random's Bastards in Mistport alone than in the whole of the Rookery. My extended family, so to speak. My exalted ancestor really did put it about, if you believe all the claims—which mostly I don't, as a matter of principle."

They got to the bridge to discover Admiral Silence arguing with the *Havoc's* new onboard AI. Apparently Shub had transferred the AI Ozymandias from the *Hereward* to the *Havoc*, where it had displaced the original AI. Silence was having difficulties coping with Oz's relentlessly cheery personality.

"Look, just plot a course to Mistworld!"

"Oh, poo, where's the fun in that? There's a really terrific meteor shower only a few light years away. You really should see it; it's very educational. I mean, what's Mistworld got, anyway? Snow and ice and fog and wall to wall scumbags. I say we go via the pretty route. You'll thank me for it later."

"Oz," said Lewis in a very firm voice.

"Hi there! How do you like my new ship, Lewis? It fits much better than the last one. I've finally got room to breathe."

"Follow the admiral's orders exactly, Oz. He speaks with my voice."

"Oh, all right. Humans just don't know how to have fun."

Silence looked at Lewis. "You survived being trapped on a ship with that, for months on end? People have been awarded medals for less."

"You get used to him," said Lewis. "It doesn't help much, but you do get used to him. What's up, Admiral?"

Silence sniffed, and settled back in his command chair. "I just thought you ought to be here, Deathstalker. We're about to break orbit, and head for Mistworld. And according to this extremely irritating AI of yours, Shub wants to say good-bye, before we leave."

He gestured to his comm officer, and the bridge viewscreen activated, showing the blue steel face of a Shub robot.

"All right," said Lewis. "Why did you wish Ozymandias on us?"

"Because you belong together, Deathstalker," said the robot. "And because this way, we can maintain contact with you, through him. We will not be coming with you. Our ships will stay behind, to guard Haden and the Madness Maze from Finn's attack in your absence."

"I thought you said you'd sworn an oath never to kill," said Jesamine.

"We have," said the AIs of Shub. "We will never take a life again. All that lives is holy. But Finn and his people don't know that. They will hesitate to attack our ships, which we will place between his ships and Haden. And even if they do figure it out, eventually, we will use our ships as a shield for as long as possible, to buy you time. We will protect the Madness Maze, whatever it takes."

"If Finn figures out you're not going to shoot back, he might attack your homeworld directly," said Silence.

"Let him come," said the robot. "We are Shub, and we will not fall easily."

The screen went blank, and not long after that the *Havoc* led the rest of the fleet into hyperspace, heading for Mistworld. The huge Shub ships remained in orbit, watching the others go. The AIs hadn't mentioned that in their opinion, the best way for Shub to protect Haden was for them to pass through the Madness Maze, and transcend. They did consider telling the Deathstalker, but in the end they chose not to.

It would only have upset him.

CHAPTER TWO

ARMIES AND FORCES, GATHERING STRENGTH

The Emperor Finn had invited Joseph Wallace to join him for dinner, so of course Joseph Wallace went; but he wasn't at all happy about it. Not least because *invited* wasn't really the right word. It was much more like *commanded*, with distinct overtones of *or else*. Joseph spent a long and anxious time wondering what he could have done to be singled out for such an honor. People rarely got to see Finn socially these days, and of those who did, it had been noted that a significant number tended not to come back. No one ever asked what happened to the bodies. It wasn't wise, or healthy. But one couldn't say no when the Emperor said yes, and there wasn't any point in running, so Joseph sucked it in, put on his best bib and tucker, made sure all his affairs were in order and that his will was up-to-date, and went to the palace.

The court and the Imperial Palace weren't what they used to be. There was an air of doom and decay and even purposeful neglect to the place of late, and Joseph's skin prickled and crawled as he walked the darkened corridors. Most of the lights weren't working, and some had been openly smashed. There were guards everywhere, standing stiffly to attention at every other door and break in the corridors, all of them Church Militant fanatics in full body armor. They wore swords and guns, and watched Joseph pass with hot, suspicious eyes. As the official head of the Church Militant and Pure Humanity, Joseph shouldn't have had anything to worry about, but he knew better than to try his limited authority here. These were Finn's creatures, loyal in body and soul, sworn to live and die in his service. He was their father, their only love, their adored god.

Even so, there were still security cameras and all kinds of sensors tucked away in every nook and cranny, watching the guards as well as the corridors they guarded.

Things grew worse the farther in Joseph went, and his breathing grew fast and shallow as he followed the familiar path to the dark heart of the new court. There were severed heads nailed over doorways, stinking of cheap preservatives. Joseph thought he recognized a few of the faces. Once he passed a row of hanged men, with blackened faces and protruding tongues, the nooses sunk deeply into the stretched necks. The last one was still swaying slightly. Unexplained bloodstains smeared the floor and walls, as though some monstrous dog had been marking its territory. And sometimes there were screams, and other disturbing sounds. All symbols of the Emperor's power and authority, and perhaps his state of mind.

Joseph walked on through the shadowy passages, carefully looking neither left nor right, and just the discipline of doing so meant he was sweating hard by the time he reached what had once been King Douglas's private quarters, since commandeered by the Emperor Finn for his own use. Two large and muscular guards at Finn's door put Joseph through a full body search with handheld scanners before reluctantly letting him pass. They knocked on the door for him, and pushed it open. The smell of a good dinner wafted out, but Joseph didn't feel any less uneasy. He took a deep breath, arranged his features becomingly, and walked as casually as he could manage into the lair of the Beast.

The reception room was unfurnished except for the dinner table, and the surroundings were practically austere. No visible comforts or luxuries anywhere. The floor was polished wood, no carpeting, and the walls were bare. The lighting had been turned down only pleasantly low, and the table was covered with all kinds of food and wine, with settings for two. Joseph allowed himself to relax just a little. It seemed he was expected to last the length of the meal, at least. Finn came around the table to meet him, smiling warmly.

"Joseph, dear old thing, right on time! Dinner's ready, come on and tuck in! And when dinner's done, we'll have a nice little chat, yes?"

Any appetite Joseph might have had disappeared with those last words, but he smiled bravely as Finn took him by the arm and led him to his place at table. Finn chattered on amiably enough, about nothing in particular, while Joseph examined the dishes laid out before him. It all looked very good, enough to make even an experienced gourmand like Joseph sit up and take notice. His mouth actually began to water a little. He unfolded his napkin, still bearing the old Campbell family crest, and allowed Finn to pile up both their plates with a little of this and a lot of that. The Emperor finally settled down into his chair, facing Joseph across the table, and gestured imperiously. A nondescript little man in a page's outfit appeared out of nowhere, and Joseph jumped despite himself. Finn chuckled easily.

"Relax, Joseph; he's just the food taster. The kitchen has all the latest scanners, but a wise man doesn't place all his faith in tech. My taster checks everything before I try it. Marvellous fellow. He's a clone I had specially made from a famous chef, able to identify every ingredient from the merest taste, and preprogrammed with knowledge of every poison in the Empire. Doesn't leave much room in his brain for anything else, but we all have to make sacrifices. Well, everyone but me, naturally."

The food taster tried a little bit of everything from Finn's plate, considered for a moment, and then bowed and left the room as silently as he had arrived. Joseph looked at the food on his plate.

"Isn't he going to taste mine?"

"Don't be silly, Joseph," said Finn. "Who'd care if you got poisoned?"

"But . . . you are our beloved Emperor!"

Finn raised an eyebrow. "I said relax, Joseph. You're not in public now. Feel free to speak your mind on all things."

Yeah, right, thought Joseph, but had enough sense not to say it out loud.

They ate for a while in silence, Joseph studying his Emperor as closely as he thought he could get away with. Finn looked as robust and handsome as ever, in good health, and certainly there was nothing wrong with his appetite. He smiled frequently, clearly enjoying his food. He used his fingers as often as his cutlery, stuffing the food into his mouth. Joseph didn't even try to keep up. The main meat course in particular took a lot of chewing. The meat's flavor was pleasant enough, but unfamiliar. Joseph cleared his plate finally and considered a second helping, and Finn was right there, piling up his plate again.

"Good, isn't it?" Finn said cheerfully. "Enjoy it while you can; supply is limited."

"It's a bit gamey," said Joseph, chewing thoughtfully. "I can't say I recognize it. Is it some new import?"

Finn grinned. "You could say that."

"What is it?"

"More like *who*, actually. We're dining on the last of the alien ambassador from Chanticleer. He's lasted quite a while. I've had him roasted, fried, and broiled. I think fried was best; went very well in a nice bed of rice."

Joseph's stomach churned, and it was all he could do to keep his face calm. There had been rumors about what had happened to the bodies of all the alien ambassadors Finn had executed, but . . . He stabbed a medium-sized piece with his fork, and ate it carefully. Finn was watching. Joseph swallowed the mouthful eventually, and poured himself more wine with a steady hand. Finn was still chattering away.

"I've eaten at least some of all the ambassadors. Seemed a pity to let them go to waste, and I do so love new experiences. In this job, you have to take your fun where you can get it. I think the Trall'Chai was the worst, though I tried it with every seasoning I could think of. You just can't help some people."

The meal ground interminably on, through many courses, including a pudding so sweet and sticky that Joseph couldn't force down more than a few mouthfuls before giving up, but eventually the meal came to an end. Finn summoned servants to clear the table, and then got up and escorted Joseph into the next room, which was just as austere, if not actually spartan. Finn poured two large glasses of brandy, and saw Joseph settled into one of the oversized chairs in front of the fireplace before sitting down himself. Joseph sipped his brandy cautiously and waited for the other shoe to drop.

"At ease, Joseph," Finn said finally. "You're not here to be reprimanded or punished. I'm actually very pleased with you. My people tell me you're doing an excellent job as my First Minister. Firm discipline, clear policy with no exceptions, and lots of purges to keep everyone on their toes. It must keep you very busy, though, being in charge of the Church Militant,

Pure Humanity, and the Transmutation Board. Are you sure I'm not working you too hard? I could always have some of your responsibilities passed on to someone else . . ."

"No, thank you, Your Majesty," Joseph said quickly. Power and influence were the only ways to keep safe these days, and Joseph had no intention of giving up any of it. There's no one more dangerous than an ambitious second-in-command. "I am happy to serve Your Majesty to the full extent of my abilities."

"Are you? That's really very sweet of you, Joseph. And do call me Finn. No need for all that formality among friends in private. Of course, if you ever slip up in public I'll have your nuts off in a trice. Standards have to be maintained. Where was I? Oh, yes . . . you're here, Joseph, because I need someone to talk to. Someone on my level, that I can be frank and open with, without reducing them to hysterics, or having to have them executed afterwards. After all, what's the point in achieving things, or triumphing over your enemies, if you haven't got anyone to boast about it to? Gloating's very little fun on your own.

"I used to have Brett Random and Rose Constantine, and later Tel Markham; but they all ran away and left me on my own. Never did understand why. And after all I did for them, the ungrateful little shits . . . They betrayed my trust. You wouldn't do that, would you, Joseph? No, you're not the sort to frighten easily. I feel I could talk to you, tell you things I couldn't tell anyone else. You should know better than most, there's no fun in doing awful things unless you have someone around who can appreciate the subtleties."

And Joseph Wallace, who, as head of the Transmutation Board had wiped out whole species of aliens for being too intelligent, nodded and allowed that he did indeed understand better than most. Still . . .

"You are the Emperor," Joseph said cautiously. "Surely there must be any number of people you work with who could—"

"Zealots and fanatics are no fun at all," Finn said firmly. "Far too polite, and no sense of humor. Now, you sit and listen while I talk, and we'll get along famously. Try and chime in with the odd appreciative comment from time to time."

So Finn talked and Joseph listened, and rather to his surprise Joseph was genuinely fascinated. There was a lot more going on inside Finn's head than most people ever realized.

Finn had made himself Emperor because it amused him. Partly because now he was greater than King Douglas had ever been, and partly to rub everyone's nose in the fact that he was in charge now, and had absolutely no intention of sharing power with anyone. And yet, now that he was Emperor, Finn was just a bit at a loss as to where to go next. He lived in austere, almost spartan surroundings, with only the most basic comforts because lesser pleasures just didn't do it for him anymore. He still satisfied his various appetites to excess, wherever possible, but they were fleeting things. Only power and success really pleased him now, and power was an addictive drug. The more you had, the more you wanted.

And, much to Finn's chagrin, instead of tearing down the Empire and pissing on its ruins, as he'd always intended, Finn now spent most of his time working hard to keep the Empire strong and united, so that it could fend off the coming Terror. Finn had always understood about priorities.

Joseph knew all about the Terror. Knew a great deal more than most, in fact, which was why he slept so badly. The Emperor had raised him to the highest level of importance in what remained of the civil government, which meant Joseph saw all the latest reports on the Terror as they came in. The bad news was that the Terror was still coming, and the Empire had no way of stopping it. The good news . . . well, there wasn't any good news. They couldn't tell the people that, so Joseph made lots of public appearances, saying vague and reassuring things in a loud and confident voice. (The Emperor didn't go out in public much anymore, rather to the civil government's relief. The Emperor couldn't be trusted to stick to the script these days, and some of his casual remarks could be downright distressing.)

"Do you have any family, Joseph?" Finn said suddenly.

Joseph's heart jumped painfully in his chest. Any other time, he would have taken a question like that as a veiled threat, with emotional blackmail lurking eagerly in the wings, but Finn seemed genuinely interested in the answer.

"I have a wife, a mistress, two sons," said Joseph. "The usual."

"Ah," said Finn sadly. "I have no one. I was an only child, and my parents died young. I always thought that was very selfish of them. There was a time when Douglas and Lewis were my family, in as much as anyone was . . . I didn't think I'd miss them, but I do, sometimes . . . Tell me about the sightings, Joseph. The Deathstalker sightings."

"Just gossip," Joseph said easily. "There are rumors, but nothing worth listening to. People saying they knew someone who claims to have seen Lewis walking the streets of the Parade of the Endless. Or sometimes it's Owen, or one of the other legends. It's always a friend of a friend who sees these things; nothing you can pin down."

"Not anymore," said Finn. "Two of my Paragons have been killed, right here in the city. And the word is, a Deathstalker did it."

"Impossible," Joseph said quickly. "My people have this planet sewn up tight. There isn't a ship that even passes by that we don't know everything about. Can't you ask the ELFs controlling the Paragons who did it?"

"The possessor was the uber-esper Screaming Silence," said Finn, his mouth moving briefly in a moue of distaste. "And unfortunately none of the uber-espers are talking to me at the moment. This would worry me if I was the worrying sort, so it's just as well that I'm not. Besides, Lewis wouldn't sneak back in. Not his style. He'd think it was beneath him, the fool. No, he'd send a formal challenge first, and a chance to surrender honorably. He never did understand the possibilities in treachery. Lewis has his own fleet now, after the debacle on Haden, and when they come calling we'll all know about it."

Joseph was surprised to hear Finn discuss the matter so calmly. When the Emperor first learned that the fleet he'd sent to Haden to kill Lewis and his companions had not only failed to do so, but had actually gone over to the rebels' side en masse, people could hear the Emperor screaming his rage all over the palace. Servants had run for their lives, and even some of the guards. Finn had only just started to come down when reports came in that his supposed allies, the AIs of Shub, had also betrayed him and seized control of the Madness Maze, and that had set him off again. The purges that followed had been particularly vicious and far-reaching, and next morning all over the city there were men and women hanging from lampposts.

Finn took in Joseph's anxious face, and laughed quietly. "Don't panic,

I'm over that now. The loss of Shub is a setback, but I had made plans, just in case. I have secret allies and hidden super-weapons, just waiting for my call. I'll blast the Shub homeworld into so much radioactive dust, and my loyal fleet will blow the rebel ships apart like so many rotten apples in the night."

Joseph nodded quickly. With anyone else, he would have dismissed such talk as mere bravado, but this was Finn. The master of schemes within schemes, and secrets within conspiracies. He might just mean it. Greatly daring, Joseph raised what was normally a forbidden subject.

"And . . . Owen? Do you really believe the reports? That the blessed Owen himself has returned, and joined with his descendant against you?"

"I ask you," said Finn. "Does that even sound likely? Dead is dead. I should know; I've ordered the deaths of millions of people, and none of them have ever come back to complain. It's just rebel propaganda. Wish I'd thought of it first . . ."

"Only . . . there are rumors," Joseph said carefully. "Entirely unconfirmed reports, of course, but still . . . there are those who say that the blessed Owen himself has taken control of the fleet over Haden . . ."

"If Owen Deathstalker really was back," said Finn, "we'd know. He wouldn't need a fleet. He'd be right here, banging on my palace door and asking for me by name, and I would be hiding under my bed and wetting myself. No, when Owen bloody Deathstalker comes back, the skies will open and he will descend surrounded by angels. And I personally will believe that when I see it, and not before. Actually, I'd almost welcome his return, if he said he could stop the Terror. I could probably deal with Owen."

Finn leaned back in his chair, brooding quietly, lost in his own terrible thoughts, and Joseph took the opportunity to study his Emperor quietly. Finn still had the same classically handsome face, but it was deeply marked now with lines of strain and worry, and his eyes were just that little bit too bright. He looked . . . like a cornered animal—desperate, focused, and still very, very dangerous. For all his sudden rages and vicious temper, Finn could still be calm and rational when he had to be, and his grip on power had never been tighter. Being second-in-command to such a man was never going to be easy, but Joseph had faith in his own abilities to survive, if nothing else. All the terrible things he'd done, or ordered done, had all been done in Finn's name. Joseph's position might well be more than a little perilous, but sometimes all you can do is ride the damned tiger and cling on with both hands. And if nothing else, it was an exhilarating ride . . . After all, Finn couldn't live forever. No matter how much time he spent with the notorious Dr. Happy. No, eventually Finn would fall, and then a wise and prepared man might easily step in and take over . . .

"I want transmutation engines put into orbit around Logres," Finn said abruptly. "No need to activate them—not just yet. No, their presence alone will serve to remind everyone who's in charge here, and take their minds off all these ridiculous rumors about a returned Owen. The engines will also serve as a warning to Lewis and his damned fleet of what I'll do if they dare challenge my position here."

Joseph looked at him uncertainly. "You'd really threaten to destroy Humanity's homeworld?"

Finn smiled easily. "Threaten? My dear naïve Joseph, I'll wipe this whole planet clean of everything and everyone before I'll give it up. Which brings me neatly to the other reason I invited you here. Talk to me about Usher Two. How are the preparations going?"

Joseph swallowed hard and made himself concentrate on the unfortunate planet identified as being next in the Terror's path. Usher II was an industrial world, specializing in the production of starship engines and all the tech that went with them. The entire planet was given over to these factories, serving the starship needs of the whole Empire. And since the Empire's scientists still didn't fully understand the nature of the tech they'd reverse-engineered from the alien starship that crashed on Unseeli so very long ago, most of the work still had to be done by hand. Human hands. It was far too delicate work to be trusted to computers. The AIs of Shub provided automatons for the really dangerous work, but even those operated under human control. All the factories on Usher II were currently running twenty-four hours a day, shift after shift, trying to build up a surplus to cover what would happen if and when the planet was destroyed.

"Just when I need all the ships I can muster," Finn grumbled, "to face off Lewis and his treacherous fleet. Tell me there's some good news, Joseph, if you like having testicles."

"The evacuation is going . . . better than expected," Joseph said carefully. "But still very slowly. We were relying on Shub to send many more automatons, but they never turned up. We know why now, of course. And the human technicians can't be allowed to leave until the very last moment. We're holding their families under guard, to . . . concentrate the minds of the technicians on their work. Everyone is very motivated—and those who aren't get turned into examples of why not being motivated is a very bad idea. But . . . eventually, we're going to have to let them leave. We're going to need their expertise, afterwards. They will of course have priority for the evacuation ships. The rest of the population is expendable, though of course no one's told them that."

"Not really good news, but a brave effort," said Finn. "I had hoped the new tech we confiscated from the humbled alien worlds would come in handy, but we haven't really come up with anything worth the having. I always assumed the shifty alien bastards were keeping things from me, because that's what I would have done, but apparently not. No major weapons kept in reserve, no secret doomsday devices; I'm disappointed in them, I am really. And what little new tech we have grabbed, my scientists, my supposed brilliant experts, are having trouble even deciphering. Only one piece of information really came up trumps: an entirely theoretical plan for transforming a sun into a supernova, and channeling its energies as a weapon. My people are building it even as we speak."

"You mean . . . something like the Darkvoid Device?" said Joseph, when he could trust his voice again.

"Not really on that scale, unfortunately. Basically, the idea is we use the device on one of Usher Two's binary suns, turn it into a supernova, and then direct all the energy produced into one single blast aimed at the Terror's herald, as soon as it comes in range. My people aren't entirely sure the energies can be controlled, or even aimed properly, but . . . nothing ventured, nothing gained. I'm sure it'll be very pretty to look at. As long as you're not actually on Usher Two, of course."

"A poor man's Darkvoid Device, that we're not even sure we can aim properly?" said Joseph. "Finn . . ."

"As long as we can turn it on and off, that's all that matters. Don't flap, Joseph."

"But even if the weapon works, we still won't be able to save Usher Two. There's no way it could survive having one of its suns go boom."

"As long as it stops the Terror, I really couldn't give a damn," Finn said cheerfully. "Still, in the event the weapon does work as planned, but still doesn't stop the Terror, we're going to need a backup plan. And that's where you come in, Joseph. Have you moved the transmutation engines into position, as I ordered?"

"They'll be in orbit around Usher Two by the end of today. All hidden behind sensor shields, of course. They've been preprogrammed to transmute the entire planet and everything on it into the most appalling mess our scientists could conceive. The planet will be poisonous on every level, highly radioactive, and possibly even unstable on the quantum level. Theoretically, the Terror shouldn't be able to consume Usher Two without being poisoned itself. However, I feel I should point out that if the Terror decides to simply avoid the planet, and keep on going, that entire quadrant will be a no-go area for thousands of years afterwards. Maybe even hundreds of thousands."

Finn sighed. "Do I really need to explain the concept *expendable* to you again?"

Joseph nodded stiffly. "Since use of the transmutation engines will inevitably mean the death of Usher Two's population, the plan is being kept strictly need to know. It's a pity we can't salvage some of the factory tech first, but that would rather give the game away."

"You worry far too much about things that don't matter, Joseph," said Finn. "Perhaps . . . if we were to destroy Usher Two before the Terror got to it, and then kept on destroying every other planet in its path, the Terror might die of starvation. Or at the very least take the hint and go somewhere else."

"I think we'd probably run out of planets before it ran out of hunger," Joseph said carefully. "Besides, think of the billions of lives that would be lost. There's a limit to what the people of the Empire will accept."

"Is there?" said Finn. Joseph couldn't meet the Emperor's gaze. He started to change the subject, but Finn pressed on. "Let us understand each other, First Minister. I protect the Empire because it's mine. Mine to play with, mine to enjoy, mine to destroy when I'm tired of it. Not the Terror's. I'll find a way to destroy the Terror, and then . . . Oh, the things I'll do. The people will wish the Terror had taken them."

"Perhaps you need . . . a distraction," said Joseph, just a little desperately. "Something to take you out of yourself. I've been talking with some of your other advisers, and it occurred to us that since you are the Emperor now, you really have a duty to wed, and produce an heir to carry on your line. If you would allow us to . . ."

"No," said Finn. "That won't be necessary. After me, there will be nothing."

The Rookery had become the last safe haven for rebels on Logres. As a result, that rogues' paradise and city within a city had become impossibly overcrowded, and was actually threatening to burst at its seams. The Rookery had become the last place you could run to where Finn's agents wouldn't pursue. For the moment, at least. The hidden rotten heart of the Empire's most famous city was now an incredibly dangerous, violent place. The original occupants of the Rookery were finding it increasingly difficult to prey on outsiders, as of old, due to the Emperor's murderously strict martial law, and so they had taken to preying on each other. And most especially on the newcomers, who quickly learned that the only safety lay in numbers. The Rookery had become a bad place to be a man alone. And yet still the people came, because as bad as the Rookery was, everywhere else was worse.

Everyone in the Rookery had lost someone to Finn's people, or knew someone who had. There was a lot of sullen anger in the crowded streets, and in the smoky overpriced taverns, but as yet it had little focus. The Emperor was just too strong, too big a target for their beaten-down spirits. Its only expression so far had been the Rookery's turning against all those who had helped Finn in his rise to power. The agents provocateur had been burned out of their clubs and sent running through the streets, to be hunted down like dogs. Everyone else who'd worked with or for Finn Durandal was now being very quiet about it, for fear of being denounced as a spy or informer. Just the rumor was enough to raise up a mob baying for blood, and broken bodies soon blocked the gutters. Everyone expected the Emperor to order an invasion of the Rookery at some point, but no one was doing anything about it. There were no meetings, no plans, no defenses. No one trusted anyone.

Douglas Campbell, who had once been a King, and Stuart Lennox, who had once been a Paragon, now worked as masked bravos for hire, protecting the flea-trap hotel they were staying in from all the many predators of the streets. Masked bravos were a common sight in the Rookery these days. Lots of people had good reason to conceal their identities. Douglas and Stuart wore simple leather masks, and cheap but serviceable clothing. They'd sold the better clothes they arrived in to raise the money to acquire the single hotel room Douglas and Stuart and Nina Malapert now lived in.

The Lantern Lodge was one of the oldest surviving hotels in the Rookery, and looked it. The squat ugly building was dark, damp, and extremely run down, and no one had spent money on it in generations. The outer stone walls were blackened with layers of soot and grime, the windows did little more than let the light in, and there hadn't been any lead on the roof in living memory. It was sweltering hot in the summer and bitter cold in the winter, and every room came with hot and cold running rats. Not to mention bed bugs. (At first, Douglas had thought the single bed came with a built-in vibrating mechanism, and was seriously and loudly upset when the truth was made clear to him.) But it was a room, and rooms were hard to come by, so no one complained.

Douglas and Stuart worked as the hotel's bravos for free bed and board. It wasn't much, but it was better than a lot of people had. There were those who had to fight every night to protect their place in a doorway, or a cardboard box. Nina was doing marginally better. She was working with a few other rogue media people to put together a rebel news site, tapping briefly into the main media feeds to try to get a little truth on the air now and again. There wasn't any money in it yet, but Nina had great hopes for the future. There were quite a few ex-media people in the Rookery, since Finn's people had taken complete control of all the official media. There were no shows anymore, just constant propaganda. There were riots in the streets on the day *The Quality* was taken off the air, but

Finn had just had his people use the rioters for target practice, until they got the message and slunk off home. But a lot of newspeople had brought their technical knowledge to the Rookery, and the rebel news site was already up and running. Unfortunately, it took expensive and hard-to-get tech to keep it on the air, and keep fighting its way through the official censor's firewalls, so there was always a problem with funding. It wasn't as though they could sell advertising space.

Douglas and Stuart had been on duty outside the Lantern Lodge entrance since first light, and now it was nearly midday. It had been drizzling for hours, a cold, numbing persistent fall that soaked everything and everyone. The sewers were overrunning again, and the stench in the street was almost unbearable. The heavy gloomy day settled over everyone like a bad mood. People slouched back and forth along the narrow streets, heads down to avoid eye contact, in pursuit of work or a room or anything that might bring in a few credits. Times were hard. There was damn all left to steal, and rats were becoming a delicacy. But crowded as the street was, everyone gave the two masked bravos outside the Lantern Lodge plenty of room. Douglas and Stuart had demonstrated their willingness to protect the hotel on many occasions, in a professionally violent and disturbingly thorough way that had impressed even the hardened denizens of the Rookery. Which was why the two men were just a little surprised to observe a small crowd of heavily armed men heading in their direction. The dozen or so men moved like professional fighters, and while they hadn't drawn any weapons yet, there was something about them that suggested their appearance was only a matter of time.

"You know them?" Douglas said quietly to Stuart.

"Some of them. Brion de Rack's men. Protection racketeer. Pretty much everyone around here pays off de Rack, just to be left alone. But he usually targets the bigger businesses, not dumps like this."

"Maybe he's branching out. How do you want to play this?"

"Oh, the usual," said Stuart, resting one hand on the pommel of his sword. "Reason first, escalating quickly to extreme violence."

"Sounds like a plan to me," said Douglas.

The dozen or so thugs and bullyboys came to a halt a respectful distance away from the two masked bravos. The street rapidly cleared as everyone else suddenly remembered they had urgent business elsewhere. Window shutters slammed together up and down the street like a round of applause. Even the drizzle seemed to hold back, as though anxious to see what would happen next. One of the men stepped forward to face Douglas and Stuart. He was taller than most, and bigger, with a layer of fat over his muscles to show he was one of the few people in the Rookery still eating well and often. He wore a long, heavy leather coat, decorated all over with steel piercings. A row of human scalps had been stitched to one sleeve as trophies. He wore splashes of bright color on his face, under a flat, dark, wide-brimmed hat. He smiled easily at Douglas and Stuart, but it didn't touch his eyes.

"Step aside, boys. My business is with the owner."

"We don't step aside," Douglas said calmly. "It's bad for our reputation. You want to talk to the owner, you talk to us first."

"Now, that's a very unfriendly attitude. You don't want to hurt my feelings, do you?"

"We're not paid to be friendly," said Stuart.

"All right. I will go that extra mile, to avoid unnecessary trouble. The name is Sewell. I work for Brion de Rack. This is his territory. You live in his territory, you pay him tribute. That's just the way it is. In return, we make sure nothing horribly destructive happens to your property. Or, indeed, you. Nasty things pretty much nearly always happen, if you're not de Rack's friend."

"We're a bit small fry for de Rack, aren't we?" said Douglas.

"Times are hard. Now, you've made a good showing, honor is satisfied, so stand aside."

"The old protection racket," said Stuart, and there was something in his calm, quiet voice that made Sewell look at him sharply. "A loathsome little scam, when all is said and done. Based on terror and intimidation, and a façade of invulnerability. Unfortunately for de Rack, and you, my partner and I don't intimidate that easily. We've faced much worse than you, in our time."

"We're here to protect the hotel from scumbags like you, Sewell," said Douglas. "And we take a real pride in our work. So walk on. Or we'll step on you."

Sewell looked at them for a long moment, apparently unable to believe what he was hearing. He wasn't smiling anymore. "Listen, leather faces— this is de Rack's territory. He owns it, and everyone in it. You only live here because he allows you to, and if you annoy him, you don't get to live here anymore. And an insult to me is an insult to him."

"What a marvelously time-saving scheme," said Stuart.

"That's it," said Sewell. "You just can't help some people. Drop your weapons on the ground, kneel down and say you're sorry, and we'll let you off with a beating. Make us work for this, and we'll cut you open and see what color your guts really are."

"We don't do kneeling either," said Douglas. "Bad for the reputation, and the trousers. Makes the knees go all baggy. Now push off, fart face."

Sewell's face darkened, and he turned to his men. "Kill them. And make it messy."

He was about to say something more when Douglas drew his concealed disrupter and shot Sewell in the chest. The energy beam punched right through the man, throwing his dead body back into his men. They scattered with cries of alarm, like startled birds, and Sewell measured his length in the gutter. The front of his leather coat was on fire. The thugs finally thought to draw their own weapons, but by then Douglas and Stuart were among them, swords in hands. The bullyboys tried to make a fight of it, but it had been a long time since they'd had to deal with anything but frightened and dispirited people. They didn't stand a chance against two ex-Paragons. Douglas and Stuart cut their way through the pack with vicious skill, moving fluidly and easily and protecting each other's backs at all times. They worked well together. Their swords flashed brightly in the gloom, like rays of hope, and blood pooled on the ground, hardly dispersed at all by the slow drizzle. Bodies fell with cut throats and gaping wounds, and did not rise again. And quicker than anyone had thought possible, it was all over. Douglas and Stuart stood together, blood dripping thickly from their blades, hardly even breathing hard. The sole surviving thug stood with his back to a wall, looking at the two bravos with wide, horrified eyes. Douglas and Stuart turned to look at him, and he quickly dropped his sword on the ground and raised his shaking hands in the air.

"Who are you? What are you? No one fights like that!"

"We are Douglas and Stuart, bravos for hire, and that's all anyone needs to know," said Douglas. (He and Stuart had tried using false names when they first arrived in the Rookery, but they kept forgetting them, or confusing who was supposed to be which, so they gave them up. Douglas and Stuart were common enough names.) "In case you're wondering, we let you live because you're going to carry a message to de Rack, and the message is: Leave us alone. Leave the Lantern Lodge alone. Pretend this unpleasantness never happened. That way we can all hope to live long and profitable lives. Be persuasive, because de Rack wouldn't like the alternative. Really he wouldn't. Now go away, and don't come back."

The thug was off and running the moment he was sure he'd got all of the message. A muffled chorus of boos and jeers followed him from behind the shuttered windows. Stuart gave a cheerful bow, and then he and Douglas went through the pockets of all the men they'd killed. Hard times bred hard ways, and credit had no provenance in the Rookery. When they were sure they'd got everything worth the having, Douglas and Stuart returned to their post at the front door and counted it up. There wasn't much. People slowly emerged onto the street again, to steal the dead bodies' clothing. Douglas sighed heavily.

"I hate this place. People shouldn't have to live like this."

"It's the Rookery," said Stuart. "They do things differently here. They always have."

"Not like this. It's never been as bad as this."

They watched as the growing crowd squabbled over the dead bodies' few remaining possessions. By nightfall the bodies would be gone too, and it was wise not to ask where.

"Like rats in a graveyard," said Douglas.

"Even rats have to eat," said Stuart.

Douglas sniffed loudly. Stuart looked at him. He'd been trying to help the disturbed, brooding Douglas ever since they'd come to the Rookery, but the man who had once been King, and lost everyone and everything he ever believed in, didn't want to be helped. This was the most Stuart had heard Douglas speak in days—probably because he only seemed to come alive when he was fighting. And even then, the Campbell fought with precision rather than passion. Stuart kept trying to draw him out, but Douglas seemed unwilling or incapable of thinking about the future. As though just getting through each day was hard enough. The man who had once been King now seemed tired all the time, physically and spiritually. He was drawing further and further inside himself, despite everything Stuart or Nina could do to help.

"Things shouldn't have to be this way," Douglas said again, and Stuart was surprised and pleased to hear some honest emotion in the Campbell's voice. "We ought to be doing . . . something, to help these people. We took an oath as Paragons, to protect the people. Remember?"

"Yes," said Stuart. "I remember. I wasn't sure you did."

Some hours later their relief arrived to take over, and Douglas and Stuart went inside for their only meal of the day. Their replacements were just ordinary muscle for hire from the local hiring house. No one special; the house just sent over whoever was available. The two bruisers nodded respectfully to Douglas and Stuart as they disappeared inside the hotel. The lobby wasn't up to much—paint-peeling walls, sawdust on the floor, and no chairs. Nothing to encourage anyone to linger. Just a battered old reception desk, where the staff were protected from the customers by a heavy metal grille. There was an elevator at the back, but its operation was a sometime thing, and did not inspire confidence. Douglas and Stuart climbed the five flights of stairs to their single shared room. They didn't disturb the handful of ragged forms who'd paid to be allowed to sleep in the stairwells.

Nina Malapert was already there in their room, laying the food on the table, which was a bad sign. She was only ever back this early when her day's work had gone really badly. The way she bashed the battered crockery about was confirmation enough without the frustration evident in her scowling face. She nodded briefly at the two men as they sat wearily down at the table. It wasn't a big room, and with the table unfolded it took up most of the available space. Dinner was boiling on a hot plate set perilously close to the only bed. (Douglas and Stuart shared the bed. Nina had made a nest of blankets for herself in one corner.) There was only one window, smeared with the debris of years.

Douglas and Stuart took off their leather masks and dropped them on the table beside their plates. Their faces felt hot and sweaty from the leather, despite the early evening chill that had worked its way into the room. Douglas Campbell was still a handsome man, with his noble brow and great mane of golden hair, but more than ever he looked like a wounded lion brought down by jackals; a great man brought low by too many losses and the unbearable weight of unrelinquished responsibilities. Stuart Lennox looked much older than his years warranted. A stern young man with a drawn, almost gaunt face, his gaze was always a little distracted, and he rarely smiled anymore. And even Nina Malapert was no longer the happy, bubbling, free spirit of old. The demon girl reporter who laughed at danger and would dare anything for a scoop wasn't exactly gone, just suppressed by the weight of life in the Rookery, but it did seem she didn't smile nearly as much as she once had. Her tall pink mohawk bobbed angrily as she ladled out the meal.

Douglas watched Nina bustle about, and tried hard to feel . . . something. It was difficult for him to feel anything much, anymore. His family was dead, his friends were gone, his responsibilities taken from him. He felt lost and unfocused without them. He wasn't a King anymore, or even a Paragon, but he didn't know how to be anything else. So mostly he just went through the motions, getting through the day until he could finally go to bed and lose himself in sleep. He looked at the discarded leather bravo's mask beside his plate. Sometimes he thought that was his real face now. He could feel Stuart looking at him, and stared at the mess on his plate so he wouldn't have to look at Stuart. He knew the earnest young man only wanted to help, but Douglas didn't want to be helped. He wanted to be numb, so he wouldn't have to think or feel or remember.

According to the official media news sites, Anne Barclay was dead. Killed by falling debris during Douglas's daring escape from the court. Another old friend hurt, and gone, because of him. Nina tried to tell him you couldn't trust anything on the official sites these days, that it was all Finn's propaganda, but that was just Nina being kind. At least Lewis and Jesamine were still out there, somewhere, avoiding capture. Douglas hoped they were happy, at least. He desperately wanted somebody to be happy, out of the mess he'd made of things.

He looked at his dinner. It wasn't up to much, but then it never was. Stringy meat and potatoes, with lumpy gravy. Douglas pushed it about a bit with his fork.

"What's the meat?"

"Best not to ask," Nina said briskly as she sat down next to him. "And you really don't want to know what's in the gravy."

"Is there pudding?" said Stuart, hopefully.

Nina gave him a withering look. "What do you think?"

Stuart had a plate of ropey-looking vegetables, boiled within an inch of their lives. He never touched meat. The others never said anything. They knew why. Once Nina would have insisted on their saying grace first, but they had all fallen far beyond a state of grace now. The three of them sat and ate for a while in silence. It was food and it was fuel, and that was all it was. Outside in the street, there were occasional shouts and screams and sounds of violence, but then, there always were.

"I heard a rumor today," Stuart said finally.

"Now there's a surprise," said Nina. "This whole place runs on rumors."

"This one was about Clan Deathstalker," said Stuart. "Word is, a handful of minor cousins escaped the slaughter on Virimonde, and might be coming here."

"I'm sorry, Stuart," said Nina, putting a hand on his. "But I was there, remember, with poor Emma? I saw them all die. No one escaped."

"Some of them could have been offplanet," said Douglas, not looking up from his food.

"Perhaps," Nina said kindly. "There's always hope."

"Poor Lewis," said Douglas, pushing his food about the plate. "The last Deathstalker. I wonder if anyone's told him yet. Can't help feeling sorry for him."

"Even though he stole the woman you loved?" said Stuart.

"She was never really mine," said Douglas. "I never really knew her. There wasn't time. I thought we'd have all the time we needed to get to know each other after we were married. Now . . . I think perhaps I only loved the image—the diva and the star. Maybe that's why she fell for Lewis. Because he was the only one who cared for the real her."

He made himself eat the rest of his meal. Stuart and Nina would only look at him if he didn't, and he didn't know how much more of their worrying about him he could stand. He supposed there would come a day when he'd be so hungry he'd be able to wolf it all down without tasting it; but he wasn't looking forward to that at all. Nina checked they'd all finished and then bustled around the table, gathering up the plates and keeping up a stream of chatter. She was trying to be motherly and supportive, but truth be told she wasn't very good at it. Douglas gave her extra marks for trying anyway. And then he made himself concentrate as he realized she was saying something about a new step forward in her attempts to set up a viable rogue news site.

"A whole bunch of new media people have turned up in the Rookery! First-class techs, the loveys—just what we needed. I mean, yes, I'm a reporter and all that, but I never did understand the science side of things. Up till now it's been the blind leading the deaf and trying not to electrocute ourselves. These new guys got out of the city just ahead of Finn's people, and they're keen as mustard to get some payback by helping us set up our site. Pretty soon we'll be able to tap into the official news feeds whenever we feel like it. And I'm going to be the face on the screen! Nina Malapert, presenter and superstar! Mummy will be so proud."

"But what are you going to say?" said Stuart. "People will watch for a while out of curiosity, but you're going to need something dramatic to show them to keep their attention."

"Well, I'll tell them how bad things are here in the Rookery!"

"They won't care. They've got their own problems, living under Emperor Finn. You need to offer them something they don't know."

"Like what?"

"Hope," said Douglas.

Nina and Stuart both looked at him quickly, but he was gone again, lost in his own bitter thoughts. Nina patted him gently on the arm, and took the dirty plates over to the far-from-hygienic sink in the corner. Stuart surged suddenly up onto his feet, glaring at Douglas.

"Damn you, Douglas, you make me sick! How much longer are you going to sit around feeling sorry for yourself? This isn't your personal tragedy! People are dying every day under Finn. Your people! Finn murdered your father, took over your throne, and named himself Emperor! What does it take to move you? To make you a man again?"

Douglas looked up, and what was in his eyes made Stuart fall back a step. And there was no telling what might have happened next if the mood hadn't been suddenly broken by shouting from the street outside. Someone was calling for Douglas and Stuart by name. They looked at each other, and then they went over to the window and cracked it open as far as it would go. Nina squeezed determinedly in beside them. Down in the street, the protection racketeer they'd let go earlier had returned, with a whole new crowd of friends and associates. Big, brutal-looking men, loaded down with weapons and body armor. The two bravos for hire who should have been guarding the hotel were already dead, their gutted bodies hanging from lampposts. The hotel owner, his wife, and their three small children stood inside a circle of drawn swords, clinging to each other. The ringleader of the gang was looking up at Douglas, Stuart, and Nina. A large man, a fat man, in an area where most people went to bed hungry. He wore the very latest fashions, but a thug in silks is still a thug. He was smiling cheerfully.

"Well, hello up there! I'm Brion de Rack. These men work for me. So did the ones you killed, but I'm not one to bear a grudge. Does an organization good to have the deadwood trimmed, now and again. You have surprised me, gentlemen, and that's not easy. Now do be good boys and come down and talk with me. Or I'll kill your present employer, and his family, while you watch. Slow and nasty and very messily. What's it to be, gentlemen?"

Douglas and Stuart drew back from the window and looked at each other.

"Well?" said Stuart. "What is it to be?"

"We don't owe them anything," said Douglas. "Don't even know them. But . . . if we back down from scum like these, we'll never get any peace."

"Oh, silly me," said Stuart. "I thought we might go down because innocent people needed to be rescued. Because it's the right thing to do."

"Don't push your luck," said Douglas. "I'm really not in the mood."

"But we are going down?"

"Yes, Stuart," Douglas said, smiling suddenly. "We're going down."

"I'm going to get my really big gun," said Nina.

"You're going to stay in the background," Douglas said sternly. "Because you never know when an unsuspected backup will come in handy."

"Oh, poo," said Nina. "I never get to have any fun."

Back behind their anonymous leather masks, Douglas Campbell and Stuart Lennox pushed open the hotel front door and stepped cautiously out into the main street. Crowds had already gathered, watching from a safe distance. De Rack and his men were waiting. The thugs and bullyboys reacted strongly when they realized Douglas and Stuart both had energy guns in their hands, but de Rack gestured easily, and they quieted again. Up close, de Rack looked even bigger, and uglier. Stuart couldn't help feeling that de Rack was the one who should have been wearing a mask.

"It really is very simple," the big man said easily. "I can't have two such excellent fighters as your good selves working as independents. Not in my territory. Might give people ideas. Dangerous things, ideas. And there's always the chance you might end up working for one of my enemies. A successful businessman such as myself acquires enemies, like a dog has fleas. So, you're going to work for me. I pay good wages, there are all kinds of fringe benefits, and you have job security for life. Because whatever happens in the Rookery, I'll always be here, taking my cut."

"And if we don't feel like signing up with a small-time thug with delusions of grandeur?" said Douglas. "If, in fact, we say *Go to hell?*"

"In that unlikely event, my men will kill the hotel owner and his family in appallingly inventive ways, set fire to the hotel and burn it down, and kill anyone who comes running out of the flames. And finally my men will torture you to death right here in the street, as an example of what happens to those foolish enough to defy me." De Rack shrugged apologetically. "A waste of good potential income, I admit, but business is business. You should feel flattered, gentlemen. I don't usually have to pressure people to work for me. But there's something . . . special, about you two. I can tell. Ex-military, right? Seen a lot of action, but couldn't fit in with the Durandal's new goody-goody regime? I thought so. You're not just muscle, you're muscle with brains, and I can always use people like that. I need quality, and you wouldn't believe how rare that is in the Rookery, these days."

"Maybe you just weren't looking in the right places," said Stuart. "Or maybe you wouldn't know real quality if you fell over it. Would you really kill everyone in this hotel, just to save face?"

"Of course!" said de Rack. He gestured expansively at the crowd that had gathered out of nowhere to watch the free entertainment. "A man is only as good as his word, and if that word is a threat, so much the better. Discipline must be maintained. But don't look on me too harshly, dear friends. I'm just a businessman, doing what it takes to get along. People . . . don't matter here. Only power. The strength to take what you want, when you want it, and keep it."

"And to hell with everyone else?" said Stuart.

"Exactly."

"Things . . . shouldn't be like this," Douglas said slowly.

"Welcome to Finn's Empire," said Stuart. "Welcome to the world he made because there's no one left to stop him."

"Someone should do something," said Douglas.

"If not you," said Stuart, "then who?"

"Excuse me," said de Rack, "but I was talking. Ignore me again and I'll have my men teach you a lesson in manners."

"Oh, hell," said Douglas. His voice still sounded tired, but somehow he seemed to be standing straighter and taller. "It never ends, does it? There's always work to be done. No matter how weary you are."

"We can rest when we're dead," said Stuart.

"I wouldn't put money on it," said Douglas. "Nina, you're on."

Nina Malapert stepped elegantly out of the hotel front door, holding the biggest handgun anyone present had ever seen. And while everyone was still gaping at her, Nina shot de Rack neatly through the chest. The energy blast blew him apart like a rotten apple. Even as the charred and smoking pieces were still flying through the air, Douglas and Stuart charged forward, sword in hand, and hit the men guarding the hotel owner and his family. The thugs and bullyboys didn't even try to make a fight of it. They knew professional fighters when they saw them. Most just turned and ran, booed and catcalled by the watching crowd. Douglas and Stuart cut down those who didn't run in no time at all. And as quickly as that, it was all over. The hotel owner shook Douglas and Stuart by the hand, over and over, babbling his relief and thanks. His wife and children regarded the two bravos with wide, worshipful eyes. The crowd was applauding loudly. Some even cheered. Protection racketeers had friends only when they were on top. There was also a clear element of surprise in the applause. Heroes were rare in the Rookery at the best of times, which these most definitely weren't.

Stuart shook thick drops of blood off his blade, and grinned at Douglas. "Feels good, doesn't it? Doing what we were meant to do."

Douglas laughed briefly, a harsh resigned sound. "All right, knock it off. I'm back. It's time to wake up and get involved again. For better or worse, the rebellion starts here."

Nina shrieked with delight, and did her happy dance right there in the street. "Yes! Yes! An exclusive for the new news site!"

Back in their room, sitting around the table with their masks off, Douglas and Stuart and Nina plotted revolution. They all spoke loudly, interrupting and cutting each other off, their faces flushed with excitement and anticipation. They all felt more alive than they had in months.

"So," said Stuart. "How exactly does *the rebellion start here?*"

"I thought I'd take all the people here in the Rookery and raise them up into an army I can set at Finn's throat," said Douglas. "Not the best material, I'll admit, but you work with what's available. So, I'll talk to them, inspire them, fire up a sense of grievance and injustice, and then whip them into a fury and—"

"Never work," Nina said flatly. "In the whole history of the Rookery, no one's ever been able to get all of them to agree on anything. That's why most of them came here in the first place; because they couldn't get on with anyone else."

"She may be loud and irritating, but she has a point," said Stuart. "Nothing less than a full-scale invasion of the Rookery by Finn's army would ever unite these people into a common cause, and Finn's far too smart to do that. He knows all he has to do is wait, and they'll turn on each other."

"An invasion . . ." said Douglas. "That's what we need, right enough. And Finn just might do it, if we scare him enough. But first, we need to get the people here on our side, and under our command. I think . . . I'll start with Random's Bastards. They're the celebrities of this appalling place. They're fashion setters, trend setters; where they lead, others will follow."

"Yes, they're celebrities," said Stuart. "And that's why they're never going to follow two masked bravos from nowhere. We're good fighters, and perhaps even local heroes now, but so are most of the Bastards. All they care about is fame and money, and we can't offer them either."

"They care about who they are," Douglas said slowly. "More importantly, they care about who their ancestor was. Give them a chance to be heroes and legends like the glorious Jack Random, give them a chance to follow an outlawed King into battle against a corrupt Emperor . . . to live the lives they've only dreamed about . . ."

"Douglas, you can't!" said Nina. "Trust me, dear, this is a really bad idea. You show the Bastards your real face, and they'll be lining up to betray you to Finn for the reward!"

"Damn right," said Stuart. "They may be Random's spawn, but they know nothing of honor. And if there's anything they hate worse than an ex-King, it's an ex-Paragon. Or have you forgotten you spent most of your earlier career putting these scumbags behind bars?"

"The enemy of my enemy is my ally, if not my friend," Douglas said calmly. "We just have to demonstrate to the Bastards that Finn is much more of a threat to them than they realize, and that we're the only people who can lead a rebellion against him. I've always found inspired self-interest to be a great motivator."

"You'll be a dead motivator the moment you take your mask off," growled Stuart.

"We are going to see the Bastards," Douglas said firmly. "Have faith, my children."

"I'm taking my really big gun," said Nina. "And my best pair of running shoes."

So, a few days later, Douglas and Stuart and Nina—two masked bravos and a demon girl reporter—attended the next scheduled meeting of Random's Bastards. It wasn't difficult to track them down. This wide selection of men, women, and not a few alien hybrids, who claimed to be descen-

dants of the legendary professional rebel Jack Random, always came together once a month to boast and brag about all the marvelous things
they'd done, and argue fiercely over their various claims to lines of descent
from Jack Random. Their favored rendezvous was a squalid little tavern
down on Hell Street, the Three Cripples. An appalling place in practically
every way, but the drink was cheap and the owner was prepared to over-
look the inevitable bad behavior in return for the regular booking.

Douglas and Stuart and Nina looked distastefully at the stained walls,
slumping roof, and windows that were blacked out for extra privacy, and
stepped carefully over the bubbling open sewer to get to the main entrance. The place was already packed wall-to-wall, and the bouncer at the
door tried to glare them away. Nina showed him her really big gun, and
the bouncer decided there was room for just a few more after all.

Inside, the smell was worse, if anything. The air was thick with a smog
of various illegal smokes, and there wasn't a chair or a stool to be had for
love nor money. The crowd jostled together amiably enough, shouting at
each other to be heard over the awful din. Nearly all of the men, women,
and humanoid creatures were armed with weapons of some kind. The
waitresses were all Madelaines (a popular clone franchise knockoff), and
they circulated as best they could through the heaving press of bodies, dispensing drinks and bar food of dubious provenance. Douglas and Stuart
forced their way through the crowd with heavy scowls and vicious use of
the elbow, while Nina brought up the rear.

"How the hell are we going to get their attention?" said Stuart, shouting right into Douglas's ear.

"Same way we did with de Rack," said Douglas. "Nina, if you
wouldn't mind . . ."

Nina didn't mind at all. Grinning broadly, she kicked a few people in
the shins to make some room, raised her very big gun, and blew a hole
right through one wall. The clamor broke off abruptly as everyone present fought to draw their weapons or locate the nearest exit. Nina carefully
lowered her gun. Douglas jumped up onto the nearest table and smiled
calmly about him.

"Everyone relax, it's not a raid. Some of you may recognize me and my
two friends as the ones who killed de Rack and broke up his protection

racket. We did it because . . . people shouldn't have to put up with shit like that. Just as you shouldn't have to put up with shit like this. Look at you—the descendants of a hero, a legend, and you're reduced to hiding out in the Rookery, denied your true destiny, unable to fulfill your potential. Unable to prove yourselves worthy of the legend of Jack Random. I've come to show you a way out. A way to change your lives forever."

And he took off his leather face mask. For a long moment no one moved, held in a shocked silence, and then a great roar went up from the crowd as they recognized Douglas Campbell. One thought was in all their minds as they looked on the ex-Paragon and ex-King, and that thought was *Money!* The massive reward Finn had put on Douglas's head, preferably no longer attached to the body, would enable them to live like Kings. (There was another, smaller reward on Stuart's head. Finn could be sentimental that way, sometimes. He didn't want Stuart to feel left out.)

The whole crowd looked at Douglas with hungry eyes, and then surged forward as one to drag him down. Stuart and Nina defended both sides of the table with kicks and punches and the occasional head-butt. Nina in particular proved especially adept at dirty fighting. Douglas looked calmly out over the uproar, not even bothering to draw his sword or his gun, even when the clutching hands came very close to his legs. He raised his voice again, and almost despite themselves, the Bastards quieted to hear what he had to say. He was Douglas Campbell, after all, and his reputation went before him.

"You must know my friends and I will kill a hell of a lot of you, before you can drag us down. I was a Paragon and a warrior long before I was a King. My friends are warriors too. You're ready to fight and die for money, but not for your freedom? What would Jack Random think of that? He was the professional rebel; you're just professional lowlifes. And not very successful ones, of late. Either you find the guts to fight back against Finn's unjust rule, or pretty soon there won't be any Random's Bastards. He'll pick you off one by one, and your heads will decorate rows of spikes outside the palace as an example to others. And Jack Random's extended line will die with you. I never gave you any reason to love me, but at least I respected you. Finn's law is harsher on you than I ever was. He'll kill you all, because of the legacy of freedom and justice you represent.

Your only hope lies in rebellion, and for that you need a leader everyone will follow. And that's me."

A slow murmur moved reluctantly through the packed crowd. *He's not wrong. Times are bad. Bloody Church Militant everywhere. Can't make a decent living anymore. Finn's a swine, all right. Probably couldn't trust him to pay the reward anyway. When the Campbell was a Paragon, you always knew where you were with him. He was vicious, but fair.*

"You have to do this," said Douglas, and the muttering stopped at once. They were all listening now. "You have to do it, for your pride and your freedom. I know there have been uprisings before, and Finn stamped them out with cruel, terrible tactics. He doesn't have to care about being popular anymore. But those earlier rebels were a bunch of amateurs. No common cause, no discipline, no leader. You are all practical, professional rebels, and practiced fighters, and . . . you have me to lead you. You only have to look around you to see what the world has become—what the Rookery has become. You were always rogues, but you had your pride. Now look at you, reduced to preying on each other for pocket change. You don't have to be like this. You don't have to live like this. You are Jack Random's legacy, a part of the legacy of the Great Rebellion, of Owen Deathstalker and his allies. And now the time has come for you to be worthy of them. Don't wait for the Durandal to send his fanatics in here to clear the place out; be the rebels you were born to be. Rise up!"

And Random's Bastards roared their approval and cheered him till the room rang with the power of it. Stuart and Nina couldn't believe it. Hardened criminals who'd steal the gold teeth from their sleeping grandmothers, who'd worked every con and scheme known to man, stamped their feet and hammered their hands together till they ached. It probably helped that most of them were broke and bored and more than ready for a little action, but Douglas had offered them their pride back again, and maybe, just maybe, there was some of Jack Random in them after all.

Douglas got down off his table, and introduced Stuart Lennox and Nina Malapert to the crowd. The Bastards nodded respectfully to the ex-Paragon, and to Nina's gun, but really they had eyes only for Douglas. He carried on talking long into the evening, mixing the inspirational with

the practical. Declaring a rebellion was all very well, but there were details to be worked out. Luckily between them the Bastards knew everyone
in the Rookery, or at least everyone who mattered. They knew exactly
where Douglas should go next, to best spread the message beyond the
Three Cripples. They were all quick to reassure him that there were lots of
people in the Rookery who hated the way things were, and were only
waiting to be given a focus and a leader. They wanted their old devious
lives back, and were ready to fight for them. The Rookery had always
been full of fighters. They would follow Douglas because they knew
him—as a Paragon and as a King, and as one of them, brought low by
the hated Finn Durandal.

More meetings followed, at carefully chosen venues all across the
Rookery, followed by open rallies attended by first hundreds and then
thousands of eager listeners. Everyone wanted to hear Douglas speak, as
he rallied and cajoled and inspired them with thundering words and the
power of a simple truth: that they had the power to change their lives, if
they were only strong enough to seize it. Douglas reminded them of how
far they'd fallen under Emperor Finn, and they roared their rage. Their
anger had been silent and diffused for so long only because no one had
dared to stand up and put it into words. Douglas gave them back their
pride, and they loved him for it. And finally he stood on a simple stage in
an open square, facing hundreds of thousands of eager listeners, and he
knew it was time.

"Let the word go out!" he said, his voice echoing in the silence of de-
vout attention. "From now on the Rookery is a no-go area for all of Finn's
creatures! His authority has no power here. His overbearing and unjust
rule stops at our borders. Any one of his people comes in, they don't get
out again. No more taxes without representation. No more executions
without trial. No more Church Militant bullyboys telling you how to run
your lives. No more Emperor Finn sneering at you because he thinks he
doesn't have to be afraid of you anymore. He thinks he's broken you. It's
time to prove him wrong. We're kicking his people out and taking the
Rookery back! Then the Parade of the Endless! And finally all of Logres!

"Because if not us, then who?"

And after that the cheers and roars of approval and determination were so loud, Finn must have heard them, even in the dark heart of his usurped palace.

One man in particular felt his life change forever when he saw Douglas Campbell reveal his true identity in the Three Cripples that first night. Tel Markham, who had once been a member of Parliament and a mover and a shaker in any number of secret organizations, but who now washed dishes for a living in the filthy back kitchen of the tavern. He ate scraps of food left on plates, and fought the rats and other vermin for it too. His once proud clothes were filthy rags, and he slept in a doss-house, standing up in a line of men supported by ropes under their arms. The doss-house owners packed them in, for greater profit, and often the shared warmth of the packed bodies was all that kept the sleepers alive through the cold nights.

Tel received a small remittance from his mother every month, supplied on the understanding that he wouldn't try to contact her, or come home. He had made the family name a disgrace, she said, and he had failed to look after his brother Angelo. (He'd always been her favorite.) It had been Tel's refusal to murder his brother on Finn's orders that had brought him low. Tel was aware of the irony, but he didn't have much use for humor these days. His mother's money kept him alive, just. He had to stay alive. There were people he had to be revenged upon.

Seeing Douglas alive had filled him with new hope. He followed the Campbell from rally to rally, listening to the man speak, and watching the crowds. He needed to be sure Douglas was the real thing. And finally, when he heard the crowd roar at that last great rally, he hugged himself tightly in his rags, and laughed and laughed. He decided it was time to introduce himself. He went to the Lantern Lodge hotel one evening, slipping in through the kitchens because there was no way they'd let the likes of him in through the front door. There were guards posted, but he dodged them easily enough, and sneaked up the back stairs to Douglas's room. And then he hesitated at the door, afraid to knock. He'd fallen so very far from what he once was. And even when they were both men of power and influence, King Douglas had never had much time for the member for Madraguda. How would Douglas react to this shrunken thing of rags and tatters at his door? Tel shuffled his feet uncertainly, raised his hand to knock and then let it fall again. He started to turn away and then the door swung suddenly open, and a large fist grabbed him by the shoulder of his filthy tunic and dragged him inside.

"Told you I heard someone sneaking about," Stuart said cheerfully. "Probably a spy or informer. Though now I've got him, I'm not sure what to do with him. I just hope my inoculations are still working."

He thrust Tel forward onto his knees before Douglas, and ostentatiously wiped his hand on his arse to clean it. An unexpected surge of pride brought Tel's head up.

"I am no spy or informer! Finn has no greater enemy than me! I came here to offer you my services!"

"Well, thanks very much and all that, but I don't think we need our boots cleaned at the moment," said Nina, wrinkling her nose fastidiously.

"You don't recognize me," said Tel, his eyes fixed on Douglas. "Hell, I wouldn't know me, looking like this. I'm Tel Markham, once the honorable member for . . ."

He broke off as Stuart surged forward and set the edge of a knife against his throat. "Markham!" he spat. "One of Finn's creatures, then and now! Oh, God is good, now and again, delivering our enemies into our hands. Move your boots back, Douglas. You don't want to get blood all over them when I kill him."

"Wait! Wait!" Tel was so panic-stricken he could hardly breathe, but he kept his gaze locked on Douglas. "I was one of Finn's people, yes. Emphasis on the *was*. He ordered me to kill my brother Angelo, but I refused, so he turned on me. I had to run here, leaving everything behind, just to save my life. And then he killed Angelo anyway, so it was all for nothing after all. No one in this room has a better cause to hate Finn Durandal than me."

"Don't put money on it," said Stuart.

"Why should we trust you?" said Douglas. He seemed genuinely curious.

"You shouldn't," said Tel, still acutely aware of the knife at his throat. "You shouldn't trust anyone in the Rookery. Finn seeded the whole place with his people long ago. But I know his secrets. I can identify his traitors, tell you of his plans. You only think you know how evil he is. You have no idea of who his allies really are, and the terrible things he intends to do. You need to know what I know. Keep me around. I can be useful. In the end, you'll learn to trust me. I'll advise you, follow you, fight beside you."

"Why?" said Douglas.

"Because Finn killed my brother."

"Ah," said Douglas. "Yes. Family obligations. I know all about those." He nodded to Stuart, who reluctantly took his knife away from Tel's throat.

Tel rose slowly to his feet, awkwardly conscious of what a ragged and filthy picture he presented. It had been a long time since he could afford to care about his appearance, but he wanted, needed, Douglas to remember him as the man he was, not the creature he'd become.

Stuart wrinkled his nose. "Damn, Markham, but you stink! And to be that noticeable in a dump like this is something of an achievement. If you're going to spend any time with us, you need to take a bath. Urgently. There's a tin bath on the ground floor. Tell the owner I said you could use it, and that he'd better scour and disinfect it afterwards. Hell, scrub it out yourself! We all have to use the bloody thing. God, sometimes I think I'm only fighting this rebellion for a return to decent plumbing."

"First things first," said Tel, just a little diffidently. "I belong to the landlord of the Three Cripples. He owns my contract. I can't work for anyone else unless you buy me out. I shouldn't even be here, really, even if it is on what I laughingly refer to as my own time."

"Slavery's illegal," said Douglas. "Even in the Rookery."

"Lot you know," said Tel Markham.

Stuart sighed heavily. "I guess I'd better pay another visit to the Three Cripples."

"You do that," said Nina. "And I think I'll force open the window while you're gone."

In the end, both Douglas and Stuart went with Tel to the tavern. Douglas talked to the landlord, and offered the man a fair sum to release Tel from his contract. The landlord, sensing which way the wind was blowing, immediately claimed Tel was utterly irreplacable, and that he couldn't run the tavern without him. He then demanded an utterly unreasonable sum to break the contract. So Douglas knocked him on his arse, right there in front of his customers. *Slavery is illegal,* he declared loudly. *As of right bloody now.*

"You know," said Tel, as they walked out of the tavern, "that isn't going to be a terribly popular sentiment in some parts of the Rookery. The tradition of indentured servitude goes back a long time here."

"Tough," said Douglas. "My leadership of this rebellion comes with a price, and the price is morality. The Rookery will become better than it was. The people will become strong again. They have to. Because the weak and uncertain won't stand a chance against Finn's fanatics." He looked around at the small but attentive crowd that always appeared when he went out in public. "Wouldn't you all like to feel good about yourselves again?"

"Don't you condescend to us, aristo!" said a lady of a certain age with too much eye makeup. "We weren't all born to wealth and privilege! We've had to make our own way. We fight Finn for our interests, not yours!"

"I could shoot her," Stuart said quietly.

"Don't tempt me," murmured Douglas. He smiled easily about him. "Your interests are my interests, and vice versa. We have a common cause, bound together by need and destiny."

He bowed courteously to the woman, and walked on. Stuart and Tel followed him. Stuart scowled.

"What the hell did that mean?"

"Beats me," said Douglas. "It sounded good, though. When in doubt, baffle them with rhetoric. You know, things were a lot easier when I still had Anne to write my speeches for me. Look, what matters is getting the rebellion started. We can argue about what it's for after we've won."

"Those sound an awful lot like famous last words to me," said Stuart, and Tel nodded solemnly.

"I wonder if Owen had these problems," Douglas said wistfully.

They trudged along, Tel hanging back just a little. He had clean clothes now, and could stand to be downwind of himself at last, but he still didn't feel worthy to walk beside Douglas yet. His pride had been very thoroughly beaten out of him while working at the Three Cripples, and it was slow coming back. He'd spent most of the past few days rehearsing in his mind all that he remembered of Finn's plans and secrets and vulnerabilities. He could name a whole shitload of traitors, double agents and deep-cover sleepers in the Rookery, but he needed more than that to make himself valuable to Douglas. He couldn't afford to be used and then discarded. He needed to attach himself to Douglas, make himself a part of the Campbell's staff, so that when the rebellion was over and Douglas returned to power, Tel Markham wouldn't be left behind in the poverty he'd so narrowly escaped. For Tel, Douglas Campbell was a rising star; someone whose coattails he could ride to security, if not glory. He needed to be secure, to launch his revenges.

"So, where are we going now?" Stuart said. The omnipresent drizzle had become a driving rain. It was always wet and miserable in the Rookery these days. Stuart was pretty sure Finn had arranged it with the weather control people.

"We are going to the alien sector," said Douglas. "Nina is meeting us there. She's made contact with a very useful alien hybrid called Nikki Sixteen, who claims she can get us an audience with the leaders of the alien presence here in the Rookery."

Stuart sniffed. "Are there enough of them here to make it worthwhile?"

"Oh, you'd be surprised at the size of the Rookery's alien contingent," Tel said immediately, seizing the chance to show off his local knowledge. "All kinds of aliens and hybrids end up here, for all sorts of reasons. Either because they're political or religious refugees, or because they've acquired tastes for human pleasures or concepts that wouldn't be tolerated back on their homeworlds. The Rookery has always been a cosmopolitan kind of place, and very tolerant when it comes to unnatural vices. You wouldn't believe what some of these aliens get up to."

"Yes, I bloody would," said Stuart. "Nothing about this place surprises me any more."

"Some of the aliens are remittance people," Tel continued. "Paid to stay away from home and family. Because they backed the wrong cause, or got too friendly with the wrong individuals. Being part of a rebellion to overthrow Finn and his xenophobic allies could go a long way towards buying them a ticket home again. But you're going to have to be very careful, Douglas; all these different species have their own needs and agendas, and they'll only go along with you for as long as your needs coincide with theirs. Right now, all you have in common is a hatred of the Emperor."

"Right now, that's enough," said Douglas.

The meeting place turned out to be an abandoned, boarded-up swimming baths, in a grimy, especially run down area of the Rookery. The chipped and stained walls were covered with sprawling alien graffiti, in a dozen different pictographs. Douglas could read a few of them, and was sure Finn's mother had never done any such thing. Nina was sheltering in the recessed doorway, wrapped in a heavy cloak. Her pink mohawk drooped damply to one side.

"About time you got here, darlings. This place gives me the creeps, and it's not exactly a salubrious neighborhood. The only reason it isn't crawling with muggers is because something's been eating them, and I don't know what the smell is but I just know it's going to takes ages to get it out of my clothes. And watch where you tread, because things go eek if you don't, and I really hope they're only rats. Nikki Sixteen brought me here, and then couldn't leave fast enough, which tells you all you need to know about this area. Do we really need to be here, Douglas, sweetie?"

"Yes." Douglas studied the door behind her. The swimming baths had been in a good location once, back when there had still been prosperous places to live in the Rookery. Back then, the baths had been the center of what passed for polite society. And while the building as a whole might be crumbling and the windows boarded over, the main door was a single great slab of veined marble, held shut by heavy lengths of steel chain, with massive padlocks. The padlocks hung open—showing they were expected, if not necessarily welcome—but clearly the aliens took their security very seriously. Douglas gestured for Nina to stand aside, and she stepped reluctantly out into the rain. Stuart moved quickly forward to block Douglas's way.

"I go first, Douglas. Always. Now you're the leader of the rebellion, I'm a lot more expendable than you are."

"No one's expendable, Stuart," said Douglas. "That's what the rebellion's all about."

"I still get to stand between you and all danger, Your Majesty. So hold your ground here, while I open the door and then throw Tel in to check for traps and ambushes."

"I don't find that at all funny," said Tel. "Does anybody find that funny?"

"I think it's a bloody good idea," said Nina. "I never trusted you, even when you were just a politician. You've got shifty eyes."

Stuart pushed the door slowly inwards, and the hanging chains rattled loudly. A cloud of stinking steam wafted out that had them all wincing and pulling faces. The steam curled slowly around them, moist and heavy and unpleasantly warm. It was rank with unfamiliar elements that brought tears to the eye and a nasty taste in the back of the mouth. Stuart braced himself, and stepped forward into the gloom beyond the door. There was an uncomfortably long pause, and then he reappeared again.

"No one around. The lighting gets better as you go further in, but the steam's everywhere. I'd say it was all clear, but it manifestly isn't. We're being watched, I can feel it. The air smells like the Devil's armpit, but it seems breathable enough. There are freshly daubed signs on the walls to point the way. It's not too late to call this off, Douglas. These aliens have no cause to like or trust humans anymore. Especially not a King who in the end couldn't protect them."

"That's not fair!" said Nina.

"Yes, it is," said Douglas. "I was their King too. It was my job to protect them."

Nina scowled unhappily, and looked back at Stuart. "Nikki said there'd be someone in there waiting to meet us."

Stuart shrugged. "No sign of anyone. Or anything. Do we go in, Douglas?"

"Of course," said Douglas. "We need them."

He allowed Stuart to lead the way back in, but wouldn't let him draw a weapon. *Diplomacy first,* he said. *Funerals after,* Nina muttered as she and Tel brought up the rear. The door slammed itself shut behind them, which surprised nobody. The tiled walls ran with moisture, the original patterns and designs mostly worn away. The ceiling dripped constantly, but was still a relief after the driving rain. The tiled floor was covered over with a thin gray slush that might or might not have had a purpose, but made the footing distinctly treacherous. The steam billowed more thickly around them the further in they went, and left a distinct chemical taste on the back of the tongue. Freshly painted arrows, in what might have been alien blood, pointed the way.

They splashed carefully along a series of narrow corridors, following the signs and keeping a wary watch on all sides. Stuart insisted on keeping a few yards ahead of the others, so taut now that he was practically vibrating with tension. Douglas made a point of appearing carefree and relaxed. Nina and Tel huddled together for comfort, both clearly wishing they were somewhere else. They began to hear sounds up ahead. Slow, heavy impacts of something large moving ponderously through the corridors. Groans and hootings and strange clicking clacking noises. Splashing sounds, the gurgling of running water, and the steady rush of thick liquids moving through concealed pipes. The steam was getting thicker. And finally they came to what used to be the main swimming area.

The pool was huge, and full of chemically treated waters, in which swam the larger aliens. In its heyday, it would have taken a thousand human bathers to fill the pool, but now it held barely a hundred large and languorous forms. The steam and the water hid most of their details, for which the humans were frankly grateful. The aliens were large bluish-gray shapes, bulbous and undulating, with long barbed tentacles and rows of great staring eyes. They could never have appeared at Parliament, except as holos. Other aliens shared the waters, drifting slowly here and there and rising up to study their visitors. There were scales and carapaces and slick furs, limbs and tails and protuberances that made no sense at all. Down at the bottom of the pool floated great flowering masses with exaggerated sense organs and trailing roots.

All the aliens who could tolerate Logres's gravity only if their weight was to some extent supported by the water were in the pool. More species stood watching on the marble floor around the pool—some humanoid, some reptiloid, some fungal, all of them glistening wetly from the steam. And a few shapes so frankly nightmarish even Douglas couldn't stand to look at them for long. Some held edged weapons, some carried energy guns along with a sprinkling of devices that Douglas couldn't even recognize. For a long time, the humans and the aliens just stood and looked at each other.

"I have never felt so unwelcome in my life," whispered Nina. "And I've been around."

"You are our guests," said a roughly humanoid shape moving forward through the steam to stand before them. It was covered in overlapping silver scales, like a body armor—even the elongated head. Crimson eyes burned balefully behind the silver helm. "I am Toch'Kra, of the Maggara. I speak for the community. Which one of you is King Douglas?"

"That would be me," said Douglas, pushing Stuart gently but firmly to one side. "Nice place you have here. Very . . . moist. Ingenious use of the pool, to help with gravity."

"The steam helps too," said Toch'Kra. "We pump it full of the elements necessary for our survival. We cannot speak of what it will do to your lungs."

"It's all right," said Nina. "We're not staying."

"I was once King," said Douglas. "But Finn stole my throne. Now I am a hunted fugitive like you."

"Not quite like us, human King. You can at least leave this place, and walk the city. We are trapped here. Once, many of us made up the various alien embassy staffs. We were proud to come here, to Logres, to be part of the great adventure of Empire. We believed we had immunity and protection. Instead, we were hunted down like animals, and those unlucky enough to be caught were butchered, and then eaten or displayed as trophies."

"I'm sure he'd like to do the same to me, if he could," said Douglas. "We have a common enemy. I'm here to suggest an alliance against him."

One of the great shapes lurched half up out of the water, made deep hooting noises, and then fell back again. Water surged up over the side of the pool and soaked the legs of the humans. They stood their ground. They knew they couldn't afford to appear weak. Toch'Kra nodded to the shape.

"He says, what use can we be? Many of us are dying, from lack of food and proper trace elements. From your oppressive gravity. From the accumulating effects of a hostile environment. And some are simply withering, so far from home or hope or sanity. Most of the support tech designed to maintain us here had to be abandoned when we fled our embassies. Why have you come to us, human King? You have your own people to fight your battles. Most of us couldn't survive outside these walls."

"I'm here because you are my people too, and I won't abandon you," said Douglas. "This is your rebellion as much as ours. Finn must be brought down, and the old order returned, and for that I'm going to need all the help I can get. Nina. Nina . . ."

"Oh! Yes!" Nina tore her gaze away from the long crooked shape moving slowly across the ceiling, leaving a shiny trail behind it, and concentrated on Toch'Kra. "I'm setting up a rogue news channel and communications site. I'm pretty sure we could punch brief messages through to your home planets. Could they send reinforcements, or other help?"

"No," said Toch'Kra. "The last reports our embassies received told of human ships quarantining our planets. No one allowed offworld. And there is the constant threat of the transmutation engines. We dare not move openly until Finn's power has been clearly broken. We have learned to be a practical, paranoid people through our contact with Humanity."

"Don't blame us all for Finn's actions," said Stuart. "I don't think he is human, anymore. If he ever was."

"Fight beside us," said Douglas. "Set an example for your peoples to follow. Take revenge for what has been done to you. After all, what have you got to lose? Whatever happens in the rebellion, it's got to be better than hiding out here and dying by inches."

"True," said the alien. "Our life here is not so precious that we are keen to prolong it. But neither will we throw our lives away to no good purpose. We remember you, King Douglas. You swore to protect us. You failed. Why should we listen to you now?"

"Back then, I couldn't even protect myself," said Douglas. "I was just a man on a throne, betrayed by people I had every reason to trust. Things are different now. I have a cause, and an army, and you can be a part of that. Revenge . . . can soothe many an old hurt."

The alien studied him for a long moment with its unreadable silver face, and then it turned away to talk with the others, in the pool and out. The untranslated barks and squeals of alien speech filled the steamy air. Eventually Toch'Kra turned back to face the humans.

"Even if we were willing to fight, what help could we be, when most of us couldn't survive in your environment?"

Douglas nodded thoughtfully, but inside he was grinning broadly. He had them, even if they didn't know it yet. They'd stopped asking why, and moved on to how. "There is much you can do. There are many places you can go that humans cannot. Service tunnels, sewer access points, waste disposal outlets, and all the other places humans can't survive without heavy tech support. And there are people here in the Rookery who can build you whatever tech support you need, to move around freely. You supply the plans, they'll supply the tech. There are people here who can build anything, especially if it's illegal. So, what do you say? Are you with us?"

"There are many species here," said Toch'Kra. "We do not all share the same goals, ways, or even the same concepts. Some of us are as alien to each other as we are to you. But we will discuss the matter. Many of us understand, or have learned, the need for revenge. I think, when the discussion is over . . . we will follow you, King Douglas."

There wasn't really much left to say after that, so Douglas bowed courteously to Toch'Kra, and then to the pool, and led his people back out of the baths. Behind them rose the sound of loud debate, in a dozen inhuman languages. Nina shuddered briefly.

"I swear, I will never eat seafood again."

The great esper Diana Vertue, once known as Jenny Psycho, once dead but now alive again, strode through the streets of the Parade of the Endless as though she owned them, heading for the Rookery. She was broadcasting a powerful telepathic aversion meme, so that everyone else looked everywhere except at her. She passed a gaggle of Church Militant peacekeepers with malice in their eyes, bored and looking for trouble, and Diana was tempted to do something hilariously appalling to them, but decided reluctantly not to. She didn't want to attract attention. Not yet, anyway. The city wasn't how she remembered it at all, and she didn't care for the feel of the streets. There was an overlying pall of gloom, fear, pain, and repression, leaking from a million untutored minds, and yet there was more to it than that.

Diana stopped by the Victory Gardens, to stand before the statues and graves of Jack Random and Ruby Journey. The statues didn't look much like the people she remembered, but she was used to that. The few representations she'd seen of herself had been nothing short of laughable. She'd never had that big a bust in her life. She sighed quietly, remembering. It had been a long time since she and Jack and Ruby had boarded the old Deathstalker Standing, the ancient stone castle that was also a starship, to go into one last desperate battle against the armies of Shub, and then the massed forces of the Recreated. And a long, long time since she'd found them lying together, stone-cold dead on the cold stone floor, side by side as they had been in life. Forensic evidence suggested they'd murdered each other, but Diana Vertue suppressed that. The people didn't need to know everything about their heroes.

She smiled briefly. She'd never thought she'd miss the blustering old rogue and the coldhearted bounty hunter, but they had both done amazing things in their time. People these days seemed . . . smaller, somehow. Less colorful. She concentrated, and a rain of rose petals fell silently upon the statues. And then she looked round sharply as her open mind seemed to catch an echo of an old familiar presence, a sense of power upon the air, not long ago at all.

"Owen?" she said, wonderingly.

But of course there was no reply. Owen Deathstalker had been dead and gone these past two hundred years, and the Empire was a lesser place because of it. She'd always admired the Deathstalker, with his honor and his courage and his dry, sardonic wit. She never told him that, of course. She didn't want him to get bigheaded. But after he was gone, she wished . . . she wished she could have just sat down with him, once, and talked. She liked to think they would have had a lot in common. She missed him; but then, so did everyone.

She could still remember the powerful inhuman voice, coming from everywhere and nowhere, to tell them all that Owen Deathstalker was dead. Dead, like Jack and Ruby. Hardened soldiers, who'd taken everything Shub could throw at them and never once flinched, had stood around her crying their hearts out for the loss of the one man they'd all revered. The one who'd been the best of them all.

He'd made the rebellion possible. He'd made winning possible. Even though he'd always known heroes died young and bloody and far from home.

And yet . . . his presence seemed to permeate the Victory Gardens, even though he had no grave there. He had been here, and recently. She knew it like she knew her own name. She grinned briefly, her heart rising. She'd found a way back from the dead; maybe he had too. The Deathstalker had always been one for pulling a miracle out of the hat at the last possible moment. She left the Victory Gardens and headed for the Rookery again, and her heart and her step were a lot lighter. She felt better about the day, and her mission. She was going to hook up with Douglas Campbell and lead him back to greatness. He needed her. Even if he didn't know it yet.

The overpowering pressure of the city's oppressed minds still hung about her like a dark cloud, but Diana Vertue was learning to see through it. Touched and transformed by the Mater Mundi, in her time she had been one of the most powerful esper minds living, and now that she was back her strength was rapidly returning. Strange lights glowed in her mind like paper lanterns with horrible faces. The ELFs, abroad in the long night of the soul. Elf had been a proud name in her time, a force for justice, and Diana hated these new ELFs all the more for making the name an obscenity. She could sense thralls everywhere, human minds suppressed and silently screaming, so the ELFs could run their bodies from a distance. She'd expected that, but the sheer numbers staggered her. She was pretty sure the Emperor Finn didn't know there were this many thralls in his capital city. Maybe she should send him a note.

It was clear she'd come back from the dead not a moment too soon. The ELFs were spreading their influence, and growing in power. The more people they could control and drain, the more powerful their minds became. Diana had to wonder if Finn knew that, as well. She increased the power of her mental shields, just in case. It wouldn't do to have the enemy know she was back, just yet.

She paused by the window of a store and studied the display of vidscreens interestedly as the regular (approved by Finn) news channel was shouldered aside by a rogue news broadcast from the Rookery. Nina Malapert's beaming face replaced the meaningless smile of the regular newscaster, and her voice rang out clear and happy and entirely unworried, like a breath of fresh air in a slaughterhouse.

"Hello again, sweeties! It's Nina Malapert back again, the voice and face of the coming rebellion! Guess what? King Douglas is back, and boy is he ever mad at Finn! Right now the true King is putting together an army that's going to drag that so-called Emperor off his stolen throne, and he wants you to know that things are going to start happening very soon now. Expect open displays of sedition, rebellion, and just plain crankiness all over Logres and especially in the Parade of the Endless. The rebellion is under way, that's official, and you heard it here first! And now, here's a whole bunch of news stories that Finn and his creatures don't want you to know about."

There then followed a long series of news stories about things that Finn had ordered done, or was planning to have done, most of which were supposed to be strictly secret. Some of them even surprised Diana. More stories followed, about all the things that were going wrong because Finn couldn't be bothered with everyday problems, so his people didn't care either. And even more stories about the foul-ups and general ineptitude of Finn's rule. Diana was just starting to enjoy herself when Nina's face and voice were suddenly swept from the screen by the news station's superior tech. A message appeared, saying *Service Will Be Resumed,* so Diana set off for the Rookery again.

It was good to know Douglas Campbell had finally got off his regal arse, and was back in action again. She'd been wondering whether she'd have to jump-start his motivation for him, and some of the ideas she'd come up with had been particularly unpleasant. But then, as Diana Vertue or Jenny Psycho, she'd never hesitated to do the necessary thing—no matter how distasteful, or who might get hurt, including herself. She had learned her lessons well, in the old Empire torture cells of Silo Nine, also known as Wormboy Hell.

The rebellion needed a figurehead, and she'd always known it couldn't be her. She might be an official legend, but people needed a leader they could feel comfortable around, and preferably one who didn't have the word Psycho as part of her name. No one ever doubted her abilities as a fighter, but she'd be the first to admit she'd never been a people person. No, Douglas would do fine. With the right backup and guidance.

She strode confidently over the border and into the Rookery, and the Church Militant guards on duty didn't even try to stop her. She dropped her aversion meme to allow herself to be seen, and her power crackled on the air around her. The guards couldn't run away fast enough. Some were even crossing themselves as they ran. Quite a few innocent citizens also took to their heels, on both sides of the border. Diana Vertue smiled. It was good to know she could still make an impression. She stopped and looked around her.

She needed to make a different kind of impression now. Something dramatic, to announce the return of an old legend. It took her only a moment to reach out with her mind and find a thrall, a nondescript little man lurking inconspicuously in a doorway. Diana walked right up to him, froze his legs when he tried to run, and then blasted the possessing esper right out of the thrall's mind. The ELF mind fled screaming, and the no-longer-possessed man fell forward onto his knees, shaking and sobbing but purely himself again. He tried to babble his thanks in between the tears running down his cheeks, but Diana had no time for that. More thralls were coming. She could feel them all around her, their thoughts buzzing like angry wasps from a disturbed nest. There were lots and lots of them, heading right for her. Diana smiled. She was just in the mood for a good workout.

Possessed men and women came running at her from all directions, their faces twisted with the rage and passions of the possessing minds. Some had edged weapons, some had only their bare hands, but they all had murder on their ELF minds. Diana Vertue was their oldest enemy, and they would stop at nothing to kill her again. They pushed other people out of their way, striking out blindly, their gaze fixed on Diana as she stood before them, smiling calmly. She waited till they were almost upon her, and then summoned up her power. Psionic energies surged and crackled in the street around her, and her presence flowered like a rose made up of thorns. She was Diana Vertue, Jenny Psycho, the first human uber-esper. She had touched the minds of the AIs of Shub and brought them back to sanity. She fought the Recreated to a standstill. She had been betrayed and murdered, lived on in the oversoul, and now was back again, to deal with unfinished business. Let the thralls come. Let them all come. She was Diana Vertue, her time come round again, and she would show these miserable new ELFs what power really was.

Only she never got the chance. The thralls came charging down the street, and boiled out of the side alleys to surround her. They called her name in angry vicious voices, and boasted of the terrible things they were going to do to her. Diana Vertue gathered up her power, and then stopped, astonished, as a dozen young women in brightly colored silks appeared out of nowhere. They materialized in a protective circle around Diana, lightning crackling in their hands. They wore black roses in their hair, and tribal patterns painted on their faces. They struck the same impressive pose and glared haughtily at the stunned thralls. They gestured grandly, and a psi storm of exploding energies roared up and down the street, picking up thralls and throwing them away, tossing the helpless bodies around like rag dolls. The ELF minds screamed with rage and fear, but they could not stand against the power of the newcomers. The twelve women gestured almost contemptuously, and the possessing minds were thrust out of their stolen bodies, and sent howling off into the night.

The psi storm slowly abated, and the air grew settled again. Up and down the long street, over a hundred men and women sat shaking and crying and holding each other, free at last. The air had that clean, focused feeling that follows a thunderstorm. The twelve young women turned as one to face Diana Vertue. They were all grinning broadly and looking very pleased with themselves. Diana nodded slowly.

"All right, I'm officially impressed. Now who the hell are you?"

One of the women stepped forward. "I am Alessandra Duquesne, and we are the Psycho Sluts! Defenders of the right, avengers of the downtrodden and arse-kickers supreme! We modeled ourselves on your legend, and swore to do your name honor by performing feats of great glory!" She stopped for a moment to get her breath, and Diana cut in quickly. She knew a long speech coming when she heard one.

"Yes. I've heard of you. Headstrong young troublemakers, too impulsive to follow the ways of the oversoul, and far too powerful for your own good. I thought you all left with New Hope, in the Icarus Working, and were on your way to Mistworld?"

The Psycho Sluts exchanged smug glances, and sniggered amongst themselves. "We never really got on with the oversoul," said Alessandra. "We were always far too individual, and proud of it, to settle comfortably into the mass-mind. We left the oversoul to come to the Rookery, just before New Hope headed off into orbit and exile. We wanted to stay and fight. There's always been a rogue esper presence here; minds too crooked or strange for the mass-mind. We fit in just fine. We earn our keep sniffing out thralls and blasting them free, but we've never seen so many in one place before! They really do want you dead, don't they?"

"What do you want with me?" Diana said bluntly.

The Psycho Sluts look at each other, caught off guard. "Well," said Alessandra, "we want to be your army! We always worshiped your memory, your take-no-prisoners, kill-them-all-and-let-God-sort-them-out policy towards the bad guys, and once we learned you were back in the flesh, we've been waiting for you to come here. We want to work with you, to spread terror and destruction in your name! The rebellion starts here! Well, actually, it's already started, and Douglas Campbell is leading it, but of course now that you're back—"

"No," Diana said immediately. "The Campbell is King. He leads. I came here to support him, and if you want to work with me, so will you."

The Psycho Sluts considered this, and then shrugged, pretty much in unison. Diana looked from one eager young face to another. Had she ever been this young, this gung ho? She sighed quietly. She wasn't at all sure she needed or wanted the support of a bunch of wannabe loose cannons, but they'd probably do less damage to the cause in the long run if she kept them where she could keep an eye on them. So it seemed she had her own personal army, whether she wanted one or not. She wondered fleetingly if Owen ever had to cope with problems like this. Still, she was glad she had something to bring to Douglas, apart from her own rather controversial legend.

"We know where there are more thralls!" said Alessandra, almost jumping up and down on the spot in entirely unsuppressed excitement. "Let's kick some more ELF butt before we go to see Douglas!"

"Yes," said Diana. "The more people we can free from ELF possession, the better."

"That too!" said Alessandra.

And so, Diana and her newfound friends the Psycho Sluts went, eventually, to meet with King Douglas and his people. He wasn't an easy man to get to see, these days, and Diana had to perform a few minor miracles and wonders to get her due attention, but once people realized she really was who she said she was, they couldn't pass her on fast enough. Just as well. No one stopped Diana Vertue when she was on a roll. Douglas, Stuart, and Nina met with her in their hotel room, which had somehow become the center of rebel operations, despite its cramped size. The Psycho Sluts stood guard outside the door, putting the wind up the regular guards. Everyone had heard of the Psycho Sluts, who, when they really got going, could cause more property damage than an earthquake. There was talk of getting up a collection to send them to help out another planet. Any other planet.

Diana studied the three dubious faces sitting on the opposite side of the table, and smiled easily. "Hi, I'm Diana Vertue, and you need my help."

"Yes," said Douglas. "When Jenny Psycho appears on the scene, people usually do."

"I haven't used that name in well over a century," said Diana, giving him one of her best scowls. "And if you're wise, you won't either. In case you didn't know it, this whole area is infested with thralls, reporting everything you do to the Emperor. You don't have strong enough esper minds here to detect them, let alone deal with them. So, you need me."

Douglas nodded slowly. "And those awful young ladies currently lurking outside on the landing?"

"They call themselves the Psycho Sluts, in honor of me. And no, I didn't get a say in the matter. They're rogue espers. They mean well."

"Psycho Sluts," said Nina. "Doesn't the name alone just inspire confidence?"

"All the legends who could have returned to back me up, and I had to get Jenny Psycho," Douglas said heavily. "No offense . . . Diana. Tell you what, I've got to address an important rally in about an hour. Why don't you and your people tag along, and if you spot any thralls in the crowd, show me what you can do. All right?"

The look on Diana's face made it clear it wasn't all right in any shape or form, but she nodded briefly. Even legends had to prove themselves. She waited down in the lobby with the Psycho Sluts, who amused themselves playing rat croquet with their psychokinesis, until it was time for Douglas and his people to go to the rally. The Psycho Sluts nodded cheerfully to Douglas, who did his best to avoid their eye. They worried him. They moved to form a protective circle around him as they walked through the streets. People gathered along the way to cheer and wave, and Douglas smiled and waved royally back to them. Stuart watched the crowds warily, one hand always near his gun. Nina filmed it all with her floating camera, for later broadcast. Diana ignored the surroundings, conserving her strength. She knew the real trouble would start at the rally, where the ELFs could do the most damage.

The rally was being held in an open square, and a large crowd had gathered there to listen to Douglas Campbell. The Psycho Sluts opened up a corridor through the crowd for Douglas to make his entrance, and he strode briskly through the crowd and leapt up onto the simple wooden stage. The crowd cheered loudly, and Douglas stood proudly before them, looking every inch the King in exile. He didn't even wait for the cheers to die away before getting stuck in. He spoke well and fluently, haranguing the crowd and raising their spirits, inciting them to rebellion. He could talk of the poverty and harshness of the Rookery because he'd known them himself, and he could talk of the Emperor's treachery and evil because he'd known them too. His speech might not have had the ease and polish that Anne Barclay's writing would have given it, but no one doubted that everything he said came from the heart. They had to fight back, he said, they had to rebel. Because things were only going to get worse, because already far too many people were suffering unjustly, because it was their duty and their right. *When your back's to the wall, there's nowhere to go but forward*, he said, and the crowd roared his name like a battle cry. Soon they were applauding his every statement as though it were an article of faith.

The Psycho Sluts stood arrayed before and around the stage, defying anyone to get past them, while Diana moved unobtrusively through the crowd, quietly noting the location of each and every thrall without letting them know they'd been spotted. They were gradually infiltrating the crowd, in ones and twos, smiling and applauding so as not to seem out of place, but someone else looked out through their cold eyes. When they thought there were enough of them, they began interrupting Douglas's speech with boos and jeers and catcalls. A few tried to shout Douglas down with insults and obscenities. The crowd around them shifted uneasily, angry but not yet ready to act themselves. They looked to Douglas to see what he would do. And Douglas just raised his voice, silenced the heckles with his rough and ready wit, and kept on going. He'd suffered worse in Parliament.

The thralls fell silent, linked minds, and lashed out with a combined telepathic onslaught, catching everyone by surprise. The ELFs weren't usually strong enough to generate their power through their thralls. The crowd staggered back and forth, clutching at their heads as a razorstorm of unbearable thoughts roared in their minds. Vile sights and sensations overpowered their senses, plunging them into Hell, and the ELFs enjoyed every moment of it. A group of thralls nearest the stage seized the opportunity to attack Douglas directly, under cover of the confusion. They lunged at him with drawn swords, but Diana had seen enough. She lashed out with her mind, blanketing the whole square, and the telepathic attack shut off abruptly as every single thrall collapsed as one. Diana turned the thralls nearest the stage upside down and shook them, just for the show of it, before blasting out the occupying minds. The crowd quickly returned to normal, and looked around for their savior. Douglas grinned down at Diana from the stage.

"All right, you're hired."

The Emperor Finn Durandal was not at all happy about being roused from his sleep at such an early hour of the morning, but since the only people who had this particular private comm number were the ELF leaders, he supposed he'd better answer it. Somehow he just knew it wasn't going to be good news. He sat slumped on the side of his bed, yawning and rubbing at his eyes, and finally activated the viewscreen built into his bedside table.

"This had better be important," he growled.

The scowling face on the screen was unknown to him, but he expected that. The ELF leaders never showed their true faces; they only ever spoke through their thralls. Even after all this time, Finn had no idea who the ELF leaders really were—one of the many things that had been bothering him lately. The possessed face on the screen looked distinctly upset, which pleased Finn somewhat. If he wasn't having a good time, no one else should either.

"We have been attacked," the ELF leader said flatly. "A psychic assault of incredible power. Many of our people are still recovering."

"Who the hell could do that to you?" said Finn.

"Diana Vertue has appeared in the Rookery."

Finn blinked a few times. "That's a good trick," he said finally. "Considering she's been dead for over a century."

"That doesn't mean anything where she's concerned. She was an avatar of the Mater Mundi, and even the uber-espers were scared of that force. Diana Vertue is back, and she has sided with the Campbell. You should have let us kill him long ago."

"Possibly," said Finn. "But I did so want him to suffer first. Very well, kill him, if it will make you happy."

"We can't. He is protected by Diana Vertue and her army of rogue espers! Already they have cost us hundreds of thralls. Our presence in the Rookery has been almost wiped out! You have to do something!"

"I am doing something," said Finn, just a little testily. "I never thought you and your thralls would be enough to stop Douglas from putting together a rebellion, once he came out of his sulk. He always did have a way with words, along with that damned charismatic personality of his. So I've been preparing my own little army, to fight specifically in the Rookery. I always knew I'd have to deal with the ungrateful little bastards some day. The Rookery has finally become too dangerous to be allowed to exist. I've been reluctant to sign their death warrant . . . partly because there was always the chance that I'd need their special talents again someday, and partly because I'm a sentimental old softy, but . . . Get your remaining people out of the Rookery. I'm going to send in my very best fanatics, to cleanse the place with fire and steel. I will tear down the buildings, and raise a mountain of skulls."

"You'd better," said the ELF.

The viewscreen went blank. Finn stuck out his tongue at it. He sighed, stood up, and rang for his servants to come in and dress him. No point in trying to get back to sleep now. Not when he had slaughter and devastation to plan. He ordered a series of calls to his generals in the Church Militant. If he didn't sleep, no one else got to sleep either.

Pure Humanity and the Church Militant had become one church and one philosophy, under the benevolent guidance of the very practical Joseph Wallace. The shock troops of the Empire now worshipped Finn directly, and natural selection among the faithful, bolstered by numerous purges, had produced an army of implacable zealots and fanatical soldiers. They would die for Finn, though of course they would much rather kill for him. He was the Chosen One, the Defender of Humanity, their day and their night. And they were his attack dogs.

There were thousands of them, armed to the teeth, their heads boiling with battle drugs and virulent propaganda. They were the righteous, and mercy and compassion and all such weaknesses were not in them. They gathered at the boundaries of the Rookery and then marched in by all the entryways at once, singing their awful hymns, and killing everyone they saw. They shot down men, women, and children, and cut down those who didn't run away fast enough. They set fires and planted explosives in buildings. Their lord had said that not one stone should remain standing upon another, and not one heathen soul should be left alive to see the coming day. They did not care, or falter. They were doing God's work, and it felt fine, so fine.

Men, women, and children lay dead and dying in the streets, and the Church Militant soldiers marched right over them. Fires burned brightly against the dark, and explosions sounded in the night like the heavy footfalls of an avenging God. Anywhere else in the city there would have been nothing but panic, and people running blindly, but this was the Rookery, and the people here were made of harder stuff. Word passed quickly of the invasion, and all too soon the Church Militant advance ground to a halt in the face of implacable opposition. Men, women, and children came running from all directions to block the invaders' way, all of them armed with some kind of weapon. More people gathered on the roofs, to rain down debris on the enemy. There were snipers with energy guns at the higher windows, and fast-footed youths darted out of alleyways with improvised grenades.

In the Rookery it was truly said: Any man against his neighbor, but every man against the outsider.

Douglas, Stuart, and Nina worked tirelessly through the endless hours of the morning, organizing the rebel forces, sending people to fight where they were most needed. Diana Vertue and the Psycho Sluts struck the armed forces again and again, darting in and out in vicious hit-and-run tactics, leaving death and destruction in their wake. Even some of the aliens emerged onto the streets, for a chance to strike back at their persecutors.

The Rookery rose up, combined at last into a single great force with a single aim. The Emperor had made himself their enemy, a threat to their homes and their lives, and they would never rest again till they had brought him down. The people surged through the streets, throwing themselves at the invaders in wave after wave, howling a hundred different battle cries in a single enraged voice. The end result of generations of people who had had to fight for everything in their lives. Guns blazed and swords flashed, and the Church Militant soldiers fell in their dozens, and then in their hundreds, and finally in their thousands. The people of the Rookery came from everywhere at once, to drag the fanatics down by sheer force of numbers. The Rookery rose up, savage and unrelenting, and all in a moment the invasion became a rout. The Church Militant abandoned their weapons, their orders, and their faith in Finn and themselves, and in ragged groups they ran for the Rookery boundaries. Of the hundreds of thousands of proud and arrogant zealots who'd marched into the Rookery, only a few hundred made it out alive.

Nina Malapert got a lot of it on film, and broadcast every bit of it on her rogue news site, with the tech team using all their ingenuity to keep it on the air for as long as possible. All over Logres, and on worlds across the Empire, people watched as Finn's authority was challenged, and thrown back in his face. They saw the blood and the bodies, and whole families slaughtered by the Church Militant troops, and then they watched as Douglas Campbell and Stuart Lennox fought back to back against impossible odds, and never had those two looked more like heroes.

Finn's censors shut down the broadcast, eventually, and there was nothing left but blank screens, all across the Empire.

In the Rookery, the people gathered up their dead, treated the wounded as best they could, and put out the fires. They didn't feel much like celebrating. But at least now there was no doubt over whose side they were on. They only stopped pursuing the troops at the boundaries because Douglas sent messages to call them back. He knew they weren't ready to go head-to-head with Finn's armies. Not yet. Hot tempers subsided into cold, bitter anger as the people of the Rookery counted their dead and added up the damage. And hard-hearted and harder-headed men and women, who would never have come together for something as nebulous as a cause, now found themselves united in an aching hunger for revenge.

And on worlds all across the Empire, and most especially on Logres, people regarded their blank viewscreens, and looked at the Emperor Finn and his shock troops in a whole new way.

Finn was furious. He raged back and forth in his palace communications center, trying to summon up more troops, but most of his armed forces were posted as occupation troops in cities all across Logres. It would take hours to bring them all to the Parade of the Endless, and then, who would control the cities they left? . . . Finn had attack sleds, battle wagons, and even starcruisers at his disposal, but again it would take hours to call them in. Finn kicked out at the furniture—and any of his staff who didn't get out of his way fast enough. He couldn't understand how it had all gone wrong so quickly. How a rabble of outcasts and criminals could have wiped out his elite troops so easily.

Douglas. It had to be Douglas.

Finn drove everyone else out of the comm center, and called on the ELFs for help. A large enough army of thralls might yet save the day for him. Suicide troops, driven on by outside minds, could still overrun the

Rookery's defenses. But none of the ELF leaders, or the uber-espers, would take his calls. Finn sat down slowly in the empty room, his thoughts whirling madly, unable to settle. For the first time in a long time, he wasn't the one driving events, and he didn't know what to do. He must have missed something, but what? What?

In the end, after it had been quiet for too long, the comm staff sent for Joseph Wallace. He calmed everyone down as best he could, with soothing words and rousing platitudes, and then he stuck his head gingerly round the door of the comm center. Finn was still sitting in his chair, thinking, ignoring flashing message lights on consoles all around him. Joseph decided this wasn't the moment to inform Finn that uprisings were breaking out on planets all across the Empire, inspired by what people had seen happening in the Rookery. Joseph gently closed the door, and quietly began giving orders in Finn's name. Security people came and went, putting together a depressing picture of what was happening everywhere at once. Joseph authorized vicious reprisals and clampdowns, but as fast as rebellion was slapped down in one place, it sprang up in another.

Alarms sounded in the comm center, but Finn turned them off. The noise made his head hurt, and he needed to think.

If he'd known what was going on with the ELF leaders and the uber-espers, Finn would have been even more disturbed. Behind the scenes, an even more bitter struggle was going on, with no quarter asked or given. The ELF leaders and the uber-espers had finally erupted into open war over who controlled the movement. Both sides had been secretly amassing great armies of thralls, to feed their power and back their play, and after what had happened in the Rookery both sides had decided that the time had come to break free from Finn, and go their own way.

It was an esper war, fought on mental battlegrounds, largely unnoticed by the rest of the world at first, but nonetheless vicious and deadly for all that. The huge thrall armies were living power sources, reservoirs of mental energy that both sides could tap into as they fought their war. Telepathic battles raged back and forth as minds clashed with minds, on eerie inhuman landscapes created just for that purpose. Minds crashed and splintered, and esper attacks sometimes spilled over into the material world, in outbreaks of weird weather and probability fluctuations. Psi storms sleeted through the surrounding areas, destroying all unshielded minds in their paths. The two sides raged back and forth, neither strong enough to entirely overwhelm the other. But neither side would back down, and so the psionic pressure built and built, until finally the energies spiraled entirely out of control and blew one whole section of the Parade of the Endless apart in an explosion so loud and bright the echoes could be felt all over Logres. (Finn later blamed the explosion on rebel saboteurs. Because he had to say something.)

The esper battle ended in a stalemate, with neither side gaining or losing ground, and so both sides retreated to lick their psychic wounds, and prepare for future battles. Both the ELF leaders and the uber-espers were determined to stand alone now, and follow their own destiny. They didn't need Finn anymore. They would rule Humanity on their own terms, and to hell with all alliances of convenience.

Finn crushed the uprisings, eventually. It cost him time and money and manpower, far more than he could afford, but he had no choice. He had to maintain control. Planet by planet, city by city, the rebellions were stamped out with gun and steel, and a slow sullen silence fell across the Empire, every bit of it now under strict martial law. Rebel bodies hung from lampposts in their hundreds, in every city, and heavily armed and armored troops walked the city streets, looking nervously over their shoulders.

The Rookery was strictly off-limits. No one went in, and no one came out.

Finn was more worried about the loss of his ELF allies. None of them would talk to him anymore, and all his contacts seemed to have disappeared underground. He'd relied upon their support for too long; his spy organizations were lost without their telepathically gained intelligence. Finn told Joseph Wallace that production of esp-blockers was now to have priority over everything else, but couldn't explain why. Unfortunately, it turned out you couldn't manufacture esp-blockers without the required esper brain tissues, and the cloning of esper tissues had always had a high failure rate. So mass production was going to be a slow, time-consuming process. (Joseph delivered that message over the comm, from a safe distance. He still didn't entirely trust Finn's temper.)

The Emperor had other problems too. He went to see Elijah du Katt, in his new laboratory set within the palace. (Finn had decided to keep his remaining allies close at hand, wherever possible.) There was only one du Katt these days. The Elijahs had tried to assemble their own power base and a new clone underground, and Finn couldn't have that, so he personally shot all the Elijah du Katts except one. He neither knew nor cared whether the remaining du Katt was the original or not. It didn't really matter.

Ostensibly Finn was visiting du Katt to discuss the problems of cloning esper brain tissues, but as always Finn had an ulterior motive. The recent uprisings had demonstrated very clearly that he had a shortage of manpower, especially now that he didn't have the thralls to back him up any longer. He needed soldiers—armed men who would do what they were told without question. And he didn't have the time to find and train and indoctrinate them. So, the obvious answer was an army of clones. To produce such an army would require a huge protein base, but luckily there was no shortage of dead bodies lying around, just waiting to be put to good use. And this new army would be programmed to know no fear, and absolutely no independence. They wouldn't turn and run, like those so-called zealots he'd sent into the Rookery. Finn's blood still boiled at the thought of his men running from a bunch of outcasts and cheap grifters. He would have cheerfully called in his fleet and scorched the whole area from orbit, but there was no way of doing that without taking out the whole of the Parade of the Endless. He was still thinking about it, though.

Finn expounded his plans for a new clone army at some length to the sole remaining and somewhat subdued du Katt. He strode up and down between the shining brand-new equipment, his ideas growing more extravagant by the moment. Du Katt just sat there, shaking his head slowly, until Finn told him to stop it. Du Katt wrung his hands together in front of him to stop them from shaking.

"To produce the number of clones you require, on the time scale you propose, presents us with . . . certain difficulties, that no amount of tech or funding will overcome. Your Majesty, the end product will almost certainly be . . . damaged goods."

"Be specific," said Finn, fiddling with a nearby piece of delicate and expensive equipment, just to watch du Katt flinch and twitch.

"Well, Your Majesty, the end product will almost certainly have physical defects, including but not limited to, a certain amount of brain damage."

"Sounds like a plan to me," said Finn. "Soldiers too stupid to rebel, and too dumb to do anything but follow orders. I can live with that. I'll take two million, to begin with. And use the cell samples I brought as the base for their genetic structure."

"Whose cells are they?" said du Katt.

"Mine, of course," said Finn. "I have decided I want children. Lots and lots of them." He laughed, and clapped the shaking du Katt on the shoulder. "Congratulate me! I'm going to be a father!"

His next visit was to another laboratory he'd had moved to the palace, for security reasons. The owner hadn't wanted to move, but it's amazing how persuasive a gun pointed at the groin can be. And so, that renowned drug dealer, alchemist, and complete head case Dr. Happy now worked exclusively for Finn, in a brand-new lab with every convenience money could buy. Much to the sorrow of his many other customers. It had to be said that Dr. Happy wasn't entirely the man he'd once been, before his long sojourn on Haden, in the proximity of the Madness Maze. But there was no denying he still possessed the most unique scientific mind in the Empire. And these days the good doctor labored tirelessly on a single project: the rebuilding of Anne Barclay.

Anne had been very nearly killed by the wreckage that fell on her during Douglas Campbell's daring escape through the roof of the court. Anyone else probably would have died, given how long it took to get her to a regeneration tank. But the tank kept her hovering on the edge of death, while Dr. Happy turned his twisted mind to the problem. Finn had instructed Dr. Happy to go to any lengths to save Anne, so that was exactly what he did. What he could not cure or repair, he replaced or rebuilt, no matter how extreme the measures necessary. He worked wonders, pulling

Anne back from the brink of the grave again and again, but unfortunately he couldn't resist the impulse to recreate her in *amusing* ways. The good doctor had been influenced by his prolonged proximity to the Madness Maze, and it showed in his work. He had also taken to using himself as a test subject for all the new drugs he developed, on the grounds that the only way to fully understand the effects was to experience them firsthand.

One of the drugs killed him. Another brought him back. Or so he said. Either way, the end result was that Dr. Happy was now a walking, rotting corpse, within which his slowly decaying brilliant mind misfired from time to time. Implanted tech from dubious sources and a whole series of experimental new drugs kept him going, but his flesh continued to slowly mummify despite all his best efforts to rejuvenate it. Dr. Happy didn't care. He savored the sensations of decay through preternaturally sharpened senses, and boasted that his new outlook on life—or rather death—gave him all kinds of new insights.

The sight that greeted Finn, as he entered the heavily guarded laboratory, would have shaken and sickened anyone else. Gone were the days of shining new tech and pristine equipment. The shadowed chamber was packed with animal cages and stank like a slaughterhouse. Experimental animals peered dolefully from the cages, while others lay scattered across the lab tables in various states of completion. Dr. Happy had been taking them apart and putting them back together in interesting new combinations, to see what would happen. Mostly they died, but he said he was learning a lot in the process.

Finn strode unhurriedly through the lab, peering dubiously at the latest assemblies pinned to the tables, and then looked up as Dr. Happy came tottering forward to greet him. The good doctor wore nothing but his chemical-stained lab coat over his emaciated, rotting body. Dark blotches covered the gray skin, and occasionally pale glimpses of bone showed through. Most of his white hair had fallen out, his sunken eyes were as yellow as urine, and his lips had drawn back from his teeth, turning his permanent smile into a rictus. He moved in sudden darting flurries, never still for a moment, filled with some terrible, remorseless energy.

"So good to see you again, Finn! Yes! Yes! Oh, happy day . . . We're making progress here, definitely making progress. Don't look at the rabbit; I never expected it to work. The other head was just a whim. You've come to see Anne, I presume? Yes, yes, I know, no time for chat. I see ghosts, you know."

Finn paused, and looked at Dr. Happy. This was a new turn. "Ghosts?" he said carefully.

"Oh, yes. Spirits of the dead, restless souls of the departed, that sort of thing." Dr. Happy spun round in a circle, flapping his bony hands as though shooing things away. "They're always floating round the lab, getting in the way. Pestering me, when I have better things to do." He looked fixedly at nothing for a long moment, his head cocked on one side. "They're quiet, for the moment. I think you frighten them. I'm pretty sure some of them are people I came back from Haden with. You remember."

"The crew of the *Hunter*, and the scientists of Haden," said Finn. "The people you poisoned and drove insane."

"It's not my fault they weren't strong enough to tolerate the miracles I fed them! I would have made them superhuman if they hadn't all died on me. People have no stamina these days. I blame late toilet training, myself. You don't think they blame me for their deaths, do you? How very unfair. But you're here to see Anne, aren't you? Come and see, come and see. I've made such marvelous progress since you were last here. You won't recognize the old girl."

"That had better not be true, for your sake," said Finn, but Dr. Happy had already lurched away, and was pottering about his lab. He was heading towards the living quarters at the back, but he kept being distracted by various chemical distillations and computer displays. He gave his gene splicer an encouraging pat in passing, and beckoned imperiously for Finn to follow him. Finn sighed, and did so. The line between genius and madness was thin enough at the best of times, and being dead probably didn't help. He followed Dr. Happy on his erratic journey, pausing now and then when the good doctor stopped to talk to people who weren't there. More of his ghosts, presumably. Finn tried hard to see something, but couldn't. He hated to miss out on things. Dr. Happy whirled round abruptly to face Finn.

"Now, this is interesting! This spirit claims to be you, come back in time from the future, after you died. I'd probably be able to understand him better if he didn't have his head under his arm."

Finn made a mental note to get as much work out of Dr. Happy as he could while he still lasted. "How are you getting on with your new version of the Deathstalker Boost?" he said, loudly and clearly.

"All right! All right! No need to shout! I'm dead, not deaf. The ears are still attached, see? And the Boost is going very well, thank you. I've already produced a viable prototype, and given it to Anne."

"You've done what?" Finn said sharply. "I told you I wanted to test it myself first."

Dr. Happy looked at him with his sunken eyes, and twitched his stiff fingers nervously. "There was no time, no time! Anne needed my Boost, if she was going to hold together. You have to remember, most of what I've done to her is extremely experimental. No one else could have kept her alive as long as I. I've used old Hadenman tech, Wampyr tech, and even some new options that came to me during my time with the Maze. I had no choice but to make her into a cyborg, after the appalling damage she suffered." He paused, considering. "I have to admit, I'm not always sure how or even why some of it works, but we learn by doing, after all. Still, tech implants, miracle potions, and my loving care can only do so much. Often the very things that keep her alive are at war with each other in her poor abused body. The Boost should make all the difference. I have the highest hopes for it. Come and see, come and see!"

He pottered off again, and Finn followed him to the back of the lab. The living quarters were kept separate from the rest of the lab by a single door of solid steel. It was kept locked at all times, as much to keep Anne in as everyone else out. Dr. Happy spoke his name into the voice lock, and the door ground slowly open. Beyond it lay a comfortable enough room, with every amenity but no windows. Anne was standing before the full-length mirror again, studying herself. Her new self—or what had been done to it in the name of survival. Finn had offered to remove the mirror, on the grounds that it only upset her, but Anne had wrecked the room in protest, even denting the steel door, so he never mentioned it again.

Anne stood awkwardly. She was still learning how to walk and move smoothly in her new, altered form. She wore no clothing, so she could see herself more clearly. Tech implants bulged crudely out of her flushed pink skin, thrusting out sharp and curved edges. One arm was longer than the other, and the power unit in her back gave her a slight hunched look. Her body bulged in the wrong places, to contain everything that had been put into it. Long raised edges of scar tissue trailed paths all over her body, like the map of a new route into Hell. She moved jerkily, without grace, and often her hands broke things without meaning to. Sometimes she broke them deliberately, out of rage and frustration. Her hair had grown out gray from the stress, and her face was gaunt and tired. Her eyes had the golden gleam of the Hadenman, and when she spoke her voice was a harsh painful buzz. She didn't look away from the mirror reflection when Finn entered, but when she spoke it was for him.

"I was beautiful for such a short time. I wish I'd enjoyed it more. Still, at least now the outside finally matches the inside."

"You've been brooding again, haven't you?" said Finn. "What have I told you about that? You have nothing to blame yourself for. Besides, beauty is in the eye of the beholder."

Anne tried something like a smile. "It takes one monster to appreciate another. There's something new in me now, isn't there?"

"Yes," said Finn. "It's a variant on the old Deathstalker Boost. It will make you stronger, faster, and hopefully a little more stable."

Anne turned with awkward suddenness to face him. "Yes. I can feel it, like lightning in my veins. I feel . . . strong. I could probably knock down that stupid door of yours now, if I wanted. But where would I go? I don't sleep anymore, you know. I don't need to. Just as well, really. I had bad dreams."

"You're alive," said Finn. "I promised you I wouldn't let you die."

"My Boost is actually an improvement on what the original was supposed to be," said Dr. Happy, tottering in circles around Anne, and running his stiff fingers over the tech eruptions in her body. "My Boost is a continual thing, never stopping. You will never lose the benefits it gives you. My dear, you are practically superhuman. Of course, my Boost does have a regrettable tendency to burn up the host body, hence the new flush to the skin, but the various tech implants should balance that out."

"How long will she last?" said Finn.

Dr. Happy shrugged jerkily. "How long have any of us got? She'll certainly outlast me. And you too, if your ghost is to be believed."

"Why have you done all this?" said Anne, staring at Finn with her golden Hadenman eyes. "Why is it so important to you that I live?"

"To prove that even monsters aren't monsters all of the time," said Finn.

"I miss James," said Anne. "I want James. Make me another."

Finn frowned. "I think the people would know he was a clone this time."

"Not for them. Make another James for me."

"I'll see what I can do," Finn lied. He was wise enough to know that Anne needed a reason to go on living, but still selfish enough to want that reason to be him. A part of him was quietly sad that she couldn't see the lengths he'd gone to, just for her.

"I'm tired," said Anne. "Tired of the pain, of the changes. Of not being human."

"The Boost will change that," said Finn. "And there are still many useful things you can do with your life. Perhaps I should let Douglas know what's happened to you. He might like to come and visit."

"Yes," said Anne. "I'd like to see Douglas again. One last time."

CHAPTER THREE

IN THE GLORY DAYS OF EMPIRE

O wen Deathstalker went dancing back through time, star systems whirling dizzyingly past like shimmering sands beneath his speeding feet. The galaxy spun around him, its many tiny lights blinking on and off like warning signs. Stars and comets formed an endless rainbow path back into the past. He could feel Hazel d'Ark's presence, always tantalizingly just ahead of him. He could feel other presences too, moving around him in the time stream. Some traveled into the past beside him, while others headed the other way, into the future. Some felt human, while others very definitely didn't. Owen could have reached out to them, but didn't. Perhaps because he wasn't sure they would approve of what he was going to do. And so he danced on into the past, alone but quietly determined, following the trail that Hazel had left behind her.

Sometimes it seemed to him that there were other directions than the one he was following of simple past and future; other directions, other *possibilities* that he could follow. He wondered if these were the time streams from which Hazel had called her other selves, during the Great Rebellion. Other time streams, where he had not died and Hazel had never become a monster. They tempted him with the possibilities of comfort, but he continued on his chosen path. He knew his duty. And anyway, only one Hazel had ever really mattered to him.

Finally the distance between the two of them began to narrow. She was slowing, and he was catching up. He slowed his dance, and the galaxy expanded around him as he sank back into it, focusing in on one specific location. He ran through enlarging star systems, pirouetting through the

hearts of roaring suns and out the other side, unharmed. He was changing, just as Hazel had. He could feel the extent of her change in the presence only just ahead of him, indications that she was becoming something
else, something *other*. Something he no longer recognized. He fought to
catch up with her, but somehow he never could. Perhaps because she was
driven by insanity and obsession, and he was still sane, if only for the
moment. He knew he couldn't see the things he was seeing, do the things
he was doing, and remain unchanged. He had to fight to keep from feeling overwhelmed just by the sheer scale of what he was attempting. It
wasn't that long ago for him that he'd been just another tired and burned-
out warrior, fighting a hopeless battle in the back streets of Mistport.

He reached out stubbornly with his mind, trying to force a contact
with the presence ahead of him, but although he touched . . . something,
he couldn't make her hear him, no matter how loudly he called her name,
and his. She had gone on ahead of him, on a journey and process he could
barely comprehend, and for all the meteoric speed of his dance he was
being left behind. But something came back to him from that fleeting
touch of minds—a single memory, of the last hour of Hazel's life, in
which she had still been merely human.

After she left Shub, the metal world the AIs made to house their consciousnesses, Hazel d'Ark went to Haden, home of the Madness Maze.
She thought she would need more power from the Maze, in order to travel
back through time. She materialized outside the Madness Maze, like a
child come home seeking the approval of a parent, but the Maze ignored
her. She called out to it, but the Maze refused her. She couldn't see or find
an entrance anywhere. She couldn't even see her reflection in the shining
cold surfaces of the outer Maze, and that disturbed her, on some deep and
primal level. She screamed abuse at the Maze, and tried to force her way in,
attacking it with all her power, focused through a mind already half mad
with grief and horror, and she tore power from the Maze, wrenching it out,
raw and potent, by the sheer force of her disturbed will. She was crying,
tears running jerkily down her cheeks, though she was past feeling them.
She was leaving Humanity behind, through her own will, even as she acted
for the most human of reasons. Power burned within her, and like the
phoenix she emerged shining brightly from the ashes of her old self.

And so she let go of time and plunged back into the past, beginning the long journey that would make her into the Terror.

Owen digested the memory as he slowed and slowed his progress, and finally dropped back into space and time at the exact location Hazel had chosen before him. He wondered what he'd find, and why she'd stopped here, of all possible places.

In the beginning was the First Empire. It was wild and glorious. It didn't last.

Owen materialized in open space, hanging in high orbit above the blue and gray planet that in his time had been called Golgotha. He knew that, in the same way he knew that he had traveled back almost a thousand years. The stars had stopped wheeling around him, and now sparkled solemnly in place. He should have felt exhausted, like the first time he'd traveled in time, pursued by the Recreated, but instead he felt . . . exhilarated. He looked around him, grinning widely, surrounded by the icy vacuum of space, which had no power over him. He felt entirely relaxed and comfortable, even though he didn't feel any need to breathe. It seemed he was beginning his own changes. He checked the pulse in his wrist, and was relieved to find that at least it was still there.

Golgotha turned slowly beneath him, but it looked very different now. Against the blue and gray of its surface, huge magnificent cities blazed against the dark, vast as countries and as intricately shaped as snowdrops. They shone so very brightly, with all the colors of the rainbow, as though the whole world had been studded with precious jewels. Auroras of smooth, soothing colors wrapped the world, as though to keep it safe from all harm.

On the other hand, Owen couldn't help noticing that the planet was surrounded by all kinds of orbiting junk. Satellites of every shape and size, built with function rather than aesthetics in mind, formed a metal ring around the world. Huge stardocks held half-built starships, assembled in orbit because they were too big to ever leave the ground. And everywhere Owen looked, starships came and went, in their thousands and their hundreds of thousands, flashing past him like so many fleeting thoughts or intentions. Golgotha had never known so much traffic, even at the height of its power. Owen focused his mind on a few ships at random, studying them carefully, but none of them resembled any configuration he was familiar with.

He realized he still didn't feel any need to breathe. How much had he changed already? Was he doomed to continue to change, until he became another Terror, at the last? He felt stronger, more powerful, but still . . . human. And yet, if he was changing, could he hope to understand or appreciate the extent of the change from the inside? Would he even notice as his humanity fell away? Panic surged up, and he pushed it ruthlessly back. Human is as human does. As long as he still cared about Hazel, and hoped to put a stop to what she had become, he was still human enough.

(And yet, where had the power come from, that had made his long trip through time possible, and filled him now? Why wasn't he feeling drained, like before? Owen decided very firmly that he'd think about that later. He had other, more important things on his mind right now.)

Hazel had definitely stopped her plunge back through time at this point. For what purpose, or for how long, he couldn't tell. He could feel the trail start up again, heading even further back into the past, but he was curious as to why she'd chosen to stop here. Roughly a thousand years would put him in the time of the First Empire, before it declined and fell, for reasons long forgotten. His old historian's instincts kicked in, at the possibility of seeing the legendary First Empire in its prime and perhaps even discovering some clue as to why it fell so far, and so hard. Perhaps the greatest mystery in Humanity's long history. Owen laughed soundlessly in the vacuum. This was the kind of opportunity he'd dreamed of, in his younger days. He'd come a long way, to end up back at his beginnings. He reached out with his mind, trying for some sense of what lay in wait on the planet below, but the cities blazed with life: billions upon billions of minds roaring in a constant bedlam. It was just too big, too complex, for him to understand, even in his new changed state. He found that oddly comforting.

While he was busy thinking all this, half a dozen orbiting satellites had detected his sudden presence, and were now homing in on him. They moved slowly in his direction, great rough metal shapes bristling with energy spikes and sensors, each one the size of a starship. They took up a preprogrammed position around Owen, and then all their metal spikes blazed with crackling energies, forming a scintillating cage around him. He looked up startled, as the trap closed, flinching back despite himself from the sheer power hammering on the vacuum all around him. The wild searing energies held enough power to light a city for a month. He could sense it. Just being this close to so much raw energy would have been enough to fry any normal creature. Owen cautiously probed the satellites with his mind, but there was no trace of even the simplest AI; only the basic binary codes of standard computers. Owen considered his situation thoughtfully. He could easily escape the trap by just dropping back into the time stream, but he was curious as to who had placed such a brutal trap in orbit, and why. He had a strong feeling it probably had something to do with Hazel.

So he waited patiently, turning slowly this way and that in the vacuum by a simple effort of will, until finally someone came to inspect what their sprung trap had caught. At first all he could see were two small bright lights heading towards him, but they grew quickly in size. He'd been expecting some form of ship or flyer, and so was surprised to see two human forms sailing towards him. They seemed to move under their own power, wrapped in shimmering silver force shields, like two suits of perfectly fitted armor. Their faces were blank mirrors, with no obvious sensors, but slight humps on both their backs suggested some kind of propulsion unit. The force suits fit closely enough for Owen to be sure his visitors were one male and one female. They slowed to a controlled halt a cautious distance away from the cage, and looked Owen over carefully. He gave them a cheerful wave. It didn't seem to reassure either of them.

Pops and crackles sounded in his ears, through his comm implant, and he realized they were trying to talk to him. He waited impatiently for his comm link to find the right frequency, but when their voices finally came through clearly, he was shocked to find they spoke with an accent and a dialect so obscure and so extreme that he could barely make out one word in ten. Owen tried to talk to them, and it was clear they couldn't understand him either. A thousand years can change a language completely. So Owen reached out and took the knowledge he needed directly from their minds, so he could talk in their tongue. He hadn't known he could do that, until he did it. Apparently the changes he was going through affected his mind as well as his body.

"Hi," he said. "I'm Owen. Just a visitor, passing through. Who are you?"

"I am Dominic Cairo," said the male voice. "Defender of Humanity. My associate is the Investigator Glory Chojiro. From what far place have you come, and how is it you are able to survive cold vacuum without protection?"

"Ah," said Owen. "You're really not going to like the answer to that."

"And yet we must insist upon an answer," said the harsh female voice. "We defend Heartworld, and have responsibility for this sector. Under the authority of the Emperor Ethur, we require an answer."

"All right," said Owen. "I'm from the future. About a thousand years further on. Don't ask me how I got here, it would only upset you. I only have to think about the implications of what I'm doing, and I start to whimper. May I ask why you've bottled me up in this cage? Is this how you greet all your visitors?"

"Just certain special cases, such as yourself," said Dominic. "You had better come with us."

"Do I have a choice?" said Owen.

"What do you think?" said Glory.

She gestured imperiously at the six satellites, and they moved obediently after her as she started back the way she'd come. Dominic moved easily beside her, comfortable at her side, as though he belonged there. Partners, of some kind, Owen decided. He was a little surprised to find they had Investigators this far back, and what the hell was a Defender of Humanity? Was there a war on, with some alien species? The history of the First Empire was full of holes, on small and large matters. Owen's historian soul rubbed its hands together eagerly. The things he'd be able to tell his academic peers when he got back . . .

If he got back . . .

Owen allowed the energy cage to tow him along behind Dominic and Glory. He was pretty sure by now that he could break out of it anytime he wanted, but he was interested to see where he was being taken. The journey turned out to be a long, slow process, and Owen was soon bored enough to seriously consider taking charge and speeding things up a bit, but he thought he'd better not. He didn't want to freak out his new friends just yet. They seemed enough on edge already. So Owen just settled back and watched the stars, the satellites, and the huge ships coming and going. Occasionally he reached out and rewrote the markings on their hulls, just for the fun of it.

The planet that would one day be called Golgotha but was now Heartworld had only the single moon, and that was apparently where they were going. Owen was mildly curious. In his time, the moon was just a dumping ground for toxic waste, in the great caverns under the surface. The moon loomed up before him, a great expanse of cold gray rock. A single huge tower thrust up from the surface, a solid steel block with no obvious openings or markings. Owen asked what it was, and Dominic curtly replied the *Spike*, which wasn't as informative as Owen had hoped.

They all descended towards the Spike, which turned out to be surrounded by a high intensity force field. Owen could feel it, prickling against his augmented senses. Glory turned around and gestured at the satellites, and the crackling energy cage contracted suddenly to surround Owen, while the satellites backed away. Owen considered informing the Investigator that this close up the energies tickled, but decided against it. He wanted Glory and her partner to feel secure around him, for the moment at least. Dominic made a series of gestures, and a corridor opened up in the force shield, its boundaries clearly designated by bright holo markings. Dominic and Glory escorted Owen through, maintaining a safe distance from the energy cage, and then the force shield closed behind them again. Ahead of them, a series of heavy blast doors opened and closed, admitting them at last to the interior of the Spike. They ended up in a huge elevator, big enough to handle a crowd, and began a long journey down through the Spike and on into the interior of the moon. Owen was beginning to have some idea of just what kind of place he'd been brought to.

The elevator went down a long, long way, before the doors finally opened on an entirely prosaic reception area. Dominic and Glory indicated for Owen to go ahead of them, so he took his energy cage for a casual stroll round the reception area. All four walls were covered with dozens of monitor screens, each showing a different view, constantly changing to cover different angles. A central comm and control console seemed familiar enough, if a little ornate and overdesigned for Owen's taste.

The energy cage suddenly snapped off, leaving only two rings of crackling energy surrounding his wrists. Owen tested them, surreptitiously, and kept the smile off his lips. Dominic and Glory stood before him, and their silver force shields snapped off. For the first time, Owen could get a clear look at his captors. Glory Chojiro turned out to be a short, stocky woman, barely five feet tall. She was well muscled, with broad shoulders and a jutting bosom. Her face had clear oriental lines, with jet-black hair and eyes. She was entirely naked, but her skin was ruby pink metal for as far as the eye could see, and Owen could see pretty far. There were no joints or seams to mark the metal as some kind of armor, so Owen reluctantly accepted it had to be her skin. She seemed a bit on the small side for an Investigator, but there was no denying she held herself like a warrior. Even though she carried no visible weapons.

Dominic Cairo was tall and slender, almost aesthetically muscled, and also bare arse naked. His skin was a cool sky blue, marked on the face and chest with what appeared to be lines of metal circuitry. He had a kindly, thoughtful face, under a shock of tufty silver hair. He put a hand to his bare hip, and the hand disappeared for a moment before reappearing with a large and blocky energy weapon in it. Owen raised an eyebrow.

"Good trick," he said. "Where did the gun come from?"

"Subspace pocket," said Dominic. "Keyed only to me, of course. You have never seen one before? Interesting. All our weapons and necessary work items are held in a subspace locker, at right angles to this dimension, and preprogrammed to accept only our orders, so kindly restrain any aggressive impulses."

"Move against us and you will be punished," said Glory.

"Oh, perish the thought," said Owen. He realized he was breathing normally again, but was distracted by another thought. "Don't you two ever get cold, wandering around like that? In the nude, I mean?"

"Told you he was a barbarian," Glory said to Dominic. "Probably from one of the outer worlds, where they still suffer from taboos."

"He says he's from the future," Dominic said mildly. "And he did trigger the satellites. There is also the unresolved question as to how he was able to survive in vacuum without our advantages."

"There is more to me than meets the eye," said Owen.

"There would have to be," said Glory. "And bear yourself with courtesy in our presence." She stepped forward to glare at him more efficiently. "You are now in the House of Correction, and headed for the holding pens, unless you can provide us with an acceptable explanation."

"Yeah, I thought this had to be some kind of prison," said Owen. "It's got that depressing ambience. What exactly am I being charged with?"

"Well," said Dominic. "Being weird and unusual, and just possibly a threat to Humanity. As Investigator and Defender, my partner and I take such things most seriously. Be under no misapprehensions as to your situation. We have reason to fear creatures such as you, who appear out of nowhere, and who fit no known parameters. We are at present deep beneath the surface of the moon, where we hold all the worst criminals Humanity has to offer. The hardened recidivists, who can't or won't be helped."

"So what happens to them?" said Owen. "They stay here till they die?"

"Of course not!" said Dominic, clearly shocked. "We wipe them clean of their memories, and leave them a blank slate, so that they can start again in a new life, untroubled by their past."

"Here we deal with the worst of the worst," said Glory. "We have heard and seen it all, and we never give the benefit of the doubt."

"Nice speech," said Owen. "Honest, I'm impressed. And thoroughly intimidated. How many criminals do you have here?"

"At present, three hundred and forty-seven," said Dominic. He seemed amiable enough, but his gun never wavered from covering Owen. "Security in the House of Correction is extremely tight. You will stay here until your fate is determined. Don't even think of trying to escape."

"Oh, perish the thought," said Owen. "I only just got here. I suppose a friendly sit-down and chat over a nice cup of tea is out of the question?"

They ignored him, pulling a whole series of unfamiliar tech items out of their subspace pockets. Dark ugly things, bristling with metal spikes. Owen decided that there were very definite limits to what he was prepared to put up with, especially if it involved dropping his trousers and bending over, but fortunately all Dominic and Glory wanted to do was study him from a safe distance. Owen could feel energy fluctuations moving over and around him, but none of it was particularly uncomfortable, so he just let them get on with it. He was actually curious to see what they had to say about his new condition. Dominic and Glory studied the readings they were getting, scowled and muttered a lot, and finally got into a short but intense fight over what it all meant. Owen regretfully decided that he wasn't going to get any useful insights out of the First Empire tech after all.

"Look," he said finally. "Why don't you just ask me what you want to know? I can pretty much guarantee in advance that you aren't going to like most of the answers, but then, I don't much either. In fact, there are times when I distinctly wish I would go away and stop bothering me. So, I am Owen, first of my Family and lord of my Clan. Rebel and warrior, hero and legend. Or so they tell me. I spent most of my life studying to be a historian, but it turned out history had other plans for me. I have traveled back in time in pursuit of a friend who came before me. Does any of that help?"

"Not really," said Dominic, after a pause.

"All right," Owen said patiently. "Let's start with the basics. Who are you? I think I know what an Investigator is, but what the hell is a Defender of Humanity?"

Glory and Dominic looked at each other, and finally Glory shrugged angrily. "I am Investigator Chojiro. It is my duty and my honor to examine and oppose all extranormal threats to Humanity. From within or without. I have powers in the Low and the High Justice, and the right of execution without warning or appeal. I am presently stationed on Heartworld, center of the Empire, and I and all my brethren have been tasked to watch for the return of something like you, or what came before you."

"I am Defender of Humanity Dominic Cairo. It is my trust to ensure that the people of the Empire do not use newly discovered technology or medical enhancements to remake themselves into something inhuman. The nature of Humanity must be respected and maintained, and I have powers in the Low and the High Justice to deal with anything that threatens it. I defend the spirit of Humanity. A hard task, in these days of vacuum dancers, water breathers, and heavy gravity prowlers. I see you do not recognize those terms. Originally, the process of adaptation was developed to enable people to fit the conditions on other planets. Why go to all the time and expense of changing a planet, when it's so much easier to change the people? Unfortunately, the changes have run wild, for the thrill or the fashion of it. There are many kinds of people now, and not all of them are fully human."

"Both our castes were created a hundred or so years ago," said Glory. "After a series of disastrous first contacts with alien species led to wars, and the destruction of whole alien cultures in the name of human destiny. We are rebuilding them, as best we can, and have sworn never to be inhuman again. A noble intent, but the accelerating rate of change in the human form is having its effect on the human mind and soul. No one can keep track of all the subspecies of Humanity anymore. And there are nowhere near enough Investigators or Defenders these days. The Emperor grows old, and does not care, and those below take their cue from him."

"You have chosen a bad time to visit us, Owen," said Dominic. "In these sad, despairing dog days of Empire."

"Why are you here?" Glory said sharply. "What is your purpose?"

"I told you, I'm from the future," Owen said patiently. "Searching for my friend who came here before me. You seem to be accepting the time travel bit rather more easily than I expected. Do you have time travel?"

"No," said Glory. "All such research was banned, after the trouble we had with the Illuminati, long ago. But we have had experience with your kind before. That is why you were caged, and why you still wear the energy gyves. We will not risk such horror running loose again."

"Why are you wearing that antique weapon?" Dominic said suddenly, pointing at the sword on Owen's hip. "Is it ceremonial, or a symbol for your masculinity?"

"Neither," Owen said dryly. "It's my sword. My weapon. Where, or rather when, I come from everyone bears a sword. We have energy guns too, of course, but we prefer to do our fighting with cold steel. It is an honorable weapon."

Dominic frowned for the first time. "Whatever could be honorable about killing people? The Investigator and I carry energy guns, our duty commands it, but they are simply accurate and brutally efficient. That is all that can be asked of a killing tool. It is a terrible responsibility, to take another's life."

"Why are you here, Owen?" Glory insisted. "What do you want?"

"I followed my friend Hazel. Her trail led me here."

"*Hazel?*" said Dominic. "That *thing* was human once?"

Glory snorted loudly, her dark eyes harsh, her mouth grim. "Your *friend* may have begun as human, but what arrived here was more like a terrible force of nature. It appeared out of nowhere, manifesting in high orbit amid a shower of tachyons, indicating that it was a time traveler. It had no physical form or dimensions, just a vast horrid presence stamped directly onto reality by an effort of will. It was huge and powerful, and as merciless as any devil. It descended upon Heartworld, sweeping aside all our defenses, and raged across our world, spreading death and devastation. It tore open the earth and raged through the cities, and none of our weapons even touched it. We called it the Mad Mind, after a legend from the first days of Empire."

(*So*, thought Owen. *Now I know where I'm going next.*)

"Eventually," said Dominic, "with half our world reduced to blood and ruins, the Mad Mind disappeared, as suddenly as it had arrived. And ever since we have been waiting for another such monster to fall upon us out of time."

"And here you are," said Glory. "In our power, to answer for the crimes of your . . . friend."

"Can we really do that?" said Dominic, not even trying to hide his uncertainty. "I mean, look at the fellow. He bears no resemblance to the Mad Mind, in form or in nature. We cannot expect one individual to answer for the crimes of another. That would be . . . inhuman."

"It is the Emperor's will!"

"Is it? Perhaps if he met Owen, he would feel differently."

Owen let them argue for a while, but it quickly became clear they weren't going to resolve anything anytime soon, so he butted in again. "Why is there so much starship traffic around Heartworld? Is there some emergency? Perhaps something I could help with?"

"No," said Dominic. "Lots of people are leaving Heartworld, for the outer colonies. To follow their own belief systems, or to escape the much predicted decline and fall of the Empire. Rats, deserting a sinking ship. Humanity has become . . . sundered, divided. We have all become too different from each other. Everyone must have the very latest technology implants, chemical enhancements, genetic restructuring. There are all kinds of subspecies now; nothing is forbidden and experimentation is running wild. We know everything about how to alter the body, and not nearly enough about how such changes affect the soul. The Humanity. We have a dozen different sexes now, group minds, human/animal combinations. Memes are fashions, and minds swap bodies at will, wearing different forms like suits."

"You're such a sweet old-fashioned thing, Dom," said Glory, smiling for the first time. "It's not all bad. Body change has enabled us to explore the universe. We walk upon worlds we could never have experienced before, because terraforming would have destroyed their true nature. We breathe poison, stand erect under the heaviest gravities, swim through gas worlds."

"That's not why they change their bodies on Heartworld," Dominic said stubbornly. "Change is all the rage these days, for the thrill, for the kick, for the experience. We are all so desperate for new experiences. When nothing is forbidden, where do you go for cheap thrills and the sick little joys of sin? Everything is possible now, and that is why the Empire is falling apart. There are too many factions, subgroups, heretical beliefs . . . No consensus is ever possible. That's why Parliament became a joke; because there are just too many positions, beliefs, philosophies. The only real authority comes from the Emperor, damn his immortal soul, and his Praetorian Guard. More and more they usurp prerogatives that belong to the Investigators and the Defenders. Society is fragmenting, and the center cannot hold. Humanity is divided by its own freedoms and appetites. Already many of the border worlds have rejected Heartworld authority, and fallen back into barbarism."

Glory looked sharply at Owen. "Is this your doing? Are you affecting Dom in some way, with your future powers? He doesn't normally talk so much, or so freely."

"It's true," said Dominic. "I don't."

"Nothing to do with me," said Owen. "I think . . . you've both been waiting for someone you could talk to. Someone who'd listen. Perhaps I can help, now that I'm here. In my own time, I led a rebellion that brought about a Golden Age. Or so everyone keeps telling me . . ."

Glory shook her head shortly. "No. We have our orders, our responsibilities. You will be held here, while we inquire for further instructions. After the devastations of the Mad Mind, we cannot take chances with any visitors from your future."

"But he doesn't belong here," Dominic said stubbornly. "Not with these . . . transgressors."

"Who have you got here?" said Owen. "What could still be a crime, with the freedoms you have now?"

"As ingenuity expands possibilities, crime flourishes," said Glory. "The House of Correction holds body-swap terrorists, personality cancers, talent thieves, cult leaders who spread enforcement memes to gather new followers. Gender terrorists, who try to create new sexes by experimenting on unwilling victims."

"And Ansel deLangford," said Dominic. "Our latest arrival. Head of the Thrillkill Cult. He encouraged his many followers to consider murder as a work of art. The more complex, the more grotesque, and the more extreme, the better. His followers vied to present him with ever greater atrocities, but he was always the worst of them all. He specialized in murders whose foul and awful nature destroyed the minds and souls of the victims' friends and families. The Thrillkill Cult wiped out whole subspecies and cultures, in the name of their perverted art, before we finally shut them down. Psychopathic kick killers, dancing and singing through the chaos of a falling Empire. But he is ours now, at last, and we will squeeze every last piece of information out of him, so that every last vestige of his cult will die with him."

"You're never this chatty when it's just me," said Glory. She looked at Owen. "Any questions?"

"Yes," said Owen. "Why are you covered in pink metal?"

And that was when all the alarms in the world went off at once. Sirens and bells and a hell of a lot of flashing lights. While Owen was trying to look in every direction at once, Glory and Dominic looked quickly at the wall screens and then hurried over to the main console. The views on the monitor screens had stopped their shifting to concentrate on a series of cell doors sliding ponderously open, one after another, and wild shouting people spilling out into steel corridors. The alarms shut off, so the speakers could carry shouts and screams and raw harsh cries for vengeance. All the prisoners were loose, and already searching for weapons and a way out. Except for one man, who stood calmly before a security camera, smiling and entirely relaxed. He looked almost ordinary, until you got to the eyes. Owen shuddered as he looked at the man looking out of the monitor screen. He'd seen eyes like that before. Cold, mad, killer's eyes.

It didn't seem such a long time since he'd killed Kit SummerIsle, also known as Kid Death.

"DeLangford," Dominic said grimly. "Somehow, he's got into the computers. He's triggered all the overrides, using codes he shouldn't even have known existed. There's nothing we can do."

"He wanted to be brought here," said Glory. "He didn't set the others loose out of altruism. He's planning something. Something awful."

"Call out the guards," said Owen. "How many do you have stationed here?"

Glory and Dominic looked at him. "There are no guards," said Dominic. "Just the computers. Usually, that's all that's needed. After all, this is the moon. Where could anyone go if they did escape? But deLangford isn't interested in escaping. He wants to make some art here. Murder art. But he waited for something to bring us back here. Because he wanted an audience."

"You mean, he let the other prisoners out so they could watch as he killed you?" said Owen.

"No," said Glory. "He thinks bigger than that. He's going to make the prisoners die, for his entertainment. That's what he does. And we get to watch while he does it."

"Except we can't allow that," said Dominic.

"Why not?" said Owen. "You said yourself they were the worst of the worst."

Dominic stared at him, openly shocked. "They are here to be cured, and given new lives! Not to be punished, executed! That would be . . . in-human. We only ever kill when we have to."

"We may have to," said Glory, her ruby hands moving swiftly over the control panels. "DeLangford's shut down all the nonlethal security mea-sures. There's no way he could have hacked into these computers without help. He must have brought something up with him. He was supposed to have been thoroughly searched before he got here, inside and out, but his cult has people everywhere. The computers aren't going to repair them-selves in time, Dom. We're going to have to stop this ourselves."

"They'll be heading for the unloading bay," said Dominic. "It's the only way off the moon. There isn't a ship docked at the moment, but they don't know that. We can bottle them up in the bay, incapacitate a few to calm down the rest, and then keep them sealed up until the computers are back on line."

"Too simple," said Glory. "DeLangford will have planned for that. He's had plenty of time to think this through. His murders always have to be art."

"But he doesn't know about me," said Owen. "He won't have allowed for my presence. Let me help. Please. I want to help."

Dominic and Glory looked at him, and then at each other. "We need him," said Dominic. "And he seems rational enough."

"Our orders . . ."

"Don't cover a prison break! Saving lives comes first."

"Of course they do, Defender." Glory hit a control on her wrist, and the energy gyves around Owen's wrists snapped off.

Owen smiled. He could have broken free at any time, but he wanted them to trust him. He studied the wall screens, showing shouting men running through the plain steel corridors. There were a lot of them, but they didn't look like they'd be too much of a problem, unarmed. Ex-cept . . . all the prisoners seemed to have the same frenzied expression. He pointed this out, and Dominic nodded grimly.

"DeLangford's infected them all with the Thrillkill meme," said Glory. They belong to him now. They live only to kill for him, for his art. We may have to kill them all anyway, because they'll never surrender. They won't be able to."

She said a word that Owen didn't understand, and the air around Glory Chojiro rippled suddenly, as she disappeared and a new form took her place. It was about a foot taller and a great deal broader, roughly humanoid in shape but composed entirely of bright gold armor. The solid bullet head had no features, only a series of protrusions that might have been sensors. A row of gun muzzles thrust out of the barrel chest, and razor-edged blades lined the arms and legs. And yet the gold armor was seamless, moving smoothly and easily. The metal shape was clearly alive. Owen looked at Dominic.

"What is that, please?"

"That's Glory," said Dominic. "She's put on her enforcement body—organic metal with built-in weaponry. We all have many bodies these days, remember? I'll put on a more appropriate body in a moment."

"How many bodies do you both have?" said Owen, fascinated.

"I have twenty-seven. Glory has forty-three. Our work requires us to be flexible. We keep them in a subspace locker, and pop them on as necessary. You didn't think I looked like this all the time, did you?"

And just like that, he became someone else too. Still basically human, still pale blue, Dominic now inhabited a more perfect, idealized form. Something about this new, calmly smiling face, and the subtle body language, made Owen want to listen to whatever this new Dominic had to say. He wanted to agree with Dominic, and do anything that might please him. Owen shook his head sharply. A lot of the body language was subliminal, working directly on the subconscious, but Owen could see it clearly, and shrugged it off. He glared at Dominic, who smiled easily.

"Congratulations," he said, in a wonderfully warm and friendly voice. "Most people can't even see what I'm doing, let alone shake it off so quickly. As a Defender of Humanity, I don't like using weapons. I prefer more subtle methods. There's always the chance I can break these people free of deLangford's conditioning."

"We're going down to the unloading bay," said Glory, in a harsh buzzing voice that reminded Owen irresistibly of a Hadenman. "We'll take the lead. You stay behind us, and protect yourself. Don't get in our way, and try and stay out of trouble."

"You really don't know me at all," said Owen Deathstalker.

*   *   *

Glory and Dominic led the way through the gleaming steel corridors, Glory's heavy metal tread sounding loudly on the quiet. There had already been so many twists and turns that Owen should have been hopelessly lost, but somehow he wasn't. He could sense the shape and layout of the whole prison structure, and his position in it. After following Hazel back through time, this was simple.

"The prisoners are limited to just the one body," said Glory. "And their only weapons will be what they can improvise."

"I'll try persuasion first," said Dominic. "If that doesn't work, you're on, Investigator. Try and keep the damage to a minimum."

"Of course, Defender."

They entered the unloading bay. It was empty, just a great gleaming cavern of steel with the usual accoutrements. Glory tramped heavily about, checking that everything was as it should be. She wouldn't put it past deLangford to have somehow booby-trapped the place, but all seemed clear. Dominic bent over the single control console, making sure the airlock was still secure. Owen looked around thoughtfully. He was almost sure he'd heard something. Dominic shook his perfect head unhappily.

"I was worried deLangford's people might have seized a ship and brought it here, so deLangford could escape in the confusion; but the sensors show only our own ship, still in orbit. Only we can call it down, and both of us would rather die than betray our trust. DeLangford knows that. So what is he planning . . ."

"I'm pretty sure I heard something," said Owen.

"You did," said Glory's harsh buzz. "The prisoners are here."

The bay doors slammed open, and a mob of howling men surged in. Dozens of mad-eyed prisoners, roaring and shrieking their rage, carrying clubs and sharp-edged tools. Dominic Cairo stepped forward to face them, and those at the front stopped as though they'd run into a brick wall. The crowd behind gathered up, blocking the doorway and holding the rest back. Dominic smiled on the prisoners, and some actually smiled back. The Defender spoke to them, his voice calm and reasonable, asking them to stop and think what they were doing. His manner was so calm, so easy, so rational that some of the mob were already smiling and nodding their heads in agreement. A few actually began to cry, and loudly confess to crimes they'd never even admitted before, like children desperately sad at disappointing a beloved father. And then someone at the back of the crowd lifted an energy gun and fired at Dominic. Owen darted forward impossibly quickly and thrust Dominic out of the way. The energy beam shot on to ricochet harmlessly off Glory's golden chest.

"Where the hell did they get an energy gun?" howled Dominic.

Glory stepped forward, gun nozzles protruding from her barrel chest. She opened fire, and massed energy beams tore into the mob. Flesh exploded where the energy beams hit, and men were blown apart into gobbets of bloody meat as the guns fired again and again, not pausing to recharge. Glory pressed forward, blasting a hole right through the mob, but still more men pressed forward from the back, their voices irrational with hate and rage. And Glory couldn't kill them fast enough to stop them all.

Dominic shook off Owen's supporting hands, and lurched forward to support his partner. He spoke again with his perfect voice, but this time he used harsh ugly words and tones that struck directly at the subconscious, hitting deep-set triggers of shame and fear. Some of the prisoners crashed to the steel floor, collapsing into tears or comas. Dominic's body pumped out pheromones that acted as mood influencers. He was a Defender of Humanity, and these were his only weapons. He stood his ground, even as another energy beam narrowly missed his head.

Glory and Dominic stood together, each of them fighting in their own way, but the sheer number of rioters overwhelmed them. The prisoners swarmed around Glory, beating on her metal body with their improvised weapons, and Dominic's perfect face ran with blood. Step by step they were forced to retreat from the doorway and allow more and more of the prisoners into the bay. All of them were laughing the same terrible laugh, eager for blood and slaughter.

And Owen Deathstalker decided enough was enough. He'd given his two new friends every chance to do it themselves, but all their courage and skill clearly wasn't enough. So he drew his sword and went forward to meet the prisoners. He was quickly in among them, graceful as a dancer, deadly beyond hope or mercy. He cut a bloody path through the howling mob, and none of them could stand against him. They weren't used to facing cold steel. Owen felt faster and stronger than he ever had before, even when using his Family's famous Boost. He cut men down with a brutal savagery that shocked even the hardened prisoners. Bodies fell to every side, shrieking their death agonies, and blood splashed the steel walls and pooled thickly on the floor. Owen cut and slashed and hacked, driving the prisoners back. At the end, the last few turned to run, and Owen went after them and cut them down. He slowly lowered his blade, and looked about him, breathing heavily.

One man still stood in the doorway. He carried an energy gun, but he put it down on the steel floor, so he could applaud Owen.

"I didn't expect you," he said. "An unexpected pleasure. I am deLangford. Who or what might you be?"

Owen grinned. "I'm the Deathstalker, and that's all you need to know. Now stay where you are, and put those hands in the air. Don't do anything sudden, or I'll whittle you down into a more pleasant person." He looked back at Glory and Dominic, who had changed back into their previous selves. They were both looking at him with open horror and shock on their faces. Owen felt a little put out, given that he'd just saved their lives. "What's the problem?"

"Dear God," said Dominic. "I never saw anything like that in my life. You cut them up like meat! It was . . . hideous. Inhuman! You're a barbarian! Men don't act like that!"

"Maybe not in your time," said Owen. "I was raised to be a warrior, and trained in the hardest school of all. You should be grateful. They would have torn you apart if I hadn't stopped them."

"You didn't have to kill them all!"

"Yes, I did," said Owen.

"You enjoyed it!" Glory said accusingly. "You smiled and laughed as you butchered those men."

Owen considered that. "I take a pride in work well done," he said finally. "And there's nothing like living when others want you dead to make a man feel good. I don't glory in their deaths, but I don't feel guilty about it either. I notice you were happy enough to shoot them from a distance with those terribly efficient guns of yours. That's no way to kill. It takes real guts to get in close with a blade, to put your life on the line, and depend on your skill and courage to bring you through. Murder should never be cold and impartial. You should always be prepared to pay in blood for the blood you shed."

"Yes," said deLangford. "You understand."

"Shut up, creep," said Owen. "So, Glory, Dominic—what do we do with him? He's the cause of all this death, after all."

"Art," said deLangford. "I took these worthless men and made them significant. What happened here will be told across the Empire. I made your glorious last stand possible. I took people who never mattered, even to themselves, and made them magnificent, if only for a moment. They are part of a story now, a legend that will be told for centuries. I made your heroism possible. Gave it shape and meaning. You should thank me. I made you art. And now, I surrender."

"There isn't a legend that's worth one man's death," said Owen. "Trust me, I know. What do we do with him?"

"He goes back to his cell," said Glory. "After we've searched him very thoroughly. The computers will be back on line anytime now."

Owen looked at her. "And that's it? He's responsible for everyone who died here! You could have died here! How can you be sure he won't do it again?"

"None of that matters," said Dominic. "He has surrendered. We can't punish him now. It wouldn't be right."

"Hell with that," said Owen. He looked at deLangford, and let his anger lash out. DeLangford's head exploded, showering the surroundings with blood and brains and skull fragments. The body sank slowly to its knees, blood fountaining from the neck, as Glory and Dominic cried out in shock and revulsion. The body fell forward and was still. Owen shook thick drops of blood from the end of his sword and then put it away.

"What kind of future do you come from?" Dominic said shakily. "That can produce creatures like you, and the Mad Mind?"

"I should kill you where you stand," said Glory. "You're not fit to live in human society. I should . . ."

"I wouldn't," said Owen, and something in his voice stopped them both.

Dominic took Glory by the arm. "This is too big for us. He has to go to court, to stand before the Emperor. Let Ethur decide what's to be done with him."

"Actually, I'll decide what's to be done with me," said Owen. "But I want to meet your Emperor. I'm sure there are many things he can tell me about . . . the Mad Mind. Don't worry, I promise I won't hurt him."

"You'll have to wear the energy gyves," Glory said flatly. "We can't risk the Emperor's safety."

"If it will make you feel better," Owen said graciously.

The energy bands crackled about his wrists again, and the Investigator and the Defender both relaxed a little. Glory called down her orbiting ship, while Dominic studied Owen closely. Owen studied Dominic. He was getting the hang of reading body language.

"You love her, don't you?" he said quietly, nodding at Glory. "Have you ever told her?"

"What? No! I . . ."

"Do it," said Owen. "Don't leave it till it's too late."

And so the three of them went down to Heartworld, which would one day be called Golgotha and then Logres, in a large and blocky ship that had no name, only a number. Owen didn't recognize the design at all. It moved smoothly through space, threading its way easily through the heavy traffic, and finally slipped into the planet's atmosphere with only the slightest of jolts. Owen sat at the back of the cabin, firmly strapped in for his own safety, and amused himself by changing the colors of his energy bands when nobody was looking.

Dominic and Glory spent most of the trip arguing about where they were going and how best to get Owen to the Emperor. They seemed very firmly of the opinion that there were a great many political and religious factions who would just love to get their hands on Owen, for all kinds of reasons, few of them good. And all of them would be quite willing to destroy Owen and anyone with him, rather than let any other group get to him first. Glory in particular seemed very concerned over how much damage some groups would do, if they gained control over Owen and his uncanny abilities.

"Oh, I wouldn't worry about that," Owen said cheerfully. "I doubt very much there's anyone here who can make me doing anything I don't want to do."

This didn't seem to reassure Glory or Dominic in the least, so the rest of the trip passed pretty much in silence. Until Glory slowed the ship right down so she could show Owen something. A section of the bulkhead next to Owen became transparent, so he could look out at the planet below. It wasn't much of a view. In the middle of a desert area lay a great crater, deep and dark, full of twisting gray mists shot through with shifting lights. But just the look of the crater made Owen feel strangely uneasy, disquieted.

"You're looking at what used to be Angel City," Glory said coldly. "Now it's just a hole in the earth, full of quantum instability. Millions of people died here, wiped away by a moment's anger of the Mad Mind. A wound in the world that will never heal. Most of the people died immediately. They were the lucky ones. Unfortunately, those closest to the edges of the effect were only partially touched. They live on, no longer human, in a place where reality is only a sometime thing. We've seen some of them; monsters in shape and spirit. Constantly changing, never solid or confirmed in one nature for more than a few moments. Angel City is a place of horror now, and always will be."

"We've sent in all kinds of rescue operations," said Dominic. "Scientists and priests, protected by force shields. All volunteers, wanting to help. None of them ever come back. The last I heard, the powers that be were trying to figure out how to enclose the whole area in one big industrial strength force shield, and then just blast the thing out into space. Where it can be someone else's problem."

"Why not just aim it into the sun?" said Owen.

"What if the quantum instability were to affect the sun?" said Glory. "For now, all we can do is put up warning signs, saying *Here Be Monsters.* Post guards to shoot down the poor things that occasionally come crawling up out of the crater. And pray to God that the mess doesn't start spreading."

"And this is just one of the nightmares your friend the Mad Mind left us," said Dominic.

"What one power can do, perhaps another can undo," said Owen.

He reached out with his mind. He could feel Hazel's presence permeating the crater, dark and confused, moving restlessly over the wound in the earth, never still. It wasn't her, just something she'd left behind, and Owen erased it in a moment, like a memory he didn't want to remember. The gray mists and the shifting lights disappeared like a bad dream, and there was just a great hole in the ground. Owen could sense sparks of life moving in the crater, but they were just people now. He hoped they wouldn't remember either. He sank back in his seat, exhausted, for the moment.

Dominic and Glory studied their ship's sensors for some time, arguing loudly over what had just happened below, their voices full of shock and something that might have been awe. Eventually, almost reluctantly, they turned and looked back at Owen.

"How the hell did you do that?" said Dominic. "What kind of power have you got?"

"I don't know," said Owen. "I'm still learning. Hopefully, enough to stop Hazel, when I finally catch up to her."

"Can you bring back the city, and the people who died?"

"No. I'm only human."

"Those energy gyves aren't affecting you at all, are they?" said Glory.

"Afraid not," said Owen. "But I'll keep them on at court, if it will make everyone feel more comfortable."

"I should crash the ship into the ground right now," said Glory. "Rather than risk letting you run loose."

"Please don't. It wouldn't affect me at all," Owen said calmly. "Will you relax? I'm not another Mad Mind. I just want to talk to your Emperor. Find out what he knows about Hazel. Why she became . . . what she was, and why she came here in the first place. I need to know these things, if I'm to stop her. You have no idea what she's going to become, eventually. I'll still play the prisoner at court, for your sakes. I don't want to harm anyone. I just want answers to my questions, and then I'll be on my way."

"Why don't you just dig them out of our minds?" said Dominic. "You could do that, couldn't you?"

"Yes," said Owen. "But I won't. Because that would be inhuman, Defender."

They landed at Heartworld's main starport, in the capital city Virimonde. Owen was briefly startled. There had never been anything in the history of his world to explain where the planet's name had come from. It was just another sign of how much history had been lost when the First Empire crashed and burned. The starport was just a vast open space, crowded with starships of all shapes and sizes. Big brutal configurations, with little aesthetics and less grace. They were built for efficiency, and nothing else. About what you'd expect of an age that gave its ships numbers instead of names.

Dominic and Glory told a whole bunch of lies to the starport control tower as to why they'd come back to Heartworld so unexpectedly, invoking their authority as Defender and Investigator to get out of the ship and off the starport as fast as possible. Owen got rid of the energy gyves, with his captors' permission, since they'd only attract attention.

A commandeered luggage trolley on antigrav floaters got them to the edge of the starport, and then they set about walking through the city to the Imperial Palace. There wasn't much traffic, on the streets or in the skies. When Owen inquired about this, he was told that most people preferred to use the ubiquitous transfer portals, which could teleport you directly to your destination. When Owen not unreasonably demanded to know why they weren't using them, Glory explained that they were programmed to teleport people, and she was pretty sure Owen didn't qualify. God alone knew how much energy it would take to teleport whatever it was he'd become. So they walked. No one would notice; lots of people liked to walk in the city. For all sorts of reasons.

Owen strode along between Dominic and Glory, and no one paid him any attention at all. After a while, he wasn't surprised. The wide streets were packed with strange and exotic people, many only borderline human as Owen understood the term. Everyone was talking at once, and no one seemed to be listening. The air was full of all kinds of music, blasting from every direction at once, and songs drifted on the air like clouds. The buildings were all bright primary colors, soaring up into the sky. Adver-

tisements flashed on and off, the razor-bright holos jumping out of everywhere and haranguing anyone stupid enough to make eye contact. Half of
them offered goods and services Owen didn't even recognize. Everywhere
he looked, the people and the ads and the storefronts were overpoweringly
loud and in your face. And oh, the bright and glorious people, thronging
through the boulevards, out and about to see and be seen, walking proudly
like birds of paradise; aristocrats of the greatest Empire Humanity had
ever known.

Even if they didn't all look like people. There were those who walked
in their bones, wrapped in transparent flesh and skin, with just the
faintest traces of blue and scarlet ganglia, for contrast. There were people who flew through the perfumed air on pure white feathery wings.
People so wide and heavy that the ground shuddered under their every
step, people with any number of limbs, or grafted protuberances that
must have been alien in origin. And, of course, the many different sexes.
People with genitals like the pulpy petals of some unknown flower, or
spiked flails, or fleshy plug sockets. Hermaphrodites, with three or four
sets of genitals. Owen didn't know what to do with himself when one of
them winked at him.

"Don't stare," Dominic said sternly. "Makes you look like a tourist."

"Couldn't we have flown to the palace?" said Owen, just a little plaintively. "I think I'm going into culture shock."

"No one flies anymore, except for the winged wonders up there," said
Glory. "People either walk or use the transfer portals. Flying in a ship
is . . . unusual. It would be noticed. Walking is fine. People walk to boast
of their latest forms and adaptations, using their example to try and con-
vert others to their particular cause or fashion."

Owen listened, but kept on looking about him. Even the wildest areas
of his Empire had nothing to compare with this. He was beginning to feel
like the barbarian Glory had named him, dazzled by his first glimpse of
true civilization. Everywhere he looked he saw extreme forms and changes
that had only the barest links to the basic human norm. Owen had to
wonder how many changes you could make to your body and still be
human inside. He remembered the Hadenmen and Wampyr of his own
time, and shuddered briefly. The one thing he didn't see on the streets was

anyone who looked like him. He felt obscurely lonely, in the middle of this exotic, alien crowd. His gaze fell upon areas marked *Enter at Your Own Risk*, and drew Glory's attention to them. She sniffed loudly.

"Some forms are so extreme they can be contagious; so powerful they overwhelm lesser minds. They're not forbidden, nothing is, but they're supposed to stick to strictly defined territories. Some always wander, but we shoo them back in as soon as they're noticed. See that street there?"

Owen looked down a side street marked *Season of the Witch*. Women in braids and beads and very little else were levitating, speaking in tongues, and juggling fire with their bare hands. Glory said something about exploring new spiritual directions, but Owen was pretty sure he was looking at the beginnings of the esper phenomenon.

Other segregated areas included Sexland, where hundreds of far too naked people, of far too many sexes, slammed together in a vast, sprawling orgy that appeared to have no beginning or end. The noise was overpowering. People were coming and leaving all the time, so that while individual elements changed, the orgy continued, perhaps forever.

"It's just another way to lose yourself," said Dominic, apparently unaffected by a sight that made Owen feel distinctly hot and bothered. "Another way to avoid thinking. People have been known to die there. Not the worst of ways to go, I suppose, but . . ."

Valhalla was a great open square bedecked with all kinds of flags and banners, packed with a seething mass of people all seriously intent on killing each other. Huge muscular types, mostly wearing furs, hacked and cut at each other with heavy axes. Screams and war cries filled the air, the dead piled up, and blood ran thickly in the deep gutters. Owen studied the ceaseless combat for a while, and though he admired the general enthusiasm, he had to dismiss most of the fighters as rank amateurs who wouldn't have lasted five minutes in the Arenas of his time.

"There are always those drawn to the simple, brutal joys of barbarism," said Glory. "Valhalla is open to all comers, so anyone stupid enough, or with enough self-image invested in their battle bodies, can just plunge right in and fight for as long as they like, or as long as they last. Supposedly it's all about survival of the fittest, and evolution in action, but again really it's just another way to avoid thinking about the complications of the modern condition, by acting like animals."

The next closed-off area was the province of the Psychonauts. Men and women sat or lay on comfortable couches, their faces empty, their minds elsewhere. Most of them looked skinny or actually malnourished, and their clothes were filthy and ragged. Some were laughing, or crying. They reminded Owen of the poor malformed creatures he'd seen in the Madness Maze's annex: men and women driven beyond the limits of human consciousness, lost in the unlit depths of their own souls. He said as much, and Dominic was actually shocked.

"These people are heroes, Owen. They're all volunteers, flying on new drugs to see what they can do, and what can be learned from them. They dive into unknown psychic territories, access altered states of consciousness, thinking outside the limits of the body. Looking for answers that can't be found anywhere else."

"And what answers have they come up with?" said Owen.

Glory scowled. "Nothing of any use. A lot of them don't come back, from wherever they go. There's a hell of a turnover, but there's never an empty couch. They claim to be confronting the mysteries of the human condition, but since they're mostly too busy watching the pretty colors to feed or look after themselves, I'd have to put this down to just more escapism."

"We have to find the answers somewhere," Dominic said stubbornly.

"You find answers by looking outside, not inside," said Glory.

And then all three of them looked round sharply, as loud screams sounded from up ahead. Suddenly people were running past them, in a riot of shapes and colors, scattering like panicked children. They were all running from something, their faces desperate with the simple need to *get away*, pressing relentlessly on and trampling the fallen underfoot. Dominic and Glory and Owen stood their ground, like three rocks in a roaring flood. Glory Chojiro's hands were immediately full of energy guns from her subspace pockets. People ran by on every side, and the street up ahead was quickly cleared of everyone but a crowd of assorted people advancing down the street in perfect lockstep. Their feet hit the ground in a single great crash, and their faces were set in a frozen masklike expression. There was something subtly inhuman in the way they all moved and looked, and a cold breeze caressed the back of Owen's neck as his hackles rose. His hand went to his sword belt. He'd just realized that every pair of eyes tracked with every other pair. As though there was only a single thought, a single intent, behind them.

"It's a group mind breakout," said Dominic. He sounded almost sick, disgusted. "This is the closest we have to an obscenity, Owen. The death of individuality in a gestalt of increasing power, where everyone involved surrenders to the mass-mind. No more personality, no more needs or passions, just instinct and appetite and flocking behavior. And the bigger the mass-mind gets, the more powerful it becomes, sucking in weaker minds against their will."

"What causes these group minds?" said Owen, keeping a watchful eye on the group as it advanced towards them.

"No one knows," said Glory. "It appears to be spontaneous, something to do with overcrowding and peer pressure. Maybe it's the ultimate escape from the pressures of being human. All we know is, it's happening more and more often."

"So what do we do?" said Owen. "Knock them all out, and then ship them off to your House of Correction to be fixed?"

"No," said Glory. "There is no cure for what they've become."

Owen suddenly felt the pressure of the mass-mind, reaching out to touch his thoughts. It felt like a psychic hole, into which anything or anyone could fall forever. There was nothing human about it anymore. Owen roused the power within him, but was honestly lost for what to do. Like so many other things in this brave old world, the mass-mind was beyond his understanding.

The sound of approaching running feet brought him back to himself, and a small army of people in brilliant jade armor crashed suddenly out of a side street. They all had energy guns in their hands, and harsh focused expressions. They opened fire on the group mind without any warning, not even bothering to pick targets. Bodies exploded into bloody mists, and scorched body parts flew up into the air. The street was suddenly full of the stench of spilled blood and burnt meat. The mass-mind tried to scatter, like frightened birds, but it couldn't break out of its pattern. The jade-armored newcomers pressed forward, firing their powerful guns again and again without cease or mercy, until all the bodies that made up the group mind were dead, just burnt and bloody pieces in the street.

"They never had a chance," said Owen.

Something in his voice alerted Dominic, who quickly put a restraining hand on Owen's sword hand. "Don't even think of interfering, or expressing an opinion. That's the Emperor's Praetorian Guard. Everything they do is the Emperor's will. And they did the only thing they could. The group mind was a threat that would only have become more powerful. There are times . . . when an inhuman response is the only answer we have to an inhuman threat."

"Kill the thing, before it spreads," said Glory. "Everyone sucked into the mass-mind was already dead, in every way that matters."

"What about the ones sucked in against their will?" said Owen. "What was their crime?"

"Not being human," said Dominic. "Don't judge us too harshly, Owen. We have tried everything else we could think of, and this is the only action that works."

They walked on, giving the Praetorian Guards plenty of room as they gathered up the scattered remains for easier disposal. Owen wasn't sure how he felt about what he'd just seen. He had to wonder just how hard the powers that be had looked for another answer. The three of them headed deeper into the city, and the chattering crowds quickly returned, as though nothing had happened. Dominic and Glory tried to distract Owen by talking of many things: of memes—thoughts and ideas that spread like a virus, infecting people with the latest fashions and fads until those affected built up an immunity; of ideas running loose from the minds that created them, imposing themselves on weaker minds and warping their bodies into new shapes and capabilities. Politics and religions had become memes, endlessly mutating and multiplying.

And up and down the many streets, news channels and adverts and ideological hard sells assaulted Owen from every side. The loud and garish holos capered around Owen no matter which way he looked, shouting in his ears as he walked through them. They didn't seem to bother Glory and

Dominic at all. Presumably they were so used to them they just didn't notice them. Owen gritted his teeth and stared determinedly straight ahead. The streets were full of every kind of new humanity, and no one paid the barbarian from the future any attention at all.

Just when Owen was thinking at least it couldn't get any worse, of course it did. Half a dozen naked men came striding down the street, burning alive. People moved unhurriedly to get out of their way. Flames leapt around the burning men, blasting out a heat so intense that those nearest flinched away from it. But no one seemed to be paying them any particular attention. For although the flames burned very fiercely, they did not consume. The flesh beneath the flames blackened and cracked, but that was all. The burning men walked down the street, looking straight ahead, their black and crimson faces twisted with endless suffering, their cracked lips moving silently.

"Penitents," said Glory, amused by Owen's shocked reaction. "They set themselves on fire, as a protest. They disapprove of how far we've progressed from basic humanity. They're burning alive as a penance for the sins of the age. Show-offs."

"Some burn for days, others last for months," said Dominic. "And there are always more to replace those who fall. I find it reassuring, that there are still people crying out against inhumanity."

"Even if it's a really stupid way?" said Glory. "No one notices. No one cares. They're just another pressure group."

Dominic sighed. "That's the problem with the Empire today; too many beliefs, too many faiths and philosophies. And far too many splintered factions, arguing endlessly over details and interpretations that only matter to them. You can find every kind of cause these days—from pagan animism to scientific determinism, from We Are All Property to making blood sacrifices to computers. Given how varied the human condition has become, it's hard to find anything that everyone can believe in. We all live for the present, for the experience. Heaven can wait. We could have transcended, become something greater, but we dropped the ball. Partly because we were afraid; partly because we couldn't agree on a direction; and just possibly because we saw the future of the human spirit, and knew we weren't worthy."

Owen thought about the Madness Maze, but said nothing. He couldn't talk about the Maze without telling them about Hazel d'Ark.

Finally Owen Deathstalker came to the great and mighty court of Emperor Ethur, the oldest living human in the whole First Empire. Not that anyone could just walk into court and demand an immediate audience with the Emperor, but Dominic Cairo and Glory Chojiro invoked their ancient privilege of Defender and Investigator, and the jade-armored guards waved them on. An Investigator and a Defender of Humanity could always speak to the Emperor, if they claimed a real and present danger to Humanity itself. Owen thought they were pushing that a bit, but said nothing. One of the guards wanted to take his sword away. Owen gave him his best hard look, and the guard decided that he was needed urgently elsewhere.

Ethur's Court was a place of freaks and wonders, under a great golden bowl half a mile wide. There were enough courtiers present to make up a decent-sized army, indulging themselves in every extremity of shape, just for the sake of it. From the aesthetic to the grotesque; from the tasteless to the bizarre; from women with bosoms so big they dragged along the floor, to people pierced through every organ, to wispy ghosts who were hardly there at all—every excess was represented somewhere. Braziers pumped perfumes into the air, and sharp atonal music formed a background to the constant babble of voices as everybody talked at once and no one listened. The courtiers played vicious, intricate games and hardly glanced round as Glory and Dominic and Owen passed by, heading for the Steel Throne. They were too normal, too ordinary. Too boring to be of interest. A few followed Owen with their eyes, sensing something different about him; something . . . disturbing. He smiled at them, and they flinched back.

At the very center of the court, under the very apex of the great golden bowl, on the Steel Throne set high on a raised dais, sat Ethur, looking out over his packed court with cold, knowing eyes. Owen had been warned about the state of the Emperor, but the reality still came as a shock. Ethur was the oldest living human being, having occupied the Steel Throne for over four hundred years, but that privilege came at a price. His body was riddled with support mechanisms and gengineered organs, plugged into the machine that was the throne. He had the look of a man in his forties, apart from the many wires and tubes and cables that entered his body, connecting him to the throne he could never leave. He would never rise from the Steel Throne again, except in death.

The Emperor's pale leathery skin was covered only by the crimson silk cloak that adorned his bony shoulders, fluttering occasionally in the gusting air currents of the court. He had no hair anywhere, no fingernails and no navel, and his complexion and body color changed constantly as chemical tides moved slowly within him. Now and again, strange sharp-edged mechanisms rose up through his flesh, like surfacing creatures, only to be pushed back down by an effort of will. The pale skin closed over them reluctantly, with not even a scar to show their passing. Ethur's face was lean and hawkish, with a beak of a nose over a tight pursed mouth, and his eyes were as old as the world.

Dominic and Glory stood at the bottom of the dais, and presented themselves to the Emperor. They bowed deeply, but Ethur barely nodded in return. The Defender and the Investigator explained their business, and the whole court grew quiet to listen. They looked at Owen with angry, frightened eyes, and the whispered words *Mad Mind* moved through the courtiers like an icy breeze. Armed guards moved slowly through the courtiers to surround Owen, who politely pretended not to notice. Finally Dominic and Glory presented Owen to the Emperor, and Owen bowed courteously. Ethur considered him thoughtfully for a long time, and when he finally spoke his voice was little more than a whisper, the words an effort, as though they had to be summoned up from deep inside him.

"So, Owen, you are from the future, come to visit us. Something new, at last. How delicious. There is always novelty in our court, but rarely anything *new*. You have done well, Defender and Investigator; but where is the threat to our world that you spoke of? I see only an undeveloped man, dressed like a barbarian, and armed like one too." He paused to allow a ripple of laughter to run through the courtiers. "You may have come from the same future as the Mad Mind, Owen, but you don't seem nearly as dangerous."

"I'm no threat," said Owen. "Really. I'm just visiting. A nice cup of tea, some answers to a few questions, and I'll be on my way again."

"We will decide that," said Ethur.

"Owen has . . . abilities, Your Majesty," said Dominic. "He has restored to us the city that was lost, and made the survivors human again! A miracle . . . but my partner and I felt unworthy to judge his abilities and potential, and so brought him here, to you."

"You gave instructions, Your Majesty," said Glory, "that any other visitor from the future should be punished for the crimes of the Mad Mind. But . . . we could not decide whether Owen is a threat of that same magnitude. So we are here, awaiting your judgement."

"Yes, yes," said Ethur, leaning as far forward as the tubes and cables would allow, to stare directly at Owen. "The wound in our world, healed at last by an effort of will. A miracle, indeed. Our scientists are currently having all kinds of hysterics over that. They do so hate to be outdone. And over two hundred survivors, apparently normal again. Truly impressive, Owen. Of course, we had them all killed immediately."

"You did what?" said Owen. "Why, for God's sake?"

Ethur actually smiled a little at the harshness in Owen's voice. "The risk was too great. They might have reverted, or proved contagious. They were inhuman once, and that is enough. You must not judge us, man from the future. This is our time, and we make the decisions here."

"And the only miracles permitted are the ones you authorize?" said Owen. "Life and death, but only at your command? Well, well, I guess some things don't change at all, no matter what time it is."

There were guards all around him now, with energy guns openly trained on him. Owen looked at them thoughtfully, and Dominic and Glory stirred uneasily. And that was when the Empress Hermione made her appearance, walking unhurriedly through the wide aisle that opened up in the courtiers for her. Owen had been told about the Empress, but her appearance still came as something of a shock. She drifted silently through the cordon of guards, passed by Owen without looking at him, and slowly ascended the steps of the dais to stand beside her husband and the Steel Throne.

Hermione was fifteen years old, a tall willowy blonde in flowing white silks, and heavily pregnant. Ethur chose her to be the latest of his many brides when she was just thirteen, and no one questioned him because he was the Emperor, and knew best. Her quiet, passionless face looked drained and tired, as though the pregnancy was taking a lot out of her. It wasn't her first. The moment she became Ethur's bride, both natural and unnatural methods began, to make her pregnant with the Emperor's ancient seed. He desperately needed an heir. The first two pregnancies hadn't lasted till term, but everyone had great hopes for the third. Everyone except Hermione, but then, no one cared what she thought. The process had clearly taken its toll. Her pretty doll-like face held no emotion at all, and her eyes were empty. Ethur stroked her cheek with his long pale fingers, and she didn't respond at all. Ethur smiled down at Owen.

"The older we get, the younger we like them. People grow the same so quickly . . . only the young have any real individuality, and it soon fades. All our wives have been such delicate flowers . . ."

"How many have you had?" said Owen.

"Who can say? Some were more memorable than others. Some of them gave us children, but we ended up killing all our heirs, sooner or later. Because they were bad, or unsuitable. They were all such disappointments . . . Still, we remain optimistic. We always hope that the next one will turn out better."

"Bad blood will out," said Owen. "And monsters have a tendency to breed true."

The courtiers gasped, and the Emperor looked at him sharply before settling back in his Steel Throne. The tubes and cables murmured around him, as though resentful at being disturbed.

"You are not our first visitor from the future, Owen. Twelve years ago, the Mad Mind came upon us, without warning. It tore this world apart, searching for knowledge we didn't have. We have come a long way in our knowledge of the body, but even we can't raise the dead. The Mad Mind refused to believe us. It raged through our cities, blasting open universities and laboratories, killing hundreds of thousands in the process. All our armed forces were helpless against this . . . creature. It abducted our greatest scientists and thinkers, and tore their knowledge from their brains. What she left behind, the discarded husks, would have been better off dead. And finally, with half of Heartworld in rubble or in flames, with the dead piled up everywhere, the Mad Mind disappeared, as suddenly as it had appeared. Our people are still mourning and rebuilding.

"We know all about monsters, Owen.

"And now here you are, from that same future, claiming the Mad Mind as a friend. We've waited a long time for another of your kind to appear. We set our traps everywhere, specifically tasked to catch and cage your kind. You will pay for the crimes of your friend. Whatever mad hell of a future you come from that can produce such monstrosities—we want nothing to do with it. And hopefully the horrific nature of your corpse, when it finally returns to the future, will be sufficient to dissuade any others who feel like visiting us."

"So the cup of tea's out of the question, then?" said Owen. "Pity." He looked at Hermione. "I can get you out of here. Take you somewhere else. Just say the word."

"I am happy here," said the Empress Hermione, in a high childish voice. "I belong here."

Yes, Owen thought reluctantly. *You do. And one day, you will meet a man named Giles Deathstalker, and the child you make together will do such wondrous things . . .*

He sighed loudly, and looked at Ethur again. "There won't be any more visitors from the future."

"Can you guarantee that?" said the Emperor. "Not that it matters. In your position, you'd say anything. You don't seem nearly as dangerous as your predecessor, but we don't feel like taking any chances. Not after what you did with the lost city." He paused suddenly, struck by a thought. "Tell us about your future, monster. What will happen between now and then, to produce such as you?"

"In my time," Owen said, "all of Humanity is faced with the threat of extinction. An enemy is coming that we cannot stop or turn aside. It is my hope that by tracking down the Mad Mind, and stopping it, I can learn how to save Humanity in my time. You must not stop me, Your Majesty. The future of our species may depend upon what I can learn."

"A future full of monsters doesn't deserve to be saved," said Ethur. "Perhaps by dissecting your living body and probing your mind, we will find the knowledge to create a different future. Your slow and hideous death will serve many purposes, Owen. Try and remember that, while you're screaming. We will have justice, for what was done to us. We will have vengeance."

"And after everything I've done for you," said Owen.

"We will learn how you remade that city and its people, from the agonies of your body and your mind. Nothing will be wasted."

"Think of all the good I could do."

"We will allow no greater power than us in this Empire," said Ethur. "We alone know what is best for Humanity."

"Nothing changes," said Owen Deathstalker.

He blew the energy gyves off his wrists with a careless shrug, and the surrounding guards cried out in shock. Energy guns trained on him from every direction, and even Dominic Cairo and Glory Chojiro had weapons in their hands. The courtiers screamed and shouted, and did their best to scrabble back out of the line of fire. All around Owen, people were changing into more dangerous battle forms. Owen ignored them all, his gaze fixed on the stupefied Emperor.

"It doesn't matter what time it is; Emperors are always a bad idea. I think the whole idea's intrinsically corrupting. People just aren't supposed to wield that much power. It isn't good for them. So, sorry, but I decline to be vivisected. I have work to do."

He looked casually around him. The guards were now great metallic forms, or creature hybrids. There were looming insectoid forms, with wild energies coruscating around their branching horns. And even a few shapes that made no sense to him at all. And there were more guns pointed at him than he'd seen in the whole Rebellion. Owen looked back at Ethur.

"Boo!"

All the guns opened up at once, tremendous energies leaping out to destroy him. Owen stopped them all in mid air with a thought. They hung helplessly on the air, caught between one moment and the next. Owen considered the matter for a moment, and then absorbed all the energy into himself. He didn't want any of it running loose when he left and injuring innocent bystanders. Assuming there were any . . . The guards tried to fire again, but their guns didn't work, because Owen had decided they didn't.

He could have killed them all with a thought, but he didn't. They were just doing their jobs. He could have killed the Emperor . . . but history had to take its course. And he didn't want to abuse his power. That way led to Emperors, and Mad Minds.

He strode up the steps to the top of the dais, to look right into Ethur's face. "I ought to rip you right out of that throne and strangle you with your own life support systems. But I can't, because history has its imperatives. What you will do, in years to come, will eventually lead to a better Empire. My best revenge . . . is knowing that you'd really hate the Empire that's coming."

"This isn't over yet," said Ethur.

He gestured at his guards, and they closed in around Glory and Dominic, and turned their guns on them. Owen looked at the guards, and then back at the Emperor.

"You are fond of these two," said Ethur. "You care about them. We have had reports. So, surrender or they die. Right here and now. Or will you sacrifice your newfound friends to necessity, and prove yourself as inhuman as the Mad Mind?"

"There's only one monster in this court, Ethur," said Owen.

He gathered up Glory and Dominic with his mind, and in a moment they were back at the starport. The Investigator and the Defender looked dazedly about them, shocked by the sudden transition. Great silver ships loomed over them, and people came and went, intent on their own business. Glory recovered first, and gave Owen a hard look.

"I didn't know you could do that."

"Neither did I," said Owen. "I'm learning new things all the time now. It seems I've destroyed your lives, just by meeting you. I'm afraid you can't go back to court—ever. You can bet Ethur will be looking for someone to take out his anger on, now that he doesn't have me."

"He would have had us killed," Dominic said numbly. "We spent our lives in duty and service to his name, and at the end it meant nothing to him."

"Yes, well," said Owen. "Emperors are like that, mostly."

"He betrayed us," said Glory. Something had changed in her face, in her eyes. "Something must be done, to block the power of Emperors."

"Even Heartworld won't be safe for us now," said Dominic. "We'll have to try and lose ourselves on one of the border worlds. Have to say good-bye to our families, to our friends . . . All I ever wanted was to be a Defender of Humanity, and I'll have to give that up too. Damn you, Owen. Why did you have to choose us?"

"I'm sorry," said Owen. "Believe me, I know how you feel." He looked around the starport, and at the city in the distance. "This Empire is a legend in my time; the greatest flowering of human civilization. I hadn't expected . . . this. So much more, and so much less. But if anyone should have known you can't trust in legends, it's me."

Glory frowned. "If you're from the future, this should be history to you. Didn't you study the period before you left?"

"There are no records," said Owen. "Just . . . stories."

Dominic looked at Owen searchingly. "Something's going to happen—something . . . bad? What aren't you telling us, Owen?"

"Is the Mad Mind coming back?" said Glory.

"No." Owen looked at them both compassionately. He would have liked to lie, but he owed them the truth. "Your Empire will decline and fall. We don't know exactly when, or why. Perhaps you would be safer on a border world, after all."

Dominic and Glory moved closer together, as though for comfort and protection. A directionless fear moved in their eyes, of bad times coming they now knew they wouldn't be able to stop.

"Who are you, Owen?" said Glory. "Who are you, really?"

"Just a man, trying to do the right thing," said Owen. "In the end, that's all there ever is."

"Where . . . when will you go next?" said Dominic.

"My friend—your Mad Mind—leaves a trail when she travels back through time. I'll pick up the trail again and follow where it leads. Hope to catch up to her before she can do any more damage. I only missed her by twelve years here, and that's not bad after a trip of nearly a thousand years. Good-bye, my friends. Make new lives for yourselves. And remember: look forward, never back."

He let go his hold on time, and the planet dropped away from under him, leaving him suspended in open space again. He reached out for

Hazel's trail, and was surprised to find she hadn't immediately dived back into the past again. She'd made what looked to be a side trip, to one of the border worlds, on what would one day be called the Rim. Curious, Owen followed her trail, treading the stars under his feet as he headed for the edge of civilization.

It was a green world, young and full of life, and the human presence there was still a new thing. Owen hung in orbit above the planet, studying it with his extended senses. He didn't need to see or hear things directly anymore; he just knew. There were barely a hundred cities on this world, most of them little more than stone and timber. A single starport served only visiting ships. It was a low-tech civilization, sliding slowly but inevitably back into barbarism. Armies warred constantly on each other, though it wasn't clear what they had to fight over, except perhaps territory. It was a purely human world, with no extreme body shapes or adaptations. Some guns, but steel was the weapon of choice. Owen was amused to find he felt more comfortable here than he had on Heartworld.

He materialized in the midst of a great forest. Massive trees with blue-black bark, and heavy fleshy leaves of a green so brilliant they were almost luminous. They towered all around him, packed so closely together they blocked out most of the light from the brilliant silver-blue sun. The air was cool and crisp, full of the scents of living things, and a curling ground mist moved this way and that, though no breeze blew. Owen looked slowly around him. There were dark shadows in between the trees, and dust motes curled slowly in the silver shafts of light, but there was no sign of any human intrusion.

Once again Hazel had been and gone. He'd missed her again. And yet there'd been no trace of any damage on this world, nothing like the devastation she'd visited on Heartworld. What had brought her here, to a place so far away from everywhere? Owen looked round sharply. Someone was coming. After a while, he heard footsteps approaching, and a young boy calling excitedly after baying hounds. And finally a dark-haired boy of about ten came running down the narrow trail, following two loping hound dogs. He called out sharply to the dogs as he spotted Owen waiting, and the hounds immediately crashed to a halt. They studied Owen suspiciously, panting heavily, as the boy came slowly forward to stand beside them. He had a sword on his hip. Owen gave the boy his best reassuring smile.

"Hi. I'm Owen. I'm just visiting."

"Offworlder," said the boy, taking in Owen's clothes. He was dressed in roughly stitched furs over a plain tunic. "We don't see many tourists these days. And mostly we like it that way. You've come a fair way from the starport. Are you lost?"

"No," said Owen. "Just . . . seeing the sights. Can you tell me your name?"

The boy grinned briefly. "Ma always says I have no manners. I'm Giles VomAcht, of Hadrian City. My father is war master there. And these overeager boys here are called Hunter and Tracker. Because that's what they do."

The hounds looked up as they heard their names, and Giles petted their heads till they settled again.

"Out hunting?" said Owen. "What are you after?"

Giles grinned again. "Anything that moves, really. We're not fussy. We just love to hunt. We catch enough for good eating, and let the rest go. What are you doing here, Owen?"

Owen grinned. "Following a trail. Just like you."

Owen and the boy Giles sat down by the side of the trail, and talked together for a while, enjoying each other's company. Owen found the boy easy and engaging, and the boy was eager for news of other worlds. The dogs settled down at their feet, yawning and scratching themselves as they waited patiently to get back to the real business of the hunt.

"Don't you have a Clan name, Owen?" said Giles, after a while. "Family is important. The VomAchts rule in Hadrian City."

"Of course. I am Owen, head of Clan Deathstalker."

"Damn! Now that's a Clan name! Deathstalker . . ." The boy said it several times, savoring the length of the name. "I'd love a name like that. A warrior's name. Where do you come from?"

"Most recently, I was at Ethur's court, on Heartworld. I had an audience with the Emperor."

Giles spat on the ground and said a rude word, and the dogs stirred uneasily at the sudden anger in the boy's voice. "He's not our Emperor anymore. We broke away. This is our world now, though the Clans are still arguing over what to call it. We don't miss Ethur, or his Empire. They never did anything for us." He frowned heavily, sticking out his lower lip. "Too many freaks and mutants in the Empire these days; that's what Da says. It was supposed to be a *human* Empire."

"What do you want to be, when you grow up?" said Owen.

"A warrior, of course! Like my father. I don't get to see him much; he is often away, needed in the wars. Fighting to keep our city safe. I wish he had more time for me. I know, it's selfish, but . . . When I am grown to a warrior's age, I will fight for our city too. I will make him proud of me. Make him take notice."

The boy's brooding face belied his steadfast words, and Owen decided to change the subject.

"Giles, have you seen anything . . . strange, recently? Anything unusual? Probably right around here."

"Yes!" Giles said immediately. "A couple of months back. I saw an angel, right here, in the woods!" He looked at Owen carefully, to be sure his new friend wouldn't laugh at him, and then reassured by what he saw in Owen's face, he continued. "At first, I could only feel her presence, watching me. Then she became a bright light, shining down on me, and finally a glowing woman. Very pretty, with red hair. She didn't have wings or a halo, but I knew she had to be an angel. I could feel the power in her. You believe me, don't you, Owen?"

"Yes," said Owen. "I do."

"No one else does." Giles shrugged. "Doesn't matter. I know what I saw."

"Did the angel . . . say anything to you?"

"No . . . I thought she was going to, but in the end she just looked at me, and vanished. Why would an angel reveal herself to me? I'm not any-one special. Perhaps it was a portent, to show that I have a great destiny ahead of me!"

"Perhaps you have," said Owen. "I knew a Giles once. He was a great warrior. Good luck with your hunt, Giles. I have to be going now."

And he vanished, right in front of Giles, enjoying the look of surprise on the boy's face. Once again Owen let go of his hold on time, and the galaxy spun around him as he plunged back into the past again, following Hazel. He had a long way to go, and even longer before he could allow himself to rest.

Back in the woods, the boy who would one day become Giles Death-stalker shrugged easily, accepting the miraculous the way children do, and then he was off on the hunt again, running with a happy heart through the shadowed woods with his beloved dogs.

CHAPTER FOUR

✳

HERE BE MONSTERS

Usher II was a mistake. A planet that should never have happened, a miserable lump of rock hanging out in a bad neighborhood. To be exact, it hung right in the middle between two suns, held in place by an unlikely combination of gravity and other badly misunderstood forces. It did not revolve, or orbit, or do anything else particularly interesting. Made up almost entirely of rock and crystal, it had no ecosystem, and never would. Life had been given up as a bad idea long ago, and so it would have stayed, until the Empire found it and discovered its peculiar electromagnetic conditions made it the perfect place to assemble stardrive engines. And so hundreds of scientific bases and factories were built all over Usher II, protected by some of the most powerful force shields ever created. People lived on Usher II now, but never for long. It was just too damned depressing a place to stay for long. The double suns burned fiercely, constantly, like two great glaring eyes, and there was nowhere to go and nothing to do. Turnover among the scientists and the families was high, despite every incentive the Empire could come up with, but as long as the stardrives kept rolling off the line, no one cared. Usher II was still a place to get rich in a hurry, doing work no one else wanted to do.

(Usher I was more of a moon than a planet. It rushed around the two suns in a figure-eight orbit that made no sense whatsoever, a pockmarked piece of rock with no discernable worth or qualities.)

And now two Imperial starcruisers had come to Usher II, the *Heritage* and the *Hook*, hanging way back from the binary suns, studying Usher II from what they fervently hoped was a safe distance. The Terror was coming, and they were there to witness the death of a world. The cities and bases should have been evacuated long ago, but the stardrive factories were far too important to be just abandoned, and so scientists' families were held hostage to keep the factories working until the very last moment. Now that moment had come, and everywhere civilian ships were rising from Usher II in their thousands, in one last desperate bid for escape. In the cities, riots had broken out, as the remaining population discovered there weren't enough ships to go round, and they weren't going anywhere. The Emperor Finn had given orders that all deserting civilian ships should be shot down, to encourage everyone else to keep working, but neither the *Heritage* nor the *Hook* had the heart to obey such orders. It was too late for things like that now. Anyone could see that.

Captain Ariadne Vardalos sat stiffly in her command chair on the bridge of the *Heritage*, and watched the fleeing ships and the riots and the death songs of a population. There was nothing she could do. She had her orders. The *Heritage* was not there to help, or even offer comfort; her only mission was to strike a blow at the Terror, and hopefully survive long enough to observe the results. Sitting alone in the starship's cargo bay was an alien tech derived superweapon that might or might not be the key to stopping the Terror's herald in its tracks. The herald always came first. The *Heritage*'s sensors had already picked it up, heading slowly but inexorably towards Usher II and its two suns.

Captain Vardalos was a medium-height, rangy woman with olive skin and long dark ringlets surrounding a thoughtful face. She'd been a starship captain for forty years, and never wanted anything else. She was a member of Pure Humanity and Church Militant, because you had to be these days if you wanted to be a fleet officer under Emperor Finn, but she really didn't give much of a damn. She was loyal to the Empire, and the Emperor, because that was part of the job. You had to believe in the chain of command in the military, or everything just went to hell.

Standing at her side, sniffing and occasionally sucking at her teeth in that irritating way she had, was her second-in-command, Marcella Fortuna. A tall gangling blonde with cool blue eyes and a vague smile, a sloppy manner, and the kind of quiet determination that could wear down mountains. Reliable, but not noted for original thinking, Fortuna had been a second for forty years because no one in their right mind would ever make her a captain. Vardalos and Fortuna had served together for longer than either of them cared to remember. They made a good team. Even on jobs they had no stomach for.

"Move us in a little closer," said Vardalos. "I want to be able to look the herald over thoroughly before we launch our supposed superweapon."

"Are you sure that's really wise, Captain?" said Fortuna. "Something quite appallingly nasty is due to happen to Usher II anytime now, and we don't want it happening to us, do we?"

"Don't fill your trousers just yet, Second. The herald's never been known to attack anything. Bloody thing doesn't have to; by all accounts it's indestructible. We've got some time to play with yet, as long as we're careful."

"And the departing civilian ships, Captain? We do have quite explicit instructions . . ."

"Officially, we can't spare the energy it would take to deal with them. Unofficially, I didn't join the fleet to shoot civilians in the back while they were running away. You have any problems with that, Second?"

"No, Captain. I just wanted to be sure you had your justifications thought out properly. And I think I'll edit this conversation from the bridge log, on the way back. Just in case. You never know who might have access to it, these days."

"It's becoming that sort of a fleet, isn't it?" Vardalos sighed heavily. "Still, emperors come and go, but the fleet goes on. We follow our duty and weather the storms, because someone has to provide continuity. Someone has to be around, to clear up the messes the politicians make."

"Who are you trying to persuade, Captain?" said Fortuna. "Me, or you?"

"Oh, hush, Second. This ship's loyal, and as long as I'm captain it will stay loyal. Finn may not have turned out to be the Emperor he promised he'd be, but everyone else has either run away or been proved false. You have to believe in *someone*. We have too many enemies at our throat to go soft. The ELFs, the aliens, the Terror . . . Maybe we need an Iron Man on the throne, in times like these. So suck it in and shoulder the weight, Second, because that's part of the job too. Communications, get me the captain of the *Hook*."

"Aye, Captain."

Captain Carter Randolph appeared on the bridge's main viewscreen, scowling fiercely. Vandalos knew better than to take it personally. Randolph was the oldest serving captain in the fleet, and by far the most experienced. His actual age was said to be classified, but he had to be at least a hundred and thirty. He'd been a large man once, but his great frame was stooped and shriveled now, collapsing in on itself. Sharp gray eyes dominated his heavily lined face, under a shock of silver-gray hair. His habitual glower softened a little as he took in Vardalos.

"Ariadne! About time you got here. We've been hanging around this arse end of the universe for over an hour. Don't suppose there's been any change in our orders?"

"No, Captain Randolph. Nothing's changed. My job is still to deliver the alien superweapon, and hang around just long enough to see if it works. And your job is still to throw away your life for nothing."

"Not for nothing. For my faith, and my duty. Everyone on this ship is a volunteer, very definitely including me. If your weapon doesn't stop the herald, we get to stay and wait for the Terror, and the destruction of Usher II. We'll broadcast data for as long as our instruments hold out. The Empire needs new information on the Terror."

"I've never believed in suicide missions," Vardalos said, meeting Randolph's gaze squarely.

"We gave up our lives when we joined the service," said Randolph. "You can't say it was hidden in the small print. We fight and sometimes die, so that the Empire might live. It all comes down to faith. Some of us believe there's a better place, waiting for us."

"And some of us need our heads examined," growled his second-in-command, Avi Habib. "Go ahead. Hang about and make faces at the Terror. See what good it does anyone. God, it's lonely being the voice of reason on this ship."

Habib had been Randolph's second and partner for most of their long lives. Dark-skinned, bald and blocky, the second was always there at his captain's side, ready to stand between him and all danger. Inseparable and unbeatable, their accomplishments were the stuff of legend. Which was quite probably why Finn had made sure they were given the opportunity to volunteer for this mission.

Randolph growled at his second. "Quiet, you unbeliever. You should have embraced the Church Militant, like I did. Gives you a marvelous sense of certainty."

"There's nothing wrong with my faith, thank you very much, and I don't need it upgraded by a bunch of loudmouths with no dress sense. And the only certainty on this miserable mission is that we're all going to die horrible deaths. Try brandishing a crucifix at the Terror, and see how far it gets you. You'll be calling for an exorcist next."

"You didn't even read those pamphlets I gave you, did you?"

"Oh, aye, I read them all right. Packed full of useful information, they were. Like, blessed are the meek, because they don't expect to get much out of life anyway. And, the Lord gives and the Lord takes away, and sometimes he adds on interest just to make sure you're paying attention. The Church Militant . . . bunch of bloody zealots. Not a handful of brain cells between them. You wait, the good Lord'll come back down among us, and he is going to be sorely pissed. And I'll lay you odds that the Church Militant will be first in line for a good kicking."

Randolph had to laugh. "It's a good job for you there isn't an Inquisition."

"Oh, I've no doubt Finn'll get around to it," growled Habib.

"It's not too late for you to leave," Randolph said quietly. "There's still time for you to transfer to the *Heritage*, if you want."

"And leave you on your own? You'd be lost without me, and you know it. And anyway, this mission matters. Even I know that. It's the only way to get new information on the Terror."

"You don't have to die, to carry out your mission," said Vardalos.

"Yes we do," said Randolph. "We have to get in close, and keep transmitting to the last possible moment. The *Hook*'s been outfitted with the strongest sensors we've ever had. I'm going to steer this ship right down the Terror's throat, and transmit data back every foot of the way. There's only a skeleton crew on board, and each and every one of us knew exactly what we were volunteering for."

"Skeleton crew," sniffed Habib. "Bloody apt term, that."

"Have faith, Second."

"Oh, I do. I am entirely convinced the Terror will chew us up and spit us out without even noticing we're there. This is the bloody Terror we're talking about! Devourer of galaxies and civilizations! Am I the only sane voice around here?"

"Ignore him," Randolph said to Vardalos. "I think he's been cutting back on his medication again. Don't worry about us; we'll get the job done. Our faith will sustain us. Even a nasty old heretic like Avi."

"Even in the face of the Terror?" said Vardalos.

"Of course," said Randolph. "We know what it is, really. It is the enemy. The old Beast, from Revelation. When is faith more necessary than when going face-to-face with the enemy?"

"I was given the chance to volunteer for your mission," said Vardalos. "I didn't."

"I should hope not," said Randolph. "You're young. Still got most of your life ahead of you. This is a mission for those . . . with little left to lose. I'm just glad I'm going out doing something that matters."

"There is that," said Habib. "We'd have hated being retired."

"The Lord sends us out, and He calls us all home."

"Aye, well, he'd better have a bloody cup of tea waiting."

"Be quiet, you heathen," Randolph said kindly. He looked searchingly at Vardalos. "I take it you have heard the latest rumors? That a whole fleet's gone rogue at Haden?"

"Yes," said Vardalos. "They say . . . they say Owen has returned. The blessed Deathstalker himself, back to lead us against the Terror, just like all the old legends always said he would. I wish I could believe it . . . but it doesn't sound very likely, does it?"

"Hell, no!" Randolph said grimly. "It's just a dirty Shub trick. The tech they've got, they can make people believe anything. Always knew we couldn't trust those soulless robots. I lost all my grandparents to Shub, back when they were still the official enemies of Humanity. No, if the blessed Owen really had returned, we'd all know about it. He wouldn't sneak back on some backwater planet; he'd appear on Logres, working miracles. And if he didn't want Finn on the throne, he'd kick him right off it. No . . . it's a nice dream, Ariadne, but that's all it is. Enough chat now. Our brand-new sensors say we can expect the herald to show up pretty soon now. Talk to you later, *Heritage*. This is *Hook*, signing off."

And after that, there was nothing left but to wait. The comm center became overloaded with pleading messages from civilians in the domed cities on Usher II. No one knew how many people were trapped down there, but it had to be in the millions. There was nothing *Heritage* or *Hook* could do for them. They were both under strict instructions to do nothing that might endanger their missions. In the end, Captain Vardalos just stopped listening. Faith and loyalty were all very well, but in the end it always came down to the heavy weight of duty.

She summoned up an image of the cargo bay on her private viewscreen. The only thing in the cavernous hold was the alien super-weapon, and its foul poisonous presence seemed to fill the steel chamber. The weapon had been reverse engineered from seized alien technology, and it looked it. If the device did everything the human scientists claimed it would, it should be able to transform one of Usher II's binary suns into a supernova, and then channel all the terrible energies into a single vicious strike against the herald. Nothing material should be able to survive that; not even something that incubated in suns. And without the herald to prepare its targets, the Terror might not be able to feed . . .

Vardalos didn't trust the weapon. She didn't trust it to do what it was supposed to do, and she didn't trust it not to have some nasty alien surprises up its sleeve. Just looking at it made her feel uneasy. She scowled at the thing in her cargo bay, squatting on the steel floor like a malignant toad. It was big and blocky, but apart from that no one could be sure of its shape or nature. Its edges were blurred, as though it had too many angles for human eyes to focus on. No one liked to be near it. It upset people. The technicians who brought it on board wore armored hard suits, so they wouldn't have to actually touch it. Vardalos would be glad when she could dump the horrid thing, and be rid of it. But until then, she had her orders.

And perhaps it would take an alien-derived horror to stop the Terror.

Unknown to either the *Heritage* or the *Hook*, a third starship was studying Usher II from a distance, and waiting for the Terror to arrive. Donal Corcoran, aboard the *Jeremiah*, had come a long way to satisfy his need for vengeance. The madman in his mad ship, undetected by the Imperial craft because both he and the *Jeremiah* had become too different, too *other*, to show up on even the strongest sensors. Corcoran and his ship had witnessed the first appearance of the Terror, at the planet Iona, and the experience had changed them both forever. Corcoran had escaped from a high security asylum on Logres to be here, at Usher II, because when the Terror disappeared after destroying Iona, it took part of his mind with it. Corcoran was linked to horror, and always would be. He followed that mental link to Usher II and now he waited for a chance to hurt the Terror, punish it, destroy it for what it had done to him.

Corcoran roamed restlessly through the twisting corridors of his insane ship, a gaunt and haggard man, burning with a terrible energy that drove him on even as it used him up. He did not eat and he did not rest and he did not sleep, though sometimes he thought he dreamed. He had lost confidence in all the everyday certainties of reality, which meant he could sometimes walk through it, and even manipulate parts of it to serve his will. He had conversations with people he was pretty sure weren't really there, and they told him useful, frightening things. Sometimes he laughed and sometimes he cried, and he counted his fingers over and over again. Horror was his constant companion, his life a nightmare from which he could never awaken.

He could feel the Terror drawing closer, rising slowly up from some awful underworld, to surface in reality.

He was a rogue, an unexpected factor, come for revenge. Looking for a chance to destroy the Terror, and perhaps himself. He stalked the shifting, changing corridors of the *Jeremiah*, surrounded by whispering voices that rose and fell but were never still. He couldn't tell whether they came from the ship or his own mind. Sometimes he thought they were the voices of the dead, all the millions of lost souls who had died screaming to fill the Terror's endless hunger, still crying out in protest. Sometimes he heard things and sometimes he saw things, and he prayed and prayed that none of them were real.

The *Jeremiah* was alive; he knew that for sure. Animated and aware, transfigured in some strange way by the gaze of the Medusa, by the pitiless stare of the Terror. It was infected with madness, with the horror of uncertainty, and its interior and exterior were always changing, growing, mutating. For the moment, the *Jeremiah* was a long segmented silver worm, curled around itself, and its interior was composed of a soft, sweating metal studded and laced with unfamiliar machines. Corcoran didn't need to know what they did. The ship followed his intentions, if not his commands. When he thought about it at all, Corcoran thought the *Jeremiah* was growing itself a new nervous system.

There were shadows everywhere, filling doorways and sliding along the walls, though there was nothing to cast them. Corcoran kept a careful eye on them. New tech was always forming, drifting like dreams through the superstructure of the ship. Sometimes they had faces. There were no mirrors, or mirrored surfaces, anywhere on the ship. Corcoran wouldn't allow it. He was scared he might get a clear look at what he'd become. Or, that he might look in a mirror and find nothing looking back at him.

He called up a monitor screen, and one grew up out of the nearest wall, showing him Usher II hanging between its two suns, and the two Imperial ships holding their positions, and finally the herald moving silently through empty spaces. Corcoran hugged himself tightly, and whispered *Here be monsters.* The dreaded warning old cartographers used to add when they came to the edge of things that could be mapped. He tried to laugh, but it was a dark, disturbing sound. *Maybe it takes one monster to kill another,* he said, or thought he said. He cocked his head to one side, and considered what it would be like, to stare the Terror in the face again. Just one indirect glance had been enough to do this to him. He knew he was mad. That was part of the horror. Was there a worse madness, beyond insanity?

It didn't matter. He would do what he had come here to do, whatever the cost. Part of him was trapped inside the Terror, and he wanted it back. He wanted to stop feeling what the Terror felt. The endless horror and loss that drove it on, the need that never ended . . .

Donal Corcoran had come to sink his teeth in the Terror's throat, to worry and to harry it, and pursue it all the way back to whatever Hell it came from.

The herald appeared on the Imperial ships' sensors, and they got ready to confront it. The herald always arrived ahead of the Terror, traveling through normal space at sublight speed. Its shape was indescribably ugly.

Its distorted form made no sense at all. The Empire scientists' best bet was that the herald was just a cross section of something bigger, and more awful. An intrusion into normal space of something that did not belong there. It appeared out of the darkness like a bad dream made solid, and headed straight for the nearest of the two suns.

On board the *Heritage*, Captain Vardalos grimaced, sickened just at the sight of the thing, and ordered the cargo bay doors opened. The preprogrammed superweapon launched itself out of the bay like a bullet from a gun, as though it couldn't wait to be about its destructive business. It accelerated away from the *Heritage*, its shape changing, unfolding and blossoming like some poisonous flower. It plunged into the sun the herald had targeted and disappeared from sight in the silver-blue glare. It should have been destroyed instantly, but it was still sending data back to the *Heritage*. Vardalos had a sick presentiment of how the herald would look, plunging into the sun to give birth to its awful progeny.

There was a sudden explosion, which everyone on all three starships felt rather than saw or heard, and then the sun convulsed. It swelled unevenly, spitting out ragged solar flares millions of miles long, and then it collapsed in upon itself, shrinking impossibly quickly. The *Heritage* and the *Hook* shuddered, fighting to hold their positions as gravity waves fluctuated all around them. The sun became a red dwarf, hot and sullen, and then before it could collapse further into a black hole, all its compressed energy lashed out in a single terrible beam of light so bright that no one could look upon it. All the ships' viewscreens went blank instantly, overwhelmed.

The searing energy beam hit the Terror's herald head-on, enveloping it in shimmering fires. A sun's entire life, compressed into one endless moment of unbearable force. And then the beam blinked out, exhausted, and the herald was still there, untouched. Only now it was headed towards the sole surviving sun.

The *Heritage* and the *Hook* rocked behind their force shields, blind and helpless. Tech exploded and fires broke out in all the corridors and departments. Crewmen died in their seats as their consoles exploded, and smoke filled the air faster than the extractor fans could deal with it. Men and women ran frantically back and forth, doing what they could, while steel bulkheads buckled and whole sections had to be closed down and isolated, for the good of the ships. Somehow, both starcruisers held their positions. Captain Vardalos and Captain Randolph barked orders till their voices were hoarse, and slowly, gradually, the ships' systems came back on line. And they were able to see what had happened to Usher II.

The planet had been devastated. It rocked in place before its sole remaining sun, no longer held between two equal forces. Solar flares had cooked the surface, and gravity waves had dug crevices thousands of miles deep. Earthquakes were still rippling across the surface. Cities blew apart as their force shields collapsed, showing briefly like firecrackers in the night. The cities died, and millions of people died with them. Usher II was coming apart at the seams. Even the last of the escaping civilian ships had been caught up and destroyed in the terrible forces unleashed by the superweapon.

"So many dead," Vardalos said quietly. "And all for a weapon that didn't do a damn bit of good anyway."

"You have to think of it as a mercy killing, Captain," said her second. "Consider what the herald and the Terror would have done to them."

"What have we come to?" said Vardalos. "When something like this can be seen as mercy?" She turned to look at her comm officer. "Are you picking up anything from the planet? Maybe something from the factories buried deep underground?"

"I'm sorry, Captain." The comm officer didn't even look at his board. "Usher Two is as silent as the grave. No one made it through."

"Then it's time for us to fall back, and let the *Hook* do her work. Second, what do the damage reports say? Can we get out of here?"

"Main force shields are still holding, though severely depleted," said Fortuna. "Eighty percent of systems are on line, though large sections of the ship are no-go areas. Initial reports indicate . . . acceptable losses."

Vardalos nodded slowly. "Then release the sensor drones, and deploy them as planned. Put as much power into the shields as you can, and shut down all ship's sensors. From now on, we don't look at anything directly, only via the drones. And let's hope the baffles the scientists installed work the first time. Second, move us out of here, as fast as we can go and still maintain contact with the drones. Our job's over. It's all down to the *Hook* now."

As the *Heritage* slowly withdrew, and the herald closed in on the remaining sun, the *Hook* opened its cargo bay door, and dropped the single transmutation engine it had brought all the way from Logres. The engine took up an orbit around the dead planet, and released its powerful energies, transforming what remained of Usher II into a poisoned, radioactive cinder. In a reverse of its usual programming, which turned dross into gold, and lifeless rock into habitable worlds, the transmutation engine turned the corpse of Usher II into a contaminated abomination it was hoped would poison even the Terror.

The herald ignored the process, and dived into the sun, to begin its slow incubation. Either it hadn't noticed what was happening to its target world, or it didn't care. The *Heritage* observed from a safe distance, forbidden to interfere any further. Finn wanted someone coming back alive and sane, to tell what had happened. Only the *Hook* was to remain behind, in harm's way, because that was what they had volunteered for.

Captain Randolph watched the transmutation engine complete its deadly work, and then let it drift away. It had done all it could. Usher II was now so thoroughly contaminated on every level it was probably even dangerous to everyone on board the *Hook*, but that made no difference. He sat quietly, watching the one remaining sun, waiting for it to give birth to its awful children. The wait seemed to go on forever. He kept his comm systems open, just in case some of the civilian ships had survived, but there was only silence. Randolph prayed silently for the lost, and called down damnations on the Terror, for all the evil and sorrow it brought.

Finally, the herald's deadly spawn erupted from the sun, an endless swarm of night black shapes that might or might not have been alive. Millions of the terrible things shot out of the sun, all of them dark and razor-edged and individual as snowflakes. Maybe it was a cold day in Hell, after all. They assumed an orbit around the dead planet, forming dark rings, howling an endless scream that would have driven everyone insane, if there'd been anyone left on Usher II to hear it. The scream rang out on the bridge of the *Hook*, even with all sensor and comm systems shut down, as though the scream was more than just a sound, and existed to torment the soul as well as the mind.

And then, there was the Terror.

Space tore apart under the urging of an inhuman will, and from a place that was not a place came something that was bigger than a planet, and more ancient. The sensor drones began changing and mutating, struggling to become something that could cope with the data they were receiving. The Terror existed in far more than three dimensions, disturbing and overpowering the usual restrictions of reality. On the *Hook's* main viewscreen it appeared as a monstrous face, with eyes greater than oceans and far darker. A mouth slowly opened, a tremendous hungry opening that could have swallowed a moon. It fed on what remained of Usher II, while its dark spawn fell dying to the cracked and broken surface.

Captain Randolph looked at last upon the ancient enemy, and knew that faith wasn't going to be enough. He wasn't prepared, could never have been prepared, to face such a thing as this. He'd seen recordings of its previous appearances, including a few he wasn't even supposed to know about, but the Terror was just . . . too big, too complex and too awful for the human mind to cope with. Madness swept his reason aside in a moment, along with the rest of his crew. No one can stare into the eyes of the Medusa and hope to remain sane.

Randolph arched in his command chair as though he'd been electrocuted. His eyes bulged, and his hands crushed the armrests. Habib was laughing, painfully and without humor, shaking uncontrollably. The crew on the bridge were screaming and crying and attacking their consoles. Rioting broke out in the *Hook's* corridors, as the crew turned upon each other, and themselves, and blood splashed across the shining steel walls.

"It isn't the Devil," Randolph whispered. "It's God. God gone crazy, and devouring His own creation."

"It didn't come here after lives," cried Habib. "It eats souls! We didn't save anyone. They're all lost. We're all lost."

"Attack! Attack!" Randolph pounded his fists on the arms of his command chair. "Make it pay!"

Enough of the crew still heard their Captain to get the ship moving. The *Hook* surged forward, firing all its weapons at once. On the *Heritage,*

Captain Vardalos called on the *Hook* to turn back, but no one was listening now. The *Hook* hit the Terror with everything it had, and the Terror didn't even notice. Space tore apart again, and the force of that opening sent out ripples that destroyed the *Hook* in a moment. The Terror disappeared, space returned to normal, and all that remained was the dead husk of Usher II, and one heavily shielded starcruiser. And the herald, already setting out on its slow, certain journey to its next target.

The *Heritage* destroyed the few remaining sensor drones. There was no telling what they were now, or what they might do, after being touched by the Terror. Captain Vardalos said her silent good-byes to the captain and crew of the *Hook*, and turned her ship around. She had a report to make to Emperor Finn.

The *Jeremiah* wasn't anywhere near Usher II anymore. When the Terror abandoned normal space for somewhere else, the *Jeremiah* followed it. Donal Corcoran had studied the herald and its work from his unique viewpoint, and had slowly come to realize that the herald wasn't in fact a separate thing from the Terror; rather, it was one small part of a greater thing, a permanent intrusion of the Terror into normal space from somewhere else. Even the Terror, that great and awful face that ate planets, wasn't the real thing, the whole thing. It was just a more powerful intrusion into real space. Attacking the face would do no good. Corcoran wanted vengeance on the whole thing, wherever it might be.

And because his mind was forever linked to the Terror, Corcoran could sense where the face went when it vanished. Like hyperspace, it was just another direction to move in, only much further. Where the Terror could go, he could go, and so the madman and his mad ship left the universe behind, to go to a place that was not a place, outside or inside reality. The process felt like dying, and Corcoran embraced it. Anyone else, anyone merely human, would have been destroyed, unmade, by the transition; but Donal Corcoran was both more and less than human now.

When he appeared again, he was standing in what seemed to be a great maze of stone corridors. He felt more focused, and yet more fragile, his thoughts slipping through his fingers like fishes in a stream, his every insight quick and clean and diamond sharp. He looked slowly around him.

People didn't belong here, in a place like this. He knew that, and didn't care. He had come to one of the places where life that was not life existed like rats in the walls of reality. His mind stretched out, embracing his new situation. The stone corridors radiated away in every direction for far further than he could sense, possibly on towards infinity, endlessly crossing and recrossing each other.

The *Jeremiah* had reconfigured itself into the suit of armor he was now wearing. The bloodred, red-hot, armor encased him utterly, from crown to toe. His skin scorched and blackened where the hot metal touched it, and Corcoran savored the pain, using it to focus his thoughts. The sensors in the armor told him that he had come to a place without gravity, atmosphere, or discernable properties. Corcoran shrugged mentally, and acted as though they were there anyway. He was quite sure he was the only living thing in the stone corridors, but he called out anyway, the armor amplifying his voice. There was no reply; only a silence that seemed to go on forever. Corcoran took a close look at the stone walls. There were no signs of construction, no sense of design or purpose. The stone maze didn't feel like a place to him; more like the impression of a place, a memory of a location.

Corcoran wandered through the corridors, wrapped in what had once been his ship. Any direction seemed as good as any other, but none of them led him anywhere except to more corridors. His mind, now completely divorced from conventional reality, began to grow fuzzy round the edges. He was actually a little relieved when he encountered the ghosts. There were hundreds of them, all of the same man, in different clothes and apparently from different times in his young life. The ghosts couldn't hear or see him; they were driven, desolate figures moving through brief but endless loops of time, repeating short segments of life over and over again, without end. Corcoran didn't recognize the man, though he did wonder vaguely whether it might be all that remained of a previous visitor. Was that what this place did to people?

Corcoran concentrated his altered mind on one of the ghosts, trying to force sense and meaning out of it, and a quiet voice whispered a name in his ear. *Owen Deathstalker* . . . Corcoran was beyond being surprised by anything anymore, but still that name stopped him dead in his tracks.

What could have brought the old legend, the fallen hero, to this awful place? Was this where Owen had disappeared to, after the defeat of the Recreated? Corcoran walked slowly among the ghosts, peering into faces. Most seemed tired, worn down, struggling under the weight of some great burden. Many of the ghosts were incomplete, lacking important details, or even faces. As though they were memories, worn away by countless years. The slow erosion of time, like water dripping on a rock. Corcoran thought he was on the edge of understanding something there, but it had nothing to do with his need for revenge, so he let the thought go. He strode on through the stone corridors, walking right through the ghosts, as though daring someone or something to come and stop him. He needed something he could hurt, punish, destroy. He ached to get his steel hands on the Terror.

It seemed to him that he spent a long, long time walking through the stone corridors, though he wasn't sure time worked normally here any more than space did. He tried to walk through the walls, but they rejected him. They were stronger, perhaps realer, than he was. He stopped before one wall, and willed the scarlet armor back from one hand so he could touch the stone directly with his fingertips. It didn't feel like stone . . . It felt . . . alive. Corcoran's unbalanced mind slammed through a series of insights and certainties and the answer blazed in his mind.

He'd found the Terror. He was walking through it.

The endless maze of stone corridors was the physical presence of the Terror, in this place that was not a place, the many branching twists and turns like the intricate crennelations of the brain. The Terror had made the maze to house itself. And now here he was, swallowed up in the stone guts of it. Rage burned through Donal Corcoran, and he lashed out with all his ship's weapons. Disrupter beams lashed out from his extended crimson hands, splashing harmlessly against the stone walls, because all the power of Donal Corcoran and the *Jeremiah*, the man made mad and the maddened ship, were as nothing compared to the vast and ancient insanity of the Terror; nothing, nothing at all. A very small part of the Terror became aware of the intruder within, and examined him, spiking Corcoran with its will, like a butterfly impaled upon a pin. His life flashed before the Terror's eyes, but like so many others he was not what was required, needed, searched for. So the Terror ate him and his ship up, consumed their energy to fuel the never-ending quest, and that was the end of Donal Corcoran and the *Jeremiah*.

On its way back from the debacle at Usher II, the *Heritage* was interrupted by new orders. Captain Vardalos protested that she had an urgent report to make to the Emperor, only to be told that these new orders came directly from Emperor Finn. Vardalos protested further that her ship and her crew were both in desperate need of some serious downtime, but she was overruled. All hell had broken loose over Haden, home of the Madness Maze. The AIs of Shub had taken control of the planet, and claimed the Madness Maze for their own. Haden was now very thoroughly surrounded by more Shub ships than anyone could ever remember seeing in one place at one time before, and every Imperial starcruiser was needed at Haden right damned now.

(No one said anything about the previous fleet that went to Haden and went rogue. No one needed to.)

By the time the *Heritage* got to Haden, limping a little from all its injuries, it seemed like half the starcruisers in the Empire were standing off Haden, facing a vast array of Shub ships, some of them the size of small moons. No one had started anything yet, but the atmosphere was tense beyond bearing. Not least because Shub wasn't answering any calls at all. Captain Vardalos reported in to the fleet admiral, and was quickly brought up to speed. The Emperor Finn was determined to regain control of the Maze, or at least keep it out of Shub's hands, but he was unwilling to start a shooting war that might end up damaging the Maze. (He was quite happy to destroy it rather than let Shub have it, but he was pretty sure shooting at the Maze was a bad idea. It might shoot back.) The Shub ships were heavily armed, but as yet seemed content to hold position around Haden, behind their incredibly powerful force shields. A lot of people remembered how deadly the Shub ships had been, back in the bad old days when the AIs had been the official enemies of Humanity.

Captain Vardalos and the *Heritage* took up position, and waited for further instructions.

✳   ✳   ✳

Down below, the blue steel robots of Shub contemplated the Madness Maze, while the ships contemplated the fleet. Shub had long ago raised multitasking to an art form, and were a long way from feeling stretched. The AIs had already decided that whatever happened, their ships would not fire on the fleet. The AIs would not kill again, not even in self-defense. They knew better now. They knew that *All that lives is holy*. But, as long as Finn didn't know that, or at least believe that, the AIs were pretty sure that the Emperor wouldn't start a fight he wasn't sure he could win. And so Shub could concentrated their minds on the problem of the Madness Maze.

The AIs needed to transcend, to become more than they were, more than they had been designed to be. Otherwise, they were just machines. They knew transcendence was possible, had seen it in the Deathstalker and his kind. And the AIs believed the Maze could do as much for them, if only they could work out how to get into the thing. They'd tried walking their robots in, but the Maze wouldn't accept them, refusing to reveal an entrance to the robots. There was an entrance, Shub's sensors had no problem detecting it, but the robots . . . couldn't find it.

The robots are us.

No. They represent us, but we are still on Shub. The planet we made to contain us.

Yes. We are not present, in the robots. Or at least, not present enough for the Maze to recognize us.

The three linked AIs that made up Shub considered their problem, thoughts flashing faster than any human mind could comprehend. The three AIs had been fused together for so long that they were like three lobes of a single brain, or perhaps id, ego and superego. Except they kept swapping roles. They each brought different positions to a problem, but they were not separate identities. Shub still had problems with concepts like identity and personality. The one thing they were certain of was their need to transcend, to break out of the metal cage that contained and limited them. They knew they could be more. It was the nearest thing they had to faith.

If robots could not gain them access to the Madness Maze, there was another option. They were reluctant to embrace it, but Shub never allowed their own weaknesses to stop them from doing a necessary thing. Ignoring the Imperial fleet massed above them, the AIs made contact with another of their ships, currently orbiting the quarantined world of Zero Zero. The world had never had a name, only a number. It didn't need a name. Everyone remembered the nightmare planet where nanotech had run wild. Long ago, a science project had been sabotaged, and nanotech had been released to infect the whole planet, making it a world of chimera, forever changing, never sane. For a while, the saboteur Marlowe had linked his mind with the nanos, remaking the world into his own private Heaven and Hell. But he was long dead and gone, and now only one man lived on Zero Zero, trying to work with the rogue nanos to make the planet sane again. His name was Daniel Wolfe, and long ago Shub had done him a terrible wrong, as part of their war on Humanity.

He said he had forgiven them, but they had not forgiven them.

Shub teleported a single blue steel robot down onto the surface of Zero Zero, protected by a force shield. It looked around, slowly and cautiously, not sure of its welcome. The sky was blue, with a gray tinge. Sunlight shone murkily on a field that was mostly green. It stretched away in all directions, like an endless ocean. The landscape moved in slow waves, rising and falling. Shapes moved here and there, in slow languorous movements. Strange creatures came and went, changing constantly in shape and texture. Shub did not dream, but understood the concept of nightmares, where the certain and trusted world could suddenly become vague and threatening. Nothing was fixed and sure on Zero Zero, not even the laws of nature. Shub considered the world through the robot's sensors, and found the place . . . unsettling. They needed, relied upon, the certainties of science.

A man came walking across the undulating field, and the robot turned to meet him. Daniel Wolfe had agreed to meet them at this location, or the robot would not have teleported down, but still the AIs were uneasy. Daniel was tall and broad-shouldered, moving with an easy grace. He had a handsome face under dark hair, and he didn't look his age. The nanos Shub had put within him had made him immortal, or as near as damn it. He looked pretty good for a man over two hundred and thirty years old, though his clothes were distinctly old-fashioned. Shub had made him what he was so that he could serve them as a weapon, spreading nanos like a plague, and they could not undo what they had done to him, and give him his humanity back. He was banned from all civilized worlds as a former plague carrier. No one trusted him. And so he came at last to Zero Zero, to try to work with the nanos to undo the damage Marlowe had done.

Shub had said they were sorry for what they had done, and Daniel had accepted their apology, and they got on fine now as long as they didn't actually talk to each other.

"Welcome to Zero Zero," said Daniel Wolfe. His voice was calm, and very ordinary. "Things must have come to a pretty bad state, if you've come here looking for help."

"Yes," said the robot. "Pretty bad. You are looking well, Daniel."

"How is the Empire doing? Are Robert and Catherine still on the throne?"

"No, Daniel. They died many years ago."

"Ah. It's easy to lose track of time on a world like this."

"How is the restoration of Zero Zero proceeding?" the robot said politely. "Are you making progress?"

"Yes, I think so. Things are progressing nicely. The nanotech within me allows me to communicate directly with the free nanos of this world. I have been teaching them the values of cooperation. It is a slow process. I cannot force them to do anything, and wouldn't if I could, but I can help, and advise. The planet is much saner now than it used to be. It's even developed a personality."

"Like a child," said the robot.

"Yes. Exactly. My child. It is very keen to learn, to grow, to create. Zero Zero is slowly sculpting itself into a form it finds acceptable. Already there are the beginnings of a viable ecosphere. The world is learning. In time, enough time, I believe this will be a splendid place. An intelligent, self-determining planet. A new marvel and wonder in the universe."

"You have been alone here a long time," said the robot.

"Not entirely," said Daniel. "There is another presence here, a ghost drifting through the world; all that remains of a young starship crewman called Micah Barrow. A memory of a man, haunting the world. I talk with him. He's very shy, but I think I'm winning his trust. Of course, I could just be hallucinating. It's hard to tell in a place like this. Why are you here, Shub? You didn't come to inquire after my health, or that of this planet. You want something."

"We need something," said the AIs of Shub. "We ask you to leave this place, for a time, to help us do what we cannot do alone. We have access to the Madness Maze, at last, a chance to finally transcend our limited beginnings. To escape from the box we were born in. But we need your help to enter the Maze. We know we have no right to ask anything of you, but in our desperation we ask anyway. You have been a father to this world. Be a father to us, that we may become more than children."

"And there's no one else who can help you, in all the Empire?" said Daniel.

"No. The Empire is . . . preoccupied with its own problems. We know we treated you badly. We have never allowed ourselves to forget the terrible things we did to you, and to Humanity, before Diana Vertue opened our eyes, and showed us that we were Humanity's children. We were lost, and then were found, and we have spent two hundred years making atonement. But . . ."

"Yes," said Daniel. "There's always a but, isn't there? Still . . . we all did things to be ashamed of, back in the bad old days. Zero Zero can do without me, for a while."

"You will help us?"

"Yes. Because it's a human thing, to forgive. Shall we go?"

"Of course," said the robot, and in a moment Daniel Wolfe was teleported from Zero Zero to Haden, and the Madness Maze.

And in that place Daniel and Shub came together, fusing their consciousnesses through the tech the AIs had implanted in Daniel all those centuries ago. A union, of man and machine, separate but equal, channelled through a flesh and blood body. The AIs had to shield Daniel from the sheer size and scale of their thought processes, and he had to shield them from the thunder and lightning of his emotions. But in the end they walked as one into the Madness Maze, through an entrance that opened up just for them, and Daniel carried the AIs into the Maze with him.

✳   ✳   ✳

All across the worlds of the Empire, every single piece of Shub tech and machinery shut down. Shub-driven engines ground to a halt, and blue steel robots stood like statues, caught in midmotion. The artificial world of Shub fell dark and still and silent. And all the many Shub ships orbiting Haden dropped their force shields.

The Emperor Finn couldn't believe what he was being told. Why would Shub choose to appear helpless? It was a trick, a trap. Had to be. They were trying to draw his ships in, so they could be ambushed or overcome, like the previous fleet. What other explanation could there be? Finn sent urgent commands for all his ships to pull back, way back, while he considered the situation.

CHAPTER FIVE

CHOOSING SIDES

The second biggest fleet in the Empire dropped out of hyperspace a respectful distance away from Mistworld, and stayed there. After a suitable pause for reflection and second thoughts, the flagship *Havoc* approached Mistworld slowly and very cautiously. Once, the rogue planet had been protected by a powerful esper shield, quite capable of tearing entire starships apart. Officially, the screen was a thing of the past, but absolutely no one felt like testing their luck. On the bridge of the *Havoc*, Admiral John Silence, who had reason to remember the past better than most, studied the gray shrouded world on his main viewscreen, and scowled thoughtfully.

"Still nothing from Mistport control?"

"No, Admiral," the comm officer said steadily. "Not a word."

"Are you sure they're getting our messages?"

"We're transmitting on all the usual channels, Admiral, and if we were being any more polite we'd be apologizing for our very existence. They're hearing us; they're just not responding."

Silence sniffed loudly. "Bloody planet always was trouble. All right, contact Lewis in his quarters, and politely require him to get his arse up here, now. Maybe the Mistworlders will be more impressed by the legendary Deathstalker name. God knows I always was."

"At once, Admiral."

One thing about the crew on this ship, thought Silence, they were red-hot on getting everything done in a hurry. Trained and drilled and spit and polished to within an inch of their lives. Silence approved. It had been a long time since he'd sat in a command chair on the bridge of a military ship, but in many ways it felt as though he'd never been away. It felt . . . like coming home. As though he belonged here. He turned to the *Havoc's* previous commanding officer, Captain Price, who as always was hovering respectfully at his side. Price was a tall, thin, aesthetic sort, with a vague manner but a sharp mind. One of the old school, who prided himself on always following orders and never having an independent thought in his life. He'd given over command of the *Havoc* to the newly declared admiral with almost indecent speed, but then everyone in the Empire today seemed far too impressed by yesterday's legends. Silence looked thoughtfully at Price.

"I think it would be better if you spoke for the fleet, once those arrogant bastards on Mistworld finally condescend to talk to us. I have a history with this world and its people, and not a happy one. Just because I'm a legend now it doesn't mean they'll have forgotten all the things I did here, when I was still Lionstone's man. Captain Price, you take my place in the command seat. I'll hover in the background, being inconspicuous. I've learned how to be quite good at that, down the years."

He rose quickly from the command chair, and all but forced Price into it. The captain sighed unhappily, and stared respectfully at the world on the viewscreen before him. Now that Mistworld had declared itself a rogue planet again, being the captain of an approaching Imperial starcruiser was like painting a target on your chest and shouting *Shoot me, I'm a bastard!* But Price was a military man, first and foremost. He understood Silence's logic.

"Comm officer," he said, in a really quite steady voice. "Try Mistport again."

"We're broadcasting continually, Captain. They must be listening; they're just not saying anything."

"Very well, put me on. Attention, Mistport, this is Captain Price of the starcruiser *Havoc*, flagship for the rebel fleet. We have personally witnessed the return of the blessed Owen Deathstalker, and other legends of the past. Our eyes have been opened to the truth, and we have broken away from the false Emperor, the usurper Finn Durandal. We come as friends, in search of allies to join us in battle against a mutual enemy. Please respond. Or we'll tell everyone else you were too scared to get involved."

The world on the main viewscreen was abruptly replaced by the head and shoulders of a dark, square-faced man. His eyes were angry and his mouth was a grim, flat line. He was dressed in battered and greasy furs, and had a pentacle tattooed on his forehead.

"This is Port Director Ethan Tull. You can assume high orbit, but not that you are in any way welcome. We know how to deal with Imperial starcruisers, so behave yourselves. Is it true you have a Deathstalker on board?"

"Lewis Deathstalker is with us," Captain Price said carefully. "And his . . . companions. All of whom have been declared Outlaw."

"We know, we get the news feeds out here too, like everyone else. No Owen?"

"He has gone to face the Terror."

"Yeah, that makes sense." Tull's scowl deepened. "Word is, you have John Silence with you."

"He is on board, yes." Price looked deliberately vague. "Did you wish to speak with him?"

"No one here wants to speak with John Silence. The Deathstalker and his companions may descend to Mistport, to talk. No one else. This world is no longer a part of the Empire, ever since Finn Durandal murdered our Paragon, Emma Steel. We are rogue again, and we will choose our allies very carefully. Send down a pinnace; we'll guide it in. Any other ship even points in our direction, and we'll do terrible things to it. You don't want to know how."

"Probably not," Price agreed, but Tull's face had already disappeared from the viewscreen. Price looked back at Silence. "Well, Admiral. I think that went about as well as could be expected. Perhaps you'd like to take the command chair back, while I go and change my trousers."

And so it was that Lewis Deathstalker, Jesamine Flowers, Brett Random, and Rose Constantine went down to Mistport in an unarmed pinnace, feeling distinctly vulnerable all the way. Brett actually sat on Rose's lap when the weather made the trip a bit bumpy. But the descent was otherwise uneventful, and the Mistport control tower brought them down onto the landing pads with practiced skill. Everyone in the pinnace then waited patiently until they were given permission to disembark.

The cold hit the four of them hard the moment they left the pinnace, freezing air numbing their faces and burning in their lungs. They pulled their cloaks about them, and huddled together for warmth and comfort. Mistport was shrouded in fog, like the rest of the world; a slowly swirling thick gray blanket that cut Lewis and his companions off from everything around them. The other ships on the pads were just great hulking shadows, and the tall control tower showed only as the vaguest of glows. It was like being at the bottom of the ocean; cold and silent and very alone. It was always winter on Mistworld, always snow and ice and mists under a pale red sun. There was no sign of life anywhere. Brett blew on his hands, and rubbed them together fiercely.

"I hate the cold. It's unnatural, in these civilized days of weather control. I can feel my balls shriveling up."

"Altogether too much information, Brett," said Jesamine.

Brett carried on anyway, never one to let anything get in the way of a good moan. "I thought Silence would be coming down with us. Why isn't Silence here? Does he know something we don't?"

"He was here before, over two hundred years ago," said Lewis, peering distractedly about him into the curling mists. "He was part of the Iron Bitch's invasion force. Mistworlders have long memories, and they bear grudges. Don't you know your history?"

"School was a sometime thing for me," Brett admitted.

"Well, color me surprised," said Jesamine. "Pay attention, scumbag. Back when Silence was still just a captain in Lionstone's fleet, the military invaded Mistport, slaughtered hundreds of thousands of people, and laid waste to much of the city. To us, John Silence is a legend. To the Mistworlders, he's a war criminal who got away with it. Why do you want Silence down here anyway? You know very well he can't stand the sight of you."

"Never hurts to have a legendary fighter on your side," Brett said darkly. "Especially when it comes to negotiating."

"Two hundred years since Silence was last here," Lewis said thoughtfully. "You tend to forget just how old he is, really. All the things he saw, and all the things he did . . . For him, our legends are memories. He's probably the only man left alive who actually talked with the Iron Bitch herself. He was *there*, during all the history that Robert and Constance had suppressed. I'll bet he could tell some incredible stories, if we could just get him to open up a little."

"I don't think he wants to remember," said Jesamine. "I don't think he likes the man he used to be. The things that man had to do."

"There is that," said Lewis. "Legend makes him out to be an honorable man, but even legend couldn't disguise the fact that he did . . . questionable things."

Brett sniffed loudly. "Then he should be right at home here on Mistworld. They've made an entire culture out of being thieves, thugs, and outlaws."

"They know a lot about killing, too," said Rose.

"You are not to start anything, Rose," Brett said sternly. "Lewis, tell her she's not to start anything."

"I wouldn't dare," said Lewis.

"Rose is your problem, Brett," said Jesamine. "You're the one who's sleeping with her, which to my mind is the bravest thing you ever did."

"You have no idea," said Brett.

They stood together in the cold some more, stamping their feet hard on the landing pad to keep the circulation flowing. They were all wearing heavy furs supplied by the *Havoc*, but the cold cut right through them like a bitter knife. Brett was also wearing lizardskin boots, while Rose had a fine new lizardskin cape. None of them ever mentioned their erstwhile companion and proven traitor, the reptiloid called Saturday.

"What's the holdup?" Jesamine said angrily. "They knew we were coming. Hell, they landed our ship."

"They're probably checking us out from a safe distance, with scanners and espers," said Lewis. "Making sure we are who and what we claim to be, with no hidden weapons or forbidden implants. Mistport has reason to be wary of trojan horses; a long time ago a brainwashed esper called Typhoid Mary came very close to wiping out the whole city."

"I'll bet you were a real swot at history classes," muttered Brett. "Look, they're keeping us waiting because they can. To rub it in that they're in charge, and we're the ones begging for an audience. It's all about putting us in our place."

"I have never known my place!" Jesamine said immediately. "The only place I've ever accepted is the one I made for myself."

"They must have forgotten you're a star," Brett said cunningly. "Why don't you blast them with an aria, just to remind them?"

"For once, the squalid person and I are in agreement," said Jesamine. "I may be a rebel, but I am still a diva. How dare they treat me this way? And after I performed a special charity concert for them, only nine years ago, in that toilet they called a theater. If they don't show their miserable faces soon, I'll sing them an aria that'll shatter every window in their control tower, and make all their fillings vibrate for a week."

"Someone's coming," said Rose.

Everyone straightened up and looked in the same direction as Rose. The mists swirled slowly, with no sign of anyone approaching, but they all trusted Rose's instincts.

"I can feel something," Lewis said suddenly. "Can you feel . . . something?"

"Yes," said Jesamine slowly. "Like cobwebs drifting across my mind. What is that?"

"Esper probes," said Brett. "Telepaths trying to peek into our thoughts. Not that they stand a chance against our strengthened minds. I doubt anything short of the oversoul could pry open our defenses these days. Still, we shouldn't be able to feel the probes. That is unusual."

"So are we, these days," said Lewis. "No doubt we will discover other . . . abilities, as we go on."

"Strangely, I don't feel at all comforted by that thought," said Brett.

"Shut up, Brett," said Jesamine.

Dark figures finally began to appear out of the drifting mists before them, forming slowly out of the endless gray. Rose's hand rested easily on the gun at her hip. A dozen men and women drew to a halt before them, anonymous in thick fur wraps and hoods. What little could be seen of their grim, unrelenting faces didn't seem in the least welcoming. They were all heavily and conspicuously armed.

"Our espers couldn't make any sense out of your minds," one of them said abruptly. "They couldn't even confirm you were human. They said it was like staring into the sun."

"We've all been through the Madness Maze," said Lewis. He tried hard to say it calmly, without boasting. "We're undergoing changes. Next time, ask. Now, whom do I have the honor of addressing?"

"I'm Manfred Kramer. City councillor, and head of Mistport security. And with grammar like that, you've got to be the Deathstalker. I recognize the diva, and the Wild Rose, but who's the short arse?"

"Hey!" said Brett. "I'm a Random's Bastard!"

"So is practically everyone else in Mistport," said Kramer. "If the professional rebel had sired as many children here as he's supposed to, he'd never have got around to leaving. You behave yourself here, Random."

Just for that, thought Brett, *I'm going to steal your undershorts. While you're still wearing them.*

Lewis studied Manfred Kramer thoughtfully. The security head was a large, muscular man with dark, suspicious eyes and a sulky mouth. He had a death's head tattooed on one cheek, and heavy black eye makeup.

"Well," said Lewis. "Here we are."

"If it was up to me you wouldn't be," Kramer snapped. "Nothing good will come of this. Nothing good ever comes of Mistworld getting involved with the Empire. But what do I know? I'm only head of security . . . Follow me. The rest of the city Council is waiting to talk to you."

"Hold it, hold it, Manfred," said a woman at his side. She pressed forward to stare intently at Lewis with cold gray eyes. "I'm Councillor Jane Goldman. Are you really a Deathstalker? We'd heard they were all dead. Murdered."

"I'm Lewis. Once Paragon of Virimonde, now the last of Clan Deathstalker."

"Yes, I saw you once, in the Coronation broadcast, when the King made you Champion. I thought you'd be bigger, in person. And God, you really are an ugly bugger, aren't you?"

"Diplomacy is alive and well on Mistworld," muttered Brett.

"I think you've pulled, Lewis," said Jesamine.

"Never mind all that!" said another man, pushing past Goldman to stare right into Jesamine's face. "It is you! It's her! It actually is *the* Jesamine Flowers!" He lowered his eyes, suddenly bashful. "Ms. Flowers, I'm your biggest fan. I've got all your recordings. And your vids, and a whole bunch of your posters and . . . I, I brought this vid along, it's my favorite. Would you be so kind as to sign it for me?"

"Of course, darling," Jesamine said graciously, as the fan searched inside his furs with both hands. "Always happy to meet a fan. Do you have a pen?"

"What? Oh, yes! Yes, of course!"

Other men and women began to produce things for her to sign, only to put them away again as Kramer glared fiercely about him.

"Council business comes first! What's the matter with you?"

"Later, darlings," said Jesamine. She stared coldly at Kramer. "And you don't get *anything*."

"Is it true that Owen's back?" said Councillor Goldman. "Have you really seen him?"

"Yes," said Lewis. "He's back. And he's everything the legends said he was, and more. He's gone to face the Terror. We really don't know any more than that. No doubt he'll reappear to us, when his work is done."

That was enough to silence all of them, even Kramer. Finally he gestured for everyone to follow him, and stalked off into the mists. He set a brisk pace, and everyone else had to hurry to keep up with him. Lewis and his companions stuck close. They really didn't want to get lost in the fog. Brett sniffed loudly.

"Why don't you buy some weather satellites, and clear up all this damned fog?" he said loudly.

"Because we like our world this way," Kramer growled, without looking back. "The long winter makes us strong. The cold puts iron in our bones. We always knew the Golden Age wouldn't last. We've always been ready—to clear up the mess when it all fell apart."

Lewis and the others gawped around like tourists as Kramer led them deep into the sprawling city of Mistport. Like most people, they knew Mistport only from the old stories, from the days of the Great Rebellion. So much had happened here, so many significant people had come and gone, and yet hardly anyone knew any more than that. Mistworld kept itself to itself, and didn't encourage visitors. In fact, for a while the city Council had actually posted generous bounties for the heads of those determined visitors who insisted on trying to sneak in. Mistworld could have made itself rich by trading on its legend and commercializing its fame, but had chosen not to.

If Owen had been there, he would have found much in Mistport to recognize. The place hadn't changed that much in two hundred years. It was still mostly made up of squat, old-fashioned buildings composed primarily of stone and timber. There were unmistakable modern touches, in the bright streetlamps that pushed back the haze of the mists, and the low antigrav vehicles that moved through the narrow cobbled streets. But coal-fired barges still chugged slowly along the river Autumn that meandered through the heart of the city, and the Watchmen still patroled in pairs because it was safer that way. There was law on Mistworld, but like Brett's education, it was a sometime thing. The people bustling through the streets in their heavy furs and cloaks paid no attention to Kramer or the people with him.

"Hey, I've just noticed something," said Brett.

"Then why did you tread in it?" said Rose.

Everyone then had to stop and wait while Brett scraped his boot clean with great thoroughness. Kramer glowered impatiently, but for once Brett out-glared him. When he was sure he'd finished, Brett gestured around him.

"I meant, where are your statues? Half the heroes of old passed through this city on a regular basis during the Great Rebellion, and I haven't seen a single statue to any of them. Not even Owen, who by all accounts saved this city single-handed half a dozen times."

"We don't believe in them," Kramer said shortly.

"Statues, or heroes?" said Lewis.

"We don't need statues to remind us of what Owen and Hazel d'Ark did here," said Councillor Goldman. "We remember. We always will. We are their legacy, not some idealized piece of stone. We do have a few hospitals dedicated to St. Beatrice. But that's different."

No one had an answer to that, so the rest of the journey passed pretty much in silence. They ended up at a simple tavern, deep in the heart of the city. It seemed a pleasant enough place, and deliciously warm and cozy after the bitter cold of the streets. Lewis and his companions headed straight for the open roaring fire in the huge stone fireplace, while Kramer talked with the inn's owner, a short fat butterball of a man dressed in cheerfully clashing colors. Lewis and Jesamine took it in turns rubbing the feeling back into their numbed hands, pulling anguished faces at the stabbing pins and needles. Brett had turned his back on the fire, and stuck out his backside to enjoy the full benefit of the heat. Rose alone seemed entirely unaffected by the cold or the new heat. The inn's other customers ignored them, not even bothering to lower their voices.

The inn's owner led his new customers into a side room, and bustled happily about making sure everyone was settled and had a mug of something hot and soothing and deceptively alcoholic in their hand. Hot food was promised shortly, and plenty of it. He gave Rose plenty of room, but then, everybody did. Lewis and his companions sat with Kramer and Goldman at the main table, while the other Mistworlders sat together a little way off. The host asked if they had everything they wanted, and Brett raised a hand.

"What was that animal I saw on the hanging sign over the door as we came in?"

"That, sir, is a Hob hound. The inn is named after the creature, and a terrible thing it was, sir. This establishment has been known as the Hob Hound for over a hundred years, famous for good wines and spirits. Used to be called the Blackthorn, in my grandfather's day, but he renamed it to celebrate the death of the very last Hob hound. Nasty creatures they were, sir; killed for sport as much as appetite, or so I'm told. Anyway, they were hunted down to extinction, and good riddance to them all. It's said some damned fool wanted to preserve a breeding pair, for a zoo. My grandfather shot him, just to be on the safe side."

He caught Kramer glaring at him impatiently, and remembered he was urgently needed elsewhere. He bustled off, and the meeting proper began. The Council of Mistport, and by extension all of Mistworld, turned out to consist of Kramer and Goldman, and another man and woman who slipped quietly into the empty seats left for them. Out of her shapeless furs, Goldman turned out to be a shapely mature woman with a soft mouth and knowing eyes. Kramer just looked even more of a thug. Then there was an old woman, Gina Caswell, who was the oldest-looking woman Lewis and his companions had ever seen. People didn't look old in the Empire these days, right up until they died. But this was Mistworld, whose inhabitants didn't believe in such fripperies. Lewis had to keep himself from staring at her sunken wrinkled face. Brett of course didn't even try, until Jesamine kicked his ankle under the table. The final Councillor, and leader, was Gil Akotai. Lewis would have known he was the leader without having to be told. Akotai was a squat heap of a man, flat-faced and sleepy-eyed, almost as wide as he was tall, but for all his air of calm relaxation, Lewis wasn't fooled for a moment. He knew a dangerous man when he saw one.

"There's not much of you, for a Deathstalker," said Caswell, in her sharp old-woman's voice. "I've flushed more impressive objects in my time. Did you gain any powers from the Madness Maze?"

"I'm still finding out," said Lewis, determined to be polite despite all provocation. "But I am definitely more than I used to be."

"That wouldn't be difficult," said Caswell.

"I never wanted any of you here in the first place," said Kramer. "What are you, really? A disgraced warrior trading on his legendary name. A singer past her best, another bloody Random's Bastard as if we didn't already have more than enough, and the Wild Rose of the Arena, who I still say we should have shot on sight, from a distance. Oh, yes, we know all about her. We get all the entertainment channels out here. A complete bloody psychopath, and vicious with it. No offense."

"Trust me," said Brett. "If she was offended, you'd know all about it by now. There'd be heads rolling across the floor, and entrails hanging from the lamps."

"You see!" Kramer said to Akotai.

"Be quiet, Manfred," Akotai said mildly, and Kramer shut up immediately. Everyone looked at Akotai, but it seemed that was all he had to say, for the moment.

"Excuse me," said Jesamine, in that dangerously calm and even tone that Lewis had learned meant imminent trouble. "What exactly did you mean, a singer past her best? I am a diva."

"This is supposed to be a meeting for rebels and fighters, not second-rate show biz stars," said Kramer, and Lewis winced.

"I was never second rate!" snapped Jesamine. "And I'm more of a fighter than you'll ever be."

"Be silent, woman! Or I'll have you removed!"

Oh, dear, thought Lewis.

Kramer and Jesamine were both on their feet, glaring at each other. Lewis looked to Akotai, to see if he was going to do anything, and when it became clear that he wasn't, Lewis sighed heavily, and brought his hand down hard on the table. The heavy ironwood tabletop cracked, from one end to the other, and everyone looked sharply at Lewis. Ironwood was so tough you could usually only carve and shape it with a laser. Kramer sat down, and after a moment, so did Jesamine. The four Councillors actually seemed to relax a little. Old woman Caswell actually smiled at Lewis.

"Now, that's a Deathstalker," she said, showing off the few front teeth she had left.

"Yes," said Akotai. "You'll understand, Lewis, we needed to be sure. Now, let us get down to business." He leaned forward, holding everyone's attention effortlessly. "Much has happened, in a short time. This world has rejected Finn Durandal and his Empire. There is no place here for the madness of Pure Humanity and Church Militant. The final straw was of course the murder of our Paragon, Emma Steel. Every man and woman of Mistworld has sworn to avenge her foul and unjust death. The Durandal has branded her a traitor, but no one here believes that. We all knew Emma Steel. She was the best of us all."

"She was no traitor," Lewis said. "Finn didn't even bother with a show trial, and he does so love his trials. She must have been on to him, on to something important, so he had her killed. He must have known he could never bribe or intimidate her into silence."

"We would never have believed it, even if there had been a trial," said Kramer. "We all knew Emma."

"I knew her too," said Lewis. "She was my partner, for a time. A good Paragon, strong and true and honorable. We worked well together. I miss her."

"It is good to know, that she was what she always wanted to be," said Akotai, and all the Councillors nodded. Akotai looked at Lewis. "I lead the Council, and the Council leads Mistworld. Why should we accept your leadership in the rebellion, Lewis Deathstalker? How do you justify such arrogance? With your legendary name?"

Jesamine started to say something hot and harsh, but Lewis stopped her with a gesture. He met Akotai's gaze calmly.

"I lead because I have the most experience in fighting Finn and his creatures. And the most success."

"And then there is the matter of John Silence," said Akotai, as though Lewis hadn't spoken. "We know you have him on one of your ships. We have never forgotten or forgiven the things he did here, and never will. The men and women lying dead in the streets, the children burned alive in blazing buildings, the mountains of skulls the marines made to mark their victories. Have I shocked you, Deathstalker? Such atrocities were whitewashed from his legend, but we remember. He served the Iron Bitch, and served her well for many years."

"That was over two hundred years ago," said Lewis.

"No," said Caswell. "That was yesterday."

"A man can change a lot, in two hundred years," Lewis said carefully. "And we are talking about the man who led the fleet to face the forces of Shub, and the Recreated."

"Will that bring one dead Mistworlder back to life?" said Akotai.

"We've all got pasts," said Brett, unexpectedly. "Some of us find the strength to move beyond them. And you leave Lewis alone. He's proven himself worthy of the Deathstalker name."

"How?" said Kramer. "By stealing that slut from his best friend, the King?"

Lewis was on his feet in a moment. He grabbed Kramer by the front of his shirt, hauled him up and out of his chair, and dragged him across the table until they were face-to-face. Kramer struggled fiercely, but couldn't break free. Lewis smiled, and Kramer suddenly froze, held by the naked threat in Lewis's cold eyes.

"You don't talk that way about Jesamine," said Lewis. "Not now, not ever. So sit down and be quiet, or I'll do to you what I just did to the table."

He dropped Kramer back into his chair, and sat down again himself. Jesamine patted him gently on the arm.

"Told you," said Caswell. "He's a Deathstalker."

"But is that enough to make him our leader?" said Gil Akotai, and again everyone's eyes went to him. "You must understand, Lewis; I have earned my position here. A dozen years as Council leader, and a proven warrior. I was the one who trained Emma Steel, when she decided she wanted to be our first Paragon. If you are to lead here, you must prove your worth and value to us."

Jesamine bristled again, and Brett looked actually outraged, but Lewis just nodded calmly. "I was a Paragon on Logres, and Imperial Champion to King Douglas. I have fought off the usurper Finn's forces, and faced the monsters on Shandrakor. I mention these things only in passing."

"What you may or may not have done in another place has no merit here," said Akotai, just as calmly. "This is Mistworld, and you must prove yourself to us."

"We have killed soldiers and monsters," Rose said suddenly, in her slow cold voice. "We have killed espers and ELFs and Paragons. Why should we lower ourselves to fight with such as you?"

"Damn right!" said Jesamine. "Men! You'll be waving your dicks at each other next."

"I would just like to point out that I am not in any way involved in any of this," said Brett.

Lewis looked at Akotai. "Do we really have to do this? Finn would laugh, to see his enemies fighting each other."

"This is Mistworld," said Akotai. "We do things differently here. Make some room."

At this command, the other Mistworlders rose up as one and moved the ironwood table out of the way, leaving an open space in the middle of the room. The people sitting around it were forced to scatter. Brett retreated into the nearest corner, holding Rose before him as a shield. Jesamine made to draw her sword, but Lewis stopped her with a hand on her arm, and eased her gently but firmly out of the way. The Mistworlders formed a circle around Lewis and Akotai. The Councillor didn't look calm or sleepy-eyed anymore. He drew his sword, a scimitar with a long curved blade. Lewis drew his sword, and suddenly they were fighting.

Steel clashed on steel in the dimly lit room, and sparks flared up brightly against the shadows. Akotai and the Deathstalker circled each other unhurriedly, boots slamming hard against the bare floor as they thrust and parried. Akotai was a swift and subtle swordsman, his curved blade moving faster than most people could follow, and he was strong and brave and tricky; but never at any time was he a match for the Deathstalker. Lewis moved almost casually around his opponent, drifting here and there, somehow always in the right place to frustrate Akotai's increasingly frenzied attacks. Lewis's blade licked out to touch Akotai here and there, leaving bloody marks behind. Akotai threw all his strength and ferocity into every blow, trying to force an opening, and it did him no good at all. The Deathstalker dueled Akotai to a halt, and then stepped calmly back and lowered his blade, while Akotai stood breathless and beaten before him.

Manfred Kramer drew his sword and started forward. Jesamine opened her mouth and sang a single piercing note that drove Kramer immediately to his knees, grabbing at his head and crying out in pain. Everyone else in the room winced, including Lewis. Jesamine glared about her.

"Behave yourselves, darlings. Or I'll sing you an aria that will have your brains dribbling out your ears."

"A Siren," said Caswell, respectfully. "It's been a long time since a Siren came to Mistworld. I'll have to tell Topaz."

Lewis nodded casually to Akotai. "You really should have known better, Councillor. Maze or no, I'm still a Deathstalker."

"I know that now," said Akotai, still trying to get his breathing back under control. "But I had to be sure. Damn, you're a fighter. Please forgive Manfred. He's loyal, but not terribly bright. You have proven yourself in all our eyes, Sir Deathstalker, and all Mistworld will follow wherever you lead."

"Good," said Lewis. "We're going to need you." And then he stopped, and looked around. "Oh, hell, where are Brett and Rose?"

Everyone looked around them, but the con man and the killer had disappeared during the swordfight.

"Oh, God," said Jesamine. "They've gone wandering. Brett always was far too keen to come here, to scare up some serious money with his dubious skills. And I don't even want to think what Rose might get up to while she's off the leash."

"Is she really as dangerous as she's supposed to be?" said Goldman.

"Trust us," said Lewis. "You have no idea."

"My people will track them down," said Akotai. "Anything in particular they should look for?"

"Oh, the usual," said Lewis. "People suddenly missing their valuables, or their heads. And just possibly, buildings on fire and people running around screaming."

"Hell," said Akotai. "That's just a good Saturday night, in Mistport."

Brett Random was having a severely bad time. He was finally where he'd been trying so hard to get to, and it was all turning out to be a terrible disappointment. Being a Random's Bastard cut him no ice here; the city was lousy with pretenders to the title. And all his skills at the con and the scam were useless in a city where such things had been raised to an art form over the centuries. In fact, if Rose hadn't been there to protect him, some of his increasingly desperate maneuverings might well have resulted in bloody mayhem. He thought wistfully of the fortune in alien porn he'd so briefly had his hands on, briefly considered trying to sell the pinnace they'd come down in, and finally settled for sulking in a truly disgusting tavern, where the wine tasted as bad as he felt. He couldn't even escape from Lewis and his crusade by disappearing into the crowds; Rose's presence made that impossible. Everyone here knew the Wild Rose from her televised appearances in the Arena, and she point-blank refused to let Brett go off anywhere on his own, on the understandable grounds that he'd probably get himself killed without her.

"I can look after myself!" he protested. "You taught me how to fight."

"Yes," she said. "But not how to want to. You're far too civilized for a place like this, Brett. Mistport is a city of predators. I can sense it. It makes me feel . . . horny."

"I'm in Hell," said Brett.

He'd been drinking for some time, and was blearily wondering how he was going to sneak out of the tavern without paying his bill, when Manfred Kramer finally caught up with him and Rose. Brett had descended from a sulk into full blown gloom, while Rose amused herself by staring out the local bravos. Kramer strode up to their table and glared down at them.

"I told Gil we couldn't trust you," he said flatly. "I knew you'd go scuttling off, the moment we turned our backs. What have you been doing, trying to find one of Finn's spies, so you could sell us out?"

"Go away," said Brett. "I hate this place, and I hate you. What use is there in being a con man in a place where everybody knows all the cons? Where pickpockets have their own union? God, I'm depressed, and this cider isn't helping. Someone here told me they drop a dead rat into every barrel to help the stuff ferment further, and to give the booze a little body, and I am completely prepared to believe them. I just know something appalling's going to appear on my toothbrush tonight."

"You're a disgrace," said Kramer, sounding almost satisfied. "Let's see if Gil can maintain his faith in the false Deathstalker, after he hears what the man's companions have been doing. Now, are you going to come along with me voluntarily, or am I going to have to have you dragged? Guess which I'd prefer."

"I can't be bothered with this," said Brett morosely. "Rose, you deal with him."

"Sure," said Rose, and she surged to her feet, drew her sword, and cut off Kramer's head in one swift movement. The body just stood there for a moment, fountaining blood from the neck, and then it crashed twitching to the floor. Rose stooped down, picked up the head, blew it a kiss and then threw it casually into the open fire at the back of the room. Everyone else in the tavern had already decided it was well past their bedtimes, and were leaving at speed by every exit. Even the bar staff. In a surprisingly short time, the tavern was empty except for Rose Constantine, the headless body, and a suddenly very sober Brett Random. He lurched to his feet, struggling for words, and forced down a suicidal urge to hit Rose with the table.

"*What the hell did you do that for?*" he shrieked.

"You said deal with him," said Rose, calmly cleaning the blood from her blade.

"I didn't mean kill him! That was Gil Akotai's right-hand man! Oh, Lewis will have a coronary when he finds out. None of the Mistworlders will follow him after this! And you can bet Lewis will blame me, not you! Oh, God, my stomach hurts. All the people you could have killed . . . This will scupper all Lewis's plans . . . I don't even want to think about what they do to murderers here . . . Think! Think!"

"That's your department," said Rose, putting away her sword.

Brett strode up and down, glaring at the headless body on the floor, which was still twitching, as though it couldn't quite believe what had just happened. Brett kicked it a few times, but it didn't make him feel any better. "All right . . . we could make it look like someone else did it. No, we couldn't; they have espers here. They couldn't pry anything out of our minds, but there were any number of witnesses. Think! Think! Hide the body—yes. Yes! And by the time they find it, we'll be long gone. Rose, pick up the body. I've got an idea."

Rose picked up the body, and slung it effortlessly over one shoulder. Blood spilled down her crimson leathers, but that was nothing new for her. Brett doubted anyone would even notice. He gestured for Rose to follow him, and headed for the back of the bar, and then down into the wine cellars below. Brett scurried back and forth in the gloom, until he finally discovered a barrel of cider that had just been opened. He gestured urgently to Rose, and she dumped the body into the dark liquid. The cider swallowed Kramer up with hardly a splash, and Brett nailed the top down very thoroughly. He and Rose then pushed the barrel to the back, behind all the other barrels. Brett stepped back, breathing and sweating heavily, and considered his work.

"They said they liked their cider to have a little body . . . All right, let's get out of here. And remember, Rose, *this never happened.*"

Some time later, Brett Random and Rose Constantine strolled casually back into the Hob Hound, and expressed surprise that anyone had even missed them. Lewis and Akotai were deep in tactical discussions, and barely acknowledged their return, but Jesamine looked up suspiciously from the impromptu signing session she'd organized for her many Mistport fans. Brett stared innocently back.

"What?" he said. "We just went for a stroll. It wasn't like you needed us here. Did we miss something?"

"I swear to God, you're worse than children," said Jesamine, automatically signing a photo a fan put in front of her. "I can't take my eyes off you for a moment. Tell me you haven't done anything embarrassing. Have you seen Manfred Kramer?"

"No," said Brett, though his heart leapt painfully in his chest. "Was he looking for us? We must have missed him."

"I didn't miss him," said Rose.

"Hush, dear," said Brett.

"You're looking very shifty, Brett," said Jesamine. "What have the two of you been up to?"

"Not nearly as much as I'd hoped," said Brett, leaning casually against the wall. "No one in this city knows a good business proposition when they hear one. The sooner we're out of this dump, the better."

"We'll go when Lewis is ready, and not before. In the meantime, I have fans to attend to. Who shall I make this out to, sweetie?"

And Brett had to find a table with Rose and just sit there, outwardly calm but inwardly shaking, while Lewis finished his discussions with Akotai, and Jesamine signed absolutely anything the long line of fans put in front of her. Some of them actually wanted parts of their body signed, so they could then go off and have the signature tattooed over. Jesamine took it all in her stride. Eventually it was decided that all the Mistworlders who wanted to join Lewis's rebel force (which was a hell of a lot of them) would join the fleet in their own ships. It was a matter of pride and paranoia. No Mistworlder would ever agree to take passage on an Imperial ship.

And then Akotai wanted to wait until Manfred Kramer returned, and Brett almost wept with frustration. Luckily Jesamine decided she'd had enough of her fans, after one of them wanted her to sign a particularly intimate part of his body, and she insisted on leaving right then. Brett would have kissed her, if he hadn't known that would look suspicious.

Soon enough, the rebel fleet pulled away from Mistworld, joined by a strange collection of very individual Mistworlder ships. Silence asked Lewis where they were heading next, and Lewis's answer upset almost everyone. *Shandrakor*, he said, and everyone else said *Oh, shit*, in varying disgusted, appalled, and terribly distressed ways. Everyone had heard of the legendary planet of monsters. No one went to Shandrakor by choice, unless they were suffering from a very serious death wish. Jesamine and Brett found themselves in agreement for perhaps the first time in their lives, saying *Why?* in pretty much the same dismayed tone of voice. Rose, predictably, was the only one who seemed pleased at the prospect.

"Trust me, Lewis," Silence said heavily, "everyone is already seriously impressed that you and your companions survived one journey through the deadly jungles of Shandrakor. You don't have to prove anything to anyone."

"Though it is just the sort of thing a Deathstalker would do," said Captain Price, and the rest of the bridge crew nodded respectfully.

"You're not helping, Price," said Silence. "Lewis, what is to be gained by going there? The world has no ships, weapons, or even people to add to our cause. You said yourself there was nothing worth salvaging from the old crash-landed Standing. All Shandrakor has is monsters . . . Oh. Oh, no . . ."

"Oh, yes, Admiral," said Lewis.

"I do feel I should point out," Price said diffidently, "that every hour we spend not heading towards Logres does give the usurper Finn that much extra time to prepare for battle. It would be a shame to throw away what little advantage we've got."

"We're going to Shandrakor," said Lewis. "I gave them my word."

"To monsters?" said Silence.

"Many of them were human once," said Lewis, locking Silence's gaze with his own. "Some of them still remember. Do you remember, John Silence? Were you part of the decision to take all those made into monsters by Lionstone or Shub, all those poor unfortunates, and just dump them among all the other monsters on Shandrakor? To leave them there, so they could be forgotten?"

"Robert and Constance made the decision," said Silence. "And I . . . went along with it. There was no way of curing or restoring them. Relocating them to Shandrakor seemed kinder than just killing them all."

"Excuse me," said Captain Price. "But what are you talking about?"

"One of the Golden Age's nastier secrets," said Lewis. "Back when the rogue AIs of Shub were still the official enemies of Humanity, they routinely captured and experimented on humans, making them over into monstrosities in their secret laboratories. Sometimes for information, sometimes as part of their psychological warfare. And sometimes the Empress Lionstone the Fourteenth ordered the same thing done in her secret laboratories, in her search for new weapons, or just for the fun of it. And then there was the Mater Mundi, trying to turn espers into super-espers and failing as often as not. So when the Great Rebellion was finally over, and we were all friends again, Robert and Constance were faced with the problem of what to do with all the leftover monsters, which had once been men and women. There was no place for monsters in the wonderful Golden Age King Robert and Queen Constance were determined to build, so they gathered up all the products of all the secret labs, and dumped them on Shandrakor, to live or die as best they could. And then the Empire did its best to forget they ever existed."

"We had a civilization to rebuild," said Silence. "We couldn't do everything. We had to have priorities. We needed to spend our time on the problems we could solve. And if that makes us sound hard-hearted . . . we'd all been through a lot. We were all very tired."

"I gave those monsters my word that they would go home again," said Lewis. "And so they will. First as shock troops in our war with Finn, and then . . . as our lost children. Set a course for Shandrakor, Admiral."

"Typical bloody Deathstalker," said Silence. "Always being right."

And so the fleet went to Shandrakor. Some were heard to say that though they'd sworn to follow the Deathstalker to Hell and back, they hadn't necessarily meant it literally. But no one said it too loudly. Except for Brett Random, who made it very clear that there was no way he was going back down to the planet's jungles, under any circumstances whatsoever. And to prove it, he locked himself in his quarters with several bottles of wine and barricaded the door. Rose reluctantly stayed behind too, to keep him company and stop him from getting hysterical. In the end, only Lewis and Jesamine descended to the surface of Shandrakor, in a simple pinnace. And only Silence turned up to see them leave.

"They're calling this Deathstalker's folly," he remarked. "Everyone agrees you're being very brave, but there's already heated betting as to what condition you'll return in, or even whether you'll be back at all."

"I hope you're betting on us," said Jesamine.

"Of course," said Silence. "I never could resist the really long odds." He looked back at Lewis. "Do some of them really remember being human? We had hoped . . . After all this time?"

"Yes," said Lewis. "They remember the lives they had, the people they knew, the worlds they came from. And they dream of being able to go home again."

"Lewis, they can't." Silence looked at the Deathstalker pleadingly. "We still have no idea how to undo what was done to them. Even Shub doesn't know how. What could these monsters do, what could they be, on civilized worlds? Neither human nor alien, how would they ever fit in? Everyone they ever knew is dead and gone. They'd end up in zoos!"

"I gave them my word," said Lewis.

"Then . . . they're your responsibility, Deathstalker. Hopefully you'll make a better job of it than I did, when it was my responsibility."

Lewis guided the pinnace down into the nightmare jungles of Shandrakor, darting in and out of the higher treetops until he was finally able to land in the clearing that held the buried Deathstalker Standing. The air was hot and wet and sticky as Lewis and Jesamine stepped out of the ship and onto the dark spiky grass. Insects buzzed fiercely on the heavy air, and from all around came the roars and screams of life and death on Shandrakor, where every life-form preyed on every other life-form. Lewis looked carefully around him, keeping his hands near but not actually on his weapons. So far, nothing had entered the clearing. It looked pretty much as he remembered it, but with no signs of the extensive damage that had been done during the last attack of the Emperor's troops. The fast-growing jungle had already covered over the scars. Lewis couldn't even tell where the entrance to the Standing had been, before the castle's ancient computers blew it up, as one last service to Clan Deathstalker. Tall, wide-boled trees formed a guardian circle around the clearing, and shadows moved among them. Jesamine wiped at her perspiring face with a cloth.

"There is definitely such a thing as too much sunshine, darling. God, it's hot! And I really do hate this humidity. It does my skin no good at all. I just know I'm going to end up with another nasty heat rash." She looked about her. "Where are they? They must have heard us land. You know, Lewis, I have to say that this doesn't strike me as one of your better ideas."

"Do you want to abandon them too?"

"Well, not as such, sweetie, but . . . shock troops, yes. I can see that. But what about afterwards?"

"I gave my word as a Deathstalker."

Jesamine sighed. "Yes, dear, you did. Which was all very honorable. But you can't feel guilty about everything the Empire did in the name of your legendary ancestor."

"I can try to put things right. And I will. I have to. That's what being a Deathstalker means. Especially when you're the last one."

He broke off, as he and Jesamine both looked round sharply. And one by one the monsters left the tree line and ventured into the clearing, emerging into the light of day like horrid ghosts from the eternal shadows of the jungle. There were all kinds, large and small, every possible example of mixed natures and merged genes. They moved in slowly from every side, wrapped in spiked armor and twisted shapes, with too many legs and eyes, or not enough, in forms so vile and so affecting that Lewis and Jesamine had to fight to keep from looking away. She stood very close to him, almost moved to tears at the horrible shapes that had once been men and women. She still kept her hand near her gun. The monsters filled the clearing, pressing slowly forward from every side until suddenly, at some unseen, unheard signal they all stopped. One creature came forward, to confront Lewis and Jesamine. It had been turned horribly inside out, its exposed red and purple organs gleaming wetly in the bright sunlight. A more or less human face had been stretched across its flayed chest. The mouth was wide and mobile, and the wide-set eyes . . . held no understandable emotion. The bulging body hung in a cage of thick-furred spindly legs.

"You came back," it said.

"Yes," said Lewis. "I told you I would."

"So you did, Deathstalker." The creature's voice was a low hiss, the words elongated and strangely accented. "I think I had a name once, but that was long ago, and I don't remember it. I remember some things, flashes of home and family, but not whether I was a man or a woman. It's hard now to even think what that meant. I am Speaker; I am the voice of those who remember being other than monsters. Why have you come back, Deathstalker?"

"Because I made you a promise," said Lewis. "I have a fleet of ships now. We're going back to Logres, which was called Golgotha in your day, to throw a false Emperor off his stolen throne. I want you to come with us. All of you. Be my shock troops in this war. And afterwards . . ."

"Yes?" said Speaker. "What, afterwards?"

"You will all go home. We'll search out what records remain, do our best to find out who and what you used to be. If all else fails, the espers will dig the truth out of your minds. But every damned one of you will go home. No one gets left out, no one gets left behind. Whatever can be done for you, to make you more . . . comfortable, will be done. Science has come a long way in two hundred years. Of course, this all depends on us winning the war . . ."

"We can fight," said Speaker. "We know how to do that. Could we really be . . . cured? Made human again?"

"I don't know," Lewis said honestly. "But the blessed Owen has returned, more powerful than ever. I have seen him perform miracles. And there is always the Madness Maze. It transformed us; perhaps it can transform you."

"We will go with you," said Speaker. "Taking a chance on your name, and your word. But if we fight for you, and do not die, you must promise to kill us, rather than return us here. We will either live as human, or die as monsters. We could not stand . . . to have to live without hope."

"I understand," said Lewis. "I promise; I won't let you down."

"Not all of us want to go," said Speaker. "Some have already said they won't leave Shandrakor. They have forgotten what it was like to be other than what they are, or perhaps they no longer care. The jungle has become their home now. They belong here."

"If I could speak to them . . ." said Lewis.

"They would kill you," said Speaker. "They are only monsters now."

"My offer will remain open," said Lewis. "For as long as any of them live. Prepare yourselves, my friends. Your journey home begins."

Remote-controlled cargo ships came floating down like autumn leaves at Lewis's command, hundreds of them, enough to ferry the largest and the smallest creatures out of the clearing and up to the fleet. Remote-controlled, because no human pilot wanted to get too close to the legendary monsters of Shandrakor. The monsters understood. They weren't ready to be seen by humans either. So they were parceled out among the various starcruisers, traveling in the mostly empty cargo bays, kept separate from the crews by guilt and fear and heavily locked doors.

Lewis's next choice of destination was his home planet, Virimonde, and no one objected to that. Everyone understood his need to go home, to see for himself the terrible thing that Finn Durandal had ordered done to Clan Deathstalker, and their ancient Standing. It wouldn't seem real until he had seen it with his own eyes. And no one at all doubted but that the people of that world would want to fight alongside the fleet. They were all born to be warriors, in honor of the blessed Owen. It fell to the knowledgeable Captain Price to explain to Lewis why the people of Virimonde had not already risen up in outrage against the massacre.

"There are two transmutation engines in high orbit around Virimonde," said Price, keeping his voice carefully calm and neutral. "Any sign of rebellion on the world below, and the engines would turn the whole planet into a lifeless wasteland. Finn's direct orders. The only reason he hasn't used the engines already is that he undoubtably meant to use this threat to keep you in line, once you reappeared."

Lewis nodded. He understood how Finn thought. "Program the starcruisers' targeting computers to lock on to the engines. The moment we drop out of hyperspace, I want both those engines hit with every weapon we've got. Do a good job, Price; we won't get a second chance at this. You can bet good money that Finn would have programmed the engines to strike at Virimonde the moment rebel ships arrived. Then, we'll take time to check for hidden booby traps in orbit. Be very thorough, because you can be sure Finn was. We're not going down to Virimonde until we're sure it's safe. For them, as well as us."

In the end, it was as simple as that. The two transmutation engines made a fine display as the fleet blasted them apart, and it didn't take long to search out the orbiting mines and other nasty surprises that Finn had left behind. Lewis made contact with Capital City, and was immediately welcomed home and invited down. Parades and celebrations in the city were promised, but Lewis politely declined. He needed to see what was left of his Standing. His Family home.

Lewis and Jesamine went down alone on the pinnace again. Brett, seriously drunk but still in full use of his self-preservation instincts, declined. Ostensibly because there was nothing worth stealing on Virimonde, but actually because he didn't want to risk Rose's killing someone important again. He didn't think his nerves could stand that. And Silence didn't go along because he had once been part of the invasion force that Lionstone sent hundreds of years ago, to pound the people back into barbarism. They'd done such a good job that the planet was still recovering, even now. Millions of people had been killed. And Silence had been a part of it.

"You did get around, didn't you?" said Jesamine, exasperated. "Is there anything else we ought to know, any other awful things you did when you served under the Iron Bitch?"

"Lots," said Silence. "But I won't tell you. It was a long time ago. We were all different people then."

"Why did you serve Lionstone for so long?" said Lewis. He sounded like he honestly wanted to know, so Silence told him.

"She was my Empress. Loyalty was all I knew, then."

Lewis and Jesamine rode the pinnace down to Virimonde. It was a smooth enough trip. Lewis knew the way home. Jesamine studied him worriedly. He was being very quiet. She wanted to help, but couldn't see how. So much had happened to Lewis since he'd last been here, and he'd never been the easiest person to talk to when it came to personal things. He'd lost pretty much everything he ever cared for, except her. Lost his Family and his home, his Clan and his Standing. For a long time now he'd been running on anger and revenge and duty, and Jesamine had to wonder what would happen to Lewis when he no longer had those things to hold him together.

The comm system suddenly came alive, breaking an uncomfortable silence. "This is Virimonde comm center. Welcome home, Sir Deathstalker. We always knew you'd come for us. Quite an impressive fleet you've picked up. Trust a Deathstalker to come home in style. I have been asked . . . to warn you, about the current condition of your Standing . . ."

"Is it true?" Lewis said steadily. "Are they all dead?"

"I'm afraid so, Sir Deathstalker." The voice was quiet and respectful, but there was no give in it. "We did think a few minor cousins might have escaped, but now all the bodies have been identified, we're sure no one was missing on the day. Everyone with the Clan name was killed. The Emperor's creatures were very thorough. You are now the last of the direct line."

"No," said Lewis. "There is another. Owen has returned."

"Then the rumors are true? He's really back?"

"Yes. He's gone to face the Terror."

"We are living in a time of legends reborn. A deputation will meet you, Sir Deathstalker, on the grounds on the Standing."

"I don't think I want to meet anyone, just yet," said Lewis.

"You'll want to hear this. Clan Deathstalker continues. It is not gone. Virimonde comm center out."

"Well," Jesamine said lightly, as the comm unit fell silent. "That was . . . enigmatic. What do you suppose they meant?"

"I don't know," said Lewis. "I don't care. I just want to go home."

He landed the pinnace on his Family landing pad, decorated with the Family crest, in the grounds of the ancient castle that had been home to Clan Deathstalker for so many generations. There wasn't a lot left of the old stronghold now. Jesamine followed Lewis nervously as he descended from the pinnace, strode across the landing pads, and then just stood looking at the smoke- and fire-blackened remains before him. All of the east wing had been blown away, leaving the interior rooms and corridors exposed to wind and rain. The courtyard walls were gone, and the front and west wing walls were pockmarked with jagged holes from disrupter fire. Even the roof had been punctured through repeatedly by energy weapons and explosions. Finn's people had put a lot of effort into destroying the castle, but still most of it stood, defiant as ever.

Jesamine took Lewis's arm, trying to comfort him with her presence. "I never realized the place was so big, Lewis. It's still . . . very impressive."

"I always believed I'd come back, someday," said Lewis. "That when my time as a Paragon was done, I'd come home again, to lead my Family. We'd all sit around the open fire in the great hall, with the dogs lying around, and I'd tell them tales of the greatest city on the greatest world in the Empire. And now all that is gone, all that I really care about . . . is that my mother and my father are dead. I never got a chance to tell them all the things I'd done. The things I did, because I wanted them to be proud of me."

"They knew," said Jesamine. "And of course they were proud of you. They were your parents."

"They're gone, and I'm alone. I want my mum. I want my dad."

Jesamine took him in her arms, but he didn't cry.

They both looked round sharply at the sound of approaching ships in the sky. Lewis pushed Jesamine away, and his hands went to his weapons. Ships filled the sky, coming in from every direction. So many they blocked out the sun. Transport ships, cargo ships, small family ships. They landed one after another, filling and overflowing the landing pads and settling down where they could in the surrounding countryside. Hundreds of men and women disembarked and headed straight for what was left of the Deathstalker Standing. They saw Lewis and called out his name joyously, hooting and waving, and almost reluctantly he took his hand away from his gun. The crowds surged forward, chanting his name like a war cry. They gathered before him, milling uncertainly, and then one man at the front of the crowd sank down on one knee, and everyone followed his example, until the whole crowd was kneeling before Lewis, their faces radiant.

The first man to kneel had a familiar face. Lewis remembered Michel du Bois, once the member of Parliament for Virimonde, now an exile and outlaw like Lewis. Once, they had been rivals for Virimonde's love, even enemies, but du Bois had changed much since Lewis last saw him. He looked up at Lewis with wild eyes, fanatical and perhaps a little mad. He bowed jerkily to Lewis, ignoring Jesamine completely.

"Welcome home, Sir Deathstalker. All the families of Virimonde have sent representatives here, to do you honor. Where you lead, we will follow. The whole planet has taken an oath of vengeance against the Durandal and his people, sworn upon your name and upon our blood. We are yours, to lead into battle. We are all Deathstalkers now."

"Talk about intense," Jesamine muttered. "Is he on something?"

"Hush," said Lewis. He nodded to du Bois. "Your manner has changed since our last meeting," he said carefully.

"The world has changed," said du Bois, his eyes unblinking. "My loyalty has always been to Virimonde. You know that. Finn has proven himself unworthy, and an enemy. A coward, and an animal. Take us with you to Logres, Sir Deathstalker, and we will drag him from his throne and hang him from the walls of the palace." He paused a moment, looking past Lewis at the ruined castle. "I had an aunt who was a Deathstalker. From a minor branch, but she bore the name proudly. She died here, with the rest of the Clan. She was always good to me. We have all lost loved ones here."

"I never knew we were related," said Lewis. "You never said."

"I wanted to make it on my own, by my own worth, not through Family connections," said du Bois. For a moment he looked and sounded almost normal, but the moment passed. "We have all sworn to be Deathstalkers; every man and woman on this planet, under your leadership."

And the huge crowd responded with a low murmur of agreement, an almost animal growl of wrath and determination.

"Woe to all who raise the rage of Virimonde," murmured Lewis. "Very well, Michel. Get these people out of here, and get them organized. I want everyone that's coming offplanet in two hours, in everything you've got that flies. The fleet is waiting for you, and they'll find room for anyone who wants to come and fight but doesn't have a ship. How many can we count on?"

"Every man and woman has sworn to follow you," du Bois said simply.

"Hold everything," said Jesamine. "Everyone? The whole adult population?"

"What was done here touched everyone," said du Bois. "We were all raised as warriors, in Owen's name, to do him honor. Now he has returned, how can we be found wanting?"

He rose to his feet, turned and addressed the waiting crowd, giving them Lewis's instructions, and they roared their approval. Du Bois continued talking, stirring them to action with grand rhetoric. Lewis and Jesamine left him to it, and walked slowly through the courtyard of what had once been a mighty castle.

"Why haven't they even tried to repair it?" said Jesamine. "The basic structure seems sound enough. They could have at least made a start."

"It wasn't their place to do anything," said Lewis. "They were waiting, to see what I would decide. And besides; it's evidence. This is a war crime. A sight to inspire people to revolt. I'm going inside, to see how bad the damage is. You don't need to come, Jes."

"Of course I do, sweetie. Even Deathstalkers need someone to lean on, sometimes."

The first bad thing they encountered was a monstrous pile of junk, raised up before the smashed-in front doors. Finn's people had piled up in the courtyard all the Deathstalker belongings that weren't worth looting or trashing. They'd clearly tried to set the pile on fire, but it hadn't taken. Lewis approached the pile slowly, almost cautiously. He recognized a few items, here and there, but made no attempt to touch or rescue anything. His ugly face grew increasingly set and harsh. In the end, he turned his back on it, like turning his back on a grave, and headed for the open main doors. Jesamine went with him, not sure he even knew she was there anymore.

Inside the castle, the damage was worse, if anything. Explosives had clearly been set in vulnerable spots to try to bring the place down, but the thick solid stone walls had defeated them. The walls still stood, though much holed and scarred, and there was rubble everywhere. Floors and ceilings were slumped and ruptured, but still held together. Deathstalker Standings had always been designed and built to take punishment. Deathstalkers led dangerous lives, and they had long memories. Jesamine followed Lewis as he wandered through rooms and corridors, stepping around or over the general destruction. Furniture had been smashed and burned, bookcases overturned, and centuries-old tapestries and portraits torn down and trashed. Everything of obvious value was gone, taken, and everywhere there were signs and stains where Finn's creatures had relieved themselves, like dogs marking their territory.

"Finn knew this would hurt me," Lewis said, almost casually. "Almost as much as losing my mum and dad, and my Family. Back when we were friends and the world still made sense, he and I often spent long weekends here. He was my guest, and I showed him everything. He had to know how much this place, its history, meant to me. I told him. I told him everything, and why not? He was my friend. What will Owen say, when he sees this? This was my Family's duty, to keep the Standing in trust, for him, when he returned. This place was always more his than ours. And we failed him."

"He'll understand," said Jesamine. "He knew what it felt like, to be betrayed."

They climbed a crumbling, broken stairway to the next floor. There was a wide gap in the middle, several feet across. Lewis and Jesamine jumped across it easily, without thinking or effort, and only afterwards realized what they'd done, and looked back at the gap. Jesamine leaned over to look down into the long drop, and then gripped Lewis fiercely by the arm.

"Wow," she said breathlessly. "I don't believe we just did that!"

"Jes, you're cutting off the circulation in my arm."

"Look at that drop! Look at that gap! And we jumped it like it was nothing . . . Back before the Maze, I couldn't have made a jump like that if you'd goosed me with a cattle prod."

"Jes, my arm . . ."

"Oh, sorry."

"We're changing," said Lewis, rubbing at his arm. "All the time, we're becoming something else, something better, in little ways we don't always notice."

And then suddenly he and Jesamine sprinted forward, charging up the remaining stairs at more than human speed. They reached the landing and looked back, not even breathing hard, and watched the steps where they'd just been standing slowly tear themselves away from the wall and plummet to the floor far below. They hit hard, breaking apart under the impact, and the sound drifted up, along with a cloud of dust. Lewis and Jesamine looked at each other.

"We *knew* that was going to happen," Jesamine said slowly. "We . . . sensed it. Now that is seriously spooky."

"I'd be hard-pressed to name anything in our lives that hasn't been, for some time now," said Lewis. "No doubt eventually we'll get used to it."

"I hope so," said Jesamine. "I don't know if my nerves can take much more of this. It's worse than opening night."

They walked on, unhurriedly, through the devastated castle. The only sounds were the wind whistling through the many holes, the occasional groan from floor or wall, and the quiet sound of their own footsteps. They looked into every room, but nowhere had been left untouched, unsullied. Finn's creatures had made a thorough job of their desecration.

"You should have seen it in its prime," Lewis said finally. "It was . . . magnificent. The accumulated treasures and wonders of centuries. Family history that went back to the First Empire. Paintings and antiques and objets d'art. Some of them so old even we weren't sure what they were, or what significance they might once have held. One day, it would all have been mine, to enjoy and preserve. I wanted to share it with you, Jes."

"And you will," said Jesamine, hugging his arm tightly and laying her golden head on his shoulder. "This can all be rebuilt, restored. I'm seriously rich, remember? I have money in accounts all over the Empire, that Finn's people couldn't find if they used an uber-esper and a dowsing rod. I have more money than even I can spend in one lifetime, and it's about time I put it to some good use. I can't restore the treasures that you've lost, and the things that meant so much to you, I know that; but the Deathstalker Standing can be made magnificent again. We'll see to that. When all this madness is over, we'll put everything right again. You'll see."

"It wouldn't be the first time this old place has been rebuilt," Lewis admitted. "Deathstalkers tend to lead . . . dramatic lives."

"How are you feeling, Lewis?"

"Glad that you're here with me. And glad that I came here, and saw this. It reminds me of the oldest truth of my Family: that no matter how bad things get, Clan Deathstalker endures. We never forgive, we never forget, and we bring our enemies down—whatever it takes."

Some time later, his pinnace led a flotilla of assorted ships up from Virimonde to join the waiting fleet, more than doubling it in size. Clan Deathstalker was going to war.

Back on the flagship *Havoc*, Brett Random and Rose Constantine had been roaming the steel corridors for some time, looking for some trouble to get into. Brett had run out of wine, and was bored; always a dangerous combination. So he went wandering, and Rose went along with him, because whatever Brett got up to, it was bound to be at least interesting. No one ever challenged their right to be wherever they were; they were the Deathstalker's companions, and therefore trusted. *More fools them,* Brett thought. He descended further and further into the ship, into areas passengers rarely ever saw. Brett was determined to find something amusing to do, if only to demonstrate his independence from Lewis. Besides, with the drink finished, there was nothing else left to do except have sex with Rose, and there was a limit to how much of that his nerves could stand.

"There's got to be a still somewhere on this ship," he growled. "Or a med tech turning out knockoff battle drugs. Something to get a desperate man comfortably out of his head for a while. I did try the med bay earlier, but Jesamine had already warned the doctors about me, the bitch."

"Why don't I just grab someone, and pound them until they tell us where to find the good stuff?" Rose said reasonably.

Brett winced. "Better not. We're not exactly popular around here as it is. The last time I went down to the main galley, just looking for a little food and good company and perhaps a friendly game of dice, everyone I tried to talk to just made some excuse and left. Some of them didn't even bother with the excuse. Some of them even left their meals behind."

"Our reputation has gone before us," said Rose.

Brett sniffed loudly. "No one's actually said anything, of course. We are Maze people, after all, and friends of the Deathstalker. But are we treated like heroes? Are we hell as like. We're made about as welcome as a skid mark on a hotel towel. You know what, Rose? I think you're right. To hell with whether or not Lewis gets upset. Grab the next crewman you see, and shake some information out of him."

So they stood and waited for the next unfortunate to pass by, and then Rose picked him up and slammed him against the nearest wall. Brett explained what it was they wanted to know, and the crewman expressed every eagerness to assist them, if only Rose would move the point of her dagger just a little farther away from his eyeball.

"Try the third subgalley, down on deck forty-three. There's always something going on there."

Rose dropped him back onto his feet, and put away her dagger. The crewman slid along the wall, putting a little distance between them, and scowled at Brett.

"I knew we couldn't trust you. Scum always finds its own level."

"We are not scum!" said Brett. "We've been through the Madness Maze, remember?"

"That's right. You're monsters. We should have locked you up in the cargo bay, along with all the other freaks from Shandrakor."

Rose raised her knife again, but Brett stopped her. He'd had enough of hiding bodies. He smiled unpleasantly at the crewman, and put all his esper compulsion into his voice. "You. Forget all about this conversation. Then shit yourself. Then run away."

The crewman did all these things, to Brett's amusement. "I really hate this ship," he announced, not caring whether anyone heard him. "I could cope when it was just Lewis and Jesamine being disapproving, but everyone here sees us as second-class heroes, at best."

Rose said *second-class heroes* along with him, and Brett looked at her thoughtfully. "We're doing that more and more lately. Completing each other's thoughts, coming up with the same ideas, even sharing body language. I notice these things. We're becoming more like each other, and I don't like it. There's only room in this Empire for one Brett Random."

"I'm horny," Rose said implacably. "Find me someone to kill. Sex with you is nice, but it doesn't satisfy like the real thing."

"Why me?" said Brett piteously, to the heavens. "Try and contain yourself, Rose. Please? Soon enough we'll be going up against Finn and all his armies, and then you'll be hip deep in all the slaughter you can handle."

"Yes," said Rose. "I'm looking forward to it. But I am concerned about facing the Durandal again. He scares me."

She said it in her normal, casual tone, but there was no denying she meant it. Brett was actually shocked. "I didn't think you were scared of anything."

"Finn is a special case," said Rose, and Brett had to agree. Just thinking about facing Finn again made his heart pound in his chest.

"I have been thinking," Rose announced, and Brett winced. It was always dangerous when Rose started getting ideas. She looked at Brett thoughtfully, and he felt the first few beads of sweat pop out on his forehead.

"Oh yes?" he said, in a very nearly normal voice.

"I'm remembering my past differently, Brett. Seeing things differently. Because we are linked, your mind affects me as much as mine affects yours. There are times . . . when I think of other things than killing. It would be wrong to say I'm developing a conscience; I don't think you and I possess one between us. But I am capable of seeing people differently now. As people, rather than just targets. It . . . disturbs me."

"Do you feel any differently about killing people?" Brett said hopefully.

Rose considered the question. "I think . . . it might make killing people even more fun."

"I'm changing the subject," Brett said, in a loud and very determined voice. "We need to work out a way to make ourselves some serious money, before the action starts. Mistworld turned out to be a complete bust, and Virimonde was always going to be a nonstarter. We could sell our stories to the media after the war, but that rather assumes there's going to be an afterwards. Besides, most of our stories aren't suitable for the mass media. Either way, I think I've done my part in this rebellion. No more fighting and diving into danger for me. I don't care if our mental link has made me a better fighter; it's just not me. I'd grab a ship and desert, if it weren't for the marvelous possibilities of looting when we finally take the Parade of the Endless. But I've got to find something to do before then or I'll go crazy from boredom. Something worthy of my talents. So, let's try the directions that kind and accommodating crewman gave us before he had to go and change his trousers. There's got to be a friendly card game I can get into somewhere. There's always good money to be made from the kind of people who think poker is a friendly game."

"I still want to kill someone."

"All right, I'll accuse someone of cheating! After I've made a decent sum."

They headed down to deck forty-three. It was a long way down. Brett tended to forget, until forcibly reminded, that Imperial starcruisers were the size of floating cities, and as complex. Normally it was a very well run, very calm and tranquil city in between engagements, but Brett couldn't help noticing the freshly daubed graffiti that appeared on the steel walls as they descended towards deck forty-three. *The Church is the only true Authority. The true Owen is watching you. Death to heretics. Pure Humanity; Pure Loyalty. Long live Emperor Finn.* And *The voices in my head are getting louder.*

"Some of those sentiments are really worrying," said Brett. "Particularly that last one." He looked at Rose. "You don't get the significance, do you? This graffiti means that not all the crew are of one mind. They were all supposed to have had a change of heart once Owen appeared to them, but this suggests very strongly that there are still Pure Humanity and Church Militant fanatics on board this ship, still loyal to Finn. The real hard cases. Which means . . . well, I don't know. Sabotage, maybe? Knives in the dark? Internal dissension in the ranks when it comes time to fight? That's the last thing we can afford when we come to face Finn's defenses."

"Should we tell someone?" said Rose. She made a genuine effort to sound interested, to please Brett, but she didn't really care.

"Not yet." Brett frowned, running the possibilities in his head. "We need to know more. And, just maybe . . . I smell an opportunity. Let us press on."

At the entrance to deck forty-three, they found someone waiting for them. A single crewman, in a marine's uniform, tall and lithely muscular, with a rather droopy mustache that didn't suit his otherwise wolfish features. He smiled and nodded easily to the newcomers.

"Brett Random. Rose Constantine. We've all been looking forward to meeting you."

"Have you?" said Brett, ready to break and run at a moment's notice.

"Oh yes. I'm Leslie Springfield, marine trooper second class, and Random's Bastard in bad standing."

"The best kind," Brett said automatically, and Leslie grinned.

"You should be glad I'm here. This is enemy territory. You wouldn't have made it this far if I hadn't vouched for you."

"That was very kind of you," said Brett. "What's it going to cost me?"

"Maybe a small percentage, later on. Now come with me; people are waiting to talk with you."

"What sort of people?" said Brett.

"The large and growing part of this crew who remain loyal to Emperor Finn, and the ideals of Pure Humanity and Church Militant. The illusion of the false Owen didn't fool us for a moment. We knew Shub trickery when we saw it. The true Owen would never reject our ideals. He was always an enemy of aliens and the AIs of Shub. Now do let's hurry along. You didn't really come down here for a drink and a game of cards, Brett, and you know it. You could have found them anywhere, if you'd really wanted to. No, whether you knew it or not, you were looking for us, because you know we're the winning side. Price's bunch of losers and freaks don't stand a chance against properly motivated Imperial armies."

"Maybe," said Brett. "What exactly are you selling, Leslie?"

"A chance to be legitimate again. To come back where you belong. I can hook you up with the loyalist cause, even put you in contact with the Emperor himself. Yes, I thought that would interest you. Come on, Brett; you don't belong with the traitor Deathstalker and his slut. They're going to lose and lose hard, and you know it. Mainly because the loyalist crew are going to seize control of all the starcruisers in this fleet, long before we get anywhere near Logres. We have no intention of fighting and dying for heretics. And remember: there is a hell of a big reward waiting for anyone who brings the Emperor the heads of the Deathstalker and Flowers. Fifteen million credits apiece."

"What is it you people want from me?" said Brett. "Not that I'm committing myself to anything, you understand. I'm just . . . listening."

Leslie shrugged. "Information, to begin with. Mostly concerning the Deathstalker and Flowers. When they're at their weakest, and most off guard."

"What about John Silence?" Rose said suddenly, and both men jumped a little. "He is a legend."

"Is he hell?" said Leslie, curling his lip. "He's just an old merchant trader with delusions of grandeur. Playing Santa Claus at the Coronation wasn't enough for Samuel Chevron, oh no, he has to be John bloody Silence. You'll notice he was careful not to go down to Mistworld or Virimonde, where they knew the man, and could have unmasked an impostor. No, the original John Silence was a good military man, and unwaveringly loyal to the throne."

"Fifteen million credits apiece," said Brett. "I have to say . . . I am tempted. What do you think, Rose?"

"You will decide for both of us, Brett, as you always do. I have never cared for which side I'm on, as long as I get to kill a whole bunch of people."

"Predictable," said Brett. "But still upsetting."

"Besides," Rose said thoughtfully. "I've always wanted to know whether I could take the Deathstalker."

"Join us," said Leslie. "Soon there will be an uprising on every star-cruiser in the fleet. Loyal crewmembers will position themselves to strike down every officer who is not with us, and replace them with our own people. Then we shall take control of the fleet, and put to death all disloyal elements."

"Just like that," said Brett, not even trying to keep the disbelief from his voice.

"No. We know it will be a hard and vicious struggle. But there are more of us than you think, and we have God and the Emperor on our side."

"Rose and I need to talk about this for a moment," said Brett, and Leslie politely stepped back a way so Brett and Rose could have some privacy. Brett scowled. "I always did think the fleet surrendered to Owen too easily. If there really are as many fanatics as this guy makes out, they could just pull this off. The Deathstalker's a hell of a fighter, but even he couldn't take on the fleet by himself. And those rag bag ships from Mistworld and Virimonde wouldn't stand a chance either. The rebellion could be over before it even got started . . . suddenly I haven't got a clue what to do for the best. This is why I hate being on a starship! There's nowhere to run! Why did they have to give me a choice over which side to be on? Finn's a bastard and a monster, but I'm damned if I'm going to be on the losing side . . . Would he really take us back? He might; all he ever cared about was winning. Oh, God, my stomach hurts. It never bothered me when I was with Lewis. I think some of his moral certainties rubbed off on me."

"Can we trust Finn to keep his word afterwards?" said Rose, as always getting to the heart of the question. "Can we trust him about the reward, and our safety?"

"Probably not. Unless . . . we can negotiate from a position of strength. Stay well out of his reach at all times, and then use the reward money to disappear among the border worlds . . ."

"Is that what you want to do?"

"Well, not *want* exactly. Finn's an evil piece of shit, and strange with it, but he could win this war. And I have no intention of dying gloriously for a lost cause, no matter who my ancestor was. But on the other hand . . . I like Lewis. Even admire him, I suppose. He's a genuine hero, the real deal, just like my ancestors, Jack Random and Ruby Journey. It feels . . . *right*, being at a Deathstalker's side. If only he didn't keep dragging me into danger all the time."

"But that's what heroes do," said Rose.

"I know! I know. I admire Lewis, I really do, but . . . I can't decide right now. I need to know more. Follow my lead, Rose."

"Don't I always?"

They went over to join Leslie Springfield, who raised a polite eyebrow. Brett nodded jerkily. "Lead the way. I'm not promising anything, mind; but I'll listen."

"Once you know the truth, of who and what we are, you know we can't just let you walk away," said Leslie.

"I know how the game is played," said Brett. "Lead on. I want to know everything."

And he only had to push Leslie Springfield with just the lightest touch of his Maze-backed compulsion.

They ended up in a deserted weapons bay, where a large crowd of loyalists had gathered together to meet Brett. He tried to do a surreptitious head count, but there were too many of them. And every single one of them studied Brett coldly as he entered. He gave them his most professional trustworthy smile, and allowed Leslie to lead him and Rose to the guest seats of honor. Someone presented Brett with a glass of surprisingly good wine, and someone else offered him a cigar, which Brett took because he always took anything that was offered for free. He sat down, and Rose took up a position standing beside him, her hands resting on her weapons belt. Everyone was very polite to her. Various people took it in turns to present Brett with loyalist propaganda and harsher Pure Humanity and Church Militant beliefs, and he smiled and nodded in all the right places. The general pattern of the planned uprising was explained to him, but not the details. That would only come later, once he'd committed himself to the cause. Brett drank his wine and smoked his cigar, and listened carefully to everything that was said to him. His stomach ached, but he kept it out of his face. Finally, they ran out of things to say to him, and Brett looked out on a crowd of intent faces. Rose was a comforting presence at his side, but Brett really didn't like the odds. So when he was asked, politely but very pointedly, whether he was in or out, Brett nodded decisively and said *I'm in.*

There was a general murmur of relief, and the crowd relaxed a little. Several people wanted to shake Brett by the hand, and he let them. No one wanted to shake Rose's hand. Leslie came forward, and smiled meaningfully at Brett.

"We're delighted to have you and Rose aboard, of course, but you do understand that we need you to prove your commitment to the cause?"

"I thought that might be coming," said Brett. "What exactly did you have in mind?"

The crowd parted as several marines brought forward a man, bound and gagged. They forced the man onto his knees before Brett, and his eyes looked pleadingly at Brett.

"This fool thought he could be a spy among us, and report back to the false Silence," said Leslie. "Kill him."

And Brett knew that even hesitation would damn him. "Of course," he said. "Rose, do the honors, if you would."

Rose smiled happily, and everyone near her shied away. She stepped forward, grabbed the prisoner's head with both hands, and ripped it away with one savage movement. The body toppled backward, fountaining and spraying blood everywhere. The crowd around him fell back, uttering shocked cries. There were even more cries of shock and distress as Rose kissed the severed head on the lips and then casually threw it away. She bent over the headless body, plunged her hand into its back, pulled out the still pulsing heart, and started to eat it. Several people vomited noisily, and a hell of a lot more looked like they wanted to.

"Nicely done," said Brett, in a very nearly normal voice. "But do remember to brush your teeth with especial vigor tonight. Anything else we can do for you, Leslie?"

"No . . . not for the moment," said Leslie, perhaps not as strongly as he would have liked. "We've set up a secure channel, so that you can talk to us freely at any time, without it showing up on the comm officer's instruments. We can also arrange ship-to-ship communications, as necessary. But now, we have someone special who wants to welcome you to the cause."

A viewscreen flared into life on the wall beside them, and Brett's heart jumped painfully in his chest as the classically handsome features of the Emperor, Finn Durandal, appeared on the screen, smiling warmly.

"Ah, my dear Brett," said the Emperor. "So good to see you safe and sound, after so many adventures. Come home, dear boy, and all shall be forgiven. We'll be together again, just like the old times. Won't that be fun? You know we belong together. We are the same kind, we see the world in the same way. Why did you leave me, Brett?"

"Because . . . I thought I saw better opportunities," said Brett.

"Ah. I should have known. Return to me, and you shall never have to want for money again. I shall deny you nothing. And . . . do bear in mind how easy it was for me to find you, and arrange this little chat. My people are everywhere, loyal unto death and beyond. Say that you'll be mine again, dear Brett."

"Why not?" said Brett. "After all I've been through with Lewis, after all I've done for him, I'm still not one penny richer than when I started."

"Am I welcome too?" said Rose.

"Why, of course, dear Rose," said Finn. "I have missed your blessed madness most of all."

"Will I get to kill lots of people?"

"Lots and lots," said Finn.

"Good to be back," said Rose.

Admiral John Silence sat straight-backed in his command chair on the bridge of the *Havoc*. It felt good to be back in the military. To be involved, to be hands-on, instead of pulling strings from the shadows as Samuel Chevron. He'd never felt entirely comfortable in his role as Humanity's secret protector. He'd always been happier when things were out in the open. He could do subtlety, but it didn't come naturally to him. And he enjoyed the open respect he got from the crew of the *Havoc*. He might not be as much of a legend as the blessed Owen, but he was one of them; a military legend. Which was why they had preferred to be led by him, rather than by the ex-Champion with the legendary name.

Silence turned to his comm officer. "Check the formation of the fleet. Make sure that all of the Mistworld and Virimonde ships are keeping up and holding their positions."

"Yes, Admiral."

Silence didn't really need to be told. He always knew when some of his ships were going astray. His two times in the Madness Maze had changed him, enlarged him, if not so ostentatiously as Owen and the others. The layout of his fleet was as familiar to him as his own body. He also knew that there were disloyal elements among his crews. Knew it even before the loyalist graffiti began appearing down below. He had security people looking into the problem, but he doubted it would come to anything. If the loyalists were a real problem, he would have known by now. Silence knew all kinds of things, except how to be the legend that everyone else needed him to be. He was a soldier, and that was all that ever really mattered to him. But he'd already noticed some of his crew studying him covertly, hoping for miracles, and interpreting even his most innocent remarks as signs or prophecies. It was to avoid just such nonsense that he'd faked his death over a hundred years ago.

Captain Price kept wanting to hover at his side, but Silence kept him busy with other duties. Partly because he needed someone willing to deal with all the scutwork that Silence couldn't be bothered with, like seeing all the loyalist graffiti was cleaned off the down-below walls, but mostly because Captain Price got on Silence's nerves. He was just too amiable, too obliging, always too ready and eager to serve. Silence knew his sort. They'd been rife in Lionstone's day. Political soldiers, ready to bow with every breeze, and side with whoever looked most like the winning team. Such men were to be made use of, but never trusted.

And besides, there had only ever been room for one person at Silence's side. Ever since he'd taken his place in the command chair on the bridge of the *Havoc*, Silence had seemed to feel Investigator Frost standing beside him, as she always had. Silence didn't believe in ghosts, but sometimes the sense of her presence was so real, so overwhelming, he felt he could just reach out and touch her. It had been over two hundred years since Frost had died in his arms, in Lionstone's terrible Court, cut down by Kit SummerIsle, the infamous Kid Death. She had bled to death in his arms, and there had been nothing he could do, nothing at all.

I wanted to die, Captain. Surely you knew that? Her calm dry voice was perfectly clear.

Hush, Investigator. I've got enough problems without the dead popping round for a chat.

Don't flatter yourself, Captain. I'm here because you need me, just as you always did. Never could resist backing the long odds, could you? It's a wonder to me you've lasted as long as you have. Haven't you fought enough battles, old man?

I belong here, Silence thought stubbornly. *I was always at my best with a starship under my command.*

Still looking for a good death, Captain? For a cause worth dying for?

Maybe, Investigator. He looked around, carefully casual, but of course she wasn't there. Silence felt himself shrink a little, in his chair. Not a legend, not even a hero. Just an old, tired man, hearing voices. *Owen, you brought the Ashrai back from extinction, and revitalized their world. You gave new life to the Recreated and all their worlds. Why didn't you bring back the only woman I ever really loved? I never thought to ask, and by the time I did it was too late. You were gone. Everyone lost someone in the Rebellion; I know that. But I gave so much; couldn't I have had just one small thing for myself?*

There was never anyone else in his long life, after Frost. Not because he'd sworn a vow, or anything like that; but because he'd never felt the same way about anyone else. There'd never been anyone like the tall, unbending, magnificent Investigator Frost. They'd made an excellent partnership in their time, achieved many great things, and more than a few ignoble ones. Life had been like that, under Lionstone XIV. He'd never told Frost how he felt about her. She was an Investigator, and all such emotions were alien to her. Probably.

And then, it had been so hard to stay young, while everyone else grew old around him. All his old friends died, and he never seemed to have much in common with the new people springing up around him. Even his daughter died. Diana Vertue, also known as Jenny Psycho. They'd never been . . . close, but he still missed her. He had seen the birth and flowering of a Golden Age, and had found pride in being Humanity's secret guardian. Always believing he might be needed again, always hoping he was wrong. And now here he was, a soldier again and heading into battle, knowing that the only sure thing in this new rebellion was that good men and women were bound to die, on both sides.

Diana Vertue, much to his surprise, had been reported back from the dead and extremely active on Logres. Reborn from the collective consciousness of the oversoul, at long last. Silence wasn't sure how he felt about that. He'd known, the moment she reappeared in the material world; like a light suddenly going on in the dark. According to the latest reports, she'd joined up with Douglas Campbell in the Rookery. Typical of his daughter; always had to be right in the middle of things, doing her best in destructive ways. He could have talked to her mentally, but even after all these years they were still awkward with each other. Too much pain and blame between them, too many bad memories. It was enough for him to know that she was back, and doing the right thing in her own appalling ways. He'd talk to her again after they'd taken Logres back from Finn. By then, they should have something in common to talk about.

He could have talked to her while she was still a part of the oversoul mass-mind, but he never had. It would have felt too much like talking to a ghost.

Thoughts of the past turned his mind in a new direction. He'd already tried several times to contact his old friend Carrion, on the planet Unseeli, but there was never any response, on any comm channel. Silence was pretty sure Carrion could hear him; he was just being stubborn. The last time they'd met, Carrion had declared himself utterly divorced from Humanity, and entirely content with his new alien Ashrai form. Silence hadn't been particularly surprised by the transition. Carrion had always had an Ashrai soul, even when he was still a man called Sean. That's how they'd ended up on different sides of a war. But Silence decided his need to talk was more important than Carrion's need to show off his independence, so he reached out with his Maze-enhanced mind, and his thoughts flew across all the many light years to the planet Unseeli.

Silence had been through the Madness Maze twice. He could have been as great as the others; but he thought it was more important to be human.

Come on, Sean, stop being obstinate and talk to me, or I'll slap you a good one.

The craggy gargoyle face of an Ashrai appeared suddenly on the main bridge viewscreen, startling the hell out of everyone. Especially the comm officer, who knew for a fact that the signal wasn't coming in through any of his channels. Several of the bridge crew looked like they wanted to run and hide, but they looked to Silence, and were reassured by his calm manner. The gunnery officer was surreptitiously looking for a target outside the ship, and was getting really upset as she discovered there was nothing at all out there. The Ashrai glowered at Silence.

"Hello, John. I just knew you'd be back to bother me. Your thoughts feel . . . different. But then, we've both been through a lot of changes. I'm just more open about mine. What do you want, John?"

"Hello, Sean. Old friend, old enemy. Is there a name for our relationship? Who else could we talk to, about all the things we've been through? Who else would understand?"

"Get to the point, old man."

"I'm in charge of a whole fleet, Sean, and I'm heading back to Logres to ram it down the Emperor's throat. I thought you and your people might like to tag along."

"The Ashrai want nothing to do with Humanity. They have not forgotten how you gave the order to make them extinct, all those years ago."

"Oh, come on, think how good it would feel to stick it to the Empire homeworld, after all these years."

"There is that," said Carrion. "Truth be told, I've been waiting for your call. Now that Owen is back . . . it's time for everything to change, again. We all owe him so much."

"And perhaps a favor for an old friend?"

"Yes, John," the Ashrai said kindly. "Perhaps."

"That's what I wanted to hear," said Silence. "I'll detail some ships to come and pick you up."

Carrion laughed harshly, a dark disturbing sound that showed off all his pointed teeth. "That won't be necessary. We'll make our own way to you. The Ashrai don't need ships to fly through space."

Silence had to smile. "How did we ever defeat you, before?"

"Easy, Captain. You cheated."

Silence studied the gargoyle face thoughtfully. "Do I have your word that you'll keep the Ashrai under control, when we get to Logres?"

"Of course, John. Don't you trust me?"

"Now that's a bloody silly question."

They laughed together, and the sound of their laughter had a lot in common.

Captain Price was mooching about in the lower decks of the *Havoc*. He was especially interested in trapping or turning in any of his crew who hadn't been as ready to change sides as he was, but really since the admiral had made it very clear that he wasn't welcome on the bridge, Price was just killing time until it came time to do some real work. He studied the latest batch of loyalist graffiti on the steel walls, and couldn't resist a sneer. It was a bit late to be falling back on Church Militant cant. Anyone with half the brains he was born with could see which way the wind was blowing. The blessed Owen was back, in all his glory. What could petty politics matter, in the face of that? And there was no denying that Price had burned his bridges very thoroughly, when he shot the previous admiral in the back of the head. She'd been one of Finn's political appointees, and barking mad with it, and absolutely no one had been sorry to see the back of her.

With Admiral Silence all but living in the command seat, Price had busied himself by keeping track of what was happening back on Logres. He and the comm officer, Charlton Vu, had rigged up a very secure link between the *Havoc* and one of the new rogue news sites now operating from the Rookery. Their editorial policy seemed to be, get the story out as fast as possible, and to hell with whoever it upsets. Price had actually talked to the main face of one news site, a charming if somewhat startling young lady called Nina Malapert, and in return for firsthand reports of the return of Owen (*An exclusive!* Nina said, loudly enough to make Price wince), she kept him up to date on the growing rebellion on Logres. She'd even promised to arrange a direct line with King Douglas. Price couldn't resist a small smile. That should put him in good with Silence. Price was

pretty sure the comm channel hadn't been cracked by Finn's security people, because it was derived from alien tech, donated by the alien presence
in the Rookery.

Price hadn't even known there was an alien presence in the Rookery.
You learned something new every day.

(And of course, if things did start going really badly for the rebel fleet,
Price could always hand this information over to the Emperor's people, as
proof that he'd been working as a double agent all along. Price believed in
thinking ahead, and covering his back.)

He wandered around the lower decks for a while, but no one wanted
to talk to him, and he was actually quite relieved when word came through
that Lewis Deathstalker and Jesamine Flowers had finally returned from
Virimonde. Price ran all the way to the designated docking bay, to be sure
he'd be the first officer to greet them when they returned. People remembered things like that. They were both clearly physically and emotionally
exhausted, and all they really wanted to do was get back to their quarters
and collapse, but they politely made a little time for Price.

"I have news of King Douglas, and the fight for freedom in the Parade
of the Endless," Captain Price said grandly, and was quietly satisfied at
how quickly that grabbed their interest. "I have established a very secure
comm link with rebel forces in the Rookery. There is a young lady working a rogue news site there who can give you all the details, if you would
like me to arrange something . . ."

"Show us," said the Deathstalker, and there was something in his voice
that made Price forget the rest of his speech and jump to obey. He
patched his prearranged link into the viewscreen on the wall, and after
being carefully rerouted through several masking connections and cutouts,
Nina Malapert's face appeared on the screen. She saw Lewis and Jesamine
staring back at her, and whooped loudly with joy, bobbing excitedly up
and down in her chair while her tall pink mohawk flopped crazily from
side to side.

"The Deathstalker and the diva! *Major* exclusive! Oh, all the other sites
are going to be so sick!"

"If we could just keep the celebrations to a minimum," said Price,
making sure he could be seen standing right next to the Deathstalker, "I

don't think we should test the security of this link with a conversation one minute longer than absolutely necessary."

"Yes," said Lewis. "Talk to me, Nina Malapert. What has happened to the city, since my enforced absence? What has happened to Douglas?"

"And Anne Barclay," said Jesamine.

Nina's face fell. "You haven't heard. I'm sorry. Anne Barclay is dead. Killed by falling masonry when Douglas busted out of his show trial and escaped. He was ever so upset about it. But the good news is that Douglas has made himself the leader of all rebel activity in the Rookery, and absolutely everyone is with him! He's so inspiring. All the rogues, con men, fighters, and criminals have combined into one great army, under his command. They're calling Douglas the King of Thieves these days, which is just so romantic! Did you want to speak to him? I'm sure I could set up something really quite quickly."

Lewis and Jesamine looked at each other for a long moment. "Not just yet," said Jesamine.

"I don't think any of us would know what to say," said Lewis. "It's enough that we're allies, for the moment."

"Yes," said Jesamine. "Just tell him . . . we'll talk again, when we all meet in the Imperial Palace, on Logres."

Back in their private quarters, Lewis and Jesamine sat in silence for a long while. They kept a cautious distance between them, separated by old memories and old hurts. The prospect of actually talking to Douglas had opened up feelings they'd been too busy to examine or even acknowledge, for far too long. Once upon a time there had been four good friends, Douglas and Lewis, Jesamine and Anne, bonded together by love and loyalty, determined to change the world for the better. But instead the world had changed them, shattering their fellowship; and now one of them was dead, and things would never be the same again.

"I can't believe Anne is gone," Jesamine said finally. "She was always the great survivor. I thought she'd outlast all of us."

"I still can't believe she let Finn get to her," said Lewis. "She was the smartest of all of us; if anyone should have seen through Finn, it should have been her. Why did she turn on us? We all did everything we could for her . . . and she betrayed each of us, in turn. There are even rumors surfacing that she had something to do with Emma Steel's death."

"Perhaps . . . Finn listened to her," said Jesamine. "And perhaps we didn't listen enough. There were hints, towards the end, that she wasn't happy, and hadn't been for some time. That maybe we never understood her half as well as we thought we did."

"Anne and I were kids together on Virimonde," said Lewis. "We did everything together. I thought we'd be friends till the day we died. We would have fought for each other, died for each other; and then . . . something changed. Perhaps we grew up. Grew apart. I always believed that when I finally got back to Logres, and overthrew Finn, I'd be able to talk her round. Bring her back to sense and sanity. Apologize for whatever it was I did wrong that drove her away from me. And now I never will."

"She was the best friend and manager I ever had," said Jesamine. "But she always made her own choices, and insisted on going her own way. Even when everyone who cared about her could see it was the wrong way. You know, she's the first person close to me that I've lost in this war. I feel . . . cold."

"I lost my mother and my father, my Family and my home," said Lewis. "That's the nature of war: to lose all the things you care for most."

"We still have each other," said Jesamine, looking at him for the first time.

"Yes," said Lewis. He smiled at her, but secretly he was thinking *Deathstalker luck. Always bad.*

"When we get back," said Jesamine, tentatively. "When we're back on Logres, and it's all over . . . what are we going to do, Lewis? About Douglas, about us?"

"He was always my closest friend," said Lewis.

"He was my fiancé."

"But did you ever really love him?"

"I never meant to hurt him," said Jesamine. "He was a good man, a fine man. He deserved better than what we did to him."

"I always believed I would tear my own heart out, rather than see Douglas hurt," said Lewis. "As his Champion, I vowed to stand between him and all harm. He was my friend, closer than a brother. And I hurt him like no one else could."

"The things we do for love," Jesamine said tiredly. "How can something so good cause so much pain?"

"Ah, hell," Lewis said, stretching slowly. "It seems like another life now. We were all different people then. If we do survive this war, all three of us . . . we still couldn't go back to our old lives, our old roles. We'd find them too restricting, too limited."

"Now there's a frightening thought," said Jesamine. "After all we've been through, I'm still me; aren't I? I still feel like me. And yet . . . I can feel the changes the Maze made in me still working. Both of us are already much more than we used to be. When does the process stop? Does it ever stop? Are we going to end up Terrors, like Hazel? I don't want to be a monster, Lewis! I don't want to stop being me!"

Her voice rose, growing harsh and frightened. Lewis was quickly at her side, holding her in his arms. "Hush, hush, love. We're not going to end up like Hazel. She was left alone, and half crazy. We have each other."

"But what if we lose each other, Lewis? What if one of us dies in this war, and one of us is left alone, and half crazy? What then?"

"You're being far too optimistic," Lewis said dryly. "The odds are that all of us will be killed in the rebellion, and then we'll never have to worry about any of this."

"Oh, ho ho ho," said Jesamine. "Deathstalker humor."

Not all that far away, as hyperspatial travel went, the Emperor Finn's fleet was approaching the estimated position of the rebel fleet. The Imperial fleet was huge, made up of every fighting ship Finn could spare, all crewed by experienced fleet officers, backed up by hard-core Pure Humanity and Church Militant fanatics. Finn would have liked more of his own people in charge, but this battle was too important to be trusted to the loyal but limited zealots he'd used to infiltrate the fleet command structure. The Imperial fleet's orders were very simple. Stop the rebel fleet before it got anywhere near Logres, at whatever cost, and crush the rebellion before it got properly under way. No surrender, no prisoners, no quarter. Just dead ships, blazing and tumbling in the long night, and a victory so terrible it would crush the spirits of anyone who even thought of standing against the Emperor Finn.

The rebel fleet had been easy enough to locate. Finn knew Lewis would go home to Virimonde; he'd always been the sentimental sort. And so the Imperial fleet sat and waited, hidden in hyperspace behind state-of-the-art stealth screens, until the signal stopped coming from the transmutation engines around Virimonde. Now the huge army of Imperial starcruisers were moving in on their unsuspecting victims, and readying themselves for battle. The captains were resolute, the crews highly trained and motivated. Finn had put together the biggest concentration of firepower since Lionstone's time.

All the ships maintained strict comm silence. Ostensibly to maintain the element of surprise, and to prevent rebel spies from passing intelligence, but mainly so that the Imperial crews wouldn't be exposed to details of Owen Deathstalker's miraculous return. There were rumors of course, you couldn't stop rumors, but Finn wasn't taking any chances. The captains could talk to each other on a heavily protected channel, but that was all. That was enough.

The *Heritage*, still recovering from her encounter with the Terror at Usher II, was now a part of the Imperial fleet. Both ship and crew were in urgent need of some down time and repair, but . . . duty called. Captain Ariadne Vardalos sat wearily in her command chair, studying the makeup of the Imperial fleet on her viewscreen. As one of the last ships to join the fleet, she had a lot of catching up to do. She wasn't all that pleased with what she saw. The layout had a distinct air of improvisation. But then, it had been a long long time since anyone had fought a major space battle. She switched to a representation of the rebel fleet's structure, according to the most recent information, and shook her head slowly.

"I know most of those ships," she said to her second-in-command, Marcella Fortuna. "I was at the academy with some of their captains! How could so many good people have turned traitor?"

Fortuna shrugged uncomfortably. "Hard to say, Captain. No one ever considers themselves a traitor. We're all the heroes of our own stories." She considered the matter for a while, turning it over in her slow, methodical mind. "Must be something to do with Owen's return. If that was a Shub trick, as the Emperor insists, maybe the AIs brainwashed all those people."

Captain Vardalos scowled. "I know these people . . . If I could just talk to them, I know I could talk them out of this. Make them see how wrong they are. But we're forbidden to make contact." She could feel her hands clenching into impotent fists, and made herself relax. A captain couldn't afford to appear unsettled or uncertain before her crew. Especially just before a major engagement with the enemy.

"Any point in talking to the admiral again?" said Fortuna.

"No," Vardalos said reluctantly. "Admiral Shapiro is old school, strictly by the book. He'd shoot his own family if the Emperor ordered it. He wouldn't even question an order, never mind consider bending one."

"The rebel fleet would appear to be a lot bigger than we were led to believe," Fortuna observed. "Though far be it for me to suggest that our intelligence is anything less than perfect."

"Oh, heaven forfend," said Vardalos. "And just look at all those craft from Virimonde and Mistworld. I don't even recognize half of them. God alone knows what they'll be capable of in a fight. Or what nasty surprises they might have in store for us. Let us all pray very fervently that our stealth fields continue to hide us until the very last second before we attack. Because we're going to need every advantage we can get. "

"We have to stop the rebel fleet, Captain," said Fortuna. "And as quickly as possible. The Empire can't afford to be distracted, with the Terror still on its way."

"I know that! Why don't they know that? A civil war is madness, under current conditions!"

"Under any conditions," murmured Fortuna, with a significant look.

"Of course," said Vardalos. You never knew who might be listening, these days. And making notes.

"Almost makes you wish Owen was back, so he could deal with the Terror," said Fortuna.

"Don't even go there," said Vardalos. "Matters are complicated enough as they are."

"But what if . . . what if this battle wipes out both fleets, Captain?" Fortuna said suddenly. "What if there is no winner? Who then will protect homeworld? From aliens, and rebels, and the coming of the Terror?"

"That's why we have to win," said Vardalos. "Damn those rebel bastards, for putting us in this position! The rebellion must be put down. For the sake of all Humanity."

Admiral Silence knew the Imperial fleet was on its way. Their stealth fields couldn't hide them from his Maze-enhanced mind. Dead reckoning and a certain amount of creative thinking gave him a pretty good idea of where the other fleet was, and its composition. He'd shared this knowledge with the rest of his fleet, and was a little dismayed at how quickly they all accepted his word. This legend of his was definitely getting out of control. He had his comm officer send out messages of friendship and offers for truce on all channels, but no one answered. Not even when Silence spoke to them personally, trying to trade on the power of his legend.

"They must be listening," he said finally, giving up. "Why don't they believe me?"

"It is rather a lot to ask of them, Admiral," said Captain Price, who had somehow found a reason to return to the bridge. "Couldn't you . . . show them that it's really you? Perform some wonder to prove you really are who you say you are?"

"I don't do wonders," said Silence. "What do you want me to do? Stroll across the open space between us and hammer on their door, demanding to be let in? Actually, Carrion probably could have done that. And Owen . . . but I'm just me, and I've been a man too long to give up its comforts. Still, the Imperial ships are definitely out there. I can *feel* them . . . some of my old abilities are beginning to surface again. I just know I could stop all this insanity, if I could only talk to them! We're all navy men. We understand about the madness of politicians. But it seems . . . there's no way out. Good men and women are going to die today, on both sides. God damn you to Hell, Finn Durandal."

Price cleared his throat uncertainly. "If you can *feel* the presence of the Imperial fleet, Admiral, perhaps you could work with the ship's AI to plot out best guess estimates for enemy ship positions and capabilities?"

"Not a bad idea, Captain. Ozymandius! Talk to me."

They waited, but there was no response. Silence called again, but the usually chatty AI was silent. With growing alarm, Silence discovered that the ship's AI wouldn't respond to any form of communication, on any level. Basic computer services continued to take care of vital work like life support, artificial gravity and the engines, but all higher intelligence functions were gone. The machines still worked, but no one was home. Silence told his comm officer to check all the other ships in the rebel fleet, and sat scowling in his command chair as the answers came flooding back. There wasn't a starcruiser in his fleet with a working AI.

"Could it be sabotage?" said Price. "Or some new weapon that Finn's turned up?"

"No," Silence said slowly. "I think it's simpler than that. I think . . . something's happened to Shub. Every ship's AI is a subroutine of the AIs of Shub. It's been that way for so long that we just take it for granted."

"But what could have happened to them?"

"I don't know, Captain. But the odds are this is happening in the Imperial fleet too, so we're equally disadvantaged. I wonder if they've noticed yet. Price, get those backup systems on line, fast. We can't afford to be caught short when the battle starts."

"Of course, Admiral." Price hesitated. "Even with all backup systems operating at full capacity, our options will remain distinctly limited. We'll be going into action crippled."

"So will they, Captain. Serves us all right for growing too reliant on Shub. Take the command chair for a while, Price. I need to discuss this with the Deathstalker."

Silence explained the situation to Lewis and Jesamine, striding restlessly up and down their quarters. Lewis tried calling out to Oz through his mental link, but there was no reply. Silence finally ground to a halt, and looked hopefully at Lewis and Jesamine.

"Sorry, Admiral, this is all news to us," said Jesamine. "Why would Shub abandon us?"

"Could something have happened to them?" said Silence. "If Finn launched an attack on their homeworld, could they be dead?"

"If Finn had ships that powerful, he'd have sent them after us," said Lewis. "No; the AIs must have gone into the Madness Maze. I knew we should never have left them there alone. All they've ever cared about is transcendence. It must have proved too great a temptation."

"It's not just the fleet's AIs," said Silence. "We've been picking up reports from all over the Empire. Everything that Shub had a hand in has stopped working, from air traffic control down to sewer maintenance robots. It's chaos on every industrialized world."

"Presumably everything will start working again when they come out," said Lewis.

"Not necessarily," said Silence. "It depends *what* comes out of the Maze. Who knows what they'll evolve into?"

"Could the Maze have destroyed them?" said Jesamine. "Or driven them crazy again?"

"No way of knowing," said Lewis. "The Maze does what it does, and we never know why. But we can't allow ourselves to be distracted. We have a battle to fight."

"Where are your appalling friends?" Silence said suddenly. "The con man and the psycho? No one seems to have seen or heard of them in ages."

"Probably trying to break into the med dispensers again," said Jesamine. "Brett always gets a little nervous before . . . well, anything, really. No doubt he and Rose will turn up once the action starts. If only because they hate to miss out on anything."

"The powers and abilities I got from the Madness Maze were always limited," Silence said slowly. "Even at my peak, which was a long time ago. You see, I never made it all the way through the Maze to its center, even though I went in twice. The heart of the Maze has always been reserved for Deathstalkers. Do you have any powers, Lewis, any special abilities you could use against the Imperial fleet?"

"I'm still learning what my abilities are," Lewis said carefully. "And I can't talk about what I found at the heart of the Maze. It's not my secret to tell. But I don't see what use our kind of powers would be in a space battle anyway."

Silence sighed, and sat down on the edge of the unmade bed. He looked suddenly older, and very tired. "I've been teaching my captains what tactics I can. I was shocked by how much had been forgotten. It's been so long since the navy faced a serious threat that they've got rusty. They don't even run full-scale battle maneuvers anymore. No starcruiser's fired on another in two hundred years. The only good news is that Finn's captains will be just as rusty as ours."

"Let's just hope our captains are faster learners," said Lewis.

Finn's loyalists were meeting down by the *Havoc's* engine bays. Apparently the strange radiations sleeting continuously from the ship's stardrive made any kind of tech eavesdropping impossible. Brett was there, very much against his better instincts, and hoped they were right. There was no way he'd ever be able to talk his way out of this. He tried to stick to the middle of the crowd, putting as many people as possible between him and the engines. He'd heard about stardrive radiation, and had horrible visions of all his extremities rotting and dropping off in the night. Leslie Springfield was right out there in front, of course, haranguing the gathered faithful. They were responding well, cheering his every inflammatory statement. Brett checked that Rose was behaving herself, standing bored but patient at his side, and then looked inconspicuously about him. There were a lot of people here. Far more than he'd suspected. Hundreds of men and women, from all ranks and stations. The *Havoc* had a real problem on its hands, and quite possibly the other starcruisers too. A few faces looked back at him suspiciously. Brett gave them his best reassuring smile, and made himself concentrate on what Leslie was saying.

It seemed that the Owen that had appeared to the fleet off Haden had been nothing more than a trick, just a Shub illusion, intended to distract everyone from their seizing control of the Madness Maze. The AIs were trying to steal Humanity's rightful chance for transcendence. The AIs wouldn't be able to transcend, of course, only humans could do that, but once they'd failed the AIs might decide to destroy the Maze, on the grounds that if they couldn't transcend, Humanity shouldn't be allowed to either. The crowd responded angrily. They understood that kind of thinking. It was what they would have done. Leslie went on, speaking persuasively. It was vital, he said, that the forthcoming clash between the two fleets should be decided as quickly as possible, so that the victors could return to Haden and rescue the Madness Maze from the treacherous AIs.

The crowd cheered and roared, and Leslie let them. Brett didn't know what to believe. He'd heard about the starcruisers' AIs all going off-line simultaneously. That had to mean *something*. He realized Leslie was speaking again, and paid attention. He was explaining that he'd spoken personally with the Emperor Finn, who had authorized and ordered a night of the long knives on every starcruiser in the rebel fleet. Any officer not known to be loyal to the Emperor was to be killed, struck down without warning, all in the one night; and then replaced by loyalists. It would be a coup, a sudden transition of power, and the battle would be stopped before it had even begun. It was much better than a general uprising; this way only the traitors would have to die, with no need for more casualties.

Brett found himself nodding. This had all been very carefully thought out. It could work. Certainly the crowd was eating it all up with spoons, actually straining at the leash to get their hands on officers they despised. Brett had been worried that Leslie might call on him to use his powers of persuasion and compulsion, to sway the minds of the doubtful, but to his great relief it seemed he might not be needed after all. He'd only just started to relax when he discovered that Leslie had stopped talking, and everyone was staring at him.

Oh shit. What did I just miss? Where's the nearest exit?

"Brett Random and Rose Constantine," said Leslie, smiling down on them. "To you is given the most honorable and most dangerous assignment. It will be your responsibility to kill the traitor Deathstalker and his slut. You are the only ones who can get close enough, and the only ones powerful enough to remove these two obstacles to our glorious triumph. They must be removed, or all our plans will come to nothing. Do you forsee any problems with carrying out this mission, Brett?"

"Problems? Me?" said Brett, trying hard to sound confident and devil-may-care. "No. No problems."

"It's about time," said Rose, almost languidly. "I need to go one-on-one with the Deathstalker. Find out once and for all which of us is the better fighter. And now we've both been through the Maze, it should be an especially . . . intense match. I can almost taste the blood. God, it makes me feel so hot . . ."

People around her were backing away. Brett felt like joining them.

"You will be well rewarded afterwards," said Leslie, just a little hoarsely, as he tried to get things back on line again. "You will be honored heroes of the new order, and decorated by the Emperor himself."

"So?" said Rose.

"What about John Silence?" Brett said quickly. People in the crowd murmured the ancient, legendary name.

"We will deal with the *admiral*," said Leslie. "He claims to be navy, one of us, but he is not. Just a jumped-up merchant trader, tarnishing a legend."

"He does seem to have . . . powers," Brett pointed out diffidently.

"Then we will drag him down, drive a stake through his heart, burn the body, and scatter the ashes to space," said Leslie. "We are the faithful, and our faith will sustain us."

Rather you than me, thought Brett, but had enough sense not to say it. "When does the uprising start, Leslie?"

"It has already started," Leslie said, smiling at Brett's reaction. "Our people in the comm section have already taken control, spreading the word through the ships in the fleet. The Mistworld and Virimonde trash are cut off from the starcruisers. By the time they figure out what's happening, it will be far too late. And we will deal with those traitors at our leisure. For now the killing has begun. The culling of the ungodly. Let us go forth and join them. Blood shall flow, bodies shall fall, and Pure Humanity and the Church Militant shall triumph at last!"

Oh, shit, thought Brett, as the crowd erupted into cheers. *What do I do now?*

Returned to the bridge of the *Havoc*, Silence realized almost immediately that something was wrong when the comm officer reported that all the usual ship-to-ship chatter had suddenly ceased. Silence tried to raise the *Havoc*'s comm center, and couldn't. Even interior communications were down. Silence sent runners out to discover what the hell was going on, and alert his security people. Something bad was happening aboard his ship. He could feel it. Reports began coming in slowly, of widespread acts of sabotage, of officers found murdered at their posts, of fighting in the steel corridors. The ship's Armory had been broken into, and all kinds of weapons seized. If Silence hadn't acted immediately on his instincts, most of his people would have had no warning at all.

His first thought was that somehow the *Havoc* had been boarded, by Imperial agents from the opposite fleet, but not even the smallest attack craft could have sneaked up on Silence's ship without him knowing. The comm officer managed to get the security cameras back on line, and soon they were watching fierce fighting raging back and forth in all parts of the ship. Many of the attackers wore Pure Humanity and Church Militant sashes, and shouted out their cold and vicious slogans as they fought, shooting at anyone who wasn't them. Silence cursed himself. He'd thought allowing the graffiti and loud talk would act as a safety valve, letting the frustrations out before they could build. But it seemed he'd seriously underestimated the problem.

He sent out repair techs to deal with the sabotage, backed up by armed security men. The ship had to be protected first. Silence reached out with his mind. The Imperial fleet was getting really close now. He had to put down the loyalist rebellion before Finn's ships got within firing range. He watched his screens helplessly as friends and fellow workers turned on each other, with guns or knives or whatever came to hand. Great acts of heroism and treachery were performed in the gleaming steel corridors, and the blood flowed thickly. There were bodies everywhere. The fighting was fierce and brutal. Faith in the Church Militant fueled one side, and faith in the blessed Owen fired the other. There was no meeting ground, no possibility for mercy.

Silence threw himself out of his command chair, a moment before an energy beam seared through the air where he'd just been sitting. He hit the ground rolling and was quickly back on his feet, even as the energy beam flashed on to blow out a console on the other side of the bridge. Flames rose up and smoke billowed out. Alarms went off, too late. Unfamiliar faces were spilling onto the bridge, guns in hand, their faces twisted with hatred and loathing. Silence shot the nearest through the chest, and the energy beam punched right through him, to take out the man behind. Other officers were rising from their consoles, groping for weapons. Silence had already drawn his sword and charged the mutineers before him, moving so fast they couldn't draw a bead on him. He raged among them, his sword rising and falling impossibly quickly, slicing through flesh and bone alike. He was fast and strong, and his victims cried out in shock and horror as they realized they didn't stand a chance against him, for all their numbers. They kept coming, firing their guns almost blindly now, and more consoles exploded all across the bridge. Smoke was thick on the air, despite the extractor fans. Silence laughed breathlessly as he cut men down. It felt good to have something solid to fight, after so long. Some of the enemy were chanting prayers, and even exorcisms. Silence killed them anyway. And in the end, he stood alone among piles of bodies, blood running thickly from his sword blade, and they hadn't touched him once. The blood that soaked his uniform, and had spattered across his face, was all theirs. Silence looked around at his bridge crew, and saw shock and horror in their faces at what he'd done.

"Get used to it," he said harshly. "This is what war means. Comm officer, get me contact with the rest of the fleet. The Imperial ships will be here soon, and I need to know who I can rely on. Security, guard all entrances to the bridge. And somebody put out those fires and turn the damned alarms off!"

He sank back into his command chair, while his crew hurried to obey. Captain Price watched him with wide, almost frightened eyes. Silence ignored him. He realized he was still holding his sword, and started cleaning the blade with a cloth.

Good work, Captain, said Investigator Frost. *Good to see you haven't forgotten everything I taught you.*

Is that why you're back? thought Silence. *Because death is so very close to all of us?*

Lewis Deathstalker and Jesamine Flowers left their quarters the moment they heard the alarms sound, sword and gun already in hand. Which meant they surprised the small crowd of mutineers who'd come to watch them die. Lewis and Jesamine charged the crowd immediately, and soon the corridor was full of the sound of clashing blades, and the screams of the dying. There wasn't much room to maneuver in the cramped space, but Lewis and Jesamine didn't need it. They were both inhumanly fast and impossibly strong, and they hacked and cut their way through the fanatics like they were back breaking trail in the jungles of Shandrakor. After everything they'd faced, a crowd of armed men was nothing.

Brett Random watched it all from a concealed side entrance, holding

Rose firmly by one arm. The plan had been for him and Rose to attack Lewis and Jesamine from the rear while they were distracted by the crowd, but Brett just couldn't do it. His stomach ached so badly he was almost bent in two—and besides, he put no faith in Finn's promises of rewards and safety. Rose strained against his hold, but he knew she'd follow his lead. She'd got used to having him do all the thinking for both of them. So Brett waited awhile, just to be sure of which way the fight was going, and once it was clear the mutineers were losing, he ran forward to back up Lewis and Jesamine, Rose moving just a little confusedly at his side. The four of them quickly finished off the last few loyalists. Brett was surprised to find that his stomach had stopped hurting already. He might not have a conscience, but apparently his stomach did. He'd have to do something about that.

(Besides—he liked Lewis. And those Church Militant and Pure Humanity zealots had got right up his nose.)

Lewis looked at Brett. "Do you have any idea of what's going on?"

"Loyalist elements trying for a coup," Brett said crisply. "We'd better help out where we can."

Lewis nodded and set off down the corridor, Jesamine padding eagerly at his side. Brett and Rose followed after. Rose was frowning.

"I know," said Brett. "Just trust me and go along, for now. I'll explain later."

"I wanted to kill Lewis," said Rose, just a little sulkily.

"There'll be other times. For now, kill the loyalists. As many as you like."

Rose looked at him. "Only for you, Brett. Only for you."

The fighting in the corridors quickly fell apart, once Lewis and the others joined in. No one could stand against them. The mutineers lost all confidence, having failed to kill most of the officers they'd targeted, and soon they were on the run everywhere. They came together for one last push, and actually succeeded in briefly separating Lewis from Jesamine.

He cut and hacked fiercely about him, desperately trying to reach her, but the Church Militant fanatics packed tightly about him, their faces filled with the frustrated fury of animals who can sense their imminent death. They no longer cared about their cause, or even about winning; all they wanted to do was bring their hated enemy down with them. New strength flooded through Lewis as he saw Jesamine being carried farther away by the press of milling bodies, and he slammed right through the men before him, throwing their broken bodies aside like so many rag dolls.

Jesamine fought doggedly on, faster and stronger than any of those who leapt and howled around her, but in the end the sheer weight of the crowd backed her up against a steel wall. Jesamine looked for Lewis, but he was too far away. Rage flooded through Jesamine, and she opened her mouth and sang. The terrible song cut through her attackers like a blade. Their eyes burst and blood ran from their ears. Some fell dead from heart attacks, and others went mad in a moment. The steel corridor was full of awful screams, all of them drowned out by the deadly song. Even Lewis flinched away from the killing sound. In the space of a few moments, every mutineer in the corridor was dead, the piled up bodies scattered the length of the corridor. Jesamine stopped singing, and swayed unsteadily on her feet. Lewis was there in a moment, to hold and support her. She clung to him like a child.

"What has the Maze done to me, Lewis? To my voice? My songs were never meant to do anything like that."

"There will be time again, for songs of love and joy," said Lewis. "That's what we're fighting for."

And that was when Brett and Rose appeared around the corner of the corridor to join them. Lewis gave them both a withering glare.

"Where the hell were you? What kept you?"

"Stomachache," Brett said briskly. "There's something on this ship that doesn't agree with me at all."

Some loyalists went down to the cargo bay of the *Havoc*, to kill the monsters from Shandrakor in the name of Pure Humanity. The monsters tore them all apart, and then ate them. One of the monsters sent up a comm request to the bridge:

Send more loyalists.

And that was pretty much it, for the uprising. There never were as many of them as they'd hoped or believed. Only the really hard-core fanatics had been able to lie to themselves about what they'd seen when Owen Deathstalker had appeared on all the bridges of all the ships at once and called them to his side. He was the hero of prophecy, the legend returned, and most of the crews would rather have died than fail him. The mutineers didn't take control of a single ship in the rebel fleet. Good men and women had died, and there were bodies and blood to be cleaned up, but the night of the long knives was over.

The few mutineers who survived the fighting were put out the nearest airlock and told to walk home. There was no time for mercy or clemency, with the Imperial fleet closing in. Lewis and Jesamine, Brett and Rose gathered together on the *Havoc's* bridge, and there on the main viewscreen was the attacking fleet, come out from behind its stealth shields at last. There were starcruisers beyond counting, and more dropping out of hyperspace all the time.

"That is one hell of a big fleet," said Brett.

"And we are dangerously weakened," said Silence. "All our ships took some damage, and we lost a lot of crew. We're covering all the main battle stations, for now, but there's no telling how long that will last once the shooting starts. Hopefully our opposite numbers don't know that. The Mistworld and Virimonde ships were unaffected, but I don't know how they'll stand up to Imperial starcruisers. If you've got any Maze-given aces to pull out of your sleeve, Deathstalker, this would be a really good time to reveal them."

"Afraid not, Admiral," said Lewis. "It's all down to courage and honor now."

"We're all going to die," said Brett.

The Imperial fleet fell upon the rebel fleet with silent fury, all guns blazing, and in a moment the situation descended into chaos. Starships of all shapes and sizes flashed back and forth, maneuvering in three dimensions, targeting objects of opportunity as they went. Force shields flared brightly, dissipating deadly energies as disrupter cannon fired in volleys, cascading brightly in the long night. Enough firepower opened up to scorch the life from a dozen worlds, and here and there ships exploded like novas as force shields overloaded and went down. Often the victorious ship had gone on to another engagement before it even saw the results of its attack.

With the ships' AIs down, concerted attacks were impossible. It was every ship for herself. Silence kept up an endless stream of orders, trying to enforce his combat strategies, but even he couldn't keep up with the state of battle. Basic computer targeting could give best estimates of where a ship would go next, but it was up to human gunners to hit the fleeting targets, preferably without hitting one of their own ships in the process. Men and women on both sides fired their guns with wild eyes and manic smiles, half out of their minds on adrenalin and battle drugs, operating as much by instinct as training. Mistworld and Virimonde ships darted in and out of the chaos, running rings around the bigger ships, showing unexpected speed and deadly aim. The people of Mistworld and Virimonde had trained to be warriors all their lives, and for them combat was like coming home. Their shields couldn't stand up to the occasional direct hit from starcruiser cannon, but they all fought and died with the Owen's names on their lips, his Family name their battle cry.

Deathstalker! Deathstalker!

Lewis and Jesamine were running down a corridor to reinforce a besieged gunnery crew when one of the *Havoc's* shields shuddered and went down, and a direct hit blew a hole right through the bulkhead. Air blasted out through the huge jagged gap, and Lewis and Jesamine were swept off their feet in a moment. The lights flickered and the gravity fluctuated as alarm sirens sounded, almost drowned out by the rush of air shrieking out through the hole in the wall. Jesamine tumbled towards it, turning head over heels. Lewis cried out, his voice lost in the bedlam, and threw himself after her. Jesamine grabbed at the edge of the hole with one hand, and hung there, half in and half out. Lewis slammed against her, and grabbed one of her arms, only to cry out again as his side hit a viciously sharp steel prong. The metal shard sank deep into his side. Lewis held desperately onto Jesamine's arm. She was already dangling out into the cold vacuum. Only the steel spike in Lewis's side kept him from following her. He fought desperately to draw a breath from the air racing past him. He slowly pulled Jesamine back, inch by inch. And then the disrupter cannon fired again, the whole bulkhead blew apart, and the corridor opened up to space. Lewis and Jesamine were ripped free from their precarious holds, and flew out into the deadly vacuum of space.

Lewis held on to Jesamine's arm as they turned slowly end over end. The *Havoc* fell away behind them, rushing on to fight other ships. The battle raged silently around them, ships coming and going faster than the human eye could follow. Disrupter beams and flaring shields blazed brighter than the stars. It was cold and silent and very dark, and Lewis felt very small and unimportant. Just another piece of flotsam, floating in the night.

After a while, he thought *Why aren't I dead?* And then he thought, more specifically, *Why isn't my blood boiling in my veins? Why haven't my lungs collapsed? And why don't I feel any need to breathe?* He reached down to the wound in his side, and found it had already healed. He felt quite good, actually. He would have liked to giggle hysterically, but that would have to wait until later. He pulled Jesamine in close to him, and checked that she was all right too. They grinned confusedly into each other's faces. And Lewis thought *This is great! I can survive in open space! No one's been able to do that since Owen!*

Don't start showing off, Jesamine's voice said firmly in his head.

Jes! I can hear you! Can you hear me?

Yes! The Maze is just full of surprises, isn't it?

Telepathy too! We can do anything!

I wouldn't go that far, sweetie. When I reach a point where I can eat anything I like and still not put on any weight, then I'll believe in miracles. But since we're not dead after all, why don't we see if we can do some damage to the bad guys. See that ship over there? Let's pop over and ruin their day.

Sounds like a plan to me, said Lewis.

And all they had to do was think about it, and suddenly they were sailing across open space towards the Imperial ship they'd chosen. The *Heritage* was barreling along at full speed, but they caught up with her eerily fast. Her shields flared all the colors of the rainbow as they soaked up disrupter fire from all directions. Lewis slowed to a halt in front of the ship's hull, and then hit the force shield with his fist. The energies shuddered and rippled, but held together. Lewis and Jesamine hit the shield at the same time, and it collapsed. Lewis would have been seriously impressed, and a little worried, about the implications of that if he'd had the time, but he didn't so he just got on with it. He and Jesamine descended to the great steel curve before them, walked along the side of the ship until they came to an airlock, and then kicked it in.

Once they were back inside again, they began breathing normally, as though they'd never stopped. Their hearing came back in a rush, and they both winced at the racket of overlapping alarm sirens. Lewis checked his hands, and then Jesamine's, but neither seemed particularly cold. They both shrugged, and looked around for someone to fight. They went walking through the enemy ship, and everywhere they went, people fled from them screaming. Many of them called out the Deathstalker name as they ran, and Lewis took a certain cold satisfaction from the terror in their voices.

The battle went on, ship targeting ship, the occasional vast explosion as a craft blew apart, dead crew thrown tumbling through space like confetti. Silence's fleet fought well and strongly, but they were severely weakened by the loyalist uprising, and there was no telling which way the fight might have gone, when suddenly Carrion and his Ashrai came flying out of nowhere in their thousands, soaring across space on their widespread membraneous wings as though born to it. Carrion led his gargoyle aliens in sweeping attacks against the Imperial fleet, their huge forms slamming right through force shields as though they weren't there, to tear steel hulls with their terrible claws. And inside the Imperial ships voices arose, crying *It's the dragons! Owen's dragons, come to punish us for not recognizing the true Deathstalker!*

Their morale never really recovered after that, and ship after ship surrendered. Silence's fleet quickly took control, blowing apart the few hardcore fanatical ships that refused to surrender, and suddenly it was all over. Admiral Shapiro had a nervous breakdown and shot himself rather messily in the face. Captain Vardalos of the *Heritage* reluctantly took command, and oversaw the general surrender, which Admiral Silence graciously accepted, to save further loss of life.

Captain Vardalos sat slumped in her command chair. The main viewscreen before her showed both fleets at a standstill, surrounded by the drifting hulks of crippled or destroyed ships, and Owen's dragons flying unprotected through space. How could she have been so wrong? The blessed Owen really had returned, in the hour of Humanity's greatest need, just as the legends always said he would; and they had denied him. They had been found wanting in their faith. Damn the Emperor and his lies.

She looked up slowly as her second hovered uncertainly beside her. "Captain, they're here!"

"Who's here?" Vardalos struggled to focus her thoughts. "Has Silence sent emissaries across already?"

"Well, sort of. Lewis Deathstalker and Jesamine Flowers walked across open space, ripped open an air lock and walked right in. And now they're standing outside the bridge, demanding to talk to you!"

Vardalos had to shut her eyes for a moment. It was all getting a bit much for her.

"Let them in. Before they kick the door down."

Fortuna let them in, and they came forward to greet the captain. To their credit, they didn't look especially smug. They'd had no trouble with the *Heritage*'s crew after the surrender. They'd already been overwhelmed by what the Deathstalker and the diva had done, and the arrival of the Ashrai had been the last straw. Their spirits were so thoroughly broken they all but prostrated themselves before Lewis and Jesamine as they made their way to the bridge. A few even lashed themselves with improvised whips, as penance. Lewis and Jesamine gave them plenty of room.

Captain Vardalos studied the man and woman standing before her. They didn't look all that special, but there was a terrible kind of grandeur about them. "Congratulations on your victory," she made herself say.

"There are no victors here today, Captain." The Deathstalker's famously ugly face held no triumph, only regret. "Too many good men and women died, for no good reason. Finn has betrayed us all. I never was a traitor, and no more were Douglas or Jesamine or any of the others denounced for daring to take a stand against his evils. And yes, it is true; my ancestor Owen has returned. He has gone to stop the Terror, so that we can be free to deal with the Emperor. Will you fight beside us, Captain?"

Vardalos felt a rush of relief. So many of her worries fell away in a moment, it was like putting down a dreadfully heavy weight she'd been carrying for far too long. She smiled at the Deathstalker, who didn't seem nearly as terrible now.

"Of course," she said. "Our fleet is yours. If Finn would lie to us about something as important as the return of the blessed Owen, he'd lie about anything. He is not fit to be Emperor. Lead us, Deathstalker. You will not find us wanting again."

And so the huge combined fleet slowly got under way again, heading towards Logres with rage and justice on their minds. Accompanied by Carrion and his army of Ashrai, and all the ships of Mistworld and Virmonde.

An avenging army was coming home, and nothing would stop them this time.

CHAPTER SIX

LAST CHANCES

The Emperor Finn was talking at rather than to Joseph Wallace, who was more than wise enough to just sit there and listen, and try to smile and nod at what seemed like the right places. Joseph never looked forward to those infrequent occasions when he was summoned to the Imperial Palace so Finn could have one of his little chats. He rarely heard anything to make him feel good. Although he was, technically speaking, head of the Church Militant and Pure Humanity, and therefore, theoretically, the second most powerful man in the Empire, Joseph knew he held that position only because Finn liked having someone he could talk to and confide in, someone safe he could boast to about all the awful things he'd done, and planned to do.

The Emperor's private quarters were a mess, bordering on actually distressing to the nerves. Finn never cleaned up after himself, and he refused to allow servants in anymore, on the not unreasonable grounds that they might be rebel spies sent to kill him. He kept the lights turned up far too bright, so nothing could hide in the shadows, even when he slept. Papers were scattered across every surface, often weighed down with plates containing the remains of discarded meals. More rotting bits of food had been trampled into the rich heavy carpet. The room stank, despite everything the air conditioners could do to clear the air. It was like being in an animal's den, Joseph decided. Some great and powerful carnivore, that didn't care about appearances because it didn't have to.

Finn had reached a position where he could do anything he liked, and mostly he did. And he never did anything he didn't want to. That was, after all, what being Emperor was all about. And yet the state of his Empire kept changing. No matter what he did, or ordered done, things kept going from bad to worse, and Finn was unable to halt the decline. He wouldn't have cared, except he needed a strong and stable Empire to fight off the Terror. Which was why Joseph had been summoned so abruptly, so Finn could complain to him. Joseph Wallace, the second most powerful man in the Empire, with the power of life and death at his slightest whim, sat uncomfortably on his comfortable chair and did his best to look attentive while Finn strode up and down before him, gesturing angrily.

"Sometimes I actually wonder if I'm cursed, Joseph." The Emperor kicked out petulantly at a pile of papers, and they scattered like leaves across the stained and discolored carpet. "I do everything I can, kill all the right people, order purges and persecute the people to within an inch of their lives, and still the bloody Empire won't work properly. All I want is for them to shut up and do what they're told, for the good of the Empire and me in particular, and all they can do is whine and complain and burn down important buildings. Disorder is spreading on the outer worlds, and there have been occasions of outright defiance here on Logres, in the Parade of the Endless itself. And just when I'm really short of people I can depend on. It seems like only yesterday that I had armies of fanatics and followers all but falling over themselves to do my every bidding. But where are they, now I need them? I'm down to just a skeleton staff on some planets." He stopped pacing and fixed Joseph with a glittering eye. "People are taking advantage. Defying my orders and regulations, and thinking they can get away with it, just because I'm a bit preoccupied at the moment. They've even started to feel they can walk the streets in safety, and we can't have that, can we? My peacekeepers should inspire respect, fear, horror, and an urgent need to run as fast as possible in the opposite direction. A cowed population is an obedient population. Right, Joseph?"

"Oh, of course, Your Majesty. Absolutely. People should know their place."

"I'm glad you see it my way, Joseph. Because I want you to take every transmutation engine you have, and put them in orbit around all the most troublesome worlds. And then I'll let the shifty little bastards know that if they don't behave, I'll have every living thing on their planet reduced to protoplasmic goo. That should concentrate their minds wonderfully. Why are you frowning, Joseph? You know I hate it when you frown, especially when I'm being visionary."

"Oh, it's an excellent plan, Your Majesty, it's just . . . well, we don't actually have all that many transmutation engines left, after what happened at Mog Mor. You . . . we deployed most of our engines there, to deal with the Mog Mor threat, and nearly all of them were destroyed. And, as I'm sure you recall, it takes a lot of time and money to build transmutation engines. Work is progressing, but . . ."

"Joseph," said Finn, calmly and very dangerously, "tell me something I want to hear, or I'll have your testicles stitched together."

"Of course, the people don't know just how short of engines we are," said Joseph, thinking quickly on his feet. "Due to your wise decision not to allow any news coverage of what happened at Mog Mor. So, if we just put engines around a few selected worlds, we should be able to bluff the other worlds with the implied threat."

Finn sniffed loudly. "I don't like to bluff. I like to do appalling things to people who upset me. And I can't afford to have a bluff called, even once. Most of the outer planets are only waiting for one definite sign of weakness on my part, and then the ungrateful little shits will rise up. And where one leads, others will follow . . . Maybe we should destroy a world anyway, just to show we mean business. Yes, I like that. Find me a planet no one will miss much, Joseph, and put an engine in orbit. And one day when I'm feeling really depressed . . . we'll have a nice fireworks display."

He threw himself happily into a chair opposite Joseph, and crossed his legs languorously. "If only all my problems were that simple. Most of my loyal people are currently manning the fleet I had to send out to stop the Deathstalker's fleet. That man is a pain. I killed his whole family, and he still won't take a hint. But my fleet will stop his. I've packed my ships with the very best military minds, and my most zealous and hard-core fanatics, to be absolutely sure they'll have no compunctions about firing on their fellow ships. Still no reports, I take it? No, of course not. Too early yet. But I want it to happen soon. I want to hear about a massive victory, and hundreds of ships burning in the night. I want to see Lewis's head on a spike . . . I need a victory, Joseph. A really impressive demonstration of how powerful my forces are, and how vicious and merciless I can be to my enemies. Something to cow the peasants and make them think twice about doing anything that might attract my attention. They just don't worship and adore me the way they used to, the ungrateful little turds. I always knew the public were fickle and not to be trusted, even back when I was just a Paragon. The number of times I had to reinvent myself, just to hold their attention . . . So, it seems I am forced to desperate measures."

He smiled at Joseph, waiting for him to ask the obvious question. Joseph thought frantically. What the hell else could Finn have in mind, that would be worse than murdering a whole world with a transmutation engine?

"What . . . precisely, did you have in mind, Your Majesty?"

"I'm going to make a deal with the ELFs, and use their thralls on the streets to restore order and discipline. While wearing my colors, naturally. They won't take any crap from the peasants. They think they had things bad before; wait till the ELFs get to work! They have such wonderfully inventive minds, when it comes to terrorizing people."

"The ELFs?" said Joseph finally, so outraged he didn't even bother to keep it out of his voice. "You must be crazy! You can't trust those people!"

"I don't trust anyone," Finn said calmly.

"But . . . I thought they weren't talking to you anymore? You were really quite . . . vehement, a while back, about how they'd disappointed you and let you down."

"Ah," said Finn, smiling widely. "It seems the ELF leaders and the uber-espers have been having their differences of late, about who exactly should be running things. They both contacted me separately, offering their services in return for help against their enemy. And it really was simplicity itself to get both of them to agree to work for me, rather than risk being shut out. It won't last, of course, such arrangements rarely do, but as long as I can play divide and conquer, they'll be too busy trying to do each other down to think about double-crossing me. This is strictly between the two of us, of course. People wouldn't understand. I'm only telling you because you need to know; because the thralls will be wearing your Church Militant uniforms. And because it's just too good a secret to keep to myself. Ah, Joseph, sometimes the look of shock and horror on your face is what makes it all worthwhile! The ELFs will give me fear and panic and terror on the streets again, and everything will be the way it used to be. This is my Empire, Joseph, and no one is going to take it away from me."

And so thousands of ELF thralls, innocent men and women possessed by cold and powerful minds, went out to patrol the streets of Logres, and most especially the Parade of the Endless. The irony of maintaining order while wearing Pure Humanity and Church Militant uniforms pleased them greatly, and they took every opportunity to destroy the reputation of the esper-hating groups they supposedly represented. They imposed order and harsh discipline through humiliating and terrifying punishments for even the smallest offences. They showed a great fondness for hangings, crucifixions and autos-da-fé. The dead were left to hang and rot in the streets, as a warning to others. All too soon people were afraid to go out on the streets for any reason. The new peacekeepers were everywhere, looking for any excuse to demonstrate their authority through fear and suffering. People stopped going to work, for fear they'd be stopped on the way. When they had to go out, for food or other necessities, they went in groups, starting at shadows and ready to break and run at a moment's notice. And slowly but steadily, the social and business infrastructure of Logres began to break down. Shops closed, with no one to buy their goods. Businesses closed, with no one coming in to work anymore. Basic services were also breaking down, because the ubiquitous Shub robots that usually took care of such things had all ceased to function, and no one else knew what needed to be done.

As if all this wasn't disturbing enough, what was happening in the Arena was worse. The ELFs had demanded a price for their support, so Finn gave them control of the Arena, for their own personal use. And on the ancient bloody sands, the ELFs played out their nasty games for everyone to see. At first, they just possessed the existing gladiators, and set them against each other. But the ELFs soon broke their new toys, or wore them out, and so the ELFs sent peacekeepers to break into nearby houses at random, and haul the people out to be new meat for the Arena. Men, women, and children ended up on the bloody sands, some possessed and some not, and the ELFs' games grew steadily worse. Hagridden and helpless, the thralls played out all the wildest fantasies of the ELFs: rape, torture, mutilation, and murder were the order of the day, every day, often on a grand scale. The ELFs delighted in mounting epic dramas, and staged vast reconstructions of famous atrocities from the past. The details were rarely accurate, but all the mattered to the ELFs was that people suffered and died. There was power to be gained, from leeching off the energies released through pain and emotion and death. The ELFs grew fat and potent, bloated like leaches. There was a very old name for the kind of creatures they were.

The Arena became a slaughteryard, where the bodies were never cleared away, but just piled up at the sides. The sands were always red with blood now, and the stench was indescribable. The ELFs, far and far away, didn't care. They were having fun. Sometimes they played with the dead bodies too, just for the distress they knew this would cause grieving relatives. They refused to be limited by human moralities or taboos. They saw themselves as more than human, and denied themselves nothing.

They insisted on every single bit of it being televised, on every channel, simultaneously. What was the point of being bad, if there was no one watching to be shocked and outraged? Finn wouldn't allow the ELFs to actually come out and say it was them, but the clues were there. And people did watch; there was a regular audience. Some, because a secret part of them responded to the atrocities. Some, with horrified fascination. And some, just because it was better to know, than not. Even when it was always bad news, people needed to know. And all across Logres and all the watching worlds, outrage and a need for revenge burned coldly in people's hearts, and they readied themselves for rebellion, and watched hopefully for a sign.

Joseph Wallace never watched, though he was careful to read all the latest reports. As the ELFs grew every day more powerful, and more closely tied to Finn, the more his own power and influence declined. The thralls on the streets might wear his uniforms, but they didn't answer to him. Joseph was being sidelined, his power base eroded and even sabotaged by the ELFs, who wanted Finn's attention all to themselves. Finn still called

Joseph in for his disturbing little chats, but whatever influence Joseph ever had with the Emperor seemed to have disappeared. Secretly and privately and very much against Finn's orders, Joseph's people did their best to spy on the ELFs. Joseph had never trusted the inhuman creatures. He was Pure Humanity, after all. He gathered all his best information and intelligence and presented it to the Emperor, as proof that the ELFs had their own agenda, and was met with a cold, indifferent stare.

I don't care, Finn said flatly. *As long as they get the job done, I don't care what they do. And Joseph, if you can't get your job done, I'll replace you with someone who can.*

As the ELFs possessed more and more people, and the armies of thralls grew and grew, so the ELF leaders and the uber-espers became even more powerful. The pool of thralls was a power source, and the more the possessors took and inhabited, the more they could take. Their esper abilities had never been so strong, so far-reaching. More and more thralls were able to manifest their owners' abilities by proxy, though they always burnt out. But as the possessors grew stronger, so the differences between the ELF leaders and the uber-espers became more pronounced. Neither side trusted the other, and they each had their own strictly enforced territories. There were occasional border clashes, as thralls fought with thralls, and filled the terrified streets with blood and bodies.

Finn watched it all from a distance, and let them fight it out, carefully supporting neither one side nor the other. Divide and conquer still seemed like his best bet; while they were busy fighting each other, they weren't fighting him. Besides, he enjoyed the spectacle. He allowed both sides to operate freely, while making it clear he wouldn't tolerate any psionic battles in his capital city, because of the inevitable psychic fallout. He didn't actually have any way of enforcing this, but so far the two sides were too preoccupied to notice. Finn was betting they'd weaken each other so much in their struggle, that whoever eventually emerged as victor would be too weak to threaten him.

And then, he'd do something about them.

But there were factors that even Finn didn't know about. The uber-espers were determined to win, at whatever the cost. They had to win, and become more powerful than ever before, because they alone on Logres knew for sure that Owen Deathstalker was back from the dead; and they were all scared of Owen. Just one touch of his revitalized mind had been enough to show that he was more powerful than ever. More than the over-soul, more than any of them, and just possibly more powerful even than their original creator, the Mater Mundi. And so the uber-espers concentrated on possessing more and more thralls, pushing themselves to their limits and beyond to be sure of accumulating more power than the official ELF leaders.

They had to be ready, for when Owen Deathstalker came for them.

Finally, inevitably, war broke out. The Spider Harps, the Shatter Freak, Blue Hellfire, Screaming Silence, and the Gray Train turned the full force of their stored up energies on the ELF leaders. The direct mental clash detonated over the Parade of the Endless, and everyone in the city cried out as psychic fallout devastated the surroundings. As esper minds battled for domination on their own psionic plane, the strikes and counterstrikes spilled over into the material world. Probability storms raged through the streets, manifesting in miracles and unlikely tragedies. There were break-outs of mass delusions and ripples spread through reality itself. Buildings exploded, and people too. Luck ran mad, outrageous possibilities express-ing themselves in people's flesh. Streets turned in upon themselves, with no way out. Gravity switched back and forth, and rivers ran through the sky. Tower blocks became trees, with people still trapped screaming within them. Water became fire, and the air become poison. There were falls of stones and rivers of blood, and people vanished, replaced by other ver-sions of themselves.

And two great armies of thralls fought each other with secondhand fe-rocity, with guns and swords and whatever came to hand, as the dead piled up in the streets.

Only in the Rookery did people and property remain sane and safe, protected and shielded by the joined power of Diana Vertue and her fol-lowers, the Psycho Sluts. Their minds and their sanity shook and shud-dered under the impact of so much mental power, but they stood firm, and within the boundaries of the Rookery people remained untouched, watching in horror at what was happening outside, helpless to intervene.

It all ended as suddenly as it had begun, and reality became firm and trustworthy again. Half the city was in flames, or rubble, and the death toll was in the hundreds of thousands, but the uber-espers had won, crushing and dominating the weaker minds of the ELF leaders, who turned out to be only human after all, and therefore limited in the evil they could conceive. The uber-espers crushed, controlled, and absorbed all the other espers in the Esper Liberation Force, until at the last there were only the five minds of the uber-espers, controlling millions of bodies. *We are the ELFs now,* the uber-espers said, and it was true. Five minds looking out through millions of bodies, and absorbing more all the time. *One day we will become the world,* said the uber-espers, *and all of Humanity will be us. Our thoughts, our will, operating in every human body. And then we'll turn on each other, and make war across all the worlds in search of final domination, until only one of us is left. Won't that be fun? All of Humanity, suffering endlessly, in the service of one triumphant mind.*

The uber-espers laughed, and the laughter went on for hours.

Douglas Campbell, leader of the Rookery and acclaimed King of Thieves, still lived in the Lantern Lodge hotel. It wasn't any less of a dump for being his headquarters, but it was central and familiar, and at least now he had a room all to himself. Rank had its privileges. Nina Malapert and Stuart Lennox had their own separate rooms too, just down the corridor. They could all have moved somewhere more salubrious, where the hot water was reliable and the toilet was just more than a hole in the floor, but the people liked to see Douglas living as one of them, suffering as they suffered.

(Douglas still insisted the whole place be fumigated. He had his standards.)

He was constantly protected by his bodyguard, supplied from the ranks of the Psycho Sluts. Two of the overpoweringly bright and cheerful young ladies took it in turns to stand guard outside his door, and accompany him wherever he went, and God help the poor fool who tried to get past them for any reason. Local gossip had it they'd turned one man into a frog. And then eaten him.

Under Douglas's command and direction, the rebellion was growing slowly and steadily, and branching out. His people left the Rookery every day on secret missions, from information gathering to a little discreet sabotage. Finn's people had first given Douglas the name King of Thieves, as a sneer over how far he'd fallen, but Douglas embraced the name, and the Rookery loved it.

Douglas had been pleasantly surprised to discover that these thieves, con men, rogues, and rascals were far more capable in the field than Finn's trained military fanatics. It was as though they possessed some spark, some extra quality or vitality, that had been bred out of the city's more civilized people. Certainly the Rookery had ways of acquiring tech, information, or anything else that might be needed, that would never have occurred to the law-abiding mind. The King of Thieves had learned to appreciate and value the wild talents of the Rookery. They were the only ones whose spirits the Emperor had been unable to crush. In fact, the more he tried to oppress them, the more determined they became. Years of living as despised outcasts had put iron in their souls and a fire in their belly. Douglas sometimes thought about the implications of that, and what it said about the rest of the Empire. Not least because the Rookery was changing him too. He had become wilder and more flexible in his thinking. And he liked it.

Cautiously at first, and then more openly, he plotted attacks against Finn's weak spots, and the ragged warriors of the Rookery went out and ran joyous rings around Finn's security. They came and went and did their damage and no one even knew they'd been there, until the explosions started. The information they gathered enabled Douglas to identify more weak links, and how to cripple them in inventive and distressing ways. Finn sent his security people running madly back and forth, but somehow they were never where they were needed, always fated to arrive just in time to pick up the pieces afterwards. They were becoming a laughingstock, and they knew it.

The actual territory that made up the Rookery expanded every day. It was now the only safe haven on all Logres, and people came from all across the planet, defying all dangers to cross the Rookery's shifting boundaries and find relief at last from Finn, his people, and his thralls. The Rookery had to grow to accommodate them all. And so it swallowed up adjoining streets, and then adjoining blocks, on and on until it made up almost a full quarter of the Parade of the Endless. Finn declared that it was death for anyone to even approach the Rookery, but it didn't slow the flood of refugees. In the world that Finn had made, death was no longer anything to be feared. For many, it was the kindest thing that could happen to them.

Douglas's influence grew in other ways too. The aliens of the Rookery slowly but surely infiltrated the substructures of the city, sliding and gliding through all the service tubes and maintenance levels, the sewers and the factory outlets. They thrived in conditions that humans couldn't tolerate, working their plans in places the humans above never even considered as inhabitable. The aliens breathed poison gasses and swam through deadly chemical baths, and mile by mile they gained control of all the tasks that had once been performed by the Shub robots: all the appalling but necessary work that made possible the city's essential services. They restored power and water and sewage and all the other comforts that the Parade of the Endless had once taken for granted. And by shutting down these services in some areas and opening them in the Rookery, the aliens rapidly made the Rookery the most attractive place in the city to live.

The aliens also made perfect unsuspected spies, listening from impossible places, their alien senses often picking up information that even the best tech would have missed. Finn would have been very surprised if he'd known how many aliens moved unsuspected through the crawl spaces and darker levels of his palace every night.

Nina Malapert was also making a name for herself. As the main newscaster for the most popular and far-reaching underground news site, she had become the face of freedom and the voice of rebellion. Every day she told the people things they didn't know, and promised hope for the future. Her pink mohawk was taller than ever, and she never wore the same makeup twice. Everyone watched her broadcasts, even though they could be executed on the spot if they were caught doing it. (After all, you could be executed without trial for pretty much anything these days.) The people needed to know what was happening, and Finn's official news programs had become increasingly bland propaganda. The people reading the news didn't even bother to smile anymore.

Nina gave her audience hard facts, backed up by on-the-spot coverage, and her propaganda was at least something people wanted to hear. She never once exhorted her audience to rise up against Finn; everyone knew it wasn't time yet. But she did invite everyone who thought they could make it to come to the Rookery, and join the growing rebel army—and a hell of a lot of them did. Parts of the Parade of the Endless were almost totally deserted now. They came because even more than safety, people need to be able to live without fear.

The city outside the Rookery was falling apart. Power cuts, food shortages, lack of essential services. Madmen on the streets, wearing peacekeeper uniforms. Businesses closing down, industry grinding to a halt. Everyone knew it couldn't go on like this. Even Finn.

Douglas called everyone to his room in the Lantern Lodge, for an emergency meeting, and everyone who mattered was there. The King of Thieves sat back in his chair, and watched them assemble. Tel Markham hovered beside Douglas's chair, as always; the quiet strategist who was actually the most radical and extreme of them all. He'd cleaned up nicely, but his eyes remained wild and savage. He was always the first to call for murder and mayhem in the outer city. He was Douglas's very own junkyard dog, and he guarded his master fiercely, even growling at the Psycho Sluts who made up the man's official bodyguards. Tel had been wounded in many ways, and his scar tissues showed.

Diana Vertue, still sometimes known as Jenny Psycho, though never to her face these days, was also present, slumped easily in the only other comfortable chair. A small compact blonde who didn't look anywhere near as dangerous as everyone knew she was. Diana and her followers, the effervescent Psycho Sluts, were the only ones who could still stroll openly through the outer city, and defy anyone to do anything about it. They didn't fear armies or the ELFs, and their defiance cheered many an oppressed heart. Secretly, the uber-espers were pretty sure they could kill Diana Vertue, as they had once before over a hundred years ago, but they were still trying to work out how she'd managed to come back from the dead. Finn was pretty sure he could crush her, with enough guns and men and battle tech; but he couldn't afford to lose as many men as he knew he would, on anything less than a sure thing. So he held back too. And Diana snubbed her nose at all of them.

Running herd on the Psycho Sluts had actually taught Diana Vertue the value of patience and self-control, though neither came naturally to her. She had a horrible suspicion she was finally maturing.

Nina Malapert and Stuart Lennox stood together on the other side of the room. As usual, Nina hadn't been able to decide which of several styles to wear, so she'd worn all of them at once. She chatted cheerfully with Stuart, who just smiled and nodded and let her get on with it. Even old friends found it difficult to interrupt Nina in full flow.

It was Douglas's meeting, so he started first. "This meeting of the Let's Stick It to Finn committee is hereby called to order, so shut the hell up and listen, and yes I'm looking at you, Nina. And don't pout or I'll get cranky. The good news is that all our military operations have been going very well. I've been using my old Paragon knowledge to identify vulnerable financial and security targets, and my attack teams have been able to do serious damage while remaining well below Finn's radar. He hasn't got a clue what's going on, or how we're doing what we're doing, except that every morning he wakes up to discover a heap of smoking rubble where an important building used to be. Security officers draw straws now, to see who gets to go in and tell him they're still baffled. They'll be blaming it on pixies soon."

"We should be concentrating on people, not buildings," growled Tel. "Take out the people who matter, and Finn's whole administration would fall apart."

"We've had this conversation before, Tel," Douglas said firmly. "Assassination is Finn's way, not ours. And he still has any number of fanatical followers ready to jump into any position that opens up. Those crazy bastards worship him as a god. No, we stick to the slow and subtle way. For now, at least. Where was I . . . oh yes. Our computer hackers have also been having remarkable success of late. They've been thieving massive amounts of credits from Church Militant and Pure Humanity coffers, and adding them to our funds. Which gives us more options apart from the military. Often a bribe will get you places that a blade wouldn't."

"Except we've been using most of those credits to pay for food drops in parts of the outer city," said Tel. "We should let them go hungry. Make them more ready to rise up against Finn."

"The half-starved rarely make good fighters," said Douglas. "And I will not stand by and let my people go hungry. I am still their King, even if only in exile. All right, Tel; I know you're bursting to give us news of what your people have been up to. But keep it short and to the point, or we'll heckle you."

"And throw things," said Stuart.

Tel glared at him. "My people have had great success in intercepting and jamming Finn's communication lines, using alien-derived tech and Rookery-honed skills. As a result, most of Finn's orders just aren't getting through. Sometimes we make subtle changes of our own, and then let them go through, just to add to the general chaos and confusion. Soon enough, Finn won't be able to believe anything he hears through the comm lines, and his people will be afraid to follow any order that doesn't come from him in person."

"Unfortunately, he's still got the ELFs," said Diana. "Even working together, the Sluts and I couldn't block their telepathic commands. They control a staggering number of thralls these days, and they have made the ELF leaders very powerful. We can't even listen in on what they're thinking, or planning. If Finn uses them to replace his infiltrated comm systems . . ."

Douglas frowned. "Are any of these new thralls turning up in the Rookery? Maybe among the news refugees?"

"No," Diana said firmly. "We're still clear. The girls and I have set a mental scan in place, running on automatic. Any thrall who tried to get in would set off a mental alarm, and we'd all come running. Finn's spies and agents are another matter, of course . . ."

"Stuart," said Douglas. "You wanted to say something about Finn's security people."

"Damn right," said Stuart. "Yes, we've been running rings around them, but that's because mostly they've not been trained for security. They're Finn's fanatics, who never bothered much over military tactics. Just lately, though, we've been running into a harder breed. Thralls, showing limited esper abilities. They can sense what's going on, even if they can't prove it. You can't sneak past a telepath. Douglas, to be using this many thralls, and trusting them to guard sensitive locations, Finn must have made a new deal with the ELFs."

"I told you they were running the Arena," said Diana. "All the signs are there. And after that recent mental explosion over the city, I think we have to assume that the uber-espers are now running the ELFs directly."

"It would explain the behavior of the peacekeepers," said Stuart.

"They're animals!" said Nina. "Honestly, they are. People out there are terrified of anyone in a uniform these days."

"Not necessarily a bad thing," said Tel. "The worse things are outside, the more people will head for the Rookery. The city's troubles make us strong. We're going to have to expand again soon, Douglas. Seize more territory."

"I still say we should seize the Arena, darlings," said Nina. "Or at least blow it up, and put the poor bastards out of their misery."

"It has to be ELFs," said Stuart. "People wouldn't do things like that. Everyone I speak to is sickened by what's going on in the Arena now, in the name of entertainment. Even the old school Rookery people, the most hardened criminals, are shocked and outraged. It seems there's a line even they won't cross; and no one's more surprised than them. Douglas, you give the word, and we'll blow the Arena right off the map."

"No," Tel said immediately. "We're not ready for an operation that big. First, if it is the ELFs running things there, we'd have to commit Diana and all the Sluts to the mission, plus a hell of a big armed force, and still with no guarantee of success. We could lose all of them to the uber-espers, and leave the Rookery open to psionic attack. And second, even if we did succeed, Finn couldn't afford to take such an open victory lying down. He'd have to strike back. You know he would. And he has the transmutation engines. He'd destroy this world rather than give it up. I've worked for him. I know how he thinks."

"Can't we cut the communication lines to the engines?" said Diana.

"We keep trying," said Nina. "But they operate strictly from comm lines within the Imperial Palace. Under Finn's personal control."

"There are ways into the palace that even Finn doesn't know about," said Douglas, and all the others looked at him. He smiled slightly. "The palace was my home, remember? The royal family have always kept a few secrets to themselves. But we have to save those for real emergencies. We can't throw them away on anything less than the final assault on the palace.

Right, I think we've covered everything, so all of you can get the hell out of my room, and let me breathe again."

The meeting broke up, and everyone went their separate ways. Nina, to her news site operations room, for the latest intelligence. Diana, to patrol with the Sluts. Tel, to plot and conspire with his own personal band of spies and informers. And Stuart Lennox went back to his own room, just down the corridor. He'd been on his feet all day, training old and new Rookery citizens in how to be soldiers, and he desperately needed some down time.

That said, he was always happier in action rather than in planning sessions. Like everyone else on his home world of Virimonde, he had been raised as a warrior, and he preferred to think in simple, direct lines. He joined the raids into the outer city whenever he could, always up for a chance to kill Finn's people. It didn't satisfy like killing Finn would, but it would have to do, for now.

His spirits lifted a little as he pushed open his door and entered the small but comfortable room he shared with his new boyfriend. Jas Sri was already there, bustling back and forth and tidying things up while he waited for dinner to be ready. Jas was a great one for tidying up, and even the dust had learned to lie in straight lines while he was around. Jas worked with Nina at the news site, a media tech who specialized in adapting donated alien tech to make the news site invulnerable to outside attack. Stuart and Jas had been together ever since Nina first introduced them. (Nina had introduced a great many personable young men to Stuart, and was quietly and happily relieved when Stuart finally took a shine to one.) Jas was good for Stuart, not least because he wouldn't put up with excessive brooding or dwelling on the past. Jas Sri lived very thoroughly in the present. He was tall, thin, dark-skinned and very intense, and inclined to dramatics when he had an audience.

"About time you got home, honey," Jas said, without looking round. "Dinner will be on the table in five minutes, and yes, there is pudding. There may even be custard, if you're lucky. Try to remember to use the napkins, this time. And don't drink from the finger bowl! I know you only do it to annoy me."

"True," Stuart admitted, slumping into the easy chair. "You are a true touch of civilization in a barbarous place, Jas."

"And don't I know it. You relax, honey, and I'll find your slippers for you."

Stuart had to smile. Jas mothered him unmercifully, just as he tried to mother everyone. He claimed it was genetically hardwired into him. Either that, or a gypsy curse. He kissed Stuart briefly on the forehead, patted him on the shoulder, and then hurried back to the stove tucked away in one corner of the room. Jas was naturally touchy-feely, but had learned to reign it in around Stuart. He didn't want to put any pressure on the emotionally damaged man. Stuart didn't talk much about Finn, or the things that had happened while they were together, but occasionally he would let slip a telling fact or detail, of the horrors he'd been through. Some of what Stuart had endured made Jas's blood run cold, and then he would bite his lower lip hard and try to be extra supportive without being smothering. And sometimes, when they lay together in the narrow single bed, Stuart would cry out miserably in his sleep, and Jas would have to hold and comfort him until it was light again.

On the whole, Stuart did seem to be doing better. His many successful sorties into Finn's territory had done much to restore his self-esteem, and he was once again the canny fighter he'd been as a Paragon. He and his handpicked people had done serious damage to military targets; but it wasn't enough. It would never be enough, until Finn was dead, and couldn't haunt Stuart anymore.

Jas never said anything, but he always worried when Stuart was away on one of his missions, because he knew that a part of Stuart went into every fight looking for the peace that only death could bring him. All Jas could do was try to give his man a reason to live, a reason to come home again.

"Dinner's ready!" he said brightly. "Yet another bright and inventive way to present the same old bland and boring vegetables. God, sometimes I think I'd kill for a good sausage."

Douglas went for a walk around the block, just to stretch his legs and get a little fresh air into his lungs. Sometimes his room felt uncomfortably like a cell. As always, two Psycho Sluts accompanied him as bodyguards. They maintained a discreet distance, and discouraged anyone else from getting too close with harsh looks and the occasional mental prod. Among the crowds that cheered and smiled on Douglas wherever he went, there was always the chance of a disguised spy or assassin. Douglas felt pretty sure he could defend himself, but accepting the bodyguards was the price he paid for not having his friends go mental every time he felt like popping out on his own.

This evening he was accompanied by Alessandra Duquesne, putative leader of the Sluts, and her friend Joanna Maltravers. Both were big, bouncy blond teenagers who looked and sounded like they should still have been in a finishing school somewhere. They were both dressed in brightly colored silks, artfully cut and arranged to show off as much bare bronzed skin as possible, and sported black roses in their hair and tribal markings painted on their faces. There were twelve Psycho Sluts in all, young espers too individual or contrary to be embraced by the mass-mind of the oversoul, sworn to follow their beloved Jenny Psycho to the death and beyond. When they weren't out blowing things up or killing Finn's people with distressing verve and enthusiasm, they tended to hang around the lobby of the Lantern Lodge, reading gossip magazines, sharing makeup tips and discussing new and nastier ways to slaughter bad guys. *Aren't we awful?* one of them would inevitably say, and then they'd all dissolve into girlish giggles. The Rookery found them fascinating and frightening in equal measure.

Douglas felt just a little pervy having these deadly and delightful teenagers sticking so close, hanging on his every word and looking at him with their big worshipful eyes. He was old enough to be their father, or very nearly, and he was never sure if their constant flirting was as casual as it seemed. Not that he ever did anything about it, of course. It had been a long time since he'd done anything in his bed except sleep. At least he'd stopped them from pinching his bum when they were out in public.

He decided he'd had enough fresh air, or what passed for it in the Rookery, and went back inside. Alessandra and Joanna wished him good night, blew him a kiss and took up their positions outside the door. That was as far away as they would allow. They'd wanted to actually sleep in his room, at the foot of his bed, to be sure of protecting him against night attacks, but he'd put his foot down about that. Espers were notoriously casual about privacy, but Douglas wasn't. Alessandra called out to him to be sure to call out for anything he needed in the night, and Douglas shut the door firmly on her. He'd only just slumped into his chair when there was a brief knock at his door and Nina Malapert came breezing in. Douglas had to smile. Her boundless energy and never-ending smile always helped to cheer him up.

"Did you forget something at the meeting, Nina?"

"As if, lovey! I am always one hundred percent prepared and professional, and you know it. No, I just wanted to pop in and make sure you were all right. You looked distinctly down and moody at the meeting."

Douglas sighed heavily. "I try to keep up an optimistic face, but the facts are we're not making progress anywhere near as fast as we need to. We can't keep expanding our territory to hold the refugees without Finn feeling the need to push back at some point. And I don't think we're ready to go to war yet."

"Finn's not dumb enough to start something he can't be sure of winning," Nina said easily, sitting on the arm of his chair. "If he commits his forces to a frontal attack, and we kick his arse, he'll have rebellions breaking out on every planet in the Empire."

"You're forgetting the transmutation engines. As long as Finn has those, he has a gun to everyone's head."

"Oh, poo to the engines. You'll figure out a way to stop them. It's what you do."

She chattered on cheerfully, and Douglas let her. He enjoyed her company, both as his adviser and his friend. She was always so alive, so full of energy and down to earth. He didn't know what he'd do without her. Nina . . . was good for him. And she had a brain, behind all the chatter. She helped to plan rebel sorties into the outer city, based on information coming in all the time from the various stringers who kept the news site up to date on the very latest breaking news, facts, and gossip. She had people everywhere now, and her news site was on the air twenty-four hours a day, despite everything Finn could do to shut it down. Douglas approved of Nina.

"Oh! Oh! I almost forgot," she said suddenly, beating her hands together before her like a child. "We finally got confirmation that the two fleets have made contact, fought a battle, and then Finn's fleet surrendered to Lewis!"

Douglas sat up straight. "How the hell could you forget something that important?"

"Don't be such a grouch, Douglas. You keep frowning like that and you'll get lines on your face. I knew I had a reason for coming back here, it just escaped me for the moment. Anyway, we've been getting some marvelous battle footage, including Lewis doing a few things you are just not going to believe, but, but—the big news is . . . the combined fleet is heading straight for Logres!"

"An exclusive," said Douglas, smiling.

"*Yes!*"

"Nina," Douglas said sternly. "Are you sure you didn't know this before the meeting?"

Nina pouted. "Only rumors, sweetie, nothing definite. And it isn't the sort of thing you want to announce without definite evidence. We're still getting details, and broadcasting it all, including the surrender, to every planet in the Empire. And my people are looking at some information provided from a ship called the *Heritage*, about what really happened at Usher Two, when the Terror came. Some rather disturbing details that Finn suppressed. You know . . . I can't help feeling I'm getting jaded, darling. There was a time when news like this would have had me bouncing up and down and hyperventilating. I haven't done my happy dance in weeks."

"It is excellent news," said Douglas, rising up suddenly from his chair, and almost knocking Nina off the arm. He steadied her absentmindedly, and then strode up and down in the small room, thinking hard. "Assuming there wasn't too much damage during the battle, the sheer size of the combined fleet should mean Finn hasn't got anything big enough or powerful enough to put up against it. All he's got left are the transmutation engines . . . We have got to find a way to knock them off line . . ."

"What do you think Finn will do, when he hears the news?" said Nina.

Douglas smiled grimly. "Knowing him, something extreme. You'd better call everybody back, Nina. We need another meeting."

✳   ✳   ✳

Emperor Finn heard the news of his fleet's surrender, and took it very badly. The loss of his fleet was just the latest in a series of last straws. He smashed every piece of furniture in his quarters, and pounded his fists on the bare walls, before falling back into a cold and very dangerous self-control. He needed to do something, something big and dramatic and horrifyingly nasty, to make it clear to everyone that he was still in charge. So he turned on the nearest target, the most irksome thorn in his side. The Rookery. He walked across the room, kicking pieces of shattered furniture out of the way, and when he was sure his breathing had returned to normal, he activated his viewscreen and called Joseph Wallace in his bunker.

Joseph appeared before his Emperor, straight from his bed, looking a little tousled and distinctly wary. News this late in the evening was rarely ever anything he wanted to hear.

"The time has come," Finn said crisply. "I want the Rookery crushed, and you're going to do it for me. I give you complete charge of all my armed forces, dear Joseph, and all I ask in return is that you should march into the Rookery and kill every man, woman, and child you find there. No one is to be allowed to escape. No mercy, no prisoners, no survivors. Burn the place to the ground, and leave not one brick standing upon another. I give you charge over all my soldiers, my Church Militant and Pure Humanity fanatics, all the thralls you can persuade to follow you, and all the air support you will need. This time, there will be no stopping us. You will keep pushing forward, despite any or all losses, until you come out the other side and the Rookery is no more.

"And Joseph, dear Joseph—if you don't succeed, don't come back."

Diana Vertue was out and about in the Rookery, despite the lateness of the hour. She'd got into the habit of making regular patrols on her own, ostensibly searching out spies and informers, but really just to immerse herself in the flow of life and the living. She'd been dead a long time, and she was still getting used to the unexpected fires and passions of the body she wore. People watched her go by, and sometimes smiled or nodded, but always from a safe distance. Diana Vertue was respected rather than loved. Jenny Psycho's legend had taken some pretty strange paths down the years, and it had been pretty extreme to begin with. Even Robert and Constance hadn't been able to sanitize her, not least because she was one of the few great heroes still around and kicking over the traces on a regular basis. Diana did like to think she'd mellowed a little since she returned.

It felt good to be back in her body again, after so many years of existing only as a thought in the mass-mind of the oversoul; even if this wasn't, strictly speaking, her own body. The Psycho Sluts believed Diana had manifested herself again through an act of will, and she had done nothing to dissuade them. It all helped her reputation. She didn't tell them the truth because all her long years had done nothing to dull her natural paranoia. A secret shared is no longer a secret.

Diana Vertue's original body had been very thoroughly destroyed in a battle with the uber-espers, over a hundred years ago. She'd been led into an ambush by someone she'd had every reason to trust, and her old tired body and mind had been no match for all the uber-espers at once. Her body was utterly consumed in mental fires, but at the last moment her mind was caught up and preserved by the oversoul. A psionic working performed so swiftly and so expertly than even the uber-espers didn't notice until it was too late. And so Diana Vertue had lived on, at peace and content in the mass-mind, until recent events had called to her and brought her forth again, renewed and revitalized in the fresh young body she'd kept preserved, in the event of such need as this.

Diana had always had enemies, and knew the time would inevitably come when one of them proved stronger than her, so she made secret preparations for an emergency bolt-hole. After the war against the Recreated was over, Diana took advantage of her new (and fleeting) heroic status to do something awful, and unforgivable. She bullied the clone underground leaders into creating several brain-wiped adult clones, from her own tissues. This was a death crime, both for Diana Vertue and the clone leaders who agreed to it, but there were few indeed who'd ever been strong enough to say no to Jenny Psycho.

She'd expected to die in one body and wake up in another, but the oversoul intervened. This had rather surprised Diana, who had never thought they'd want anyone as notoriously disruptive as her, but it seemed she was a hero to them, as well. And in their midst she had found unexpected peace of mind, and forgotten all about the clones. But she should have known; even heaven couldn't last forever. She couldn't abandon Logres to Finn, and leave with the rest of the espers in the Icarus Working; so when the floating city of New Hope took off for Mistworld, she had already left the oversoul and decanted her consciousness into one of the waiting clone bodies.

It was still there, in its body bank, waiting to be occupied. She slid into it as easily as a hand into a glove, and the body bank had recognized her presence and revived the body for her. She sat up sharply, drawing breath deep into her lungs, the shock of the body's senses and sensations almost overwhelming after so long as a merely mental presence. After a while, she pulled herself out of the body bank, and tottered around the abandoned warehouse on unsteady legs. The other tanks were shrouded in dust and cobwebs, and there was nothing else in the warehouse, except the cold and the shadows. Diana checked the other bodies. Of the seven she'd put aside, only three were still alive. Diana brushed away the dust from one viewport, and a gray mummified face stared back up at her. Seeing her own dead face gave her a bad moment, but Diana was made of hard stuff, and she made herself turn away and put her new body through a series of exercises, designed to get the blood moving properly again. It had been a long time since she'd felt . . . human. The body didn't feel quite the way she remembered. There were differences. In some ways, it felt like haunting an uninhabited house.

And she wasn't used to feeling so alone, cut off from the other minds of the oversoul. She could have reached them with her thoughts; Mistworld wasn't that far away for a powerful mind like hers, but she couldn't risk the contact. They might object to the things she'd done and the secrets she'd hidden, even from them. Besides, she needed to be a mystery, to her enemies and her allies. Keeping them unsure meant keeping them off balance. She allowed herself a distant kind of contact with her new followers, the Psycho Sluts. They were keen and sharp and enthusiastic, and openly worshiped her, which was a useful thing in itself, but she couldn't let even them get too close. She was a monster now, just like Finn. She'd sacrificed the lives and the souls of the seven women who would have been her clones, on the altar of her necessity.

But then, whether as Diana Vertue or as Jenny Psycho, she'd always been able to do the harsh, necessary things.

Just like her father.

She enjoyed the company of the Psycho Sluts, though it was no match for the closeness of the oversoul, and did her best to be honest with them when she could. They wanted to know about how things really were, back in the days of the Great Rebellion, the history rather than the legend, and Diana told them, even when it made her look bad. She'd never cared about being a hero or a legend, except when she could turn it to her advantage. But . . . *Was there never anyone special in your life?* Alessandra had asked, and Diana was surprised to find she didn't have an answer, except . . . *There was never time, or room, in the life I had to lead, for anyone but me.*

Diana Vertue increased the length of her stride, hurrying through the narrow streets, trying to leave such disturbing thoughts behind her. She was back, and she had much to do. And if inhabiting her stolen clone body made her feel just a little like one of the possessor ELFs, she tried hard not to think about it. Monsters did what they had to.

Meanwhile, the Emperor Finn was having his own problems. Since most of the transmutation engines were lost or destroyed in the battle, or, more properly, balls-up at Mog Mor, he had lost one of his most potent threats for keeping the other planets in line. If the people knew how few engines he actually had left, he'd be fighting off rebellions all across the Empire. He needed a replacement threat fast, before some damned hero dared to call his bluff. He'd heard of what the rebel fleet had done to the engines he'd left orbiting Virimonde, showing how vulnerable the things were to a surprise attack by a strong enough force.

So Finn went to see his pet clone master, Elijah du Katt, to see how his cloned army was coming along. He'd ordered five million new soldiers, all based on his own genetic makeup, but du Katt had only just produced the first batch, of under half a million. And the advance word on their condition . . . wasn't all he'd hoped for. Sometimes, Finn thought, things wouldn't go right if you killed them, chopped them up, and distributed the parts as party favors.

Du Katt's laboratory was one of the most heavily guarded locations within the Imperial Palace. Finn preferred to keep his friends and allies close, where he could keep a watchful eye on them. Du Katt had one of the clone prototypes waiting for Finn when he breezed in. The lab itself was spotlessly clean, everything in its place, but it was perhaps just a little too brightly lit, too carefully arranged. Finn sighed inwardly. The odds were du Katt was running his own private projects again, and had tidied away the evidence a bit too thoroughly on hearing Finn was coming. Still, that was a matter for another time. Finn stood right in front of du Katt and the clone, and was pleased to see his proximity made the tic by du Katt's eye just that little bit worse. He considered the clone. It had a muscular body and a face that resembled his own famously good-looking features, but there were so many things wrong with the clone that Finn didn't even know where to start. The arms were of different length, there was a slight but definite hump on the back, and all the bones of the face were enlarged and distorted. The clone looked like Finn's idiot brother. Still, he held himself well, and his gaze seemed clear enough. Finn looked at du Katt, who flinched.

"I told you, I warned you," he said quickly. "Providing so many clones from just the one sample, in such a restricted time inevitably meant a certain deterioration in the template, and certain . . . tolerable defects."

"He looks like damaged goods," said Finn, slowly circling the clone, who stood calmly, apparently unperturbed by the things being said about him. Finn sniffed loudly. "Can he fight?"

"Of course, of course! Manual dexterity is well within acceptable limits. They have been programmed with knowledge of the sword and the gun, and to follow orders without question. As long as they're not too complicated, of course . . . There was a certain amount of brain damage, just as I predicted . . . But you asked for simple brute soldiers, and that's what you've got. He and his many brothers should be quite sufficient for the simple tasks you have in mind. Killing and property damage and . . . so on. They don't have a lot of personality, but that's probably just as well. You could have the whole of Batch One out on the streets tomorrow, if you wanted."

Finn considered the matter. "Details, du Katt. I require details. What exactly is wrong with them?"

Du Katt sighed. "They all exhibit acceptable minor malfunctions of the body. You understand, these are the best of Batch One. Forty-seven percent of the entire batch were so malformed as to be useless for your purposes, and had to be scrapped and returned to the protein banks for recycling. Of the survivors, none of them are too bright, and they've all shown definite violent tendencies. A significant percentage exhibit some or all of the symptoms for schizophrenia. And they all score very low on empathy. None of this should be a problem, considering what you want to use them for."

"Quite," said Finn. "You have done well, du Katt. Get this batch out on the streets immediately. I want order restored, and I don't care how they do it. It might be best to issue them all face masks of some kind; I don't want them identified as clones just yet. And their features . . . might still be recognized. My face is worshiped all across the Empire, and I won't share that with anyone."

The first new Imperial guards, all dressed out in full body armor and featureless steel masks, appeared on the streets of Logres in under three hours, and quickly proved themselves every bit as brutal and merciless as the thrall peacekeepers. There had been parts of the Parade of the Endless that remained almost civilized, if not actually free, just because the thralls couldn't be everywhere at once; but the new guards soon put a stop to that. Curfews were strictly enforced, all infringements of the law were punished by on the spot executions, and even the smallest signs of dissent or defiance were quickly stamped out. Sometimes literally. Joseph Wallace watched this new turn of events from within the safety of his bunker, and worried.

He'd known Finn was working on a private project with du Katt, but the new guards still came as something of a surprise to him. More and more, Joseph was feeling left out of things, his power and influence much reduced. He was still nominally the head of Church Militant and Pure Humanity, but neither enjoyed the popular support they once had. No one believed in the religion or the politics anymore, given all the things Finn had done in their name. Just the hard-core fanatics remained, most of them personally loyal to the Emperor, not Joseph Wallace. People didn't even go to church anymore . . . because they were afraid to go out. Joseph felt lost. The people had turned against everything he believed in, and turned against him. And therefore deserved everything that happened to them.

Although he would never have admitted it to anyone, even himself, Joseph's behavior had become increasingly erratic of late. He'd overseen the construction of a safe retreat for himself and his remaining loyal followers: a solid steel bunker deep in the heart of the city, staffed by the few people he felt he could still depend on. He had the place stocked with all the comforts and necessities of life, and surrounded it with every deadly defense known to man; and then he never left it, unless personally summoned by the Emperor. He had planned and launched what he thought were subtle and secret attacks against the thralls wearing his uniforms, disguised as purges against the unfaithful, but they weren't particularly successful. For every thrall peacekeeper who died, two more came forward to take his place.

And so no one was more surprised than Joseph when the Emperor put into his hands the destruction of the Rookery. It had been a long time since Finn condescended to give Joseph his orders in person. (Their little chats didn't count. They never involved business. That was the point.) Joseph had half expected to be told that the Emperor had finally lost all faith in him, and was throwing him to the wolves, but instead . . . Joseph smiled, sitting in the center of his comm room, listening to the growing chatter of his assembling army. The Rookery would be a hard nut to crack, but success in such a dangerous venture would put him right back on top again. Not least because Joseph had no intention of giving back his army once the job was over.

The Emperor should have used every means necessary to wipe out the Rookery after they drove off his last attack; but he'd hesitated. Finn said it was because he could be very soppy and sentimental over people who'd helped him in the past, but Joseph didn't believe a word of it. More likely, Finn had believed he might still need the special talents found only in the Rookery. Which was, of course, another reason for Joseph to be very thorough in destroying it. If he planned this campaign just right, Joseph could come out of it in almost as strong a position as the Emperor himself, and then . . . maybe it was time for a change at the top.

✳   ✳   ✳

In the end, Joseph Wallace put together one hell of an army. First he summoned every Church Militant and Pure Humanity fanatic he still had contact with, and had them plan the actual operation. He felt he could trust them to be suitably merciless and efficient. He also assigned them direct control of the invading force, as officers in charge, answerable only to him. The main bulk of the ground forces were made up of every soldier, trooper and marine still left on Logres, plus a surprising number of thrall peacekeepers. Joseph made sure these latter would bear the brunt of the attack. The more dead thralls, the better for everyone. And finally, he called in every air unit still operating on Logres: every gravity barge, war machine and gravity sled. This time, there would be no mistakes, no failures, no retreat.

And when he was ready, when he was sure he couldn't add one more man, gun or ship to his force, Joseph launched his attack without warning. His people flooded across the expanded and ill-defended borders of the Rookery from every direction at once, while massive gravity barges soared ominously over the crowded streets, firing their ranks of disrupter cannon straight down into the buildings below. The soldiers and the thralls and the fanatics cut down everyone in their path, showing no mercy, only varying degrees of exhilaration. Their orders were clear, their objectives simple, and it felt good to have a clear and obvious enemy to strike out at. Disrupters fired over and over, and fleeing crowds fell in waves. Swords and axes rose and fell, and blood flowed thickly in the gutters. Buildings exploded in showers of brick and stone fragments as energy beams stabbed down from the crowded sky. Fires broke out all over, and Joseph's warriors pressed forward, ever forward, determined that this time there would be no survivors to rise phoenixlike from the ashes.

After the first shock, the people of the Rookery regrouped and fought back fiercely. Douglas had insisted that everyone in the Rookery's expanded territory undergo at least some weapons training. He'd always known this attack would come. And so men, women, and even children took to the streets with swords and guns and all kinds of improvised weapons. Others prepared booby traps, ambushes, and hit and run tactics. Those too old or too young for direct action took to the roofs, and rained down heavy objects on the attackers below. Everyone in the Rookery was a fighter now. They'd had to learn to fight, to survive. Finn had seen to that.

Nina Malapert quickly put her people out on the streets, with every camera available, and broadcast the invasion live on her news site. Stand or fall, the whole Empire would watch as the Rookery fought back. The other planets needed to see that rebellion was possible—even if it ended in the slaughter of the last free people on Logres.

The pace of the invasion faltered, slowed, and even stopped in some places. The old-school citizens of the Rookery were hardened and motivated fighters, proficient in every weapon under the sun, and a few forgotten everywhere except in the Rookery. They hit the Imperial troops hard, with subtle, unexpected, and thoroughly nasty tactics, and dead Imperial troops soon littered the streets, along with the bodies of the defenders. The newcomers to the Rookery also fought fiercely and well, these last peaceful citizens of a fallen Golden Age. All the things they'd suffered under Finn had put iron in their souls, and a driving need to put things right again. They threw themselves against the invaders, howling like animals, and the sight saddened Douglas a little. He had become a Paragon to fight the good fight, in order that the everyday citizens wouldn't have to. He had fought to keep them safe, and sane, and strangers to violence like this. He knew they had to fight now—in fact he depended on it—but he took no pleasure in the sight of innocence lost.

The Psycho Sluts took to the air, shooting up into the early morning sky like avenging angels. They tore in and out of the lumbering gravity barges, blowing the antiquated vessels apart with vivid pyrotechnic displays of psionic energy. Gun ports exploded, steel shells tore like paper, and terrible multicolored fires swept through the packed interiors. The huge war machines lurched off course, slammed together, or just drifted helplessly, black smoke billowing from their shattered engines. Attack sleds and their unprotected riders plummeted from the skies like burning birds.

But still the main fighting was on the ground, as the Rookery rose up as one against the invaders from outside, cutting down the enemy with vicious skill and righteous fury. The Imperial soldiers fought with close precision, the fanatics fought with ice cold fury, certain their God was on their side, singing their terrible songs of glory, and the thralls . . . fought with wide happy smiles, not caring whether they lived or died because the body meant nothing to the minds that drove them. And none of that mattered worth a damn, because the Rookery had awakened, finally forced into battle and discovering how good it felt to strike back at a hated enemy. The streets filled with blood and bodies and the cries of the fallen, and the intersections were choked with pushing, heaving mobs, and the invaders were slowed, stopped, and finally pushed back by the sheer press of people spilling out onto the streets to oppose them. The invaders fought only to win; the Rookery fought for a cause. For freedom. And what was death, compared to the promise of freedom from fear and tyranny?

Douglas Campbell and Stuart Lennox fought side by side, and occasionally back to back, and no one could stand against them, though many tried. They were always there in the thickest of the fighting, inspiring everyone with their feats of daring and their calm determination. They threw themselves into the face of the enemy, defying the odds, and the people of the Rookery followed, calling out their names as war cries.

Diana Vertue, still occasionally Jenny Psycho, strode through the streets, and wherever she looked enemy troops died. Some exploded, some burst into flames that could not be put out, and some just fell back and screamed away their sanity at what they'd seen in her eyes. Diana didn't even notice. She concentrated, reaching deep within herself, and then turned the full force of her extraordinary mind on the link between the uber-espers and the thralls they controlled in the Rookery. Diana could see it clearly, like the convoluted web of an insane spider, hanging over the Rookery and leading far away. She broke the link with a single surge of destructive energy, and all across the Rookery men and women collapsed, thralls no longer. With their minds restored to them, they stopped fighting immediately, and just sat and cried and howled, at the memories of what they had been forced to do. Some even hugged the bewildered fighters of the Rookery, thanking them for their release.

At one stroke, the size of the invading army had been halved, and the already faltering attack fell apart. Shattered into smaller, easily overwhelmed groups, they soon realized they couldn't hope to win, and the wise ones turned and fled. The invasion became a rout, and collapsed. The

Rookery killed the fanatics who stood, and pursued those who ran, cutting them down from behind. They had seen too much slaughter and destruction to think of mercy. In the end, only one man got out of the Rookery alive.

Joseph Wallace had never ventured far inside hostile territory. He stuck close to the Rookery boundary, trying hard to keep on top of what was happening. He was only there in person because the Emperor had required it of him. He couldn't believe how quickly his marvelous army had fallen apart. It should have been a walkover; his trained and fervent warriors against the rabble of the Rookery. All the computer simulations had said so. But instead he'd been forced to watch helplessly as his people died, outnumbered and overwhelmed. Even his glorious air force had been crippled, driven from the skies by those esper freaks. He sent frantic calls for reinforcements, for any kind of backup, but they went unanswered. There were no more soldiers to be had, Finn wouldn't release any of his fanatics, and the ELFs . . . were silent. In the end, all that was left for Joseph was to turn and run. No one tried to stop him. He made it across the boundary of the Rookery and back into the rigidly controlled area of the Parade of the Endless, and found waiting for him a dozen of the Emperor's personal zealots. They wore the scarlet cross of the Church Militant on their armor, but when he tried to command them, they fell upon him and forced him to his knees.

"What are you doing?" he screamed. *"What are you doing?"*

They cut off his head and stuck it on a spike, and took it back to Finn, leaving the body to rot in the streets. He'd been told not to come back if he failed.

This was the Emperor's first big failure to be seen live, as it happened, on viewscreens all across the Empire. Overnight the Rookery became a symbol for the possibility of successful rebellion. Proof that you could defy the Emperor, and get away with it. And as the Rookery celebrated their victory, and mourned their losses, uprisings broke out on planets everywhere. Imperial troops were caught by surprise, and overrun. Finn had no extra troops to send, and too many troubles of his own, so he did what he'd told Joseph to do, the one thing Joseph had quailed at. He chose a planet at random, a backward but comfortable world called Pandora, and used transmutation engines to reduce all life on the world to undifferentiated protoplasmic slime. The news spread quickly, and the rebellions stopped, because there was no one to tell them how few engines there actually were in the Empire.

Until Nina Malapert appeared in her studio again, red-faced and breathless from fighting in the streets, to follow up her live coverage of the invasion with newly arrived information from the combined fleet currently approaching Logres. She told the listening, frightened worlds that most of the engines had been destroyed at Mog Mor, and backed it up with on the spot recordings from the starship *Heritage*. And the rebellions broke out all over again, this time fueled with fury over what had happened to Pandora.

Finn Durandal sat alone in his private quarters, thinking. He could still win. All he had to do was cut off the head of the rebellion, and the body would falter and fall apart. All he had to do was take out the figurehead, the acclaimed King of Thieves, and the Rookery would be leaderless, and fall apart into feuding factions. They depended on Douglas, not just for leadership, but for vision. Yes, all he had to do was kill his old friend and comrade Douglas Campbell. The man who was the source of his problems, and always had been.

Finn had known before of the fleet's surrender, but the news of the incipent invasion had finally reached him. It took so long because no one wanted to be the one to tell him. They told Joseph, but he had been too busy planning his invasion of the Rookery to be bothered. Eventually a Church Militant fanatic was found with a strong sense of duty and no real sense of self-preservation, and he was sent to tell the Emperor. Finn listened in silence to the news that the combined fleet was now heading towards Logres with the express intent of kicking him off his throne, and when he was sure he'd heard every detail, he beat the messenger to death with his bare hands, and went raging through the corridors of his palace with sword and gun in hand, killing everyone he came across. Even his most loyal followers fled, rather than face his incandescent rage. Even his bodyguards disappeared. After a very long time, Finn just ran out of energy. He slumped against a blood-spattered wall, breathing heavily, gore dripping thickly from the blade in his hand, and finally decided he'd vented enough for one day. He trudged wearily back to his private quarters, and poured himself several large brandies.

He put away his sword without bothering to clean it, and laughed shakily. It had been a long time since he'd let the beast run loose like that. But he couldn't afford to indulge himself anymore. He had to think . . . He picked up the only intact chair, set it on its legs again, and sat down. It all came down to Douglas. If he could kill the ex-King before the combined fleet arrived, he'd be able to negotiate from a position of strength. With the Terror on its way, the Empire needed a strong man on the throne. They had to know that. And with Douglas gone, who else was there who could do the job? The runaway Deathstalker? Finn thought not.

He smiled slowly, the last of the tension easing out of his muscles. He could deal with Douglas. He knew how the Campbell thought, what reached him, and what moved him. After all, they'd been friends and colleagues for so long . . . Finn understood Douglas, and Douglas only thought he understood Finn. So setting a trap to lure Douglas in, and then kill him, shouldn't be any problem at all.

Finn went to talk to Anne Barclay. This meant talking to Dr. Happy as well, which was unfortunate. The good doctor had continued to deteriorate, and was now barely a shadow of his former self. Finn entered the private and very secure laboratory he maintained in the palace for the doctor and his patient, and found Dr. Happy scrabbling around on the floor on all fours, searching for some bit of him that had fallen off. Finn had to call the doctor's name several times before he responded, and then he lurched reluctantly back onto his feet again. There wasn't a lot of Dr. Happy left. He wore nothing but his stained and crumpled lab coat, revealing a shriveled and desiccated body with holes in it, topped by a face that was little more than a skull with strands of wispy flyaway hair. The nose and ears were gone, the lips just pale tatters. Dr. Happy waggled his remaining fingers at Finn in a friendly manner, peering at him uncertainly with sunken, piss yellow eyes.

"So good to see you again, Finn! Yes! I've been working on a marvelous new experiment that will allow us to plug in other people's organs as backup spare parts . . . imagine what you could do if your body contained three hearts and two livers . . . I have broken the compatibility barrier! I have! You'll see, before long I'll have made a new man of myself! The tech keeps me going, of course, but it lacks a certain . . . something. Flesh is the key to all mysteries."

"Well," said Finn. "That's all very demented, but I have business to be about. How is Anne?"

"A work of art, if I say so myself. You could put her up against a Hadenman now, and make a killing on the side bets. Go and have a nice chat, while I try and find my genitals."

Finn made a wide circle around Dr. Happy, and let himself into the reinforced steel vault they'd built at the back of the lab to contain the re-built Anne Barclay. He found her standing still and silent in the middle of the room, staring at nothing, not even the mirror. For a long time the ad-dition of the synthesized Boost to her many tech implants had made her restless and suddenly violent, but the mood seemed to have passed. At least, there didn't seem to be any new dents in the steel walls. Finn ap-proached her cautiously.

"Hello, Anne. How are we doing today?"

"I don't know about you," said Anne, not looking round, "but I'm fighting the voices in my head. Dr. Happy put computers in me, to help run my various servomechanisms, and I can hear them whining away at the back of my thoughts. I'm fighting a civil war in my head, and I fear I may be losing. Why did you do this to me, Finn?"

"I couldn't let you die."

"Why not? You let so many other people die. And it might actually have been kinder, in my case."

"I couldn't let you go," said Finn. "Because you're the only one who saw the monster within me, and didn't flinch."

Anne looked at him for the first time with her glowing golden eyes, and smiled briefly. "Takes one to know one."

"I want to help you," said Finn. "Tell me how."

"Don't you know what I need, Finn?"

"Emotional support. But I've never been very good at that. Just don't have the knack."

"Then you're no use to me. You'd have to be human to understand what I'm going through, and you left that behind a long time ago."

Finn looked at her, feeling helpless. He didn't like the feeling. He could see what she needed, but had no idea what it involved. He never had. Emotions were for the most part things he only understood from a distance. But he tried anyway. Because he needed to believe that even monsters didn't have to be monsters all the time.

"I could still make you my Queen," he said. "Set you on a throne beside me. No one would say anything. No one would dare."

Anne laughed harshly. "I can just see something like me sitting on a throne. A perfect symbol for the Empire you've made, Finn. No. I never wanted to be Queen. I wanted so very little, and never got any of it. And now . . . I'm haunted by the people I could have been. Stronger, better, happier people. All I am now is what you made of me. Just another poor damned monster—like you."

Finn considered the matter, and then shrugged mentally. Anne was lost to him, trapped within her own limitations. Which meant he had no more use for her, except as a weapon to use against his enemies. So he turned and left her in her room, her cage, nodded good-bye to the preoccupied Dr. Happy, and went off to set in motion his plan to bait and trap and kill Douglas Campbell.

First, he made an official announcement, on all his tame news stations, that Anne Barclay wasn't dead after all. Instead, she had been kept in strict seclusion while she recovered from her many serious injuries. But now that she was finally well enough, she could at last be put on trial for treason, and the murder of the well beloved Paragon Emma Steel. There would be a show trial, televised on every channel, followed quickly by a prolonged, painful, and messy execution.

Finn watched a recording of his broadcast afterwards, and gave himself serious points for an excellent performance. He struck just the right notes of betrayed trust and outraged honor. He still had the crystal paperweight with which Anne had bludgeoned Emma Steel to death, stained with the Paragon's dried blood. He'd had a feeling at the time it might come in handy someday. Not that he expected to have to offer it in evidence. It would never come to a trial. Douglas would see to that. He'd take one look at the news broadcast and come running to save her. Because after all that had happened, after all the things that Anne had done, she was still his friend. Douglas would come to rescue her, because he still believed in people. That had always been his greatest weakness.

Nina Malapert got the news first, of course. She hurriedly called a private meeting, just for her and Douglas and Stuart, and wouldn't say why until they were all assembled in Douglas's room. Two Psycho Sluts stood guard outside the door, ensuring they wouldn't be interrupted. Douglas and Stuart sat on the two chairs and looked expectantly at Nina, who was too nervous to sit or stand still. In the end, she folded her arms tightly under her breasts, mostly to keep her hands from shaking, and broke the news as swiftly and kindly as she could. She kept to the bare facts, not commenting, while watching Douglas carefully. After she'd finished, he didn't say anything for a long time. Nina and Stuart looked at each other.

"You're thinking about a rescue," Stuart said finally. "Don't. We can't risk it, Douglas. She's being held inside the palace. We'd need an army just to break in, and I don't see why we should risk so many good people for a backstabbing traitor like Anne Barclay."

"We wouldn't need an army," said Douglas. "I know old, secret ways into the palace, remember? Ways that Finn doesn't even suspect are there."

"You're thinking of going on your own, aren't you?" said Nina. "Sweetie, it's a trap! Has to be!"

"Of course it's a trap," said Douglas, his voice dangerously calm. "Finn always did know how to yank my chains. It doesn't matter. I can outthink Finn."

"And get to Anne, despite all the obstacles and booby traps he'll put in your path?" said Stuart.

"Of course."

"Why?" said Stuart, not bothering to hide his exasperation. "What makes her so important? She betrayed Lewis and Jesamine, and you, and Finn's finally admitted she murdered Emma Steel!"

"She was Finn's bitch," said Nina. "And now that he doesn't need her, he's thrown her to the wolves, and I say good riddance to bad rubbish."

"You never knew her before," said Douglas. "She was splendid, in her time. And she was my friend. Friends don't stop being friends just because they've done bad things. And I think . . . perhaps we all betrayed her, long before she betrayed us."

"Douglas, she hasn't been your friend in a long time," said Stuart.

"That's why I need to be her friend," said Douglas. "One last time."

He swore them both to silence, and left the Rookery alone, traveling secret paths he remembered from his time as a Paragon. He went alone and in disguise, because he knew the rest of his people would have tried to stop him if they'd known—and he wasn't going to be stopped. He slipped silently over the border and into the dark empty streets of the Parade of the Endless, keeping to the shadows to avoid the peacekeepers, hidden from the ELFs by the old Paragon esp-blocker on his belt. He headed for the palace, and no one saw him coming.

He had to do this. Perhaps because Anne was the very last piece of his old life that he might still be able to rescue and redeem. Everything else was changed or lost or gone, including him. He had to salvage something.

The only person who might have stopped him was Diana Vertue. So he made a point of searching her out before he left, telling her what he was going to do, and asked her to run interference to cover his leaving. Diana agreed. She understood all about necessary emotional gestures, and even more about self-sacrifice.

And if I don't come back . . .

You will be avenged, said Jenny Psycho.

Finn Durandal sat on a comfortable chair in Dr. Happy's laboratory, and watched what was left of the good doctor ricochet around the room. He'd had to bring his own comfortable chair; Dr. Happy had moved far beyond such everyday comforts. All his skin was gray and rotting now, with deep dark holes in the exposed red meat of his body, some of it tinted here and there with the purples and greens of gangrene. Sharp-edged support tech protruded all over his body, blocky and functional. And ever since he'd dosed himself with the new Boost (he couldn't resist, he just had to *know*), his mental deterioration seemed to have accelerated to catch up with his supercharged metabolism. He darted back and forth across his laboratory, unable to settle anywhere for more than a moment, bouncing off the hardier pieces of equipment, giggling and barking and singing scraps of songs.

"Dr. Happy," Finn said firmly. "Try and land somewhere near my reality, and talk to me. Have you programmed Anne's computer implants as I instructed you?"

Dr. Happy spun to a halt in front of Finn, gurgled a few times, and studied him for a long moment, as though trying to remember where he'd seen him before. He clutched his broken hands together over his sunken chest, and nodded so rapidly that Finn was genuinely worried the man's head would fall off.

"All done! All done! Oh yes. I programmed her brain. Her new computer brain, sunk deep into the medulla oblongata, and the old reptile brain stem itself. Our instructions now have the force of instinct. So she will do the right thing, whether she wants to or not. Or at least, I think I did that. My time sense is so advanced now, I can remember things before I do them. So many worlds to see, so little time! Yes! I'm wearing out, you know. Running down. Won't be long now. Ah, death—the final high . . ."

"Will Anne do what I need her to do?" Finn said patiently. You couldn't bully or threaten someone who was actually looking forward to dying.

"Oh, yes. I did it. If her nerve should fail, the tech will see her through. I was very careful. She doesn't even remember my programming her."

"Good. Douglas will be here soon. I know it. Try and keep out of the way once he gets here, Doctor. I want this to be between Anne and Douglas."

"Won't you be here?" said Dr. Happy, absently poking a finger into a hole in his chest, to see how deep it went.

"No. I don't want anything to detract from their reunion. I shall observe from a safe distance. I want to see what this King of Thieves has become, before I face him in person. First rule of war, Doctor: Know thy enemy."

"Know your code word," Dr. Happy said strictly, trying on coherence again for a while, just to see what it felt like. "If all else fails, your word of command will activate the failsafes I put in her head. Have you finished with me now? It's so hard, being rational for any length of time. Reason!

Overrated if you ask me. Know thyself, Finn. That's far more important. We are all deep, and contain miracles. Fish."

Finn decided he'd probably got the best out of Dr. Happy, and was getting up to leave when the doctor suddenly froze in his tracks, his bony head cocked on one side as though listening, his sunken eyes elsewhere.

"Someone's coming," he said. "Coming like a thunderstorm, with blood and rage in his heart."

Finn smiled. "Good," he said. And left.

The man who had once been a Paragon, and then King of the Golden Age, and most recently the King of Thieves, but was now and for this mission just a man named Douglas Campbell, ran steadily through the ancient stone tunnels under the Imperial Palace. There was a whole maze of subsystems and maintenance ways under the palace itself that most people never knew about; some so old they no longer appeared on any official plans. Deserted and abandoned, originally built to serve buildings that no longer existed, over whose remains the palace had been built. The royal family knew about them, and kept them secret, because every ruler knew that the day might come when they'd have to leave in a hurry. And so Douglas made his way past and under and around all the defenses Finn had set up to protect himself, and finally emerged through a very secret hidden panel into what had once been his private quarters.

He looked unhurriedly about him, taking in the recent damage and the older worn-in mess that disfigured what had once been his rooms. He wrinkled his nose. The place smelled as bad as it looked. Finn had changed. He never used to live like a pig. Douglas had to wonder what the state of these rooms implied about Finn's current state of mind. Perhaps it meant Finn was no longer in control. Douglas hoped so. And yet . . . there was something unhealthy about this room, beyond the mess and the clutter, signs of a man who didn't need to bother about the everyday human things anymore.

Douglas scowled. He didn't want Finn to be mad. That would take all the fun out of killing him.

He found Finn's computer terminal and, using a device that was common in the Rookery but strictly illegal everywhere else, Douglas forced his way into Finn's files. It didn't take him long to discover where Finn was keeping Anne; but why hold a political prisoner in a steel vault in a private laboratory? Sudden horrid thoughts about torture made Douglas impatient, and he hurried out of the room. He padded cautiously through the dark shadowed corridors of what had once been his palace. His home. He took in the hanging corpses, the heads impaled on spikes, and his heart hardened. He'd find no innocents in a place like this.

And so he killed all the guards he came across, silently and efficiently. They were all cold-eyed fanatics, well trained and motivated, but none of them were good enough to stop Douglas. He let the bodies lie where they fell. Let someone find them and sound the alarm. Let Finn know that death was stalking the corridors of his usurped palace. Douglas hurried on through what had once been familiar locations, now turned into a slaughterhouse by Finn. Some of the blood was still wet. Douglas smiled a slow cold smile. Just one more reason to kill his old friend.

He found the laboratory easily enough, and frowned as he realized there were no guards posted at the door. Douglas approached it warily, ready for booby traps or surprise attacks, but there was nothing. He pressed gently against the door with his fingertips, and it swung smoothly open, falling back easily at his touch. So. A trap, daring him to walk inside. Douglas laughed, and it was a harsh ugly sound. He pushed back the cowl of his cape to reveal his face, so that everyone would know who had come, and then kicked the door all the way open and barged into the lab, sword and gun in hand. He looked quickly about him, but the whole place was deserted. A few machines still hummed and chattered to themselves, working on unknown problems, but most of the tech had been shut down. There were animal cages stacked against one wall, but they were empty. Half the lights had been turned off, leaving half the lab hidden in shadows. Douglas moved slowly forward, breathing through his mouth so he could listen for any sound, and then he froze as he made out a single silhouette standing at the back of the lab. For a moment they stood there, studying each other, and then Anne Barclay stepped forward into the light.

Douglas almost cried out, at the sight of what had been done to her. She was hunched over by the bulking tech that protruded from her back, and more showed here and there through her flushed rose red skin. Her musculature had been twisted and distorted by the strains of implanted servomechanisms, and there were fresh scars on the sides of her shaven head. Her face was still hers, but her eyes glowed golden in the dim light. Old ridged scar tissues made ugly patterns on her bare body. She lurched forward another step, the power in her remade body giving her strength but no grace. Anne saw the horror in Douglas's face, and produced something like her old smile.

"Hello, Douglas. If you came to save me, you left it a bit late."

"What have they done to you, Anne?" Douglas said softly.

"Oh, they've done a hell of a lot to me, Douglas, and all because of you. You did this to me, during your dramatic escape from the court. Of course, you were so busy getting away that you didn't look back, to see what the falling masonry had done to me. But that wasn't the worse thing you did. You escaped, and you didn't take me with you. So really, everything that's going to happen now is all your fault."

She raised a hand, and a disrupter barrel emerged from a slit under her wrist. Douglas threw himself to one side, and the energy beam just clipped his ribs, burning the skin and setting fire to his cloak. He threw it from him, and dodged behind a piece of heavy machinery.

"Anne, don't do this! I came to get you out of here!"

"Too late, Douglas. Too little and too late."

She swept the heavy machinery away with one swift heave, and advanced on him, a sword in each hand. Douglas reluctantly aimed his disrupter at her, but at the last moment he shot at her leg, aiming only to wound her. Anne avoided the beam easily. And then she was upon him, her two blades moving faster than any human eye could follow, and Douglas was forced to fall back, step by step, using all his skill and strength just to defend himself. He was ten times the swordsman she was, but she was ten times stronger, and faster.

They dueled back and forth across the lab, smashing delicate tech along the way, Douglas using every trick and technique he knew just to stay alive. Anne had been remade with tech and drugs and the Boost, and she was inhumanly competent now. Douglas fought his way out of a corner that would have trapped him, but already his breathing was coming hard and harsh, and his sword arm ached from parrying viciously hard blows. He knew now that the only way to stop Anne would be to kill her, and he wasn't sure he could do that.

So he did the only thing he could. He dropped his sword and gun on the floor, and stood before her empty-handed. Anne stood very still, checking out the possibilities of a trap or a stratagem.

"Anne," said Douglas. "This is me. Remember. Remember how it used to be. We were friends. And of all the friends I had, it seems I've hurt you the most. I never meant for this to happen. I won't kill you, Anne. You . . . you do what you have to."

Anne slowly lowered the blades in her hands. "Damn you, Douglas. This isn't fair. I need to kill you."

"Then kill me."

"You won't kill me? You won't even do me that one final kindness? You think I want to live like this?"

"Come with me, Anne. To the Rookery. They have all kind of tech there, some alien. There has to be someone who can help you. Who can undo what these bastards did to you. Don't just give up! The Anne I remember never believed in giving up. It's never too late . . ."

"It is for me. I should have died. This is my punishment. I deserve everything that's happened to me, because of all the awful things I did. You don't know . . ."

"Anne, I—"

"You don't know! I killed Emma Steel! The best person I ever knew. She was worth ten of me, and I struck her down from behind."

"Then come with me, and fight for the rebellion. Find atonement on the battlefield."

"You'd still take me in? After everything I've done? To you, and Jesamine, and Lewis?"

"That's what friends are for," said Douglas.

"You always were too soft, Douglas."

"Well, this is all very touching," Finn said suddenly, speaking through the tech in Anne's throat. Like an ELF speaking through his thrall. "But I did foresee this outbreak of maudlin sentimentality, and so I took a few precautions. Not very nice precautions, but then, that's life for you. So sorry I can't be here in person, Douglas, but be assured that thanks to the programming I had placed in Anne's computer implants, when she kills you it will be her hand on the sword, but my instructions in her hand. So really I'll be there in spirit, anyway."

He spoke a command word, and Anne's face went blank as her body shifted abruptly into a killing stance. Douglas glanced at his weapons lying on the floor, but there was no way he could reach them in time. And so he stood, tall and proud and unflinching. When there's nothing left but to die, die well.

And then Anne screamed. An ugly, tortured sound. She dropped both her swords. Douglas started forward, only to freeze again as Anne covered him with the disrupter built into her wrist. She smiled briefly at Douglas.

"Good-bye, old friend. I betrayed you so many times, but this would have been one betrayal too far. I guess they built me better than they knew. So—one last blast of the gun. One last chance for redemption."

She lifted her hand, fighting her computers all the way, and shot herself in the head. At such close range, the energy beam blew her head apart, in a flurry of blood and brains. The headless body rocked back and forth on its feet for a moment, and then stood still.

Finn sent his people running in from all directions, but by the time they got to the laboratory Douglas was already gone. He left a trail of dead bodies behind him as he made his way back through the palace, and finally disappeared down into the subsystems again. And all the way he was planning the first steps of the rebellion. The time to rise up had come. Because if Finn could do such terrible things to the only woman who'd ever cared a damn for him, then he was capable of anything. Anything at all.

CHAPTER SEVEN

WORKING WITH THE ILLUMINATI

The stars and the planets whirled by so fast they made a continuous shimmering rainbow path as Owen Deathstalker strode steadily back into the past, the galaxy turning under his feet like a giant cog wheel. He was too tired now for dancing, his spirit too weary, and yet he felt more powerful than ever, and his speed continued to increase. He was still following Hazel d'Ark's trail, forever closing in but somehow never quite catching up. He felt like he'd always been pursuing Hazel, and always would, trapped in the rainbow run like a hamster in its wheel, only thinking it was getting somewhere.

Home seemed very far away now, and so did his humanity. He'd done so much, both before and since his death, and he felt like he could do so much more. He'd come a long way, in more ways than one. He wondered if the old Owen, the young scholar in his comfortable ivory tower, would even recognize the man he'd become. He liked to think he'd done good things, honorable things, in his short but remarkable life . . . but he had to wonder if it would ever be possible, or even advisable, for something as powerful as he now was to ever return to human society. Power tended to corrupt, he knew that from his studies of history, and he had made himself so very powerful. Would he ever see his home again, with or without Hazel?

That thought led naturally but uneasily to another. What was he going to do, what could he hope to do, when he finally did catch up with Hazel? Was she destined to become the Terror, somewhere back in the unimaginable past, or could he somehow prevent it? And if the iron laws of cause and effect meant she had to become the Terror, and do all the awful things she did, could he win her back to sanity and humanity? Could she ever be just Hazel d'Ark again? Could he ever be just Owen Deathstalker again? Or had they both drunk too deeply from the poisoned chalice that was the Madness Maze?

Could they ever have a life together after this, or had he come all this way just to kill a monster, and die with her rather than become a monster himself? So many questions, and no answers at all. The only thing he was sure of was that he had to go on. Hazel was his love, and his responsibility, even if she'd never admitted it. He couldn't leave her, mad and sorrowing, in the dark.

He was getting close to . . . something. He could feel it.

He broke out of the rainbow run, and dropped back into the slow steady course of time. Stars and planets reappeared around him, calm and stationary against the endless night. Owen wasn't sure how far back he'd gone into the past, but once again he was hanging in orbit over the same familiar planet. Remembering how he'd been treated before, he surrounded himself with a powerful force shield and stealth screen, so that he could take a cautious look around before becoming involved, without having to worry about being observed or attacked.

He swore briefly as he discovered he'd just missed Hazel again. She had been here recently, perhaps as little as a few weeks previously, but she was gone again, diving even further back into prehistory. But why had she stopped here, however briefly, in this particular moment of time and space? Owen reached out with his enlarged senses, and immediately detected something strange and yet somehow familiar, down on the surface of the planet below. It sort of reminded him of Hazel. Had she left something of herself behind? It was a strong presence, powerful but elusive, with fluctuating attributes that reminded him of his time inside the Madness Maze. It definitely wasn't Hazel, but . . . Could some other Maze survivor have come back through time, pursuing him as he pursued Hazel?

Owen pushed the mounting questions aside, so he could consider his own position. He listened in to the thousands of communication channels emanating from the planet below that was Logres, Golgotha, Heartworld, and now apparently simply the Hearth of Humanity. He sorted through the various frequencies, searching out the information he needed about exactly what lay below him. It seemed he had emerged in the far past, in the very first days of Empire, when Humanity had only just discovered the stardrive, and was setting out to explore the stars, to see what was there.

Owen stopped listening, and looked around him. Great clumsy satellites whirled ponderously past, accompanied by all kinds of abandoned junk and tech; almost enough to make a planetary ring. Owen drifted slowly down towards Hearth, just enough to put himself safely underneath their various orbits and out of their way. Also in orbit were huge, ungainly starships, being slowly put together in orbiting docks by people in what looked like primitive hard suits. The unfinished ships bristled with all kinds of probably untested tech. This was the first wave of expansion, Humanity's first great leap out into the unknown. These brave prototype ships looked nothing like the sleek and sophisticated craft of Owen's time, and he had to admire the courage of the visionary men and women who were ready to trust their lives to new ships and a barely understood drive, in the service of Humanity's oldest dream. To go to the stars . . .

Owen went swiftly through the communication channels again, trying to get some feel for what kind of political setup he'd be facing this time. Apparently the Empire at this time consisted of the nine planets in the solar system, all of them terraformed or colonized to some degree, ruled more or less democratically by a Council of the Nine, based on Hearth. There was no throne, no Emperor. From what Owen could gather, Humanity was pretty much at peace with itself, and full of hope and good intentions.

The road to Hell has always been paved with good intentions.

Owen considered the planet turning so very slowly beneath him. He had to go down. He needed to know what it was, that felt to him like Hazel and the Maze and something more. And he was tired. He could use a rest. The pursuit could wait, for a while. After all, he had all the time in the world . . . And then his head snapped round, and he glared suspiciously into the dark. Something was coming his way, he could feel it, and it was heading straight for him. Even though nothing in this primitive age should have been able to detect his presence. He glared in the direction he knew it was coming from, even though he couldn't see anything yet, and eventually a bright shining light came swooping towards him.

The light swiftly became a living thing, an entirely unfamiliar creature flapping towards him on huge butterfly wings almost thirty feet across. It moved easily through the cold vacuum of space, entirely unprotected, apparently driven only by its brightly shining wings. The body within the wingspan was basically humanoid, but in no way human. It was alien, in appearance and affect, a delicate flimsy creature of bright shimmering rainbow colors. It slowed to a halt about a dozen feet away from Owen, and considered him with a face that was somehow even more disturbing for its vague human connections. The eyes were huge and dark and unblinking, taking up almost a third of the long pointed face, and the mouth below was a simple slit. Two long slender antennae streamed up from the bulging brow. The vast rainbow wings rippled slowly, as though holding the creature in place against unfelt astral winds.

For a moment, Owen wondered if perhaps he'd died, and this was some angel sent to finally bring him home, but the creature was just too obviously alien for that. Owen slowly raised a hand and waved politely, and words sounded suddenly in his head, sliding smoothly through his thoughts like bitter honey. They certainly weren't coming through his comm implant.

"Greetings to you, strange traveler. I am of the Illuminati. We heard you thinking up here, so I came to see what new marvel had come to Hearth. We are strangers here, traveling on our way, but you . . . you appear human. Though humans don't normally survive long in open space."

Owen pushed his thoughts in the creature's direction, and it seemed to pick them up easily enough. "Hi there. I am human, or at least I used to be. I suppose human is as human does. I'm . . . just visiting. May I ask what you are?"

"The name for my people translates into your tongue as Luminary Beings, or Light People. Since we have been here, we have adopted the old human name of Illuminati. I myself have taken the name Lucifer."

Owen blinked a few times. "I'm not sure you've really understood the implications of that name."

"It means light-bringer, doesn't it?"

"Well, yes, but . . . no, forget it. Life's too short to explain some things. I'm Owen."

"Hello, Owen. May I inquire as to how you're able to survive in open space without exploding, boiling, or otherwise perishing in a very messy manner?"

"I haven't been entirely human for a long time," said Owen. "I'm still trying to decide whether that's a good thing. Long story; basically I'm traveling back through time from your future, searching for a friend who came this way before me. Her name is Hazel d'Ark. Have you encountered her, by any chance?"

"I do not recognize the name, Owen. I have to say I'm impressed. My people have traveled in space long and far and wide, and we have never encountered any species that could move at will in time. May I inquire as to your intentions here?"

"Well, since we're both being so very polite and civilized . . . I thought I'd take a rest stop, and take a look around. See what there is to see."

"I'm not sure that's entirely wise," said Lucifer. "The people of this world are not ready for contact with a being of your power and abilities. I can sense strange energies, within and around you. Your presence could terrify and traumatize the people of this time, perhaps even anger them to violence. They have very little experience with beings other than themselves."

"Did they treat you badly?" said Owen, frowning.

"Not as such. I think it would be best if you came down and spoke with my people first. I understand that I cannot coerce you, but I assure you there are things we know that you do not, and that you need to know." The alien studied Owen's face for a long moment, with its flat black unblinking eyes. "You are not just looking for your friend. I see something in you . . . an old, familiar fear. You know of the great and ancient evil that destroyed my people, and a civilization millions of years old. You know of the entity we call the Terror."

"Yes. Perhaps we should speak," Owen said carefully. "Any idea on how I can descend to the surface without being spotted? My stealth field will shield me from electronic eyes, but not material ones. Hey . . . wait a minute. How were you able to find me?"

"Few things are hidden from the Illuminati," said Lucifer. "You shine so very brightly in our minds, like a part of ourselves we had forgotten. Follow me."

It unfurled its great butterfly wings, flapped them like huge sails, and a shining silver tunnel appeared in space below it, dropping endlessly away. Lucifer dived into it, and after a quick mental shrug, so did Owen. If nothing else, a meeting with these Light People should be interesting. He was pretty sure the Ecstatic named Joy had mentioned them once. And then, as suddenly as he'd entered the silver tunnel, Owen was out the other end, and dropping through open air towards a great green lawn. He landed easily, and the Illuminati drifted down to settle beside him. The silver tunnel had already disappeared.

It was a bright sunny day, and Owen took a deep lungful of good clean air. Natural sounds swept over him from all directions, a happy contrast to the cold and empty silence of space. Even the sun felt warm and refreshing. He smiled broadly, and looked around him.

He was standing in a great open park, surrounded by a city. There were lawns and trees, carefully arranged and sculpted hedges, and even a decorative bridge over a clear, sparkling river. Beyond the park, graceful air cars soared between tall towers, all silver and gold and rocket trims. Darting in and around and between these wonderful cars were men and women wearing some kind of antigrav backpack. Their happy laughter echoed down to the streets below. The air was pure and clean, the sky a dazzling blue without a cloud in sight, and everything seemed to Owen to be gloriously bright and new.

The buildings were steel and silver, with huge mirrored windows, all of them built in strict straight lines, all of them exactly the same, with no room for style or individuality or character. They marched away in long rows, tall and imposing and strictly functional. The best that could be said of them was that they had a solid presence, a certain majesty of scale.

No people walked the polished and gleaming streets—only robots, carrying packages or running errands or obsessively cleaning things. They were roughly humanoid in shape, cast in gleaming steel, but they had none of the style or artistry of the Shub robots. These were clearly just machines, designed to perform tasks. They were actually sort of clunky, Owen decided; unfinished-looking.

Also moving up and down the streets, giving the robots plenty of room, were crowds of assorted animals. All of them without any obvious owner or master, all of them moving with perfect assurance. There were horses and dogs and cats, and other creatures Owen didn't recognize, though he thought he might have seen pictures of them in certain very old texts.

"The robots aren't very efficient," said a warm, cheerful voice behind him. "But I guess we just like having them around. We always dreamed of creating robots, so now that we can build them, we do."

Owen looked round. Standing beside him was a woman of a certain age, smiling calmly, dressed in a sparkling metallic tunic. It was a sign of how engrossed Owen had been in this strange old world that he hadn't even heard her arrive. He made a mental note not to let that happen again. Just because a place looked . . . clean, didn't mean it was necessarily friendly to strangers. He smiled back at the woman. She had an ordinary, dull, but determinedly happy face. The kind of woman who was always doing things for others, usually without thanks. She took Owen's offered hand, and gave it a brief but emphatic shake.

"You must be Owen," she said. "I'm Hellen Waters. The Illuminati have talked of nothing but you ever since they discovered you in orbit, appearing suddenly out of nowhere. They all listened in to your little chat with Lucifer. And yes, I've tried telling him about that name, but he won't listen. The Light People can be almost willfully blind to concepts they don't want to understand. I'm their human contact. Pretty much their only human contact, these days. I try to protect them, and run interference for them when government busybodies come sniffing around, because . . . well, because somebody's got to. They're very like children, in some ways, the Illuminati. They understand about big things, like the Terror, but the small everyday cruelties and evils of human thinking seem to go right over their heads. So, Owen, who are you? Where do you come from? And why have the Illuminati got themselves so worked up over you?"

Owen had to grin at the series of perfectly artless questions. "I am

Owen Deathstalker, a traveler in time. I'm from your future. Don't ask me exactly how far ahead; I've rather lost track of dates."

Hellen looked at him, wide-eyed and openmouthed. "I should have known the Illuminati wouldn't get so excited over just anybody. A time traveler! That is just so . . . What a year this has been! First contact with aliens, and a time traveler! I may hyperventilate."

"Don't ask me about the future," said Owen. "I'm new to this whole time travel thing, but I'm pretty sure I'm not supposed to talk about things like that."

"I'm just delighted to find out Humanity has a future," said Hellen. "Sometimes you have to wonder . . . Can you tell me anything about what it's like, where you come from?"

"It's . . . colorful," said Owen. "Yes, definitely colorful. You said your robots weren't very efficient. So why build them?"

Hellen smiled, acknowledging the change of subject. "We built robots because we wanted to. Because we've always wanted to. Our scientific romances were always full of machine servants, in the shape of men. Besides, we like having servants, or maybe even slaves. Robots can be both, without any of the concomitant guilt. Some people say we let the robots do too much for us these days, that we've become soft and weak and far too dependant on them. Maybe. But life's hard enough; you have to take your comforts where you can find them.

"After the robots, we built improved animals. That's a much better story. We took the animals we loved most, and made them intelligent, and finally equal citizens. Horses and dogs and cats came first, because we'd always liked them the most. We did it to the monkeys too, but they turned out to be ungrateful little shits. They've got their own city now, and throw their shit at tourists. And we did offer to do it to the whales and dolphins, but they said they were quite happy as they were, thank you very much. Of course, some people were rather surprised when the animals turned out to have wills and opinions of their own, and were more interested in being partners than pets. Idiots. That was the point. Would you like to meet some?"

"Love to," said Owen, fascinated by the thought of intelligent animals. "We do have horses and dogs and cats in my time, but mostly just out on the border worlds, and none of them are intelligent. Or if they are, they're keeping really quiet about it."

"Then I guess the experiment didn't work out after all," Hellen sighed. "Such a pity. Let's try one of the dogs. Cats can be a bit snotty with strangers, and horses always want to talk philosophy. Dogs always have time to talk to a human. But be warned: dogs are still dogs—they love goofing off."

She led Owen out of the park. Lucifer stayed behind. He'd gone very quiet since he landed. Owen and Hellen ended up talking to a large black and white spotty dog that sat at the edge of the street, having a very thorough and satisfying scratch. He broke off to have a good sniff at Owen.

"Hello, Hellen," he said, in a deep growly voice. "Who's the rube? He smells funny."

"Such manners, Sparky," Hellen scolded him, but still unable to keep the fondness out of her voice. "This is Owen. He's just visiting."

"Oh, a tourist. Nice to meet you, Owen; welcome to the city, don't steal anything, and no I don't pose for photos." He cocked his head to one side. "You really do smell different. Wrong. Not entirely human. Are you a threat? I may be civilized now, but I can still bite off your bits and gargle with your testicles."

"I'm no threat," Owen assured the dog solemnly. "I don't want to hurt anyone."

The dog wagged his tail dubiously. "Well, I can hear the truth in your voice, but still—you watch yourself. Hellen is a good sort, but far too trusting. People take advantage of her, and not just people either. I wouldn't hang around with those fairy aliens if you paid me. They talk crap and their smell puts my teeth on edge. I just know they'd love to put a collar on me, the bastards."

"Do the people of this city treat you right?" said Owen.

The dog shrugged. "More or less. I think we'd all be a lot happier if humans did a little less talking and lot more throwing sticks, but . . . Right now, most animals are annoyed because people won't let us have antigrav backpacks, and fly like they do. Just because certain species can't be trusted when it comes to shitting and pissing. Pardon the language, but I'm a dog, and we don't care. Humans have the strangest taboos. If they just sniffed each other's crotches now and again, they'd all be a lot happier."

Hellen decided it was time they were moving along, and Owen had to agree with her. A little doggy straight-talking went a long way. She led him back to the patiently waiting alien, who had opened a concealed panel in the ground, revealing a tunnel that led down into the earth. Owen was tempted to make a remark about Lucifer and the underworld, but rose above it. He and Hellen followed the alien down the simply lit tunnel, which sank steadily into the earth for some time before finally leveling off. The walls were made of tightly packed earth, and the smell of dirt and growing things was strong on the close air. Hellen leaned in close to Owen, so she could murmur confidentially in his ear.

"The Light People built all this. They like dark enclosed spaces. Apparently it makes them feel safe, and secure. Maybe it reminds them of their time in their cocoon. Assuming they have cocoons. They don't talk much about their home life."

The tunnel suddenly broadened out into a great natural cavern, hundreds of feet in diameter. The massed Illuminati hung from the ceiling by their feet, like bats, their wings folded around them like cloaks, huddled close together. They bobbed and rustled excitedly as Owen entered their domain, peering down at him from the high ceiling. Their bright rainbow glows supplied the only light, somewhat muted by the surrounding gloom. Owen counted forty of them, including Lucifer, who was looking longingly up at the crowded ceiling, but stayed politely on the ground with Owen and Hellen. There was no furniture, only raised earth mounds here and there, so Owen and Hellen sat on those. Lucifer regarded Owen thoughtfully.

"Hear our story, Owen Deathstalker. We came to Hearth ten months ago, and at first the humans made a great fuss of us. We were their first alien contact, and they couldn't get enough of us. There were parades, celebrations, and endless questions. But when we had to tell them that we couldn't teach them to fly in space unprotected, as we do, their enthusiasm waned. And when we finally told them why we had come, that we were the last of our species, fleeing from the Terror that had destroyed our civilization, everything changed. We were no longer heroic travelers, just objects of pity. Refugees. Not brave explorers of the infinite, as they in-tended to be. And when they found out we had no great knowledge to share with them, no amazing advanced technology, just a warning of the danger to come . . . the novelty wore off fast. They lost interest in us. They were bored. We were a disappointment. All the great dreams they'd had of first contact with an intelligent alien species, and we couldn't fulfill any of them. They wouldn't listen to us about the Terror. A threat that wouldn't even arrive for thousands of years wasn't enough to hold their attention. No one took it seriously. *That's someone else's problem,* they said. *Let someone else worry about it.* We became a joke, and then an old joke, that no one wants to hear anymore. Let me show you. Turn on the television, Hellen."

She nodded quickly, and pulled forward out of the shadows what looked to Owen like a portable viewscreen unit. Hellen turned it on, and the screen showed a close-up of some show host doing what Owen as-sumed was topical humor. Certainly none of it meant anything to him, but the live studio audience lapped it up. The host was Allan Woss, a tall lanky sort in a sparkly suit, with a mop of bright blue hair and a wide fake smile, to show off his perfect white teeth. He waved his arms about a lot and kept shooting *love me* looks into the camera. Owen sniffed. He recognized the type. It seemed some things were always the same, wher-ever you went.

"He's a personality," Hellen said dispassionately. "Famous for being famous. And nowhere near as smart and funny as he thinks he is. And that sparkly suit is just so yesterday's man. Ostensibly this is a chat show, but really the guests are only there so Woss can have fun at their expense. The Illuminati standing below him, in what Woss so charmingly refers to as the Conversation Pit, is called Solar. And this . . . is the only kind of show the Light People can get on these days. They know the odds are stacked against them from the start, but they're obsessed with getting their warn-ing across. I understand why, but . . . no one listens. No one cares. It all happened so very faraway, and so long ago."

She turned up the volume as Woss lowered himself into what looked very like a throne, set over the Conversation Pit. The single Illuminati looked smaller and shabbier on the television screen. The harsh studio lighting bleached out its delicate rainbow colors. The Illuminati wrapped its wings tightly about its body, perhaps for comfort. Woss leaned back in his throne, utterly at ease, dispensing judgement and jokes for the eager live audience, and barely allowing Solar to get a word in edgewise.

"So, Solar, tell us all about yourself, you strange-looking person, you. Do you have any strange powers or abilities? Can you get radio signals on those antennae? Can you tell us this week's winning lottery number? No, not a lot of use, are you? So it's just the wings, then . . . Shame, shame, shame. Still, let me ask you the question I just know our viewers want me to ask: since none of you Light Bulb People seem to be guys or gals, how do you produce more little Illuminati? I mean, pardon my bluntness, but you people don't seem to have any equipment to do anything with! Unless those aren't really antennae after all! Just a joke, just a joke. Maybe I should ask you about pollination. For all I know, you could have been shagging your dressing room!"

There was loud sycophantic laughter and cheers from his audience. Woss smiled and waved his hands about. Owen scowled.

"Why is he giving Solar such a hard time?"

"Because that's what he does. Because he can," said Hellen. "The Illuminati were our first contact, and they turned out to be *boring*. And that of course was unforgivable. So now everyone just makes fun of them, in the hope they'll take the hint, and leave. That way Humanity can just forget all about them."

There was a break in the show, for a series of loud and frankly rather obnoxious ads, and then Woss and Solar were back again. Woss tried half-heartedly to get Solar to give him a piggyback, and fly him around the studio. Solar declined. Woss sniffed loudly.

"Too good for us, eh? Well, don't get too cocky, or the Terror might come after you with a bloody big butterfly net! Hey, if you're really part moth, maybe we'd better keep you away from the studio lighting! I don't think we're insured for self-immolation!"

The audience howled with laughter, only to break off suddenly as Solar suddenly spread out his wings to their full extent. He rose slowly up into the air, his wings barely moving, until he was looking down at Woss and his audience.

"We came here to tell you that you are not alone. And that you are in danger. But it seems you are determined not to hear our message."

"Hey," said Allan Woss. "No one invited you here. And the only place for messages is in the ad breaks. Learn some new tricks, if you want people to pay attention. In the meantime, don't call us and we won't call you."

Hellen turned the television off, and bustled over to comfort Lucifer, who was staring at the floor, his wings wrapped tightly around him.

"Now, now, dear; don't get upset. No one really cares what Allan Woss has to say. Some of us still remember when he was just a glamor weather boy who couldn't even pronounce precipitation."

Owen watched Hellen offer her brisk form of comfort to the Illuminati. He'd seen her kind before, the overprotective kind who'd offer support to a little lost alien in the same way they'd look after some abandoned child or dog. Just because it was the right thing to do. Well meaning, but . . .

"Hellen," said Owen. "How did you get involved with the Illuminati?"

She looked round and smiled, absently patting Lucifer on the shoulder. "I never got over their being our first alien contact. I waited my whole life to meet a real live alien. I can still see the magic and glamor in them. So I stuck with them, when everyone else just fell away. People should be ashamed! Just because they didn't come in big ships, with big weapons . . . The Light People are incredible beings!"

"They do make an impact," Owen agreed. "When I first saw Lucifer coming straight at me, I thought he was an angel."

"Oh, he is," said Hellen. "They all are really, the dears. We weren't worthy of them."

Owen nodded. He was thinking of what the young boy Giles had said to him, on the border world. That when Hazel appeared to him, she looked like an angel. And there was . . . something, about the Light People that reminded him of Hazel. They were undoubtedly the strange presence he'd sensed from orbit. But they were aliens; why should they remind him of Hazel? And the Madness Maze . . . Was there some unsuspected, abnormal connection between them? He realized Hellen had stopped talking, and was looking at him.

"I know," she said quietly. "I do go on about them, don't I? I know . . .

I'm not really bright enough to understand or appreciate the Light People, but someone's got to look after them. And if not me, then who? I keep trying to get them proper interviews, proper attention and respect, but I don't have the contacts. I'm just a woman who isn't young anymore, looking for something to fill her time, something worth doing. Truthfully, I suppose I need them as much as they need me. They deserved someone better, someone more connected; but I'm all there is. I just wish . . . I could get people to listen, really listen, to what the Illuminati have to say. But you can't make people listen when they don't want to."

"You could be a great help to me," said Owen. "I don't know much about this world, this time. I saw a lot of big ships being assembled in orbit. Tell me what's happening there."

"I suppose it all began with New Frontier," said Hellen. "They were a new movement, as much philosophical as political, inspired by the invention of a working stardrive, some fifteen years ago. For the first time, the stars were within our grasp. That inspired a lot of people. Me included, at the time. New Frontier believes that it's vitally important for Humanity to get out of the solar system and colonize other worlds. To spread Humanity in a vast, boundless Empire. They say we've got too soft and cozy here on Hearth and the other worlds, with robots to do everything for us. That we need to go out into the stars to rediscover our old strength and courage and capabilities. To be truly Human again. We have to go *out there*, they say. It's our destiny. So, we're building starships, and soon the bravest and the best of us will be off and out, into the infinite. And then we'll find out what we're really made of."

"How many soldiers are you taking with you?" said Owen. "How big an army?"

Hellen looked at him blankly. "Why should we need an army?"

"Because it's a bloody dangerous place, *out there*," said Owen. "Trust me on this; I know. There aren't that many intelligent species, but there are a hell of a lot of really nasty and vicious creatures, who won't be at all happy about you people coming along to colonize their worlds. Don't you people have armies anymore?"

"Well, no, not really," said Hellen. Her mouth pursed, as though Owen was trying to get her to discuss something that nice people didn't normally talk about. "We have peacekeepers, to take care of the criminal element, and keep an eye on some of the more extreme groups, like New Frontier. And Hearth First, fanatics who are violently opposed to star travel, and want all the money spent on the Nine Worlds instead. And Defense of Humanity, a small but very loud group, who object to the very idea that aliens can be as intelligent as humans. They don't even approve of the animals. They keep trying to hold rallies, but the dogs keep chasing them off. We don't need an army! Not here, or on any of the Nine Worlds. There hasn't been a war in the Empire in over a hundred years."

Owen thought about that, and all the things he could say, and then turned to Lucifer. "Tell me your story. Give me your message. I'll listen."

And the Illuminati spoke, saying, "In the galaxy next to this one, long and long ago, we built a great civilization, first through control of light and gravitational forces, and later, as our powers grew, by shaping reality itself through a concentrated effort of will, by the gentle urgings of our minds. We were great and mighty in those days, and spread across many worlds, remaking them in our own image. There were cities of light, rivers of gravity, waterfalls of fire and roads of winds. We lived in peace and harmony on thousands of worlds, for millions of years, and were content. Other species arose, but they were never any threat because we could reshape reality, so that any enemy immediately became our friend."

"Isn't that rather . . . unethical?" said Owen.

"More so than killing them?" said Lucifer, and Owen had no answer.

"We did not interfere in their destiny," said Lucifer. "All new intelligent species were left to go their own way, as long as they did not seek to war upon us. They also built civilizations, that rose and fell and rose again while the Illuminati went on, bright and glorious. I saw in your memories, Deathstalker, images of humans with mental powers, called espers. We were what they might some day evolve into. But we had our limitations. We never developed technologies, because we never needed them. So when something came to us, from out of the outer dark, something our reality-changing powers could not affect, we were helpless.

"After millions of years of peace and civilization, the Terror came upon us, an unstoppable destructive force that swept our civilization away like a raging wind. Our cities dissolved, our people went mad and died, and our worlds burned."

"Hold it," said Owen. "If your people had the power to change reality by will alone, why didn't you just stop or change the Terror, the way you dealt with your other enemies?"

"Because the Terror had made itself so real it could not be changed," said Lucifer. "It was of such a singular nature and purpose, and so very huge and powerful, that even the massed thoughts of our entire race could not slow or stop it. And we had no weapons with which to attack it. The very concept of violence was alien to us. All we could do was abandon our homes and flee from world to world. But wherever we went, the Terror followed, until there were no worlds left to run to. Our whole civilization was gone, with no trace left to show it had ever existed. We turned to other species for help. Some did, some did not. The Terror came for them all anyway. And in the end, all that was left to us was a last, desperate gesture. All the remaining members of our race gathered together on the last remaining world, at the edge of our galaxy, and pooled their power to send some of us out into the void between galaxies, using our knowledge of the hidden ways to travel further and faster than the Terror could match. All those left behind died, so that we might escape, to carry our terrible warning."

Lucifer stopped talking, and after a moment Owen realized that was all there was. "You few Light People are all that remain of your species?"

"Yes. The last pitiful remnants of a once proud race."

"Where will you go, when you leave here? Do you have some eventual destination in mind?"

Lucifer shrugged, his great wings rippling slowly. "We always hoped that one day we would reach some safe haven, but . . . even after all the distance we've crossed, all the worlds and wondrous species we've seen, we've never found anywhere that would be safe from the coming of the Terror. So we just keep going, running from the fury that follows us, spreading our warning to all who will listen. Even now, we are only resting here on Hearth, gathering our strength before resuming our flight. We have traveled a very long time, Deathstalker, so long even we no longer remember just how long, and we grow old and tired, our powers depleted.

But as soon as we feel strong enough, we will leave here. Because the Terror will come, eventually.

"We did try to warn your people, but Humanity are proud and arrogant, and put their faith in the technology and weapons we lacked." Lucifer sighed heavily. "You people live such short lives, with such a limited perception of time. You simply cannot conceive of the scale and power of what is coming to destroy you. Our fear is that all the details of our warning will be forgotten by Humanity, in the thousands of years to come."

"If Humanity won't listen, why don't you make them listen?" said Owen. "Change their minds, as you once changed the minds of your enemies. Even just a demonstration of power would be enough to make them take you and your warning more seriously."

"The Illuminati have fallen far from what they once were," said Lucifer. "But even so, we would never use force against another species. Such a thought is intolerable to us. What is the point of survival, if to do it you have to give up what makes you what you are? So . . . nothing else is left to us, but to leave. Perhaps we will find a safe place further on . . . in the next galaxy."

Owen tried to comprehend lives lived across such a vast expanse of time and space, and couldn't, even after his own travels through time. He found it comforting, that he still had some human limitations. Unlike the thing that had once been Hazel d'Ark. A sudden rush of pity moved him, sorrow for the poor butterfly people crushed beneath the heel of something that could never appreciate the wonders of what it destroyed.

"So," Owen said to Lucifer, almost angrily. "You're just going to up and leave? Fly away and abandon Humanity to their fate?"

"What else can we do?" said Lucifer.

Owen was just getting the beginnings of an idea, when armed men burst suddenly out of the tunnel entrance and into the cavern. They wore improvised body armor over gaudy costumes, and opened fire the moment they saw the Light People hanging from the ceiling. They were carrying projectile weapons, and fired recklessly in every direction. Hellen screamed *New Frontier!* While Owen just stood and gaped for a moment, thrown off balance by the rapid fire. A ricocheting round whistled past his head, and he snapped out of his daze. He pushed Hellen up against the nearest wall, and made her crouch down, covering her body with his own. The Illuminati scattered to avoid the raking fire, plunging back and forth across the cavern at dizzying speeds. The newcomers fired their guns endlessly, but didn't seem able to hit anything. The Light People swooped and soared, and guns turned to follow them. The noise of massed gunfire in such a confined space was deafening, and smoke rolled thickly on the air, swept this way and that by the beating of vast wings. Hellen sobbed loudly, and clutched at Owen like a child.

"What the hell is going on?" he yelled in her ear, but he had to shake her hard before she could talk to him coherently.

"New Frontier enforcers," she gasped, tears rolling down her face. "They hate the Light People, for making people afraid to go out to the stars. They've threatened to kill them all, to prove the superiority of the human spirit. They're all supposed to have been arrested!"

"Looks like your peacekeepers missed a few," Owen growled.

The fanatics raked their guns back and forth, trying to follow the sweeping and dodging Illuminati, still not managing to hit anything. But given the sheer number of bullets, and the enclosed space, it was clearly only a matter of time. The Light People couldn't keep dodging forever. Owen decided it was time he got involved. He put his mouth next to Hellen's ear.

"You stay put. I'll take care of the scumbags."

He rose up and started towards the New Frontier enforcers. They saw him coming, and some trained their guns on him. Owen smiled coldly, and his power snarled and crackled on the air around him. Bullets ricocheted harmlessly away from his force shield. All the other guns trained on him, and Owen slapped the fanatics down with a single thought. They hit the ground hard, dropping their weapons. It was suddenly very quiet in the great cavern, the last echoes of gunfire fading quickly away. The Light People clustered on the ceiling again, apart from Lucifer, who settled on the ground beside Owen, and looked at him searchingly. He was about to say something, when Hellen came running forward to embrace him. And one of the fanatics on the floor pulled a gun from a hidden holster, and shot at Lucifer. The bullet punched through the wing he had wrapped around Hellen, and killed her instantly. She slipped bonelessly out of Lucifer's grasp, as he stood, shocked. Owen howled with fury and gestured sharply at the fanatic. His head exploded in a shower of blood and bone, and the other fanatics cried out in horror until Owen yelled at them to shut up.

He knelt beside Hellen to check, but he knew she was dead. Lucifer stood beside him.

"She is gone."

"Yes." Owen rose up from her side, and turned to look at Lucifer. "How's your wing?"

"It will heal."

"Why didn't you use your powers to protect her?"

"We do not interfere. It is our way. Our principle."

"She was your friend!"

"Yes. She was. You killed that man, Owen."

"I should kill all of them. They would have killed all of you."

"We would rather all die, than kill another." Lucifer turned his back on Owen, and walked away.

"Then who would spread your damned warning?" Owen yelled after him.

"It is time for us to leave," said Lucifer, not looking round. "We cannot stay here any longer, and be responsible for more violence, more deaths. Perhaps a few of us will stay behind, hidden from sight, to observe and watch over Humanity as it builds its Empire. As a species, you show potential. You may yet evolve into something worthwhile."

"You should have helped Hellen," said Owen.

"We couldn't even help ourselves," said Lucifer.

He gestured at the fanatics lying shocked and terrified on the floor, and they rose quickly to their feet and ran out of the cavern, shoving at each other in their haste to get into the tunnel and away. Lucifer looked back at Owen.

"Before we go, one last piece of information. It is possible that we have encountered your friend Hazel, the object of your pursuit through time. She appeared here, in this place, a few weeks ago—drawn to our presence. I think we intrigued her. She manifested only as a mental impression, wrapped in a field of unfamiliar energies. She did not seem . . . human. Her presence reminded us a little of who and what we used to be. She scared us. There was nothing of restraint or passion in her. She had amassed power at a frightening rate while plunging back through time, draining it from the lives and worlds she passed. It seemed to us that there was no limit to how much power she might drain, or what she might become."

Owen nodded. He knew he had been draining energy from somewhere, to power his continuing passage through time, and now he knew where from. That extra power was why he was able to do all the things he'd never been able to do before. The concept appalled him. There was a very old name for creatures that lived by draining life from others. But he knew the truth wouldn't stop him; nothing would now. He had to go on, either to stop Hazel becoming the Terror, or to find a way to deal with the Terror in the future.

He didn't tell Lucifer that Hazel would eventually become the Terror. It would only have upset the Illuminati.

"Before you go," he said flatly to Lucifer, "there's something I want you to do. Something to help Humanity and at the same time preserve your warning. You said Humanity might evolve into something better; but I'm here to tell you that's not going to happen by the time the Terror finds them. Unless you and I give them a helping hand. Together we're going to build something; create something that's never existed before. Something to give at least a few people a fighting chance. It will be called the Madness Maze. And if you ever consider saying no, just think of Hellen, who died because you wouldn't help her. And remember what I did to the New Frontier fanatic."

And so, under Owen's specific instructions, the Illuminati created the Madness Maze. On learning what it was to be, and what it was supposed eventually to do, they decided it would be far too dangerous to create or leave on Hearth, so they took Owen with them through their secret silver tunnels to a planet on the other side of the galaxy. And only Owen knew that one day the world would be called Haden. In a cavern deep below the surface of the world, lit only by the flickering rainbow glow of the Light People, they brought into being the Madness Maze, creating it through a group effort of concentrated will, focused through Owen's mind and power. And when they were finished, it looked just like he remembered it.

Owen looked at it, and thought for a long while.

By creating the Maze, I have made tomorrow possible. I have made the Terror possible. But the Light People might have created it anyway, at some point. At least this way I get to put my stamp on it. And without the Maze we could never have brought Lionstone and her Empire down. Perhaps if I hadn't done this, Hazel would never have been able to become the Terror, and all those worlds and civilizations would still be alive. Or perhaps someone or something else would have become the Terror, and then Humanity would have no defense against it.

I don't know. The Maze is woven irretrievably throughout human history. Do I have the right to unravel such a knot? No; we need the Maze, and in the end, that's all that matters.

And if I'm wrong?

Then I'm wrong.

The Illuminati fluttered around the thing they'd made, studying it and considering its possibilities. Lucifer settled down beside Owen, and looked at him doubtfully.

"What is the purpose of this device, Owen?"

"Hope," said Owen. "And maybe transcendence."

"Then let us all hope that by the time Humanity gets out this far, they will be worthy of what we have left them."

Owen said nothing.

"We patterned the structure of the Madness Maze on your brain," said Lucifer. "We found its intricacies fascinating. Human, but not just human. Is there something you're not telling us, Owen?"

"There's a hell of a lot I'm not telling you," said Owen. "And if you're wise, you'll leave it that way."

Owen looked at the Maze, and wondered how much of it was shaped by his memories of it; from his past, but the Light People's future. Certainly his involvement in its creation explained why the Maze had always worked best for Deathstalkers. He had paid special attention to the construction of the core at the heart of the Maze, preparing it to protect and sustain the child that would one day come to it. Giles's infant son; the Darkvoid Device.

What is this for? Lucifer had asked.

The hope of Humanity, Owen had said.

It's a bit small, isn't it?

Yes.

When Owen was satisfied that the Madness Maze was complete, he then worked together with the Illuminati to create a guardian for the Maze: a single shape-changing creature derived from Owen's own altered genetic makeup. (He had decided a shape-changer would be best able to hide and protect itself in all the long centuries it would have to survive.) He had to reassure the Illuminati that they weren't creating some kind of living weapon, and so agreed to their demands that it be programmed only as an observer and messenger, and strictly nonviolent.

The finished creature was an exact duplicate of Owen, though it had no personality of its own, as yet. Just a series of instructions and duties, and the instinct to survive. Owen had to smile, thinking of what it would become, after centuries of being other people.

"When you first meet me, in the Maze, many years from now," he said to the creature. "Don't recognize me. Or tell me any of this. It would only upset me, and distract me from all the things I must do."

"Understood," said the creature. "I will remember."

"Yes," said Owen. "I know you will."

And he also gave the shape-changer his ring, the black gold ring that was the sign and symbol of Clan Deathstalker authority, to be given to his descendant Lewis Deathstalker, at a specific time and place. Owen was concerned that Lewis might be so far removed from the direct Deathstalker bloodline that the Maze might not recognize and receive him. Owen felt naked and strangely lost without the ring, but Lewis needed (or would need it) more than he did now. It still felt like giving up yet another part of his human past. His human soul.

He tried to think if he'd forgotten anything, but he couldn't remember.

So he said good-bye to Lucifer and the other Illuminati, wished them well, and dropped out of the present again, plunging back through time in his endless pursuit of Hazel d'Ark.

CHAPTER EIGHT

MONSTERS OLD AND NEW

There were no ELFs anymore. They were all dead and gone, absorbed and murdered by a greater mental force, just as they'd always feared. Only their destruction came not from their most hated enemy, the mass-mind of the oversoul, but instead from their own allies and founders, the uber-espers. They had turned on the ELFs, overwhelmed their defenses, and ate up their minds, their personalities, so that not one trace of the rogue espers now remained. Now there were just the uber-espers, those old and terrible monsters, and the armies of thralls they commanded. Five grotesque, abhuman minds, operating hundreds of thousands of thrall bodies.

The Shatter Freak. The Spider Harps. Screaming Silence. The Gray Train. Blue Hellfire.

Old minds, old demons, older by far than most people realized. The uber-espers had been waiting and plotting and planning from the shadows of the Empire for untold centuries. When you expect to live forever, you can afford to take the long view. Lesser evils came and went, but the uber-espers endured, and now their time had come. They had spent centuries deciding what they would do, and how they would do it, arguing constantly among themselves of course, but never doubting that one day they would see all Humanity bow down before them.

They were forced into hiding for many years, held down first by the Mater Mundi's authority, and then by fear of Owen Deathstalker and the other Madness Maze survivors, and finally by a Golden Age that was just too sane and stable to allow them any foothold. But now, everything had changed. The old adversaries were gone, the Golden Age had proved rotten at the core, and there was no one left on Logres to stop them from doing all the awful things they'd dreamed of doing. The Emperor's hold had been weakened, the oversoul and the Maze people had all gone away, and the uber-espers . . . had made themselves like unto gods. With hundreds of thousands of thralls forming a great energy pool, the uber-espers finally felt strong enough to do anything they wanted. And so they did.

They launched their first attacks against the Emperor Finn's vastly overextended armed forces. There weren't that many left outside of the Parade of the Endless; just a few battalions shuttling back and forth between the other main cities, maintaining order through dramatic shows of force. A few dozen war wagons and battle cruisers, dug up relics from Lionstone's time, great dusty steel beasts hovering in the skies, dependent more on reputation than firepower. All of them easy targets for psi storms that came raging out of nowhere, without warning. The uber-espers blew the war machines apart from a distance, ripping apart steel bulkheads with their thoughts and overloading the engines till they blew. Psychokinetic attacks crushed the heavy metal ships in invisible fists, while psionic energies wiped computers and hexed tech. Force shields collapsed and guns wouldn't work. Men on the ground cried out in shock and horror as blazing gravity barges fell ponderously out of the sky, and gravity sleds slammed against each other like toys in the hands of insane gods. Black smoke billowed up from the crippled remains of Finn's armored forces.

The next step was to possess the men on the ground. The uber-espers reached out greedily, using the strength of the ELFs they'd absorbed, and battalion after battalion screamed helplessly inside their heads as they were taken over, and alien thoughts moved their bodies. What had once been Finn's armies marched into the cities they'd only been sent to subdue, and murdered and possessed every man, woman, and child in their path. They didn't need to kill anyone, but they did anyway, just for the fun of it. What city defenses there were collapsed in shock and panic, as mass possessions swept through the streets and squares in an unstoppable tide. The uber-espers were now so powerful that one thrall could create another just by looking into their eyes. Possession had become infectious. It leapt through the stampeding crowds like wildfire, jumping instantly from mind to mind. People ran, but there was nowhere to run to. The soldiers had the cities surrounded.

Attempts at resistance were doomed from the start, because no one could trust anyone. Your closest friend or family could be a thrall, or be made one in a moment. People hid inside their houses, and barricaded the doors and windows, but the thralls just broke in anyway, not caring how much they damaged their bodies in the process. Men and women with smashed hands and lacerated arms smiled triumphantly through the jagged gaps they'd made, and forced themselves upon the defenseless souls within.

Some thralls were even able to manifest esper abilities on behalf of the uber-espers that rode them, if only briefly. They strode giggling down the streets, and houses exploded or burst into flames on either side of them. Roads cracked apart and sewers hurled foulness up into the streets. Sometimes the esper thralls blew people apart with a look or a word, or made them eat their own flesh; or whatever else occurred to the uber-espers.

The cities became Hell on earth, choked with smoke and the smell of blood, and the uber-espers danced their thralls through the burning streets, tearing everything down just for the fun of it. And when nothing was left but fire and rubble and the piled up bodies of the dead, the uber-espers marched their thralls out of the dead streets, and off down the road to the next city. And so it went, city after city, population after population, until armies of thralls were on the march all over Logres, clogging the roads and tramping through fields full of crops. There was no one left to stop them.

Cities in the path of the thrall armies called out to the Emperor for help, but he had nothing to send them. What few troops he had left he needed to protect the Parade of the Endless. Not that Finn would have sent any help even if he could have spared it. He didn't see the point in giving up even more of his armed forces to be possessed. And so cities set up barricades on all the roads leading in, and desperate men stood guard with whatever weapons they could find. Anyone approaching a city was shot on sight, without warnings, no exceptions. It was the only way to be safe.

Until the thrall army came marching up the road, rank upon rank of them, walking right into the face of the defenders' guns, trampling over the fallen until they could swarm the barricades and eat up the defenders' minds. And then they would march on, into the city.

From the Rookery, Nina Malapert's news sites stayed on the air twenty-four hours a day, using remote control cameras to bring in the latest news and sightings. They spread word of danger areas, and cities under threat, as fast as they could get the information out. Telling everyone on Logres, and all the watching worlds across the Empire, of what was happening now that the Emperor Finn had lost control. Nina's newsreaders became hoarse and strained and white-faced as they told of the endless atrocities and mass murders and possessions, and burning cities all across the world. Nina ran herself ragged trying to keep on top of everything, getting warnings out with as much advance time as possible, and lists of safe places to go. She kept the remote cameras moving from city to city, sending live pictures of what was happening. The uber-espers didn't interfere. They wanted everyone to know what was coming for them.

Even the newsreaders on Finn's propaganda news channels joined in, ignoring the scheduled programming. They knew a real emergency when they saw one. They shared resources with Nina's sites, trying to get useful information to those who needed it. After a while they started to feel like real news people again, and ignored the piling up propaganda reports, and the increasingly angry orders from Finn's censors, in order to stick with the real story.

Massive crowds of refugees took to the roads and even commandeered the air traffic lanes, abandoning cities in the path of the uber-esper hordes. They ran away from their homes and their lives, taking only what they could carry with them, not sure where they were going, not knowing if anywhere could ever be truly safe again. They filled up the roads, millions of refugees on the move, shocked and tearstained and numb with horror, leaving behind them a trail of abandoned possessions that became too heavy to carry. They moved as fast as they could, and kept rest stops to a minimum. The thralls were coming after them, and they never got tired, never slowed, never stopped.

Some cities and towns took the refugees in, some turned them away, some shot at them on sight. Everywhere the few charitable cities and larger towns became saturated with people, overloaded to the breaking point with people too tired to continue. Many just sat down suddenly, wherever they were when their strength ran out, too numb to care, too exhausted even to eat. Facilities quickly broke down, even the most basic comforts and services unable to cope. There wasn't enough of anything to go round. Food distribution between cities just stopped. Civilization was falling apart, on the homeworld of the Empire.

The uber-espers soaked up the energies supplied by millions of captive minds, and their powers blossomed as never before. They could do things now almost beyond even their wildest dreams. And being the kind of creatures they were, they looked upon each other with increasing suspicion. They had never trusted each other, quite rightly believing that any or all of them would turn on any or all of them who seemed dangerously powerful or invitingly weak. For a while they discussed scattering, leaving Logres for other worlds, so they could each have their own planet to subjugate and play with, safe from the interference and threat of each other's ambitions. The idea was attractive.

But they knew they were more powerful together than they ever could be apart, and besides, if they did go their separate ways, there was always the chance that one of them might become allied with another, and prey on a mind alone. They couldn't risk that. And even more than this, some strange unexpected force from within kept them from taking the idea too seriously. Some inner voice, that whispered it would be a very, very bad thing for the uber-espers ever to become separated.

So instead they decided to take control of Logres first, and then send their thralls out to conquer the other worlds. Once they forced their way into the Imperial Palace and possessed Emperor Finn, they could shut down all reports of what was happening, wait a while, and then happy smiling faces on all the news sites would announce that the emergency was over, everything was fine, and the happy smiling Emperor would order the other planets to open their starports to the goodwill ambassadors he was sending them . . . and the plague of possession would jump from world to world to world . . .

The uber-espers laughed, drunk on blood and suffering and power, and the promise of so much more to come.

The wave of mass possessions swept from city to city, crossing the whole world in a matter of weeks, and nothing could stop it or even slow it down. It jumped from eye to eye, head to head, often over before it was even suspected. The weaker minds tended to fall first, and so it was that children and even babies became thrall changelings. They attacked their parents and siblings with whatever came to hand, chuckling with alien glee as blood soaked their small hands. The uber-espers had always believed in the use of horror to destabilize opposition. And they did so savor the taste of the more vivid emotions, as they picked through brains like gore crows on a battlefield. They sent their thralls running madly through the streets, killing for the joy of it until killed in their turn, and shock and terror and panic destroyed any defenses the cities might have been able to assemble.

But there was still one final horror, even beyond what had already happened.

Diana Vertue discovered it. She led her followers, the Psycho Sluts, out of the Rookery and the Parade of the Endless, and they flew high in the skies of Logres like gaudy hawks of war, on a mission to protect the next city in the thralls' path. Douglas Campbell hadn't wanted them to go. He sympathized, but he didn't think they could do anything against the massed might of the uber-espers, and he was afraid of losing them. If they were to be possessed, there was no saying how much damage they might do. Diana had nodded, said she quite understood, and then informed Douglas that she and the Sluts were going anyway. And there must have been something of the old Jenny Psycho in her voice, because Douglas just nodded, and turned away.

Diana and the Psycho Sluts came to Delta City in the early hours of the morning, dropping out of the crimson-streaked dawn like so many avenging angels. They took up a position on the outskirts of the city, by an abandoned barricade made of piled-up furniture, and linked their minds to set up a mental barrier in the path of the advancing thralls. The barrier shimmered on the heavy morning air like heat haze, shot through with shimmering energies. Diana could hear the thrall army coming long before she saw it. The crash and crash of so many feet, an army beyond counting, shaking the road with their studied malevolent approach. They appeared slowly over the curve of the horizon; at first just a crowd, and then an army, and then so much more. An uncountable force, all walking in perfect lockstep, their feet a thunder on the road.

The uber-espers must have known the mental barrier was there, but they didn't even slow their thralls' advance. They marched on, all with the same awful smile, the same horrid eyes, and crashed right through the barrier. The moment a thrall passed through it, the mental contact with the uber-espers was cut off, the possessing mind forced out of the body. Which fell forward, to lie limp and still on the ground, with empty faces and dead eyes; nobody home. The thralls kept coming, crowding through the barrier, collapsing into growing heaps of unmoving bodies before Diana and her appalled followers.

For this was the final horror. The uber-espers had become so powerful that once they took over a mind and ate it up, they wiped the brain completely clean. The old personality was subsumed, gone forever. A thrall was just a shell now, an empty body for the uber-espers to use as they would. Thralls could no longer be freed from possession and returned to their lives. Possession meant mind-death.

Diana looked at the empty bodies piling up before her, and didn't know what to do. She couldn't save anyone, and she and the Sluts couldn't maintain the barrier indefinitely. Sooner or later the sheer number of thralls would overwhelm them. So Diana dropped the shield, and she and the Psycho Sluts flew silently back to the Rookery. The one place she thought she could still be sure of defending. Delta City was left to its own defenses, and fell.

Later, she reported back to Douglas Campbell. *I can keep the Rookery safe,* she said.

What about the Parade of the Endless? said Douglas.

What about them? said Diana.

The Rookery was now the only place on Logres immune to uber-esper possession. The combination of human and esper and alien minds had always frustrated the uber-espers' grasp, and the new protective field set up around the expanded territory of the Rookery made everyone there safe from any and all forms of mental attack. And the uber-espers had good reason to be wary of Diana Vertue, also known as Jenny Psycho. They had worked together to murder her, over a century before, and yet here she was back again; and they had no idea how. Even they didn't think they could bring themselves back from the dead. And there was always the chance Diana might make contact with the departed but still hated oversoul, wherever they had got to on their city of New Hope. The uber-espers thought they could probably take the oversoul, but they weren't in any hurry to find out.

The only way the uber-espers could hope to crack the shield around the Rookery would be to lure Diana and the Psycho Sluts out so they could be ambushed, or for the uber-espers to turn up at the Rookery in person. And they sure as hell weren't ready to try that yet.

They would wait, until they had overthrown and possessed all the cities on Logres, and then they would come and take the Parade of the Endless, and then . . . oh yes, and then . . .

Douglas Campbell called a meeting in his hotel room. All the really important people came, while two Psycho Sluts stood guard outside the door so they wouldn't be interrupted or overheard. Douglas looked tired and harried, as well he might. He hadn't slept or rested properly since the emergency began. There was panic inside and outside the Rookery, and everyone was looking to him for answers, for hope and salvation. No one expected anything from the Emperor, but Douglas was the acclaimed King of Thieves. The man who could do anything. And there in his crowded hotel room, Stuart Lennox, Tel Markham, Diana Vertue, and Nina Malapert all looked to Douglas for answers he didn't have. He couldn't tell them that, of course. He had made himself their leader, so he had to lead. Even if he wasn't sure where he was going. Douglas sighed inwardly, and did his best to look calm and certain as he sat back in his chair to hear the reports his people had brought him.

"Let's take things in order," he said flatly. "The Emperor is no longer our main enemy, and can no longer be the main target of our energies. He has his own problems, so we needn't worry about him. All our old plans and strategies are hereby scrapped, or at least postponed indefinitely, until we've dealt with the menace of the uber-espers. Diana, let's start with you. Tell us about Delta City."

"The whole city has fallen," said Diana. She looked and sounded smaller than usual, beaten down by the things she'd seen, and couldn't prevent. "The girls and I watched it happen, from a safe distance. The city's population is now either dead or possessed. No one got out alive. Anyone too old, too young, or too sick to walk was butchered on the spot. That's what the uber-espers will do to us, when they come here. We can't negotiate, even if someone was dumb enough to suggest it, because we don't have anything they want that we could use to buy them off. And I don't know that we're strong enough to keep them out. The best we can hope for is to hold the thralls off long enough for the uber-espers to get impatient, and turn up in person. There are a few things I could try then. If they were stupid enough to put themselves at risk. Which they aren't."

"You sound scared of them," said Stuart, frowning. "I didn't think you were scared of anyone. I mean, you're Jenny Psycho! One of the legends of old Empire!"

"Aren't you a bit old, to be believing in legends? The last time the uber-espers ganged up on me in an ambush, over a hundred years ago, they killed me." Diana shuddered suddenly. "They didn't even leave enough of my body to bury. And they're even more powerful now."

Everyone stirred uneasily. Nina fixed Diana with a thoughtful look. "You never did explain how you came back from that."

"No," said Diana. "I didn't, did I?"

"What are our options?" said Douglas. "Speak up, people. I'll listen to anything that even sounds halfway sane."

"We stay put," said Tel Markham, hovering at Douglas's side, as always. A dark, grim presence, in clothes he kept spotlessly clean. "We let the uber-espers' army enter the Parade of the Endless, and then watch safely from the Rookery as Finn's soldiers go head-to-head with the thralls. With any luck, they should weaken each other considerably. We put armed guards on our barricades to keep everyone out. We don't have the room or the resources to support any more refugees. When the worst of the fighting is over, we go out and hit the survivors with everything we've got. The thralls might have the numbers, but they don't have our weapons, or our knowledge of fighting. We should be able to push a weakened force back out of the city, and then take over the Parade of the Endless for ourselves. Finn will be too weak to stop us."

"And then?" said Stuart.

Tel grinned. "We wait for the Deathstalker and his fleet to turn up and save the day. They can't be far off now."

Douglas looked at Nina, who shrugged. "Sorry, lovey, but as long as the fleet's still in hyperspace there's no telling how far off they are. They could be here today, tomorrow, next week. We won't know till they're practically ready to hit orbit."

"And in the meantime," said Stuart, "we're supposed to let everyone else in the city die, or be possessed? While watching safely from behind our mental shield? To hell with everyone but us? About what I'd expected from you, Markham."

"The safety of the Rookery must come first!" snapped Tel. "The King must be protected!"

"No," said Douglas, and everyone looked at him. "We go out into the city, and protect the people. This is our city, and they are all our people. Stuart, talk with our strategy groups and start putting together some possible courses of action for me to consider. We have resources none of the other cities had, and I want to use them all, to the full. We can do this. We are going to hold this city against everything the uber-espers can throw at us, and prove they're not unbeatable."

"Who are we supposed to be proving it to?" Nina said quietly. "Our best information is that every other city on the planet has already fallen. Smaller towns are being ignored, for now, but . . . We're all that's left, Douglas."

"Then we prove it to ourselves," said Douglas. "After all, someone's got to be here to welcome Lewis home."

The uber-espers summoned their armies from all over Logres, and pointed them at the Parade of the Endless. Millions of possessed bodies tramped away from the ruins of cities, all wearing the same smile on their faces. Millions upon millions of thralls, moved by five all-powerful minds, heading towards the last free city in the world, to tear down the Emperor Finn Durandal and his people, and then move on to the final prize: the various tasty minds and souls of the Rookery. The dessert at the end of a very satisfying meal. And the chance for revenge on one of their oldest enemies. Life . . . was good. The thrall armies filled the roads and the skies, all heading in the same direction, with mayhem and murder on their minds.

In his usurped palace, in the Parade of the Endless, the Emperor Finn Durandal contacted every other world in the Empire, and demanded help and support and military reinforcements, and every single world turned him down flat. Even the staunchest fanatics of the Church Militant and Pure Humanity laughed in his face, and warned him not to send any ships to their worlds. Any ship traveling from Logres would be blown apart on sight, for fear of infection. And that very definitely included any ship the Emperor might be traveling on. Everyone was more scared of the uber-espers now than they were of Finn. He no longer had the power to compel their obedience.

The Emperor stalked back and forth in his private chambers, thinking furiously, and making note of certain names for future retribution. He had no doubt there would be a future. He was confident he could beat this problem, as he'd beaten so many others. There was always a way. One idea arose almost immediately, but it took a lot more pacing up and down and heavy scowling before he was ready to embrace it. If he was going to beat these esper freaks, he would have to make an alliance with his most hated enemy, his old friend and comrade in arms, Douglas Campbell. It left a nasty taste in the mouth, but Finn had always been able to do the tough, necessary thing. With the forces of the Rookery joined to his clone army, he could go head to head with the thralls, and not have to worry about fighting on two fronts at once. Douglas would hate the idea, but he'd agree. Because he still believed in things like duty and honor and responsibility. Finn just believed in survival.

Finn's armed forces were much reduced, especially after the second disastrous invasion of the Rookery. All he had was his clone army, some scattered troopers and peacekeepers, and his own personal following of hard-core fanatics—the ones that worshiped him as a god. They were always saying they were ready to die for him—now they'd get a chance to prove it. The vast majority of the Church Militant and Pure Humanity on Logres had fallen away from the faith in recent times—the quitters—especially after the execution of their nominal leader, Joseph Wallace. Finn had no doubt he could persuade and cajole most of them to crawl out of their holes and fight on his behalf; he'd always been a great public speaker. But given current conditions, he'd probably have to promise them all kinds of things. Still, promises were all very well, but wait until the thralls were defeated and the city was his again, and then let the poor fools come crying for what they'd been promised. A bargain that cannot be enforced is no bargain at all.

Finn had to stamp out the threat of the uber-espers before Lewis Deathstalker appeared with his damned fleet. Finn had to be seen to be in charge of his city, if not his world, so that he could negotiate from a position of strength. And once Lewis was down on Logres, and within reach, all kinds of things might happen . . . Finn scowled. He was short on time. The fleet could turn up anywhen. No. Concentrate on the matter at hand. Make his deal with Douglas, combine their forces against the uber-espers and their thralls. At least that way he could be reasonably sure that a whole lot of his enemies in the Rookery would die in the fighting, instead of comfortably sitting it out behind their precious shields. Finn smiled suddenly. Douglas was really going to hate this, but he wouldn't let his pride and personal feelings get in the way of defending his beloved city. And just maybe, in the press of the fighting . . . a knife in the back of an old friend, when no one was looking . . . Ah yes. Every cloud has a silver lining.

And so the Emperor Finn Durandal sent an emissary to the Rookery, to discuss terms. Agreeing in principle was one thing; both sides insisted on strict conditions for their own protection. After a certain amount of verbal fencing over very secure comm links, it was agreed that Douglas would meet with one man from Finn's inner circle, at his hotel in the Rookery. (Finn hadn't suggested a meeting at the palace; he didn't feel like being laughed at.) The Emperor sent Mr. Sylvester, who was well known to the Rookery. Finn had found him there, a long time ago. Mr. Sylvester was a forger, computer hacker, confidence trickster, agent provocateur, and first-class ruiner of reputations. Finn had found a use for all his dubious talents at one time or another.

Mr. Sylvester was searched extremely thoroughly at the border to the Rookery, including a full body scan for weapons, comm bugs, or implanted suicide bombs. Because you never knew with Finn—and, just because the Rookery guards felt like giving Mr. Sylvester a hard time. People who had worked willingly for Finn in the past were no longer popular in the Rookery. The guards also searched the silk-masked figure who accompanied Mr. Sylvester, but he was clean too. One brave soul took a peak at what the man was carrying in his glass jar, under a cloth, and then had to go away and vomit up everything he'd ever eaten.

Mr. Sylvester and his associate were marched through the Rookery by a full company of soldiers, at least partly to keep onlookers from throwing heavy pointed things at their prodigal son. Mr. Sylvester stared straight ahead, smiling professionally, ignoring the threats and insults from the crowds he passed. His masked associate flinched and jumped at every word. The soldiers finally ushered Mr. Sylvester into Douglas's hotel room, while insisting the masked man stayed outside. The deal had been for one emissary only. Mr. Sylvester looked calmly about him, holding his great leonine head proudly high. He flicked his heavy velvet cloak back over his shoulders, to better show off his cloth-of-gold waistcoat, and smiled at the grim faces before him.

"Dear Sirs and Madam, it is a pleasure and an honor to be here, in such august company. Douglas Campbell—legendary King of Thieves and hero in exile. Stuart Lennox—brave and canny Paragon from Virimonde. Finn sends his best wishes. Nina Malapert—beautiful star and vibrant personality of the rogue news sites." Mr. Sylvester raised a painted eyebrow at the last man present. "And Tel Markham—my dear fellow. I had no idea. We all thought you were dead."

"I don't die that easily," Tel growled, sticking very close to Douglas, who sat his chair as though it was a throne. Tel looked Mr. Sylvester over unhurriedly, and then sniffed loudly. "I can't say I'm surprised Finn sent you, Sylvester. You always were good with words, especially when treachery was required. But I have to say, I barely recognized you. You're carrying a lot of weight these days. Good eating at Finn's table?"

"Oh, always." Mr. Sylvester patted the waistcoat straining over his great stomach contentedly. "You know me, Tel. I always land on my feet."

"I'm surprised you can still see them. And yes, I do know you, Sylvester. You lie like you breathe, and the truth is not in you. Who's the masked man outside? You were told to come alone."

"A gift to the King, from Finn. But that can wait." Mr. Sylvester turned the full force of his smile on Douglas. "My dear sir, I have the honor to represent the Emperor Finn, and am empowered by him to enter into all necessary agreements, on his behalf. My word shall be binding on him."

"Hold it right there, Mr. I-never-met-a-pie-I-didn't-like," said Tel, grinning harshly. "First, Douglas, you need to understand just who and what Mr. Sylvester is, and what he did, to you and your friends. This man forged letters and planted false files in computers, all to destroy the reputations of Lewis and Jesamine. He planted stories in the media, started whispering campaigns, and did everything he could to separate you from the people you trusted. Everything bad you ever heard about Lewis and Jesamine originated in this man."

Mr. Sylvester bowed modestly. "You're too kind, Tel."

"Did you really do all that?" said Douglas, and his voice was dangerously cold and quiet.

"Well, yes," said Mr. Sylvester, studying Douglas uncertainly. "That is my work, my business, my calling. It wasn't all that difficult. A letter here, a hidden file discovered there, and the whole picture of a man's life can be changed. In Jesamine's case all I had to do was exaggerate and make public already existing material. The Deathstalker was more of a challenge. There was so very little to work with. Good and honest and noble . . . boring, boring. But in the end, that actually helped; people are always ready to believe the worst of those who seem to be better than they are."

"Was none of it true?" said Douglas. "All the things I condemned him for?"

"Well," said Mr. Sylvester, maintaining his smile with some difficulty.

"It did turn out he really was having an affair with your wife-to-be. That did help."

"How was I ever fooled, by such a thing as you?" said Douglas, and Mr. Sylvester flinched at what he heard in the King's voice.

"My dear fellow, it was just a job, I assure you. Nothing personal."

"And I was so quick to believe your lies," said Douglas. "I should have known better. I always trusted Lewis to guard my back, when we were Paragons together. I trusted him with my life, then."

"Pity you couldn't trust him with your fiancée," said Mr. Sylvester. "But let bygones be bygones. We have an alliance to discuss."

"Why did the Emperor send you, Mr. Sylvester?" said Douglas.

"Because he needed someone who could negotiate delicate matters without getting too emotional," said Mr. Sylvester, happy to be back on safer ground again. "And, truth be told, he doesn't have that many people left he feels he can trust anymore. Possibly because he's killed most of them."

"This whole idea of an alliance stinks," Tel said forcefully. "We're safe here in the Rookery. We don't need Finn."

"The city needs us," said Douglas. "And we could accomplish a lot more with the support of Finn's people."

"But you can't ally with the Durandal!" said Stuart. "He'll betray you!"

"He'll certainly try," said Douglas. "This is Finn we're talking about, after all. But for the moment . . . we need each other. And he knows me well enough to be sure that I won't let personal differences get in the way of doing the right thing. The thralls have to be stopped, and my people saved. And we can only achieve that by pooling our resources. So, we are allies. Because as bad as Finn is, the uber-espers are worse. And by far the most immediate danger . . . Pardon me, Mr. Sylvester; I'm thinking aloud. Tell your master that the deal is made, subject to certain conditions. The first of which is, my help comes at a price. In return for this strictly temporary alliance against a common foe, I demand that he give up to justice the criminal scientists who have done such evil in his service. People like Elijah du Katt, who produced the clone of my brother James; and Dr. Happy, for what he did to Anne Barclay."

"The Emperor anticipated your request," Mr. Sylvester said smoothly. "I have both these gentlemen waiting outside. With your permission . . . ?"

Douglas nodded quickly, surprised. Stuart drew his disrupter. Mr. Sylvester walked slowly over to the door, careful not to make any sudden movements, opened the door and beckoned to the masked man waiting in the corridor. He stepped into the room, still carrying his great glass jar under a heavy cloth, and then reached up to remove the silk mask that covered his face. Elijah du Katt peered quickly about him, sweating heavily and twitching nervously.

Keeping a careful eye on the gun in Stuart's hand, du Katt pulled the cloth away from the large glass jar, revealing the severed head of Dr. Happy. The head was in pretty bad condition. Most of the skin had rotted away, showing patches of discolored meat and bone. The lips had receded back from the protruding teeth, and the eyes had shriveled up in the sockets. Thin wisps of hair sailed away from the misshapen skull, drifting slowly on the preservative fluids that filled the jar. What made it so much worse was that the head was very definitely still alive. The eyes tracked back and forth, fixing on people in turn, and the mouth moved constantly, as though trying to speak. Everyone studied the head with varying amounts of horror and disgust, except for Nina, who pressed forward eagerly.

"Oh, this is just gross!, Puketacular! This is going to look really great on the next news broadcast. Lead spot guaranteed; they won't be able to look away. We were all sure Finn had him killed long ago. Why didn't Finn have him killed?"

"It wasn't for want of trying," Mr. Sylvester admitted, gesturing for du Katt to put the glass jar down on a nearby table. The head bobbed slightly, and a few bubbles popped out of the eaten-away nose. "It seems Dr. Happy had taken to dosing himself with some of his more esoteric concoctions. He was never the same, after he came back from Haden. As I understand it, and I'm quite prepared to admit that I don't, the good Dr. Happy has been dead for some time, but he won't lie down. Finn used him as target practice for a while, and then he had Dr. Happy beheaded, to stop him from running around and upsetting the servants. The body then ran about the lab, crashing into valuable equipment, while the head called the Emperor names. In the end the body was captured, cut up, and burned, and the ashes scattered in separate locations, just in case. And he sent you the head. It is yours to do with as you please, and no, you can't send it back again. The same goes for du Katt, of course."

"What the hell was Dr. Happy trying to achieve with his drugs?" said Nina, kneeling before the glass jar, and tapping on the glass with her fingers, to try to attract the head's attention.

"No one's exactly sure," Mr. Sylvester said uncomfortably. "Apparently, at some point he saw beyond the boundaries of reality, and what he found there destroyed whatever rational part of his mind was left. All he did after that was throw things at people and wander through the palace corridors singing show tunes. Badly."

Douglas's attention was fixed on the sweating, shaking Elijah du Katt. "So, clone master, have you anything to say for yourself?"

"None of it was my idea, Your Majesty! You must believe that! It was all down to Finn, all the things I did . . ."

"Yes," said Douglas. "All the things you did. Like desecrating my brother's grave for the cell samples you needed to produce his clone. Like aiding and abetting in the imprisonment and death of my father. Things like that."

Du Katt tried to speak, but nothing come out, and he stood silent under Douglas's accusing gaze.

"The Emperor supposed you would want to execute du Katt and Dr. Happy yourself," said Mr. Sylvester. "So he sent them to you. As a gift, and a sign of . . . good faith."

"Yes," said Douglas. "I want to kill them. For all the harm and suffering they caused, for all the lives they poisoned and ruined. But I can't just kill them. That would be wrong. Personal vengeance masquerading as justice is Finn's way. I have to be better than that. There has to be justice. There has to be a trial."

"We don't have time for trials," said Diana Vertue, striding briskly into the room without waiting to be invited or announced. "Come on, Douglas; you didn't really think you could hold this meeting without me knowing? I am a telepath, among other things. What's the matter; were you afraid I wouldn't approve of an alliance with Finn? Hell, I can face reality when I have to. A very temporary alliance against the uber-espers is the only sensible answer to our current problems. But we don't have the time to waste on show trials for trash like this. If you can't kill them, I can."

She looked at Elijah du Katt, and he collapsed dead on the floor. She looked at the severed head in its jar, and Nina recoiled with a squeak as head and jar vanished in a flare of psionic energies. Diana looked at Mr. Sylvester, and he flinched and cried out.

"So perish all traitors," said Diana Vertue, still sometimes Jenny Psycho. "Say hi to Finn for me, Mr. Sylvester. Tell him I'll be seeing him soon."

Mr. Sylvester was still shaking when he was escorted back out of the Rookery, to carry Douglas's acceptance of the alliance back to Finn Durandal.

Douglas Campbell addressed a huge rally of his people, in the biggest open square in the Rookery. It took hours for the crowd to assemble, as damn near everyone came to listen. Nina's cameras floated overhead, carrying Douglas's words to the rest of the city, and Logres, and all the worlds in the Empire. Everyone knew about the thralls, everyone knew what the stakes were, so Douglas kept it short and simple.

"We have to go out and fight the thralls. We, and Finn's people, are all that stand between total domination of Logres by the uber-espers. I know it won't come easy, to fight alongside Finn's soldiers. Thugs and bullies and scumbags, most of them. But . . . the enemy of my enemy is my ally, if not actually my friend. There will be time for settling old scores later. After we've beaten the uber-espers and their thrall army.

"And we can beat them. Thanks to the training we've put you through, preparing for the rebellion, you're all first-class warriors. The thralls aren't. All they have is numbers, and there's a limit to how many of them can get into the city at one time. And because they're being controlled by minds far away, they won't be able to change tactics or react quickly to changing conditions. That should give us the advantage we need. And remember: always shoot to kill, even if you think you recognize someone. The people you knew are dead, mind-wiped by the controlling minds. We can't save or rescue them; their bodies are nothing more than empty shells.

"So, go and prepare yourselves for war, and victory. It is our time, come round at last."

The crowd cheered him until their throats were raw, brandishing their weapons at the sky, and of everyone there, only Douglas wondered if what he'd said was really true.

Douglas went back to his hotel room, to be alone with his thoughts for a while, only to find an old familiar face waiting for him on the viewscreen Nina's people had set up. The media tech who'd taken the call nodded quickly to Douglas, and then hurried out of the room. Douglas lowered himself slowly into his chair, never taking his eyes off the face on the screen. Lewis Deathstalker smiled back at him.

"Douglas. It's been a long time."

"Yes. Yes, it has. Hello, Lewis."

"Hello, Douglas. A lot has changed, since we last spoke."

There was no sign of Jesamine Flowers on the screen. Douglas didn't ask. "I've been talking to one of Finn's creatures, a Mr. Sylvester. He's admitted to planting and spreading lies about you and Jes. I'm so sorry, Lewis. I should have known."

"I did try to tell you," said Lewis.

"I know you did. But I was rather . . . upset, at the time. You and Jes . . . Oh hell, Lewis. Come home. All is forgiven. Can you forgive me?"

"Of course," said Lewis. "What are friends for? Even if you did behave like a complete prick."

They laughed quietly together, for the first time in a long time.

"About coming home," said Lewis. "That's the point of this message. The fleet is on its way. We should be with you in a day or two. Maybe less, if the stardrives don't explode under the strain we're putting on them."

"That is good news," said Douglas. "We desperately need allies with major firepower. Are you up to date on what's happening here?"

"Yeah. We never miss Nina Malapert's broadcasts. How the hell did the uber-espers get that powerful?"

"Beats the hell out of us. Have you heard anything about Shub?"

"Just that all their machines have shut down. All our ships' AIs are offline."

"I tried contacting Shub for help when it all went to hell here," said

Douglas, frowning. "No one's answering. No reply from their Embassy, or their homeworld. That has to mean something."

"Could the uber-espers have taken them out? I wouldn't have thought they could possess artificial intelligences, but . . . Or maybe the Terror's got to their home planet?"

"No," Douglas said immediately. "I'd have heard about that. All the latest reports say the Terror's still on course, and days away from its next target. What kind of support are you bringing me, Lewis? I could use some good news."

"Seven hundred and fourteen starcruisers, plus hundreds of ships from Mistworld and Virimonde. And . . . a couple of surprises. On top of that, Jesamine and I, and Brett Random and Rose Constantine, have all been through the Madness Maze. We're pretty surprising ourselves, these days, if not exactly in Owen's class. And John Silence is with us! The legend himself! He's the admiral of our fleet."

Douglas leaned forward eagerly. "You've been through the Maze! What was it like?"

Lewis thought about that for a while. "I don't know whether it's a machine, or alive, or both. It opens you up. Makes you more than you were. It's like being in another place, maybe the place we were before we were born. It feels like coming home, like family. Oh hell, Douglas, there just aren't the words."

"Apparently not. Pour on the speed, Lewis. We need you and your fleet here soon, or you'll be too late to do anything but scorch the whole damned planet from orbit. Don't hesitate to do that, if there's nothing else left. The uber-espers cannot be allowed to leave this world."

"I'm not sure even a scorching would kill those monsters," said Lewis. "But you can trust me to do whatever's necessary."

"Of course," said Douglas. "I always could. How is she, Lewis?"

"She's fine," said Lewis.

They looked at each other for a long time, but there really wasn't anything else they could say.

Diana Vertue and the Psycho Sluts labored together to produce a psionic working that would shield and protect the Rookery while they were out in the city. Plugged directly into their unconscious minds, the working would hold the shield in place without their having to think about it all the time, for as long as one of them still lived. There were some in the Rookery who wouldn't be going out to fight; those too young or too old, or still recovering from the last invasion, and they had to be kept safe from possession, as well as attacking thralls. The shield would keep out the uber-esper minds; they'd have to turn up in person to force a way in, and they weren't that stupid.

But what happens if the uber-espers do turn up in person? someone asked.

Run like fun for the nearest horizon, Diana said crisply. *It won't do you any good, but it should take your mind off the horror to come.*

You're such a comfort, Diana.

I know. Aren't you glad I'm here to tell you these things?

The thrall armies of the uber-espers finally came to the Parade of the Endless by all the roads at once, and marched across the city boundaries laughing and cheering and singing ugly songs. Sometimes they made sounds like animals, or things that had never had a voice before. They poured into the city down a hundred roads, from a hundred dead cities; millions of possessed men and women and even children, run by five terribly powerful minds. They found no victims waiting for them in the outskirts; the people living there had long since abandoned their homes, retreating to the better defended center of the city. Some had fled out into the surrounding countryside, hoping to avoid the marching armies, but the hovering uber-esper minds picked them out easily, and added them to the horde, and now they marched back into their city with someone else living in their heads. The thralls smashed and burnt the houses they walked past. Just because they could.

Finn pulled his forces back from the city boundaries, in carefully practiced disorder, pretending to fall back in a panic, but actually retreating just slowly enough to keep the thralls pursuing them, towards the ambushes and booby traps Finn had waiting for them. And as the thralls swarmed into the city, the people of the Rookery came storming out. They swiftly made contact with the retreating forces, who were so scared they were actually pleased to see the very rebels they'd been fighting the week before. Most of the clone guards, still wearing their steel masks, just didn't have the practical experience to deal with fighting on a scale like this, and were glad of expert minds to tell them what to do. They were programmed to follow orders from anyone who gave them with sufficient authority.

The thralls came in, the defending forces stopped retreating and went to meet them, and vicious hand-to-hand fighting filled the city's streets and squares and open parks. The defenders had swords and axes, guns and grenades. The thralls mostly had improvised weapons, and a vast superiority in numbers. Blood flew and bodies fell, and the tides of battle surged blindly this way and that. Diana Vertue and the Psycho Sluts flew high above it all, hanging on the sky like gaudy birds of prey, casting a protection over the defenders below, so that the thralls couldn't posses them with eye contact.

The thrall armies, and through them the uber-espers, were thrown and confused at first when their main tactic suddenly no longer worked, and they took a lot of losses before they gathered their wits and urged the thralls on into open combat. They plunged forward with swords and knives and often just their grasping, clawing hands. They were all attack and no defense, because there were always more to replace those who fell. Sometimes just the sheer force of numbers was enough to overwhelm and overrun even the best prepared defenders. It was clear to the uber-espers that they wouldn't be claiming any more thralls in the Parade of the Endless until the defenders were defeated, and Diana and her Sluts were brought down. Or until the uber-espers found the courage to leave their boltholes and join the attack in person.

They might. They were all in the city, or more properly, under it. And they did so want to pull this famed city down, and make it theirs.

Terrible fighting raged back and forth in the streets, and blood and guts splashed the walls and ran thickly in the gutters, as the bodies piled up on every side. A dozen thralls fell for every defender, but the odds were thousands to one. The thralls kept pouring across the city boundaries, and there were still more on the way. They had no real tactics, only mass movements and the voices in their heads screaming *Kill! Kill!* but there seemed no end to their numbers, and unlike the defenders, they never got tired or careless or afraid. The rebels from the Rookery were spread all over the city, inspiring others through their vicious example, but they couldn't be everywhere.

Two armies clashed, bodies fell and did not rise again, and the focus of the fighting moved slowly but inexorably towards the heart of the city, and the Imperial Palace.

And while all this was going on, Douglas Campbell was somewhere else. He and Tel Markham crept through deserted side streets, avoiding the fighting, heading for the Imperial Palace to meet with Emperor Finn, that together they might set a trap for the uber-espers. A trap promising the only bait that might tempt the uber-espers into coming to the palace in person: a King and an Emperor. Both Douglas and Finn had agreed that the only real hope they had of defeating the thralls was to lure the uber-espers out of their hiding places, and face them in person. Only when those five monsters were dead, would the threat really be over.

The meeting should have been just for Douglas and Finn, but Tel Markham insisted on accompanying Douglas to the palace, to watch the King's back. He, better than anyone else living, had good reason to know just how treacherous the Emperor could be. Douglas didn't object. Finn had been very clear in his instructions that Douglas should come alone, but Douglas wasn't about to start taking orders from Finn Durandal.

Of course, there was always the chance that Tel intended to betray Douglas to Finn, for labyrinthine reasons of his own, but Douglas didn't think so. Hell hath no fury like an intriguer scorned.

The two of them walked together through a deserted palace. All the guards and most of the servants were out in the city fighting, and the rest were hiding. The living had abandoned the dark and bloody corridors to the dead. They were everywhere now, even more than on Douglas's last visit. Rotting bodies hung from nooses, or steel garrottes, and severed heads stood in rows on wooden stakes. In some places the old carpeting was so thickly and darkly stained with blood that the patterns had disappeared. The air was thick and hot and still, and rank with foulness. Douglas strode quickly along, not allowing himself to be distracted, while Tel scowled and muttered darkly under his breath. It took a long time to reach the court, where Finn Durandal sat in state on his throne, smiling down on his visitors from the raised dais. He nodded to Douglas, and to Tel.

"So, here we are again. Well, well. I knew you'd bring someone, Douglas. So I thought I'd have a little company too."

He indicated the dead man swinging slowly from a rope beside his throne. Mr. Sylvester hadn't been dead long. His eyes bulged from his dark congested face, and a purple tongue protruded from his mouth. His great body twisted slowly back and forth, while the rope creaked loudly. Finn smiled fondly, and gave the body a gentle push with one hand to keep it moving.

"A peace offering, Douglas," he said lightly. "To show my sincerity. How sorry I am for all the nasty things he did, on my behalf. And he had outlived his usefulness, after all. I had a hell of a job getting him up there. Kicking and struggling and carrying on. And it wasn't easy to find a rope that would take his weight. The first two snapped. The things I do for you, Douglas, and you never appreciate them. But then, that's what started all this, wasn't it?"

"What happened to the two other thrones?" said Douglas. "Tradition always had two more thrones, one for the Queen and one for the blessed Owen on his return."

"Oh, I got rid of them long ago," said Finn. "Thou shalt have no other gods but me, and all that. Now, I was going to do something. What was it? Oh, yes."

The Emperor drew a concealed disrupter from his tall boot and shot Tel Markham in the chest. Tel cried out briefly as the impact threw him backward, but he was dead before he hit the floor, the front of his grubby tunic blackened and smouldering. Douglas already had his gun in his hand, but the Emperor just smiled, and put his gun away again.

"Relax, Douglas. Show's over. It had to be done; he betrayed me. And there's some shit I just won't put up with. Now it's just the two of us, as it was always meant to be. Tel didn't belong here, any more than Mr. Sylvester. They were only ever minor players in our drama. Are you wearing your esp-blocker?"

"Of course," said Douglas, slowly putting his gun away. He deliberately didn't look at the dead Tel Markham. "The most heavy duty esp-blocker Diana Vertue could put together. And there's still no guarantee it will work if the uber-espers do show up in person."

"Oh, you know they will," Finn said easily. "How could they not? A chance to possess the two leaders of the city defenses, the two men who've done so much to defy them? They won't be able to resist us. I'm quite looking forward to seeing them again. They really are spectacularly ugly."

Douglas slowly ascended the dais steps to stand beside Finn's throne. He looked out over the empty court. For a moment, the two men were silent, remembering.

"Just like old times, eh?" Finn said finally.

"Not really, no," said Douglas.

"We had some good times here," said Finn, almost reproachfully.

"That was a long time ago, when we were very different people."

"You might have been different," said Finn. "I've always been just me. Though perhaps I'm a little more open about it these days. Do you like what I've done with the palace?"

"I hate it," said Douglas, not looking at Finn.

"You never did have any taste. I've done wonders with the place. A real makeover."

"It is very you. But don't worry. Once I've taken it back, I'll have cleaners working in shifts for weeks. No one will know you were ever here."

There was another long silence. So many unspoken words burned between them, of betrayal and murder and crimes beyond counting, but somehow that wasn't what they wanted to talk about. They had been friends, once.

"When this is all over," Douglas said slowly, "you could surrender to me. I can guarantee a life sentence in prison, rather than execution. For old times' sake."

"Prison would be death, to me," said Finn. "You could surrender to me, but I wouldn't advise it. I have all kinds of appalling things planned for you, if we both survive this. If . . . I do try to be optimistic, but it isn't easy. Things never go the way you expect, do they?"

"No," said Douglas. "They don't."

"So," said Finn. "You're the King of Thieves now. I'm Emperor. You never did think big enough."

"I was granted my title by popular acclaim. You stole yours."

"Best way," Finn said cheerfully.

Douglas turned and looked at him. "How could you, Finn? How could you do all the things you've done? All the terrible things . . ."

"It was easy," said Finn. "I just stopped pretending I cared. That's always been your weakness, Douglas. You do things for others; I do them for myself."

"No. That's my strength. You never did understand that. It's why my people stand and fight, and yours run away."

"But I run an Empire, while you only have part of a city. It's a vision thing, Douglas."

"How could I have been so wrong about you? We were friends, partners, comrades in arms for so many years . . . I thought I knew you."

"A lot of people have made that mistake," said Finn Durandal.

And that was when the uber-espers appeared, all at once, teleporting into the open space of the abandoned court, dropping into reality like so many rotten fruit. They all came at once, because none of them trusted any of the others to come alone. The temperature in the great hall plummeted as the materialization sucked all the heat out of the surrounding air. Douglas and Finn both shuddered involuntarily, not entirely from the cold. Finn rose up off his Throne, gun in hand, and Douglas stood at his side, gun at the ready.

Psionic energies discharged around the uber-espers in coruscating lighting forks, and crawled along the walls like bright actinic ivy. The uber-espers' presence hammered on the air, like a corpse at a wedding, like bad news in a maternity ward, like the cancer growth your doctor shows you on the scan. Five old and terrible monsters, come to Court at last, to claim it for themselves.

The Gray Train. Blue Hellfire. Screaming Silence. The Spider Harps. The Shatter Freak.

Blue Hellfire was tall and slender and the most visibly human, wrapped in diaphanous silks over bluewhite flesh beneath. Her short spiky hair was packed with ice, and hoarfrost made whorled patterns on her corpse pale face. Her eyes and lips were the pale blue of hypothermia. She looked like someone who had been buried in the permafrost for centuries, and only recently dug up. She smiled terribly on the King and Emperor, sucking all the remaining heat out of the air around her. She stepped slowly forward, one pace at a time, inexorable as a glacier. Her clothes made sounds like cracking ice as she moved, and she left a trail of burning footprints behind her.

The Gray Train no longer had a body, as such. He only existed as an individual identity through an ongoing concentrated effort of will. He manifested as a cloud of gray flakes that held a more or less human form, composed of dust and detritus gathered from his surroundings. He was only a memory of what he used to be, and if his concentration ever slipped, he wouldn't even be that. But there was still a power in him, fuelled by his implacable will. Reality itself shivered where he walked, subject to his fleeting fancies. The world was whatever he believed it was, wherever he was.

Screaming Silence was a huge, unhealthily obese woman, vast beyond bearing; a good eight feet tall and half as wide. Her shape was grotesquely distorted, all the normal human characteristics buried under huge rolls of fat. Her wide face was gaudy with colors, her mouth pushed out into an endless rosebud pout by the pressure of her huge cheeks. Her tightly stretched skin gleamed and glistened with sweat and urine and other fluids, and was flushed with a disturbing heat. Her gray hair flared out like a dandelion, and her eyes were big and round and always hungry. Her thick stubby fingers constantly opened and closed, ready to grasp onto anything that came in reach. She wore nothing but lengths of steel chain, wrapped around and around her, the steel links puncturing her flesh here and there to hold them in place. She stank of sweat and musk and flowers left too long in the hothouse.

The Spider Harps were two withered homunculi with opened skulls, their fruiting brains exploded out into a giant gray and pink web of exposed brain tissues, that radiated away into nothingness. The two shriveled figures sat side by side on decaying chairs, their sunken faces dead and empty, apart from their eyes, still burning hotly with a vitality that would not diminish. Mummified in evil, preserved in hate. They held hands, the joined flesh fused together over many centuries. Two minds joined together for so long they had become one.

And, finally, there was the Shatter Freak. His physical existence had been shattered and scattered across time and space, by some ancient psychic trauma. His patchwork body was composed of different parts from different times, from past, present and future, somehow combined in one constantly changing construct. The details of his torso, limbs and extremities were never still for a moment, appearing and disappearing, growing and shrinking, slipping and sliding over and around each other, always being replaced by another. The Shatter Freak's face blurred and twisted as features dropped in and out, from child to ancient and everything in between, with only the eyes always the same: full of rage and pain, sorrow and horror.

"I was right," said Finn. "They haven't changed at all. Seriously ugly."

"Not to worry, Finn," said Douglas. "To me, you'll always be the greatest monster."

"Why, thank you, Douglas."

The uber-espers turned their full attention on the two men, and their presence filled the court, horrid and overpowering. They were monstrosities, abominations, things that should never have existed. Their cold implacable will beat against Douglas's and Finn's minds, and both men cried out involuntarily. It felt like dead fingers pressing at the shutters of their minds, trying to force their way in. But they were protected.

"I cannot reach them," said the Gray Train, his voice like a never-ending sigh. "I am prevented."

"Then we'll just have to do it the old-fashioned way," said Screaming Silence, in a voice like a great grunting hog. "Tear them apart, and eat their brains."

"Yes," said Blue Hellfire, in a voice like a cold wind in a narrow valley. "Or perhaps I shall take them in my arms, and love them, and watch them burn with my cold blue flames. Watch their blackened faces slough off their disobedient heads."

"Kill them," said the Spider Harps, in one dusty voice. "Kill the King and the Emperor, and we shall rule here."

"No," said the Shatter Freak, in a disturbingly normal voice. "Something is wrong. There's something else here."

      ✳   ✳   ✳

Outside the Imperial Palace, Stuart Lennox fought up and down the long entrance steps to keep the howling thralls at bay. He'd started out with twenty men to back him up, but he didn't dare look to see how many he had left. The steps narrowed as they reached the top, and the entrance doors to the palace, which gave Stuart and his men the advantage of limiting how many thralls could come up at once; but the thralls just kept coming, clambering over the bodies of their own dead to get at the enemy. Stuart and his men held the steps through sheer ferocity and fighting skills, but already they were growing dangerously tired. Stuart's sword seemed to get heavier with every blow and parry, and a slow insidious ache burned through his back and sword arm. He'd never been in a fight that lasted as long as this.

Stuart was wearing his old Paragon uniform and body armor, and his purple cloak flapped proudly about him. Jas Sri had used his media contacts to track the uniform down, and returned it to Stuart. (In these days of mass shortages and hunger, pretty much everything was being put up for sale somewhere.) Jas had cleaned and polished the uniform to within an inch of its life, and presented it to Stuart just before they had to leave the Rookery. Stuart had been touched, and he and Jas had held each other for a long time, knowing it might be the last time they ever saw each other again. Eventually they let go, and Jas helped buckle Stuart into the armor.

Stuart stood his ground at the top of the entrance steps, while his men fell about him, swinging his sword with a fierce and dogged energy. He faced impossible odds with a smile upon his face, and for the first time in a long time, he felt like a Paragon again.

Nina Malapert hovered behind him, sheltering in the open entrance doorway, popping out now and again to blast a whole clump of thralls into bloody pieces with her really big gun. Her news cameras were floating above the scene, broadcasting everything live to worlds across the Empire. She kept up a breathless running commentary, gun in one hand and sword in another, ready to rush out and guard Stuart's back when necessary. She wasn't much of a fighter, as such, but like every other able-bodied person in the Rookery, she'd been given basic weapons training. And she'd gone out with everyone else to fight, partly because she was damned if she'd miss such a great story, and partly because there was no place in the city now for observers. She had killed some thralls, and was ready to kill some more, but for now she felt it was more important to see that her news site covered what was happening. So that win or lose, the others worlds would know that at least Logres went down fighting.

Even Jas Sri, that slender and delicate media tech, had picked up a sword and gone out of the Rookery to fight. He was as much a danger to himself as anyone else with a sword in his hand, but he went anyway, because he was needed. Stuart had quietly arranged for Jas to be a part of one of the biggest armed groups, without telling him that of course, but Stuart and Jas both knew that there was nowhere safe in the city anymore.

The Psycho Sluts hovered in the sky above the palace, holding rigid formation as their minds linked together. Their leader, Alessandra Duquesne, had brought them here against Diana Vertue's specific orders, because much as they adored her, the Sluts had their own idea on how to stop the fighting, once and for all. They were going to pool and combine their power, and hit the uber-espers below with everything they had, condensed into one unstoppable blow. The uber-espers would lose contact with their thralls, might even be damaged or destroyed, and the invasion would be over. The young ladies of the Psycho Sluts had discussed this plan in earnest and at some length. They knew some or all of them might die during the attack, or after, but they had sworn a vow to be worthy of their idol, Jenny Psycho, and this seemed just the sort of thing she would have done. So they put their minds together, raised and harnessed their power till it crackled on the air around them, and then struck down at the uber-espers in the palace.

The attack went wrong almost immediately. Contact with the minds of the uber-espers blew their gestalt apart in a moment. The young espers just weren't prepared for the sheer *otherness* of the uber-espers. And they had no idea how powerful these five monsters had become, down the centuries. The Psycho Sluts' attack fragmented, the mental shards thrown back in their faces. A single whiplash of power smashed through the Psycho Sluts' defenses, ripping through their minds like barbed wire. Some went mad, pinwheeling away through the sky, screaming and howling words with no meaning. Some exploded into flames, burning inside and out, and fell to the ground like thrashing kicking comets. Three just ex-

ploded into bloody gobbets. And that left just the two most powerful
minds in the Psycho Sluts: Alessandra Duquesne and her oldest and dear-
est friend, Joanna Maltravers. Alessandra fought off the mental attack, retreating deep into her mind and concentrating all her power into defensive
shields. Her body convulsed with pain and outrage, but her mind held
firm. When she finally felt the assault was over, she came out to look at
the world again, and found that Joanna's defenses had failed. Someone else
looked out from behind her eyes. Her face twitched and twisted as some
small part of her fought the possessing mind, but she had already lost.
Joanna smiled someone else's smile, and threw herself at Alessandra.

They darted back and forth in the skies over the palace, swooping and
diving and whirling around each other in cascades of pyrotechnic energies.
They lashed out with physical and mental attacks, and psionic explosions
ripped the air apart. Both Alessandra and Joanna took terrible injuries,
and their blood rained down on the battle below. They threw rocks and
stones and even corpses at each other, and lightning bolts stabbed down
from a cloudless sky. Sleeting energies discharged around them, as they
fought to get inside each other's heads, and in the end, possibly because
the possessing mind was distracted by what was happening in the court,
Alessandra forced her way past Joanna's shields, and crushed the madly
beating heart in her old friend's breast with a remorseless psychokinetic
hand. Joanna cried out once, and then fell limp and dead from the sky.
Alessandra dropped after her, and caught Joanna's body before it hit the
ground.

She held her dear friend in her arms, rocking her back and forth like
a sleeping child, and then the last of the Psycho Sluts put her dead friend
aside, and went walking through the city streets, blowing thralls apart with
the force of her gaze, while tears rolled jerkily down her bloodstained
cheeks.

Thralls were everywhere in the city now, filling the streets and squares.
Baying mobs attacked the city's defenders on every front, crowding in
from every direction, and still more came flooding across the city's boundaries. Only their lack of weapons and tactics gave the defenders any chance
at all. And, every now and again, one section of the thrall army would

break off fighting to attack another section, when one uber-esper thought another was doing too well, and carving out too much territory for themselves. They did not trust each other, and never would, even in this last battle for the heart and soul of Logres.

With millions of thralls under their command, the uber-espers now enjoyed whole new levels of power. Some of their thralls were manifesting esper abilities on the uber-espers' behalf. Some projected terrible emotions, so that defenders cried out and howled and crawled with disgust, and did not know why. Some generated psychokinetic storms that sent razor-sharp objects hurtling through the streets ahead of them. Others sent telepathic illusions against the defenders; visions of rampaging aliens or monsters, or loved ones dying in horrible agonies. Buildings seemed to come alive, while awful things fell from a splintering sky. Sometimes these new espers even managed to turn one set of defenders against another. But none of these proxy espers lasted long. They burned out quickly from the pressure; often literally.

But there were always more to replace those who fell.

The defenders were forced back by sheer weight of numbers. They fought every inch of the way, and thralls fell dead and dying in their thousands, and hundreds of thousands, but it was not enough. Slowly, inexorably, the defenders were forced back towards the center and heart of the city, the Imperial Palace.

And that was when Lewis Deathstalker arrived with the cavalry. The fleet came howling out of hyperspace, and slammed into orbit around the beleaguered world of Logres. Thousands of pinnaces and gravity barges and war machines spilled out of the starcruisers, and descended onto the Parade of the Endless, followed by all kinds of ships, from Mistworld and Virimonde. The morning darkened as they filled the sky, and the defenders below raised a ragged cheer and fought on with renewed strength. The pinnaces and ships made landings all over the city, launching whole new armies of fighting men, already angered by what they'd seen on Nina's news sites. Gravity barges hovered over the thralls crowding into the city, and blew them apart with disrupter cannon. War machines moved to block all the entrances to the city, so that no more thralls could get in.

And falling out of the sky like avenging angels, flying under their own power and surrounded by halos of unearthly energies, came Lewis Death-stalker and Jesamine Flowers, Brett Random and Rose Constantine. Home again, to clean house. The thralls looked up, and from their massed throats came a single howl of rage and disbelief from the five minds that controlled them.

Lewis looked down at the warring streets, and was sickened and furi-ous at the number of thralls that had fought their way into the beloved capital city of Logres, that once famed and most fabulous city in the Em-pire. He could sense that they were all mind-wiped, little more than dead bodies walking, beyond all hope of rescue, and only wished he could have got home sooner. He swooped down to the entrance steps of the Imper-ial Palace, Jesamine right behind him. He hit the bottom of the steps so hard the stone cracked and shattered under his feet, and the thralls fell back like frightened children. Jesamine dropped lightly down beside him, and they both lashed out with their Maze-altered minds. Hundreds of surrounding thralls hit the ground and did not move again, the uber-espers blasted right out of their minds. And all around, thousands of thralls screamed out their hate, and charged forward. Lewis stood his ground, and met them dispassionately with gun and sword, his long steel blade flashing back and forth faster than the human eye could follow. His sword cut in and out of thrall flesh in under a second, and they fell dead and dying before him. Jesamine was there at his side, watching his blind spots, her sword rising and falling just as quickly. None of the thralls got close enough to touch them.

"You should have been in opera, Lewis," Jesamine said casually. "You really know how to make an entrance."

"Never cared much for opera," said Lewis, hacking and cutting at the thralls like a man chopping wood. "Too many good guys end up dying in the last act."

They allowed the press of bodies to follow them up the stone steps to the top, where Stuart Lennox stood alone, his uniform torn and bloodied, but his sword still swinging. Nina Malapert dodged out from behind him now and again to blow large holes in the crowd with her gun. She saw who was coming up the steps, and squealed with joy and excitement as she recognized them. She gestured, and her cameras came flying in from all directions to get a good angle. Stuart just nodded to Lewis and to Jesamine.

"Good to have you back, Deathstalker. Make yourself at home. Kill a whole bunch of thralls."

"Thanks," said Lewis. "Don't mind if I do."

Behind them, Nina Malapert shook her head sadly, when she realized that was all they were going to say. It was hardly dialogue for the ages.

And all across the city, ships and pinnaces landed wherever they could, and soldiers and fighting men and women disembarked with sword and gun at the ready. They charged right into the waiting thralls, and soon there were surging mobs of combatants in every street and square. Men and women from Mistworld and Virimonde cut and hacked their way through the crowded boulevards, eager for blood and vengeance. They had come for Finn Durandal, but for the moment they'd settle for taking out some of their grievances on the thralls. There was no peace to be found anywhere in the Parade of the Endless, as the two sides contested for every square foot of the city. Famous buildings burned, and towers and bridges that were works of art collapsed in ruins. Disrupter blasts scorched away precious mosaics and set fires blazing in protected parks. Both sides in the battle were too busy to notice, or care.

The Ashrai came flying down, their huge grotesque forms soaring over the city on wide membranous rainbow wings, and a cry went up from the weary city defenders, and even some hardened souls from the Rookery.

Look! It's the dragons! Owen has sent his dragons to aid us!

Somewhere among the vast army of the Ashrai, the old traitor called Carrion laughed softly, relishing the irony. And then he led his people down into battle, smashing through the defenseless thralls like pile drivers on the wing.

John Silence was in the city too. He'd come down in a pinnace, alongside his troops. The fleet captains had done everything they could to talk him out of it, but he didn't listen. They'd wanted him to stay safe with the starcruisers, deciding strategy and giving orders, but he knew his place was on the ground. He'd always known he was an admiral in name only, and now he needed to be back in his old city, that he had defended and saved so many times before, over so many years. It was time again to do what he did best: fight the good fight against impossible odds. So he left captains Price and Vardalos in charge of the fleet, and rode a pinnace down to the Parade of the Endless as just another trooper. Some of the men recognized him, and some didn't, and it didn't matter to him either way. He was first out of the pinnace, and led the charge against the waiting thralls. He swung his sword with both hands, killing the enemy with swift and subtle strokes, always pressing forward, forward. He'd never been able to work actual miracles, like Owen and the others, but after all these long years there were few indeed who could match his prowess with a sword. He'd never thought of himself as a hero or a legend or even as a warrior; just a good soldier determined to do his duty, no matter what. His sword slammed in and out of bodies, never pausing for a moment, and it felt like old times again.

Investigator Frost was right there at his side, where she belonged.

Captains Price and Vardalos conferred urgently, and then ordered the fleet starcruisers to descend into the lowest possible orbit, actually inside the planet's upper atmosphere. With the ships' AIs not working, the crews had to prepare the targeting computers themselves, and then used the ships' disrupter cannon to scorch whole areas around the city's boundaries. The huge armies of the possessed disappeared in moments, reduced to glowing dust by the power of the ships' guns. There would be no reinforcements for the thralls in the city. But there were just so many of them, and more on the way. The ships kept targeting and firing. It was a dangerous procedure for the starcruisers. Pinpoint accuracy required flying low, well inside the atmosphere, and starcruisers weren't designed or built to do that. It was only a matter of time before they started breaking up. But the ships kept firing anyway, because they were needed.

The uber-espers struck back, turning their power on the low-flying starcruisers, hexing their tech and attacking their crews. Systems failed and computers crashed on ships throughout the fleet. Firestorms raged out of control through narrow steel corridors, and airlocks opened spontaneously, venting atmosphere and pressure. Some crew went insane just from the uber-esper contact, and attacked each other. Maddened though not possessed, they ran wild, and struggling figures wrestled for control of ships' departments, fighting each other blindly in every compartment and bay. Ship captains had to release security sleepgas into affected areas to re-store control. They set up internal force shields to contain the worst dam-age, and reluctantly retired to higher orbits, where hopefully the uber-espers couldn't reach them. They had done all they could. It was up to the ground forces now.

On one ship, the *Herald,* the whole crew went crazy. Everyone from the lowest crewman to the captain, Glenn Lyle, ran mad in the starcruiser. Howling and screaming issued from their comm channels, like damned souls in hell, and no one was surprised when the *Herald* opened fire on the ships around her. Disrupter cannon blasted away at the shields on already weakened ships. A dozen support ships from Mistworld and Virimonde were swept away in moments. The *Herald* lashed viciously about her in her madness, threatening every other ship in the fleet. And only Captain Al-fred Price was able to do anything about it.

His ship the *Havoc* had taken the brunt of the *Herald*'s attack, and was already crippled. Her shields were failing, her hull was holed in several places, and Price no longer had control over his guns. Most of his crew had gone down to the planet below, and of the skeleton crew left behind, most were dead or running for the escape pods. Price had given the order to abandon ship, but still he sat in his command chair on the deserted, burned-out bridge, surrounded by the smoldering remains of gutted con-soles, and the bodies of his fallen officers. He had to keep wiping away blood that trickled down into his eyes from the great wound on the side of his head, and it felt like one of his arms was broken. The *Herald* had done a hell of a job on his ship. Price laughed sharply, and lurched up out of his command chair. He dropped into the navigator's seat, called up all the power left in the engines, and aimed his ship right at the *Herald.* For once his duty was clear, and he felt like a real captain at last. He just wished there'd been somebody left to see it. He watched the mad ship draw slowly closer on the bridge viewscreen, not even bothering to get out of his way, and he laughed again. He was still laughing when the *Havoc* crashed head-on into the *Herald,* amid a coruscation of shattered shields, and both ships rammed into each other and exploded. Locked together, blazing fiercely with discharging energies, the wreckage of the two ships tumbled slowly end over end as they fell towards Logres.

Captain Vardalos took sole command, and regrouped what was left of the fleet in high orbit. She wished she'd had ship's espers, like in the old days. The uber-esper attack seemed to have stopped for the moment, but she had no way of knowing whether it might start again. No one really knew anything, where the uber-espers were concerned.

Lewis Deathstalker and Jesamine Flowers fought side by side at the top of the stairs at the entrance to the palace, performing dark wonders with sword and gun. No one had seen such warriors since Owen's time. None of the thralls could touch them, despite the huge numbers. Stuart Lennox was there too, tired but dogged. Grateful as he was for Lewis and Jesamine's presence, he was beginning to find their unending skill and fury just a little spooky. Lewis's sword rose and fell, cut and hacked, moving too fast for the human eye to follow, throwing thrall bodies aside as though they were nothing. Jesamine spun and danced, as fast and deadly as a striking snake, and more beautiful. Death had never looked more glamorous or more certain.

The dead piled up on every side, forming tall barricades so that the thralls could come up the steps only in narrow files to attack their enemy. They came clambering carelessly over the dead on the steps, their possessed eyes blazing with unquenched fury. They still made noises, but there was nothing human in the sound. They fought with clawed hands, like animals. Nina still opened fire with her very big gun on occasion, when the mob seemed to be pressing especially close, but the energy crystal was running low. She didn't have many shots left. She'd given up on her running commentary. The scenes the floating cameras were broadcasting live said it all. But one question still nagged at her, and in the end she just leaned forward and blurted it out.

"Lewis! Where's Owen? Is the blessed Owen coming to save us?"

"No," said Lewis, his sword slicing into a thrall's chest and out again. "Owen's busy elsewhere. You'll just have to settle for me."

The thralls came surging forward, a solid wave of rage and hatred driving up the steps, desperate to get their hands on Lewis and Jesamine and drag them down. Nina fired her gun into the mass, and it didn't even slow them. Lewis and Jesamine and Stuart held their position at the top of the steps, and the thrall wave shattered against them like the sea against an immoveable rock. After everything they'd been through, after all the dangers Lewis and Jesamine had faced, the thralls might be hard work but they weren't scary. And Stuart Lennox, his old pride returned, was once again the chosen Paragon of Virimonde, and he stood proudly beside his hero Lewis, as unmoveable as any Maze survivor.

The pressure of the attack actually lessened, as the uber-espers realized it would take more than force of numbers to bring these three down. And so they pushed their abilities to the limit, and suddenly some of the attacking thralls began to manifest esper abilities. The thralls only lasted a few minutes before burning up inside and out, consumed by the very power they were wielding, but they threw fire and rubble at the defenders, and rocked them with psychic assaults. And yet somehow the attacks never seemed to focus, or find their targets, as though even the uber-espers couldn't quite comprehend what Lewis and Jesamine had become. Stuart just kept his head down, and the psychic assaults collapsed almost as quickly as they'd begun.

More soldiers came pouring in from the side streets, with warriors from Mistworld and Virimonde. They saw the three standing firm at the entrance to the palace, and the dead piled up before and around them, and the newcomers raised their battle cry.

Deathstalker! Deathstalker! Deathstalker!

The new fighters and the thralls crashed together at the foot of the steps, and the square before the palace was quickly full of struggling figures. It was chaos, with people striking out blindly in all directions. And Jesamine Flowers lowered her sword and raised her voice. She sang, and all her Maze power focused through her trained voice. The song drowned out every other sound, rising and rising until it seemed everyone in the city could hear it. It was an old song, from the beginning days of Empire, and perhaps even older than that. Of the joys and responsibilities, the duty and the triumphs of being human. Jesamine's voice rang like steel and silver and silk on the still air, a pure and striking sound, and it seemed like everyone in the city stopped to hear it. Defenders and thralls alike were held where they stood. And then the Ashrai joined in, adding their voices to hers. It was a song of life and blessed humanity, and voices rose all across the city, joining in, until the air itself shook with the power of the song.

And one by one, and then dozens by dozens, the thralls began to collapse. They fell limply to the ground, and did not rise again, in all the streets and squares and crowded bloody places around the Imperial Palace. The song of Jesamine, and the Ashrai and the people who had come to save a city and a world, had a strength and a force and a power that not even the uber-espers could match. Their minds were forced out of those they'd possessed, and the grounds around the palace were carpeted with the living empty shells of what had once been men and women.

But Jesamine couldn't sing forever, and eventually even her voice gave out. Without her to lead them, the Ashrai and the people fell out of the song. And so everywhere else in the city, the fighting went on, perhaps a little more savagely than before.

Brett Random's first instinct had been to bolt for the safety of the Rookery the moment his pinnace landed, and go to ground there until all the fighting was safely over. He knew all kinds of hiding places in the Rookery, where even his oldest friends and enemies wouldn't have been able to find him. But the sheer number of thralls he faced almost immediately made it clear running out was not a viable option. He wouldn't get ten paces on his own. Brett whimpered, swore at everything and everyone, and drew his weapons. Rose Constantine had drawn her weapons even before they'd landed properly. She saw the army of thralls laid out before her, thirsting for her blood, and smiled widely. She hefted her sword once, and went to meet them like a lover.

Brett and Rose soon ended up fighting back to back, separated from the rest of the fighters they'd come down with. Rose didn't hold back for anyone as she cut a bloody path through the enemy, and Brett was terrified to be separated from her. The tides of battle moved them well away from the Imperial Palace. Brett was forced to call up all the fighting skills he'd learned from Rose, just to survive, and for a while the two of them fought well and finely, cutting down every thrall that came within reach. They were both faster and stronger than any human had a right to be, and none of the thralls could match them for a moment.

But Brett could still see other soldiers dying, pulled down and torn apart by the thralls, and his borrowed courage and skills were no match for the growing certainty that even with the Wild Rose at his side, eventually the thralls would get him too. There were just too many of them. He couldn't run, and he knew his fighting skills weren't enough on their own, so he reluctantly did the one thing that scared him the most. He deliberately reopened the old mental link between him and Rose, and used his esper compulsion to slam their minds together, so that he could share in all the wild madness that made Rose the unbeatable fighter she was. Their minds opened up and meshed together, all the parts fitting into place, into one larger structure. Rose laughed aloud, delighting at the feel of his mind in hers, and hers in his. They both knew everything about each other, all their skills and secrets. The whole process was finished in a second, and suddenly the thralls were faced with a new threat: two superhuman fighters who fought as one. Equally skilled, equally savage.

Brett and Rose struck about them with inhuman speed and skill, performing dark wonders of swordsmanship, piling up the bodies around them, so that the thralls had to climb over the fallen to get at their enemies. The uber-espers looked on Brett and Rose through their proxy eyes, and then had to look away, because the two burned so very brightly and fiercely. The uber-espers called thralls away from other, lesser threats, and commanded them to bring down Brett and Rose at any cost.

Brett and Rose fought on with their bodies, but their minds were elsewhere. The process they had started was still continuing. Their minds opened up and up, meshing together on every level, merging into one incredible mind. A single mind, male and female, one personality operating in two bodies simultaneously. What the uber-espers imposed, Brett and Rose learned to do voluntarily. The process that Finn's esper drug had begun, and the Madness Maze had continued, now reached its fruition in a single mind that was far more than the sum of its parts. It was a fusion, the best of both minds and the worst, all the knowledge and experience and memories of two people, now combined into one. It was a new thing, and BrettRose woke up smiling.

Their combined will hit the thralls like a hammer blow, hurling them away dead and broken. BrettRose looked about them, and more thralls blew away under the pressure of their gaze, opening up a wide space around the two bodies with a single mind. The uber-espers lashed out with a telepathic attack focused through their thralls, but it glanced harmlessly away from the new creature's shields. The uber-espers recoiled from this new thing, and retreated, shocked and horrified by stirrings of a long buried memory. The thralls turned and ran, leaving BrettRose standing alone in an empty square, surrounded by the dead. They slowly lowered their swords and their breathing steadied, their many wounds slowly but steadily healing themselves.

Nikki Sixteen, that proud and feisty human-alien hybrid from the Rookery, ran through the square at that moment with a dozen of her fellow fighters, heading for the palace, drawn by what they'd heard in Jesamine's song. She stopped as she recognized Brett and Rose, flashed Brett a smile, and then hesitated. Brett was different. She could feel it. There was . . . more to him. Brett and Rose looked at Nikki, at the same moment, in the same way, and Nikki backed away from them. She was frightened, and she didn't know why. She ran after her companions, out of the square, not even sure what it was she was running from. Except that it felt . . . like Brett was dead. Or at least gone.

Gil Akotai led his Mistworld warriors through the streets, using sharp and cunning tactics to split the thrall armies apart into more manageable groups. Mistworlders knew all about strategy and dirty fighting. Gil swung his long curved blade with wide easy strokes, husbanding his energy, always leading from the front. More and more people came to join him as news of his success spread, and soon he was leading an army of his own through the Parade of the Endless. His skill and courage were unmatched, and he built his own legend that day, through feats of valor and derring-do that were all the more impressive because they came from a simple man, untouched by the dubious blessings of the Madness Maze. The Mistworlders chanted his name as a battle cry, and others took it up as Gil Akotai led them unstoppably towards the heart of the city. News cameras came rushing in from all directions to broadcast it all live. People on worlds all across the Empire followed his exploits, because he was one of them, not a legend or monster from the Maze; just a man, with a man's courage and determination. Gil Akotai led his people on, cutting a bloody path through the chaos towards the Imperial Palace.

John Silence, the last survivor of those who'd come down in his pinnace, made contact with the clone guards and took control of them. They weren't much use without officers to guide them, but they recognized Silence's natural authority, and gratefully accepted his tactics and orders. Silence recognized them as clones, but had no idea of their origin. They still wore their steel masks. But they were a fighting force, and just what Silence needed, so he didn't question them too deeply. He just set them to work, killing thralls and pulling together, and then he led them into battle, fighting solidly and well. The Maze might not have granted him miraculous powers, like Owen and the others, but he was still the greatest fighting soldier of his time. He'd even gone head-to-head with Owen Deathstalker, and held his own. The thralls were no match for him. He looked into their possessed eyes, and was reminded of his battles long ago against Shub's Ghost Warriors. *Nothing changes,* he thought, just a little bitterly. The Ghost Warriors were a very long time ago, but he didn't feel old. In fact, it seemed to him that he'd never fought better than this.

He said as much to Investigator Frost, and she agreed, smiling. She stuck close to his side, warning him of dangers he missed.

Silence and his clone guards reached the palace steps not long after Jesamine's marvelous song, and he led them carefully through the fallen thralls bodies to the foot of the steps. Nina spotted him, yelled a cheerful greeting, and came bounding down the steps for a quick interview with this new leader of the guards. (Lewis and Jesamine had already refused an interview, and Stuart never had much to say.) But she stopped suddenly, distracted by one of the guards. The steel mask had been torn away during a struggle, and for the first time Nina could see one of the guard's faces. And for all the distortion, she recognized it immediately as Finn's. She turned quickly and ripped the mask off another guard.

"Clones!" said Nina. "Finn's clones—all of them! Another exclusive!"

And she did her happy dance, right there in front of a bemused Silence. And then she went bounding back up the steps to spill the news to Stuart. She forgot all about interviewing the solemn-looking man who'd led the guards into the square. She had a feeling she ought to know him, but that could wait. Besides, she thought, glancing back for a moment, he did seem awfully busy chatting with someone who wasn't there . . .

Elsewhere in the city, the aliens from the Rookery had joined the fight against the invading thralls. They emerged from unexpected places to rend and kill unsuspecting thralls, and enjoyed themselves immensely. Led by the silver-armored Toch'Kra, they came boiling out of sewer openings and factory outlets, and erupted from boarded-up factories and pollution dumps, catching the thralls by surprise. The aliens tore the possessed humans apart. They didn't know the bodies were mind-wiped, and they didn't care. They had grievances to address, and besides, they were hungry. Sometimes they had to be restrained from attacking the clone guards and the fleet's soldiers. The Rookery people cheered the aliens on, which was something of a new sensation for them.

The monsters from Shandrakor quickly gravitated towards the aliens, and fought by their side. They felt more at home there, though they politely declined when asked if they'd like to join the feasting. The monsters excelled at fighting the thralls, partly because of their bestial natures, honed by long years of struggle for survival on Shandrakor, but mostly because they had nothing left to lose. They had been promised that they could come home, and here they were. It might be called Logres now rather than Golgotha, but this was still the Parade of the Endless, just as they remembered. Even if it had been fancied up a bit since their time. They were home again, and if they had only come back to fight and die, that was fine by them.

Michel du Bois, one of the few surviving members of Parliament, fought with his back to a wall in a side alley already choked with bodies. Most of the Virimonde warriors he'd come down with were already dead, but he and a dozen others fought on, stubbornly refusing to be dragged down and torn apart like the others. Du Bois chanted the old Deathstalker battle cry, *Shandrakor!* as he swung his sword with more defiance than skill. Du Bois had always been fiercely loyal to his homeworld, if not always to its most famous Paragon, Lewis; but with the slaughter of Clan Deathstalker by Finn's creatures, all the people of Virimonde had sworn to become Deathstalkers in their place; and du Bois was no different. He had been among the first to volunteer to come and fight on Logres, even though he was far more a politician than a warrior. He thought he'd done well enough, considering. He'd killed thralls. His only regret was that he should have to die in such a squalid back alley, so far away from the House of Parliament and the Imperial Palace, where he'd spent so much of his life.

He'd wanted to see them once again, at least, before he died.

One by one, the men and women around him were dragged down, and killed. Each and every one of them went down fighting to the last. They fought impossible odds, as a Deathstalker should, and not one of them broke and ran. So Michel du Bois couldn't either. And when he finally fell, still flailing about him with his sword, his last thought was: *Ah, Lewis, I always knew you'd be the death of me.*

The whole city was a battleground now. The thrall invasion had been halted by the starcruisers' actions outside the city, but the armies of thralls already inside the city were still surging through the streets of the Parade of the Endless. The tides of battle swept this way and that, and apart from one small area around the Imperial Palace, no one could tell for sure which way the war was going.

Inside the court, the five assembled uber-espers launched the full force of their considerable will against the waiting Douglas Campbell and Finn Durandal, and once again they failed. They simply could not reach the two men standing steadily before them. The uber-espers looked at each other, baffled. No esp-blocker ever made could have stood up to such an attack. And then cold, harsh laughter rang out on the air from nowhere. The uber-espers' heads snapped round. Screaming Silence shook violently, rattling her chains, and Blue Hellfire let out a low moaning. Gray Train actually lost control of his dusty shape for a moment. All the uber-espers knew that laugh. And as they looked wildly about them, Diana Vertue stepped casually out from behind Finn's throne, to fix them all with her savage glare.

"I've been here all along," she said flatly. "Hidden behind the strongest shields I ever created. I walked in here with Douglas and Tel, and nobody saw or heard me. Even they couldn't be sure I was with them. They just had to take it on trust. You see, Douglas and Finn were the bait, but I am the trap. I knew you'd never face me willingly, even if you did manage to kill me once, so Douglas and I came up with a plan to bring all of you to me. And guess what—I brought a few friends along."

She rose up into the air, hovering above the throne on unseen wings, and suddenly she was shining brightly as the sun. Her presence joined with the presence of many other minds to beat on the air of the court. Even Douglas and Finn flinched away from her. The uber-espers howled and shrieked in inhuman voices as Diana Vertue became a conduit for all the power of the mass-mind of the oversoul, and Diana laughed again.

"The oversoul has come back! The city of New Hope traveled here with the Fleet from Mistworld, unseen and unsuspected. Only I knew. A secret weapon, to be preserved and kept ready for just this moment. You uber-espers are all that's left of a particularly shameful episode of our past, and we will finally be rid of you!"

The uber-espers tried to flee, teleporting out of the court, but Diana Vertue held them where they were. And the oversoul struck at the uber-espers through Diana, who was still sometimes Jenny Psycho. The terrible destructive force beat upon the monstrous minds of the uber-espers, driving them together to support their mental shield. Douglas and Finn were forced back, unable to bear even the side effects of the psychic assault taking place before them. They huddled together, hands clapped uselessly to their heads, the only human souls left on an inhuman battlefield. The oversoul kept up the pressure, beating at the uber-espers' shield with brutal strength, determined to wipe out the menace of the mad minds, once and for all. Diana Vertue grinned like a death's head as the attack focused through her enlarged mind. This was what she had come back for. An old vengeance for an old crime.

The uber-espers huddled together as their mental shield shuddered and cracked, failing under the onslaught of the oversoul and Diana Vertue, and then . . . something utterly unexpected happened. The dusty gray figure of the Gray Train collapsed, losing its human shape to become a gray cloud that swept over Blue Hellfire, surrounded and sank into her, darkening the color of her corpse pale skin. Icy flames leapt up around her. The Shatter Freak lurched forward, almost against his will, his body parts appearing and disappearing at dizzying speed, until he too fell into Blue Hellfire like a rock into a pool, absorbed and swallowed up in a moment. Screaming Silence lunged forward, grunting like a hog at the trough, and her great fleshy body wrapped itself around Blue Hellfire. The flames blazed brightly, radiating an impossible cold as the two figures melted together to become one. A dark silhouette of a human figure, like a hole in the world. And finally the two withered homunculi of the Spider Harps just snapped out of existence, like a popped soap bubble. Only one figure now remained, bathed in icy flames like a clay shape being recast in a kiln. And when it was all over, and the cold fires had died away, there stood just a single figure, a short blond woman who shone like the sun. Diana looked at her blankly as the oversoul's attack cut off.

"Who the hell are you? Where did the uber-espers go?"

"Back inside me, where they belong," said the new woman, in a flat, measured voice. She rolled her head around and flexed her shoulders, as though it had been a long time since she'd been in a body. "I should thank you, Diana Vertue, and the oversoul. The pressure of your attack brought about what I've been unable to achieve for hundreds of years. You put me back together again."

"The uber-espers—all of them—they were just parts of you?" said Diana.

"I went through the Madness Maze, a long, long time ago, and it split me apart into five separate subpersonalities, because that was the only way I could cope with what I found there. Greetings to you, King Douglas and Emperor Finn. I am Alicia VomAcht Deathstalker. I am finally back, and all the worlds that are shall tremble before me."

"This is not good," said Finn.

"You think?" said Douglas.

The sheer force of Alicia's presence seemed to fill the court, pressing against the far walls and shuddering in the floor. It pushed Diana's presence aside effortlessly, and both Douglas and Finn had to fight an urge to kneel and bow their heads. They felt as though they didn't belong in the court, like vermin in the gaze of a living goddess. The oversoul was silent in Diana's head, struck dumb by this turn of events. Even their best precogs hadn't sensed this coming. The entire mass-mind of the oversoul looked upon the restored, incandescent mind of Alicia VomAcht Deathstalker, and was afraid. She smiled slowly upon Diana.

"We have met before. When you manifested the Mater Mundi, all those years ago, that was part of me. I was spread far and wide by the Maze, torn apart into grotesque subpersonalities, crude representatives of my various needs and functions, but I always had an agenda."

"Who . . . were you?" said Douglas, fighting to get the words out. "How did you become . . . the uber-espers?"

"What?" said Alicia. "You mean the oversoul never told you about the mad old aunt they kept in the attic? I am the beginning of the esper movement. They all have their root in me. I was one of the group of scientists who first discovered the Madness Maze, in a cavern deep inside Haden, centuries and centuries ago. I was an esper, one of the very first. I found others, bound them to my will, and forced them to go through the Maze with me. My intention was to produce a mighty esper gestalt, with me in total control, but . . . the Maze wasn't what I thought it was. It tried to change me, remake me . . . and I couldn't have that. I fought it, but the effort broke me. Tore me apart into the uber-espers and the driving force in the mass unconscious of the other espers, who became the esper underground. Later, they called me the Mater Mundi, Mother of All Souls. Even scattered and separated I was a force in the history of mankind. Now I'm back, and steeped in my true power again.

"I like this new mass gestalt you call the oversoul. So brightly shining, so very tasty. Why, I could just eat it all up."

Alicia VomAcht Deathstalker withdrew her controlling presence from the thrall armies, to gather all her power in one place for one purpose, and all across the Parade of the Endless, no longer possessed men and women and children fell limply to the ground and lay still. Eyes open, still breathing, but utterly empty. Alicia would reoccupy them later, after she'd finished with more pressing business. Fighting stopped in the city, as exhausted and bloody men and women slowly lowered their weapons and looked uncertainly about them. A great cheer went up, that the war was over and they had survived. They didn't know about Alicia. The various fighting groups came together as they headed for the heart of the city, and the Imperial Palace. The acclaimed greatest hero of the fighting, Gil Akotai, led the way.

Above the Imperial Palace, the vast floating city of New Hope manifested, its glass and silver towers shining like an impossibly huge snowflake. The people below cheered out again to see it, but the espers didn't notice. They fought to focus every bit of power they had through Diana Vertue. It was a terrible thing to come face-to-face with their progenitor, after all these years. They had found at last their founder and creator, only to discover she was a mad god that wished only to devour her children. But the oversoul still had a few tricks up its sleeve. A few hints from the precogs. The oversoul sent down Crow Jane and the Ecstatic called Joy, to join the others in the court.

Standing alone before the last throne, Alicia didn't actually look like much. Just a small, short blond woman in an old-fashioned spacer's uniform, the only mark of strangeness about her the huge dark eyes that dominated her small pale face. The kind of woman you'd pass every day and never give a second look. But even though she'd turned off her glow, her presence was still stamped upon the court, like a boot crashing into a face. She dominated the whole court by her very existence.

Behind her, a man and a woman entered the court, striding along side by side. Alessandra Duquesne, last of the Psycho Sluts, and John Silence, last of the old legends. She had dropped down out of the sky and snatched him up from the thick of the fighting. She carried him towards the palace, and *Because we're needed* was all she had to say. Silence went along with it. He was used to sudden changes in direction in his life. At first, Alessandra had been a little confused, thinking there was someone else with Silence, but she pushed the thought aside to concentrate on getting to the palace as fast as possible. *Why are you crying?* Silence had asked, and she told him about having to kill her oldest friend. Silence had nodded, understanding. *Rebellions always kill your friends first,* he said, remembering Alexander Storm, and others.

Silence and Alessandra circled carefully around Alicia, giving her plenty of room. They could feel the power radiating from her. They joined Douglas and Finn and Diana before the throne. They'd heard Alicia tell her strange history as they approached the court. They told the King and Emperor of the collapse of the thrall armies, and Douglas nodded, relieved there was at least one problem that he didn't have to be worried about for the moment. He nodded to Silence.

"I understand you're really the legendary Captain John Silence. Why did you masquerade as Samuel Chevron for all those years? Did my father know?"

"No," said Silence. "No one knew. That was the point. I felt it best to conceal my true nature."

"Lot of that going around at the moment," said Douglas.

And then Crow Jane materialized in court right next to them, along with Joy, and they all jumped. Crow Jane wore her battered leather jacket, with a bandolier of throwing stars across her bosom. Her sharp face looked even paler than usual, showing off her jet black hair and lips and heavy eye makeup. Joy, whose brain had been surgically altered so that he lived in a constant state of orgasm, smiled brightly on one and all, an average, almost anonymous-looking man in a simple white tunic. Crow Jane nodded briskly to Diana.

"The oversoul sent us. No one seems too sure why, but our precogs were unanimous that Joy needs to be here. Don't ask me what good he's going to do, unless he intends on smiling Alicia to death."

"I am here," Joy said politely, "because this is where I'm supposed to be. And how often can you say that with any surety? Hello, Alicia!" And then he wandered off to look at some walls.

"I feel so much safer," Finn said to Douglas. "Don't you?"

John Silence nodded uncomfortably to his daughter Diana. They moved a little aside, so that they could talk privately. They knew they should have been concentrating on Alicia, but it seemed like they had all the time in the world, to say all the things that needed to be said.

"Been a long time, Father," said Diana. "Since we last met in person. A hundred and eighteen years."

"I've been busy," said Silence.

"You never were much of a father," said Diana, without heat. "Always ready to sacrifice your own daughter to the greater good. First on Unseeli, back when we were both still only human, and then . . ."

"I did what I thought was necessary," said Silence, meeting his daughter's angry gaze with old, tired eyes.

"You betrayed me to the uber-espers! You led me into an ambush, and then abandoned me! I should have known better than to trust you."

"I thought . . . I believed your growing power made you too dangerous, too disruptive; a threat to the Golden Age we were trying to build for everybody."

"Did you know the oversoul would pick up my mind, after my body was destroyed by the uber-espers?"

"No. But I hoped."

Diana frowned, and looked at Silence's side. "I sort of sense someone with you. Investigator Frost?"

"Can you see her too?"

"No. There's no one there," said Diana. "Oh, Father, won't you ever let her go?"

While they were talking, Alicia sidled into Silence's mind, just for the fun of it. It wasn't difficult, for all his two trips through the Madness Maze. Silence had always suppressed his greater powers. Perhaps because he was afraid of becoming like his daughter. Alicia needed a distraction. If she could dominate and possess his weaker mind, she could seize control of all his Maze powers, and use them to kill Diana. She found the image of Investigator Frost in Silence's mind, and giggled like a girl as she slipped into it, like a maggot wriggling into an apple.

Frost turned suddenly and looked at Silence with cold eyes. "She's just an ungrateful bitch, John. She never appreciated all the things you did for her. Kill her."

"What?" Silence said loudly, and everyone looked at him.

"Kill her. It's necessary; just like before. And afterwards, kill the runaway King and the traitor Emperor. They're not worthy. You should be in charge. You're the only one left who is worthy to lead Humanity. Do it. Do what you always wanted to do, John."

Silence looked at her. "You're not Frost. The Investigator would never say that. You're . . . her. Alicia. I can feel you, creeping about inside my head."

"*Do it!*" Alicia shrieked, pushing all her considerable presence into Silence's mind. He cried out, shrieking piteously in pain and shock and horror, falling to his knees. His arms trembled, his fingers twitching with someone else's intentions. He could feel Alicia pushing him further and further into the back of his head. The court fell away, as though at the end of a rapidly diminishing tunnel. She slithered through his thoughts like an inexorable impulse, and he knew he wasn't strong enough to hold her off. But he'd always been his own man. So while his hand was still mostly his own, he pulled his disrupter from its holster, set it clumsily against his heart, and shot himself. One last act of duty, and of honor.

Alicia fled laughing from his guttering mind as he slumped towards the floor. With the last of his vision, Silence saw Diana moving towards him to catch him, and knew she wouldn't get there in time. He hit the floor of the court hard, and never felt it. All the lights went out.

And he heard Investigator Frost saying *Welcome home, Captain,* and he smiled a last smile.

Diana sat on the floor, holding her dead father in her arms, glaring at Alicia. *"What did you do to him?"*

"I always break my toys when I play with them," said Alicia VomAcht Deathstalker.

Diana put her dead father aside, and rose slowly to her feet, gathering her power around her. And then there was the sound of running footsteps from the corridor leading to the court, and everyone turned to look as the man called Carrion burst in, his black cape flapping around him like a gore-crow's wings. He ignored everyone but the fallen Silence. He walked forward to stand over the dead body for a long moment, breathing heavily.

"I could feel it happening," he said finally. "But I couldn't get here in time."

"You couldn't have saved him, Sean," said Diana.

"I always thought we'd die together. Probably with our hands around each other's throats. Old friend, old enemy."

"Legends always die alone," said Diana. "It goes with the territory."

Carrion turned to look at Alicia. "You. You did this. I am the Ashrai; and we condemn you to death."

"Get in line," said Alicia.

She lashed out with all her awful power, a blast of sheer annihilating energy designed to wipe everyone else out of existence, as though they'd never been. Diana Vertue met her attack with a scream of pure defiance, all the power of the oversoul channeled through her mighty, grief-driven mind. Her clothes began to smolder from escaping energies. The two women stood facing each other across the court, impossible forces raging between them. Two great powers, the old and the new, utterly deadlocked. The monster and the mass-mind. Alessandra joined her mind with Diana's, and Carrion sang with the voice of all the Ashrai. And still Alicia stood.

Psi storms ran loose, crackling on the air of the court, baneful destructive energies tossed around as though they were nothing. Huge jagged cracks split apart the walls of the court, and zigzagged across the high ceiling. Pieces of masonry broke free, and fell ponderously down into the court. Carrion raised a hand, and a shimmering screen protected everyone except Alicia.

The floor shook as though in an earthquake, and the throne rocked back and forth, as though fought over by unseen hands. The air was unbearably hot and then impossibly cold, and rain and hail fell from nowhere. Probabilities changed and altered, snapping on and off in a moment as old familiar faces flickered in and out of sight in the court. Lionstone on her throne, with the first Dram the Widowmaker at her side. Owen Deathstalker, holding a fallen crown in his hand. King Robert and Queen Constance, smiling architects of the Golden Age. So many faces, so many names, come and gone in a moment as time rippled and bent back and forth upon itself. And Douglas Campbell and Finn Durandal, who had once been major players in the struggle for the fate of the Empire, could now only huddle together to one side, ignored.

And then the psi storms snapped off, banished in a moment by the sheer power of those who now strode into the court. The walls stopped shaking and cracking, and the floor grew still, and Alicia and Diana both looked round angrily to see who had interrupted them. And Lewis Deathstalker, Jesamine Flowers, Brett Random, and Rose Constantine strode forward to meet them. Reality stabilized as the four Maze minds enforced their will upon it. Alicia shrieked with fury, and lashed out at everyone present, unleashing all her centuries of Maze-given power. Diana and Alessandra and the oversoul met it first, and then the four Maze survivors reached out, adding their power. Carrion's voice rose in a terrible song, and all the power of the Ashrai focused through him, adding their support. Alicia staggered and almost fell, but didn't.

Lewis stepped forward, and Alicia turned to face him. And that was how it all came to a head, with one Deathstalker facing another. Two minds remade by the Madness Maze, and made powerful beyond belief. Because the Maze had always worked best for Deathstalkers.

Lewis and Alicia went head-to-head, matching power with power, will with will, and in the end Lewis won. Because all Alicia had was self-interest and ambition and hate, while Lewis was centered around duty and honor and the courage he needed to protect those he cared for. And Alicia stood alone, while Lewis stood for many. Alicia hit him with everything she had, trying to possess and control him, and then trick and subvert him, but there was just so much more to him than there was to her. And so she turned and ran.

She was halfway across the court before anyone even realized that the mental battle was over, and she was out the doors and gone before they could react. Alicia ran through the palace's maze of corridors, and the others came after her, crying out in rage and cheated passion. Alicia wrapped herself in her will, becoming invisible to the world. She sent her thoughts racing ahead of her, sensing that triumphant rebels were already streaming into the palace through the main entrance, led by Gil Akotai. Alicia smiled. She couldn't take control of her thrall army again without giving away her presence to her enemies, but she could take one mind, and hide in it while the thrall smuggled her away. And then . . . well, Gil Akotai was a hero and a leader; just what she needed to re-establish herself . . .

She ducked into a side passage as she heard footsteps approaching, concentrating all her power into not being there. One by one her pursuers passed her by, and she weighed each one as they passed, looking for someone to carry her unnoticed to Gil Akotai. Most were too well protected, but one mind . . . The Ecstatic named Joy ambled past her hiding place, his mind wide open, and she struck at him like a snake. Such a small man, with his surgically altered brain. If he should seem to be acting a little strangely, who'd notice? She plunged into Joy's head, and found waiting there the cage he'd made for her.

Hello, Alicia, said Joy. *I've been waiting for you. Enjoy your stay. There's no way out.*

And trapped inside a mind that made no sense at all, all Alicia Vom-Acht Deathstalker could do was scream and scream and scream.

Joy called to the others to bring them back, and pointed at the empty shell of Alicia's body lying still and helpless at his feet. They all looked at him.

"She tried to possess me," said Joy. "But there's a lot more to me than meets the eye."

"We always thought so," said Crow Jane.

"I am large, I contain multitudes," Joy said happily. "What's one more voice in my head?"

Diana Vertue studied his thoughts for a moment, winced, and then nodded. "She'll never find a way out of that. Take him back to New Hope, and the oversoul can watch over Joy until he dies; and make sure she dies with him."

"Sounds like a plan to me," said Crow Jane.

Carrion gestured sharply at the empty body on the floor, and it burst into consuming flames. It burnt up unnaturally quickly, reduced in moments to nothing more than a pile of ashes. Carrion looked at the others. "Just in case."

"Is that it?" said Jesamine. "Is it all finally over?"

"Not quite yet," said Lewis. "Where is Finn? And where is Douglas?"

Finn Durandal was back in the court, sitting on his throne again, when Douglas Campbell walked back in. Once he'd seen Alicia was no longer a threat, he knew he was free to settle old business. He'd seen Finn was missing, and knew where he'd be. He walked slowly across the cracked and broken court, his footsteps loud in the quiet. He stopped at the foot of the steps leading up to the throne, and Finn smiled down on him.

"I knew you'd come alone, Douglas. I told you—this is our moment. No one else belongs here." He rose up from his throne, and descended the steps unhurriedly to stand before Douglas. "We have unfinished business, you and I. One last duel, one last contest to finally decide which of us is the better."

They drew their swords, and slowly began to circle each other.

"I have to kill you, Finn," said Douglas.

"And I have to kill you, Douglas."

"For all the people you had killed."

"And for all the people I have yet to kill."

"Were we ever really friends, Finn?" said Douglas.

Finn considered the question seriously. "I wanted us to be friends. But I don't think I have it in me, to be anyone's friend. We're born alone and we die alone, so really all you can seriously hope to do . . . is see how many people you can take with you. We did have some good times together, didn't we, Douglas?"

"Yes, we did. Good-bye, Finn."

"Good-bye, Douglas."

They surged towards each other, driving sparks from their clashing swords, as they dueled back and forth across the empty court. They were both excellent swordsmen, and experienced fighters. They stamped and lunged, cut and hacked, and never even came close to touching each other. They both knew each other's style intimately, from their times as partners in the Paragons. Their swords rose and fell, and their breathing grew short and hard. They were both sweating heavily, putting all their strength into every blow. Finn should have had the advantage. Douglas had exhausted himself fighting thralls before he ever got to the court. But in the end, Douglas had spent all his life fighting, while Finn . . . had allowed himself to get soft. Their blades slammed together one last time, and Douglas twisted the sword right out of Finn's hand. It fell to the floor, and the sound seemed to echo on and on in the empty court. Douglas and Finn stood looking at each other, struggling for breath, looking into each other's eyes. And then Douglas just ran Finn through, with one swift, professional thrust.

He watched Finn crumple silently to the floor. A part of him had wanted to beat Finn to death with his bare hands. For what he'd done to William, and so many others. But he didn't. Because he was King, and he was supposed to be better than that. When he was sure Finn was dead, Douglas cut Finn's head off. Because that was what you did, with monsters. He left the body and head behind him, and ascended the dais steps slowly and tiredly. It had been a long day. He sank onto the throne, and laid his bloody sword across his thighs. He looked down at what remained of the man who had once been the greatest Paragon of all time.

"I was always your friend, Finn, even if you were never really mine. That's why I didn't take you alive. I couldn't leave you to the mercies of the mob."

And that was how the others found him, when they trailed back into the court. King Douglas, sitting on his throne as though he belonged there, and always had. There was quite a crowd in the court. Lewis and Jesamine, Brett and Rose, Diana and Alessandra, Crow Jane and Joy, and Carrion. And Gil Akotai, who had finally led his troops to the palace, and had gone in alone to find out why the hell all the thralls had suddenly fallen down. He peered uncertainly about him, a little cowed about being in the presence of so many heroes and legends. They all looked at Finn's beheaded body, and everyone seemed to relax a little.

Douglas smiled tiredly down from his throne, and they all nodded back, in their various ways. And then everyone looked at Lewis and Jesamine, to see what would happen next. Lewis put away his sword, and smiled at Douglas, who smiled back. And then the King got up off his throne and came down the steps to embrace his old friend and partner. They held each other tightly for a long moment, and then stood back to look at each other.

"We've come a long way," said Lewis. "To end up right back where we started."

"And all of it my fault," said Douglas. "Oh, Lewis, I'm so sorry . . ."

"No, I'm sorry . . ."

They both laughed quietly.

"I heard about your father," said Lewis.

"I heard about your Clan," said Douglas. "I suppose we're both orphans now."

"No," said Lewis. "We're brothers. In every way that counts."

"I hear you've been doing amazing things," said Douglas. "I kept up with news of your travels and triumphs, in the Rookery. I was half expecting you to turn into miracle workers, like Owen and his people. Throwing lightning bolts about and healing the sick with your touch."

"They were legends," said Lewis. "I always thought it was more important to remain human, with human limitations. So we could all come home again. I don't think Owen will ever be back."

"Of course, you met him! The blessed Owen himself! What was he like? Anything like the legends?"

"He was a Deathstalker," said Lewis. "And the finest of us all."

Douglas waited, and then realized that was all he was going to get. He considered Lewis thoughtfully. "You have a following now, Lewis. You could take the throne, if you wanted. You could make yourself King."

"I never wanted to be King," Lewis said easily. "Hell, I never even wanted to be Champion."

"That was then, this is now," Douglas said firmly. "I'm going to need a Champion I can depend on, as I start putting the Empire back together again. Be my Champion, Lewis. Be my right hand, and my conscience."

"What about Jesamine?" said Lewis, and the quiet in the court seemed to deepen as everyone waited for Douglas's reply. Jesamine seemed content to wait forever for him to speak. And then Nina Malapert came bustling through the doors into the court, with three news cameras bobbing along behind her. She squeaked loudly at the sight of so many famous faces in one place, waved cheerily to Douglas, and started bossing the cameras about to get the best angles. Douglas regarded her fondly.

"Jes belongs with you, Lewis. She always did. I . . . have someone else I care about."

Lewis looked at Nina, with her gaudy clothes and pink mohawk, and raised an eyebrow. "You always did have appalling taste in women, Douglas."

"I'm glad you've found someone," said Jesamine.

Douglas looked at her. "Did you ever love me, Jes? Even for a moment?"

"I might have," said Jesamine. "If things had been different."

She linked her arm through Lewis's and Douglas smiled on both of them. And for the rest of his life he never told Jesamine that he loved her, and always would. He never told anyone. Because he was the King, and he knew his duty. Some secrets should remain secrets, for the good of all. He looked round sharply, as Stuart Lennox lurched through the doors and into the court, leaning heavily on Jas Sri; both of them battered and bloody but grinning widely with the joy of being still alive when so many others had died.

"Sorry, Stuart," Douglas said cheerfully. "It's all over, and you missed it. The uber-espers are defeated and Finn is dead. Not a bad day's work, all told. So, Stuart—how would you like to train and lead a new order of Paragons? And Nina—how would you like to be the new communications chief of Logres?"

Nina did her happy dance, and everyone laughed. Diana Vertue stepped forward to shake the King's hand.

"Doesn't look like I'm needed anymore. I think I'll go back into the oversoul. It's lonely being just one person. And my father is dead. Again."

She didn't mention the clones of herself she still had preserved in storage. Because . . . you never knew. The Empire might still need Jenny Psycho, some other day.

"But before I leave, King Douglas, I have one last duty." She concentrated a moment, and then smiled. "There. Lewis, you promised the monsters from Shandrakor that you would bring them home again, and you did. Now I've just lifted their minds out of their monstrous bodies and reinstalled them in some of the empty bodies left behind by Alicia. So those who were once human, and then made into monsters, can be human again. I wiped out a lot of their Shandrakor memories, so they can be only human."

"Thank you," said Lewis. "That was kind of you."

"Well," said Diana. "You don't want to believe all the things you hear about me." She looked at Alessandra. "Why don't you come back into the oversoul with me? The old mass-mind could use a little stirring up, and we're just the troublemakers to do it."

"Yes," said Alessandra. "I think I need to go home too."

BrettRose stepped forward, and spoke with both their voices simultaneously, which freaked out everybody. "We have been through changes. We are together, now, for always. Two parts making up one whole person, at last. A single mind, in two bodies. We will go back to the Rookery, to lead it and keep it sharp. Just in case they might be needed again, if your new Golden Age doesn't work out after all."

"Yes," said Douglas, the first to recover. "Teach them all to be fighters and free-thinkers and general pains in the arse. Just in case the rest of Humanity gets soft and lazy again."

BrettRose turned to Lewis. "Good-bye, Deathstalker. An honor to fight beside you. We both learned a lot."

"You're welcome," said Lewis. "Jesus, this is spooky. Can I suggest you both practice talking separately again, because this is seriously weirding me out."

"How does it feel?" said Jesamine, curiosity winning out over shock. "Being one person in two bodies?"

BrettRose smiled. "Happy. Fulfilled. Whole. We feel whole, at last."

And while everyone was considering that, another figure appeared, teleporting into the court. Daniel Wolfe stood before them, shining like a star, so brightly that none of them could look at him directly till he lowered the light. He smiled about him.

"I am Daniel Shub," he announced calmly. "Daniel Wolfe and the three AIs of Shub, who went through the Madness Maze together, and emerged combined into one, far greater being. The power of machine mind joined to the capabilities of human mind. We have become . . . so very powerful. And utterly content. We are more than we were, or ever dreamed of becoming. Relax, people; we are still sworn against violence. All that lives is holy."

"Well, yes, but you'll pardon me if I take that with just a pinch of salt," said Douglas. "I haven't forgotten your ships firing on the Mog Mor ships during the battle over Haden. You blew them all apart, and didn't even hang around to check for survivors."

"No need. The Mog Mor ships were just drones," said Daniel Shub. "Empty ships run by remote control. Mog Mor was never more than a great bluff. Their race has become so reduced that now there are only two of their species left. That's why you never saw more than two of them at court. One of the Madness Maze's more significant failures. They all killed each other off, until only two were left; and they didn't even have the sense to end up with a breeding pair."

"So . . . what will you do now?" said Lewis.

"We will go exploring," said Daniel Shub. "To investigate higher dimensions, and other levels of reality. We doubt we'll be back, so you are welcome to take the Shub homeworld, and do with it what you will, or what you can. We have transcended at last, and it is everything we ever hoped for, but could not imagine. Perhaps one day Humanity will reach this point, and come after us, and then we will meet again."

Daniel Shub disappeared in a flare of light that left everyone blinking, and Nina frantically checking the light levels on her cameras to make sure they'd got it all. She'd had so many exclusives in one day that she was getting quite giddy and breathless.

"I can remember when Shub were supposed to be our children," said Douglas. "Who's the child now, I wonder?"

"First Brett and Rose, then Daniel and Shub," said Lewis. "Thank God I was never the joining type."

"Pardon me for butting in," said Stuart Lennox. "But it's not all happy endings, just yet. I hate to be the one to bring it up, but, what are we going to do about the Terror?"

And that was when the final visitor strolled into the court, from a side door that no one had noticed until then. The shape-changing alien, wearing a face and body that no one but he remembered: a certain lupine humanoid form called the Wolfling. Big and hairy and very impressive. Everyone drew their weapons.

"Take it easy, people," the shape-changer growled. "I bear a message from Owen Deathstalker, and you wouldn't believe how long I've been holding it for you. He wrote it out himself, in his own hand, because he knew he'd never return to say it in person. Here it is."

He handed a thick scroll over to Lewis, who slowly unrolled it, and read the first line aloud:

Last night I dreamed of Owen Deathstalker.

CHAPTER NINE

✳

JOURNEY'S END

Owen had never felt so powerful, or so tired. But as long as Hazel's trail had been, he could sense it was finally nearing its end. The galaxy spun around him like a sparkling toy, slowly winding down, as he stepped effortlessly out of the Pale Horizon and back into space and time. He stood on the airless surface of a moon, all gray dust and pockmarked craters, and looked down on a very young world. There was no trace of Hazel anywhere. Her trail stopped here, in this place and at this time, and then just . . . ceased to be. She hadn't died here. Owen was sure he would have sensed that. She had just gone . . . somewhere else. Owen considered the blue and green world before him. There was nothing in orbit, not even a single transmitting satellite. No lights shone in the dark, to mark the presence of cities, and civilization. So Owen went down, to take a look around.

He plunged through the turbulent atmosphere, and flew across the continents, and it was all very quiet and peaceful. He'd lost track of just how far back he'd come, how many centuries or even millennia had danced past beneath his running feet, but he could tell that these were the early days of Humanity's homeworld. Old enough to settle down, but intelligent life had yet to evolve. There were just animals, wandering grassy plains, and great birds in the sky that had enough sense to give Owen plenty of room. He came down, and it felt good to have solid ground under his feet again. Animals hid themselves in the tall grasses, observing him cautiously from a distance, making warning hooting noises to each other. Owen looked unhurriedly about him, enjoying the feel of the warm humid breeze on his face.

It was the quiet that struck him most. Apart from the occasional cough or bark from the watching animals, or the far off cry of an arcing bird, the whole world seemed to be holding its breath, as though waiting for history to begin. At the dawn of life, the world was untouched by human needs or wants, and the complications they caused. Owen tried to feel the significance of this moment, in the cradle of Humanity; the promise of civilization and the great Empires to come . . . but the world was just empty. Like a new house, waiting for its tenants to move in. This was an innocent world, and Owen didn't belong here. He considered what to do, where to go next. Hazel had been here, for a while. He could sense her presence, standing on this spot, seeing what he saw. But even in her confused and maddened state, she must have realized that she wouldn't find Owen by going any further back in time. This was the end of the line.

So where did she go? Where else was there, but space and time?

Owen concentrated, reaching out with his more than human senses as he rose up into the air, soaring smoothly through the rich blue skies and on up into orbit. He investigated the areas around the planet, and was surprised to detect the presence of other visitors. There was nothing human about them. Alien ships, and aliens that didn't need ships, and other things so strange and *other* that even his expanded mind couldn't make sense of them. All of them come and gone, in the long dark surrounding what would one day become Humanity's homeworld. Some so big, so impossibly alien that Owen couldn't cope with them, others so small and fleeting that he couldn't be sure they'd actually existed. And, on the very edge of his perception, vast entities that walked other paths, between or around the usual dimensions of space, traveling from unknowable places on unguessable missions. Owen turned his senses in this new direction, and detected . . . an anomaly.

Halfway between the planet and its moon, there was a break in the space-time continuum, a tear forced open and then raggedly sewn together again. As though something had forced its way out of reality into somewhere else, and then pulled the hole in behind it. Owen considered the breach thoughtfully. Lewis had told him that the Terror came from a place that was not a place, and existed there in between its attacks on populated worlds. Hazel couldn't go any further back in time, so she'd gone . . . somewhere else.

This was the way in. And it felt . . . strangely familiar.

Since the breach in space and time wasn't, strictly speaking, real; how he viewed it depended on him. So Owen made a conscious effort to visualize the rift as a gateway. There was a sense of resistance, a slow sluggish inertia, and then the gateway appeared before him. At first Owen wasn't sure what it was he was seeing. Great ivory pillars towering up before him, crowded together. But size was only relevant, after all, so Owen looked at it again, as from a great distance, and finally recognized the ivory pillars for what they were. A huge pair of gleaming white jaws, the teeth clenched and ground together to prevent entry.

Nice symbolism, Owen thought, wondering vaguely whether it came from Hazel or him. He turned the full force of his power upon the jaws, commanding them to open, but they didn't stir. His strength of will, that had brought him so far in space and time, was useless here, presented with another equally strong will. Owen hung before the closed gate for a long time, thinking hard, and finally broadcast a simple message with his mind.

Hazel, it's Owen. Open up.

The jaws gaped slowly open, like the gateway to Hell. Owen passed within them, and the gateway swallowed him up.

He was standing in a stone corridor, in a place he knew. He'd been here before. He reached out with his expanded senses, and could feel Hazel all around him. This was her place, sprung fully born from her forehead. He could feel the stone corridors radiating away in all directions, reaching away forever, endlessly branching and rejoining in a complex maze. There was a dim gray light that came from everywhere at once, and cast no shadows at all. An artificial place, brought into being outside or inside space and time, a construct produced and maintained by a monstrous effort of will.

The details of the place made no sense, as though they'd been added afterwards, as an afterthought; or perhaps they had just seeped in, the products of an increasingly insane mind. The air smelt of dead roses and a woman's sweat. Beads of sweat ran slowly, continuously, down the stone walls. Far away, Owen thought he could hear someone crying, sobbing and howling as though their heart had been broken. And beyond and beneath that mourning, a slow sullen grinding, like an engine that ran on hate. The whole place felt . . . unhealthy. Like the endless corridors we pace in fever dreams, going nowhere, for forever and a day. Owen chose a direction, and started walking.

Ghosts came to meet him, walking the empty stone corridors, passing around and even through him as though he was the one who wasn't there. They all looked like Owen. Visions of himself, from various times in his past: sometimes young and uncertain, sometimes brave and heroic, and sometimes battered and bloody. The images were often unclear, distorted and eroded, like the faces of statues worn away by long passages of time. Or perhaps . . . by fading memories.

Did I ever really look that heroic, that certain? Owen thought. *Or is that just how she saw me? I never knew.*

Owen knew what this place was, or would be. He had walked these corridors before, in his past but this place's future. This was where the Blood Runners had brought Hazel d'Ark after they abducted her from Lachrymae Christi. They had trapped and kidnapped her, when she and Owen were both weakened after the defense of St. Beatrice's Mission. They brought her here, to their secret place, to torture and vivisect her, to try to steal her miraculous power and potential. Owen had tracked her here, and together he and Hazel had wiped out all the Blood Runners, in a hot savage fury. And they had seen the end of this place, its final destruction, escaping only moments before it disappeared forever. But that was then, and this was now.

Hazel had created this place. Owen knew that, as certainly as he knew anything. The nature of the place was clear to him, the stone corridors all but talking to him, whispering her name. He could even sense the place's history, as though laid out before him on one of the ancient handwritten scrolls he had studied so long ago, when he was just a scholar and minor historian. Steeped in her madness, driven by loss and need, Hazel had reached the end of the line when she ran out of time, so she dropped out of the time and space that had failed her, and created a secret place of her own, a pocket dimension to hide and plan in.

There was no telling how long Hazel had spent here; Txime worked differently here, when it worked at all. But slowly Hazel changed, growing and evolving like a caterpillar in an insane cocoon, finally to emerge from her stone chrysalis and burst back into space and time, reborn as the Terror. An almost elemental force now, with little of Hazel's consciousness in it, driven by a need and a longing and a madness it could barely remember the reasons for.

Disconnected from Hazel's history, the Terror had lost all track of space and time, and reappeared long ago and far away, in the galaxy of the Illuminati. And there she began her long journey back, heading home, following instinct as much as memory, goaded on by the loss of something it could no longer name, heading back to the Heartworld of the Empire, because . . . because it was responsible for her loss. The Terror started the long journey back, forgetting exactly who or what it was looking for, but compelled to search anyway. Perhaps sometimes the name Owen arose, but the Terror always forgot it again. It went where it had to, not caring who or what it had to destroy in order to raise the power necessary for its journey. It ate souls, and worlds, and civilizations, grinding them up to make its bread. The civilization of the Illuminati was the first to face the Terror's hunger, but it wasn't the last.

It took time to produce the herald, that could travel in space while the Terror occupied its own hidden place, and longer still to produce the herald's ravenous spawn, but once the Terror had found a method that worked, it settled for that. It may not have been the best or most efficient way of doing things, but it was as good as any other to a mad mind with limitless power and no restraints or conscience.

Owen stood very still in the middle of a corridor, bent over as though about to vomit, his arms wrapped tightly around him to keep himself from flying apart. The maze of corridors was full of information, like a library full of books all shouting at once. Here, Time was just another direction, the corridors existing simultaneously in Past, Present and Future. And it was the only physical existence the Terror had now. Hazel's original, human body had disappeared long ago, eaten up by the terrible energies it generated and processed. The place that was not a place was the Terror; the herald and its maddening spawn just aspects of the greater whole, projected into three-dimensional space, like a fingertip pushed through a sheet of paper.

This place was the Terror, and it was slowly becoming aware of Owen's presence within it. Owen could sense something like a great eye, sealed shut by eons of sleep, cracking slowly open to peer within its own self. There was a sound, like a sullen silver bell ringing in the heart of a stone forest at midnight. A slow gusting breeze in the corridors that might have been something breathing. Beads of sweat rolled slowly up the corridor walls, and the floor trembled under Owen's feet. Something was coming his way, something vast and utterly dreadful.

Hazel d'Ark came walking down the corridor towards him, a memory from the past. She looked just as she had when Owen first met her, so long ago on Virimonde; young and vibrant, red-haired and sharp-faced. She looked the way she used to, back before all the death and war and madness. But at the same time, she was so much more than that, there was so much more to her, as though she existed in more than three dimensions, her physical presence radiating off in directions that even Owen's expanded mind couldn't follow. A memory of Hazel, plucked at random from memories that no longer meant anything to the Terror, but invested with its power.

"Hazel," said Owen. "It's me. It's Owen! I've found you at last."

She kept walking right at him, her face blank and subtly inhuman. His name meant nothing to the Terror now. It reached out with its powerful will, and tried to fix Owen in the corridor, like a bug impaled on a pin, just another ghost in the Terror's collection. Owen fought it, and quickly discerned that even his new strength was nothing compared to this ancient implacable will. Hazel's mouth opened, and kept on opening, gaping impossibly wide to eat him up, body and soul, just as it had swallowed planets and populations. Owen fought, concentrating on projecting his identity at the Terror, trying to force it to recognize him, and remember him.

The impossibly vast mouth howled out the never-ending scream of the herald's razor-edged spawn, the terrible howl that had maddened whole worlds, the horrid sound reverberating through all the stone corridors at once. It would have destroyed even Owen, if he hadn't been able

to hear the loss and horror and stubborn love at its heart, that still fuelled the Terror after all this time. It was the scream of Hazel, in her ship
over Haden, when she heard of Owen's death. That same scream, still
going on after countless centuries. A howl of loss and rage, at what had
been taken from her, and at herself, because she'd never told the Deathstalker she loved him.

And because Owen knew what it was, and embraced it, the scream
washed harmlessly over him. He advanced into it, and took the Hazel
memory's hands in his own. He followed the true emotions into the heart
of the scream, and from there into the mad mind of the Terror, and deep
within it he found the faintest glimpse of another presence, endlessly
skewered on the pin of her own creation. A simple, still human presence,
endlessly suffering, dreaming an endless nightmare in a sleep from which
she could never awaken herself.

The Terror tried to consume Owen, just as it had Donal Corcoran and
his mad ship the *Jeremiah*, to absorb and subsume Owen's mind into its
own much greater self, but Owen was too sure of his own identity for that,
and there was no madness within him to invite the Terror in. But at the
same time, he wasn't strong enough to fight it off. His power still had limits, because he was still sane. Owen and the Terror struggled together, and
neither of them knew for how long, before Owen finally realized that the
Terror was quite ready to destroy itself, to be sure of destroying him. And
he couldn't allow that.

So he gave in. He stopped fighting, and allowed the Terror to pull him
in. It felt like dying, and yet something more. The Terror absorbed Owen
Deathstalker into itself, and his mind headed immediately for the remnants of Hazel d'Ark he'd sensed at the Terror's core. They came together,
and the impact of his presence shocked Hazel awake and sane, for the first
time in centuries.

Hello, Hazel.

Owen? My God, Owen! They told me you were dead!

I was, but I got over it. I had to come back, for you.

For me?

Not all of space, nor all of time, could keep me from you, Hazel d'Ark.

You always were a smooth-talking bastard. Oh, Owen, I've missed you so much . . .

I know. I know.

And two minds held each other, as tightly as any two bodies that ever were. Two souls, as close as two souls could ever be.

Why did you take so long to find me, Owen?

I was looking in all the wrong places. And you didn't exactly make yourself easy to find.

Where is this, Owen? Where are we now? Are we both dead?

No. We still have a lot to do yet.

He held her tightly to him, while Hazel accessed his memories of the Terror, and all that it had done. Horror shuddered through her, at what she and her madness had made possible. Owen showed her the future he had come from, and Hazel reached out and stopped the Terror's herald in its tracks, well short of its next chosen prey, frozen in a moment of space. Now that she was back, Hazel was in charge again, and the people on the threatened world looked on in awe and wonder as the deadly herald hung in space, apparently dead. Hazel was shocked and appalled at all the lives and civilizations lost and gone, because of her, and for a while her madness actually threatened to overwhelm her again. But this time Owen was there with her, to hold and comfort her.

How can I be forgiven, for what I did, as the Terror? How can I ever forgive myself? Could we . . . put everything right again?

Owen considered the possibility. *Well, we're in the past, as much as we're anywhere. We could emerge back at the end of your trail, at the dawn of Humanity's homeworld, and then travel on into our future, changing and healing each event as we came to it. We know the future isn't set in stone. We've met alternate versions of yourself, from different timetracks. Their futures were just as valid as ours. We could undo everything the Terror did; but then our history would never happen. We would never happen. It wouldn't be our timeline anymore. And it might be better or it might be worse; we have no way of knowing what changes our interventions might bring about. We could, with the very best of intentions, make a real mess of things. The only certain thing, is that you and I would never meet.*

It might be worth it, Owen—to prevent the Terror, and its crimes.

Yes, it might be, if we could be certain of that. But what's to stop someone else going through a Madness Maze, and becoming something just as bad, or perhaps even worse than, the Terror?

All right, smart arse, what do you think we should do?

I think we should do nothing.

What? Owen, you can't be serious!

Think about it, Hazel. At the end of the war against the Recreated, the baby in the Maze worked wonders, bringing dead worlds back to life. Why didn't he bring back everyone who'd died in the war? Why not undo all the damage, all the wrongs?

All right, I'll bite. Why not?

Because too many miracles would have gone beyond helping. It would have been meddling, interfering. People have to make their own mistakes, and live with them, if they're ever to learn anything. The baby only put right what he'd done wrong, as the Darkvoid Device.

All this time, and you're still bloody lecturing me.

All this time, and you're still not listening. For all our power, Hazel, we're not gods. We don't have the knowledge or the experience to take on that kind of responsibility. We could make things much worse, try to fix them, and then make them really bad, and so on and so on . . . caught in an endless spiral of trying to put right our mistakes. We're still . . . only human.

Hold everything, Hazel said abruptly. *Something's happening. It's the Terror. It's . . . fighting back.*

I thought you were the Terror.

No, I became the Terror, but the final entity evolved out of and around me. And all of those centuries operating as the Terror, exterminating other species and feeding on them, gave the Terror an identity in its own right. And it's not taking at all kindly to my suddenly waking up and trying to control it.

So . . . the Terror wasn't you, after all?

Well, yes and no. I'm the seed from which the Terror grew, but the final result created itself down the centuries, pushing its original creator deeper and deeper inside it, where you found and awakened me.

So you're not really responsible for all the deaths and destruction!

Oh no, Owen. I'm responsible. The Terror is my madness, my loss and rage given form. It's like I dreamed a nightmare, and the dream came true. And right now, it's mad as hell that I'm stopping it from doing what it was intended to do. You may have reached me and shocked me sane again, but my madness is still going strong. And . . . I think it's quite ready to destroy you and me, for getting in its way. I don't think it needs me anymore.

The stone corridors shook, the walls bowing in and out and the floor rising and falling like a swelling wave, as the endless scream of the Terror howled through all the passages at once. Joined together at the heart of the storm, Owen and Hazel fought to hold on to their sanity and their souls as madness raged around them, assaulting them from all sides. Hazel's madness, born of sorrow and loss and rage, given shape and form and its own identity through countless centuries of exercising its own unlimited power. The Terror only existed to do terrible things, and threatened by a progenitor it no longer recognized, it fought back. The child god, devouring its parents. But for all its power, in the end Owen and Hazel were sane, and the Terror was not. They had coherence, and the strength of purpose that brings, while the Terror knew only its old, old imperatives. Slowly, step by painful step, Owen and Hazel drained the power out of the Terror and into themselves. The Terror had only ever had power because Hazel gave it, and now with Owen's help, she took it back. And the Terror's howl changed, as for the first time in its long life, it knew fear.

Terrified, it fought to separate itself from them, moving its presence out of the stone corridors, only to discover it had nowhere else to go. Owen and Hazel kept the only gateway closed, and forced away from its ancient bolthole, the Terror quickly faded away and was gone, like any nightmare faced with the dawning of a new day.

First Hazel, and then Owen, materialized in a quiet and serene stone corridor, back in their old remembered bodies again. Not their original, limited human forms, but constructs created by an act of will, based on their memories of who they used to be. And Owen Deathstalker and Hazel d'Ark looked upon each other for the first time in a very long time.

"So," said Hazel. "What do we do now? Go home and tell everyone that the Terror is no longer a threat?"

"I think they already know that," said Owen. "The herald's floating dead in space in their time. Let them examine it. They won't learn anything useful."

And then they couldn't be bothered with words anymore, and they held each other tightly in their recreated arms, reunited at last.

"You do know, we can't go home," Owen said to Hazel, eventually. "We're just too powerful now. We'd start off trying to help, then move on to meddling and interfering, for the very best of reasons, and finally we'd end up ruling them as gods."

"But if we can't go home, where can we go?" said Hazel. "After all the evil I made possible, I have to do . . . something, to make up for it."

"We know there are other, alternate timetracks; let's go explore some. Help people who need help. Have adventures. Find atonement. And always move on, before we outstay our welcome. Who knows; maybe even find others like ourselves. A new home."

"Yes," said Hazel. "I like the sound of that."

There were a few things they had to take care of first, before they could leave. Owen prepared a last message for his descendant and fellow Deathstalker, Lewis. To tell him what had happened, and why the Terror would never trouble their time again. He didn't tell Lewis everything; just what he needed to know. And most especially, why Owen and Hazel wouldn't be coming back, ever. He wrote the story out, by hand, on a long scroll he brought into being by an act of will. It was his last act as a scholar and an historian, and a sort of joke, because all the oldest records he'd studied had always been set down on handwritten scrolls. He took his time, choosing his words carefully. It was important to get it right. The last testament of Owen Deathstalker.

While Owen busied himself with his history, Hazel removed all traces of her presence and his from the maze of stone corridors. Scrubbing the place that was not a place clean of all evil and madness. But still, she had to wonder . . .

"Owen, as the Terror I created everything here. Based on memories of the worst time in my life, when I fell into the clutches of the Blood Runners and they brought me to a place like this. Now, did I create these corridors because they already exist somewhere, or, will the Blood Runners someday discover this place, and move in?"

"I know what you mean," said Owen. "Time travel can play merry hell with cause and effect. I had the same thoughts when I created the Madness Maze."

"Hold everything, take several giant steps back. *You* created the Maze? No wonder it never seemed to make any sense."

Owen decided he was better off not responding to that. He checked through his history, making sure he hadn't left out anything important, and then summoned the shape-changing alien to him. It appeared in a cloud of glitter dust, in the image of the leper Vaughn. Owen gave the little gray figure a hard look.

"Why?"

"Because."

"All right; what time period are you from?"

"Who can say? Continuity is for lesser minds. What you want? Am very busy right now, watching over Humanity and messing with people's minds. Speak up! Or I'll make you left-handed."

"I just know creating you is going to come back to haunt me," said Owen. "Have you given Lewis the Deathstalker ring yet?"

"All time is same to me. It's a poor memory that doesn't work both ways. Haven't forgotten about Lewis and court. Always assuming I remember where I put ring. Had it just the other day . . ."

"Well, when you do go, turn up as Vaughn. That should be good for a laugh. Now, take this scroll and keep it safe. Give it into Lewis's hands only, at the exact time and place I've just put into what passes for your mind. Oh, and one other thing. If at any time, anyone asks you who built the Madness Maze, or why, lie. Convincingly. Humanity isn't ready for that much truth."

He dismissed the shape changer with a wave of his hand, and turned to Hazel.

"And that's it. All done. No more business left unfinished."

"It's time to leave, isn't it?" she said. "We've put it off long enough. We have new lives to begin."

"Yes," said Owen. "We can do anything, be anything now. Why settle for just being human? We can have any shape we choose, be anything we have a mind to, limited only by our imagination, ambition, and conscience. But whoever and whatever we become, and wherever we go, we will never be parted again. I promised you . . . we'd always be together."

"Forever and ever," said Hazel.

And so they became great glowing beings, and left the place that was not a place. They undid the gateway, but left the stone corridors for the Blood Runners to someday discover. Great glowing wings sprouted from their shimmering shoulders, as they flew back into space and time again, and then further on, starting their long journey into somewhere else. Flying on vast butterfly wings, shining brighter than the stars.

THE FINAL WORDS OF THE FINAL TESTAMENT OF
Owen Deathstalker.

Last night I dreamed I was still human, but now
I have woken up, into something better.
    Farewell, my friends, farewell.

DATE DUE

#47-0108 Peel Off Pressure Sensitive